Embrace what
you're afraid of...

FEAR THE DARKNESS

With a choked howl, he grasped her hands and jerked them over her head, pressing them against the quilt as he slowly forged a path into her tight body.

"Yes," she breathed against his neck, her legs tightening around his waist. "Oh, God, Caine."

His eyes squeezed shut as he struggled to rein his savage desire. With care he pulled back, bending his head to the side. "Your teeth, Cassie," he managed to rasp. "I want to feel them on my neck."

She didn't hesitate as she sank her teeth back into the base of his throat, sending a jppolt of pure adrenaline through his system.

He surged back into her slick heat, his harsh groans matching her soft sighs as he found a steady pace, his hips rolling upward with each thrust.

Her teeth clenched harder on his neck as she lifted to meet his quickening onslaught, her nails raking across his back.

He forgot to breathe, his heart thundering in his chest.

Deep inside, his wolf howled in primitive satisfaction . . .

Books by Alexandra Ivy

WHEN DARKNESS COMES

EMBRACE THE DARKNESS

DARKNESS EVERLASTING

DARKNESS REVEALED

DARKNESS UNLEASHED

BEYOND THE DARKNESS

DEVOURED BY DARKNESS

BOUND BY DARKNESS

FEAR THE DARKNESS

MY LORD VAMPIRE

And don't miss these Guardians of Eternity novellas

TAKEN BY DARKNESS in YOURS FOR ETERNITY

DARKNESS ETERNAL in SUPERNATURAL

WHERE DARKNESS LIVES in THE REAL
WEREWIVES OF VAMPIRE COUNTY

Published by Kensington Publishing Corporation

FEAR
THE
DARKNESS

ALEXANDRA IVY

ZEBRA BOOKS
KENSINGTON PUBLISHING CORP.
http://www.kensingtonbooks.com

ZEBRA BOOKS are published by

Kensington Publishing Corp.
119 West 40th Street
New York, NY 10018

All Kensington titles, imprints and distributed lines are avail-
able at special quantity discounts for bulk purchases for sales
promotion, premiums, fund-raising, educational or institu-
tional use.

Special book excerpts or customized printings can also be
created to fit specific needs. For details, write or phone the
office of the Kensington Special Sales Manager. Attn.: Special
Sales Department. Kensington Publishing Corp., 119 West
40th Street, New York, NY 10018. Phone: 1-800-221-2647.

Zebra and the Z logo Reg. U.S. Pat. & TM Off.

ISBN-13: 978-1-4201-1137-8
ISBN-10: 1-4201-1137-X

First Printing: September 2012

10 9 8 7 6 5 4 3 2 1

Printed in the United States of America

To Chance and Alex:
the lights of my life.

And David,
who always understands.

Prologue

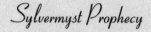

Sylvermyst Prophecy

Flesh of flesh, blood of blood, bound in darkness.
The Alpha and Omega shall be torn asunder
and through the Mists reunited.
Pathways that have been hidden will be found
and the Veil parted to the faithful.
The Gemini will rise
and chaos shall rule for all eternity.

Chapter 1

The abandoned silver mine in the Mojave Desert wasn't the first place someone would expect to encounter Styx, the current Anasso.

Not only was he the King of all Vampires, but at six foot five of pure muscle with the stark beauty of his Aztec ancestors, he was one of the most powerful demons in the world.

He could command the most luxurious lair in the area with a dozen servants eager to do his bidding. But he wanted his trip to Nevada to be as discreet as it was brief, so ignoring the protests of his companion, he'd chosen to spend the day waiting for his meeting with the local clan chief in the forgotten caves.

And, if he were honest with himself, it was a relief not to be stuck with the formal ceremony his position demanded. He was a fierce predator, not a damned politician, and the need to play nice gave him a rash.

Besides, it was always a pleasure to yank Viper's chain.

Styx made a brief survey of the empty desert that surrounded them, absently knocking the dust from his leather pants, which were tucked in to a pair of heavy boots. A black T-shirt was stretched over his massive chest with a tiny amulet threaded on a leather strip wrapped around his thick neck. That was his only jewelry besides the polished turquoise stones that were threaded through the dark, braided hair that hung to the back of his knees.

His dark eyes glowed with a golden light of power in the thickening dusk as he at last turned toward his companion, barely hiding his smile. Unlike him, Viper, the clan chief of Chicago, had no love for "roughing it."

Dressed in a black velvet coat that reached his knees with a frilled white satin shirt and black slacks, he looked like he was on his way to the nearest ballroom. An impression only emphasized by his long hair the pale silver of moonlight, which was left free to flow down his back, and his eyes the startling darkness of midnight.

Styx was raw, savage power.

Viper was an exquisite fallen angel who was no less lethal.

With a pointed glance toward the Las Vegas skyline that glowed like a distant jewel, Viper met Styx's gaze with a sour grimace. "The next time you want me to join you on a road trip, Styx, feel free to lose my number."

Styx arched a dark brow. "I thought everyone loved Vegas."

"Which was why I agreed to this little excursion." Viper tugged at his lace cuffs, managing to look immaculate despite his hours in the dusty cavern. "You failed to mention I was going to be staying in a damned mine instead of the penthouse suite at the Bellagio."

"We've stayed in worse places."

"Worse?" Viper pointed toward the rotting boards that did a half-ass job of covering the entrance to the tunnel. "It was filthy, it smelled of bat shit, and the temperature was a few degrees less than the surface of the sun. I've visited hell dimensions that I enjoyed more than that godforsaken inferno."

Styx snorted. The two vampires had been friends for centuries, a remarkable feat considering they were both alphas. But over the past months their bonds had grown even closer as they'd been forced to confront the increasingly dangerous world.

The Dark Lord—or Dark Prince or master or a hundred other names he'd been called over the centuries—had been effectively banished from this dimension long ago and kept in his prison by the Phoenix, a powerful spirit who was being protected by the vampires. But he refused to take his imprisonment gracefully.

Over the past months he'd become increasingly relentless in his pursuit of smashing through the veils that separated the worlds, not only allowing his return, but giving a free pass to every creature that inhabited the numerous hells.

Only a few days ago the bastard had nearly succeeded.

Using one of the twin babies he'd created to use as a vessel for his grand resurrection, he'd transformed from a formless mist into a young, humanlike female. It'd been creepy as hell to see the ultimate of all evil looking like a pretty cheerleader.

Thankfully, Jaelyn had managed to drain the Dark Lord before he could pass through the Veil, but Styx knew it was only a temporary reprieve.

Until the Dark Lord was destroyed, there would be no peace.

Which was why he was standing in the middle of the desert with a pissed-off Viper instead of waking in the arms of his beautiful mate.

"You're becoming as soft as a dew fairy in your old age," he mocked.

"I didn't become clan chief to rut in the dirt like some animal."

"Pathetic."

Viper glanced toward the distant glow of lights. "Are you at least going to tell me why we couldn't stay in one of the hundreds of hotels just a few miles away?"

Styx turned to scan the seemingly empty landscape. Not that it was truly empty. At his feet a lizard crawled over a rock oblivious to the owl hunting in silence overhead, or the snake that was coiled only a few feet away. More distantly a coyote was on the trail of a jackrabbit.

The typical sights and sounds of the desert. His only interest, however, was making sure there were no nasty surprises hidden in the shadows.

"I prefer not to attract unwanted attention to our presence in Nevada," he explained. "Something that would be impossible with you in a casino."

"All I want is a warm shower, fresh clothes, and a ticket to the Donnie and Marie show."

"Do I have *stupid* tattooed on my forehead?" Styx turned to stab his friend with a knowing gaze. "The last time you were in Vegas you nearly bankrupted the Flamingo and ended up banned from returning to the city by the clan chief."

A reminiscent smile tugged at Viper's lips. "Can I help it if I had a streak of luck at the craps table? Or that Roke is a humorless prig?"

The distant hum of a motorcycle sliced through the thick night air. "Speaking of Roke," Styx murmured.

Viper muttered a curse as he moved to stand at Styx's side. "That's who we're meeting with?"

"Yes." Styx narrowed his gaze. "Do you promise to behave?"

"No, but I promise I won't kill him unless he—"

"Viper."

"Shit." Viper folded his arms over his chest. "This had better be important."

"Would I have left Darcy if it weren't?" he demanded, the mere mention of his mate sending a tiny pang of longing through his heart. Over the past months the beautiful female Were had become his very reason for living.

With a throaty roar of power, Roke brought his turbine to a halt and, sliding off the elegant machine, he crossed to stand before them.

Dressed in black jeans, a leather jacket, and moccasin boots that reached his knees, he was not as tall as Styx, although they shared the same bronzed skin and dark hair that brushed his broad shoulders. His features were lean with the high cheekbones of his Native American bloodlines and a proud nose. His brow was wide and his lips generously full. But it was his eyes that captured and held attention.

Silver in color, they were so pale they appeared almost white, the shocking paleness emphasized by the rim of pure black that circled them. They were eyes that seemed to pierce through a person to lay bare their very soul.

Not always the most comfortable sensation.

Especially for those who didn't particularly want their soul laid bare.

Which was . . . yeah, pretty much everyone.

"Styx." Offering a low bow, Roke's movements were liquid smooth as he slowly straightened and with stunning swiftness hurled a dagger to stick in the ground not an inch from Viper's expensive leather shoes. "Viper."

Viper growled, giving a wave of his hand to dislodge the dirt around Roke's feet. All vampires could manipulate the soil, a necessary skill to protect them from the sun or to hide the corpses of their prey, but Viper was particularly skilled, and in less than a blink of an eye, Roke was buried up to his waist.

"Are you two done playing?" Styx demanded, his icy power biting through the air.

The clan chief of Nevada climbed out of the sandpit and dusted off his jeans, his expression as inscrutable as ever. "For now."

Viper made a sound of impatience. "Why are we here?"

Styx nodded toward their companion. "Roke has something he believes we should see."

"His collection of blow-up dolls?"

"Christ. Enough." Styx bared his massive fangs in warning. He didn't know what the hell had gone down between the two clan chiefs in the past and right now he couldn't care less. He didn't have time for their bullshit. "Roke, show me."

"This way."

In utter silence the three vampires ghosted through the darkness, moving with a speed that made them all but invisible.

They were nearing a line of rugged hills when Viper made a sound of impatience. "As much as I adore running through the barren desert, do we have an eventual destination?" he muttered.

On cue, Roke came to a sharp halt, pointing toward the desert floor just in front of them. "There."

Viper rolled his eyes. "Man of few words."

"Preferable to one who doesn't know when to shut it," Roke countered.

"Agreed," Styx said dryly, shifting so he could study the ground where Roke was pointing. It took a long moment to recognize that the lines etched into the dry dirt were more than just the scribblings from some human. "Oh . . . shit."

"What the hell?" Viper tilted back his head as he caught the lingering scent. "I smell pureblooded Were."

"Cassandra," Styx said, easily recognizing the scent of his mate's twin sister, who had recently been revealed as a powerful prophet.

"And Caine," Viper added. "Why would they be in the middle of the Mojave Desert?"

Now that was a hell of a question.

The pair of pureblooded Weres had been missing for weeks, despite Styx's best efforts to locate them. An unbelievable feat considering he possessed the best trackers in the world. Of course, if the rumors were true, then the two Weres were already beyond his reach.

Which made any clue as to how she'd been captured or how to retrieve her from her current prison priceless.

"I'm more concerned with what they left behind," he admitted, prowling around the edges of the strange symbols.

Viper frowned. "An etching?"

Styx shook his head. "It looks more like a hieroglyph."

"A prophecy," Roke said with a quiet confidence.

Styx turned to study the clan chief with a searching gaze. "Can you decipher it?"

"Yes, it's a warning."

Viper frowned. "You're a seer?"

Roke shook his head, his gaze trained on the lines etched into the ground. "There's only one prophet. But I was sired by a wisewoman who taught me to read the signs left by our forefathers."

Of course. Styx abruptly understood precisely why he was standing in the middle of a desert. "So now we know why Cassandra chose to travel to Nevada," he said wryly.

"Why?" Viper demanded.

He pointed toward Roke. "Because it was the one place to make certain her message would be understood."

Viper snorted. "She could have sent a text and saved us a trip."

Styx's attention never wavered from the silent Roke. It was impossible to judge how the vampire felt about being pulled into the battle against the Dark Lord.

But then, he no doubt realized that it wasn't a choice. Styx wasn't the head of a damned democracy. He led his people by cunning and brute force when necessary.

"How did you discover this?"

"A cur stumbled across it two nights ago," Roke promptly answered. "There are no Were packs in the area so he came to me with the information."

"How many others did he tell?"

Roke instantly understood Styx's concern. "None, but it's been here at least two, maybe even three weeks." He grimaced. "It's impossible to know how many others have seen it."

A pity, but there was nothing to be done, Styx silently conceded. "Could anyone else interpret it?"

Roke paused before giving a shake of his head. "Doubtful."

Viper crouched down, studying the desert floor with a frown. "What does it say?"

Roke moved forward, careful not to disturb the marks as he pointed toward the strange etching closest to them. "This is the symbol for the Alpha and the Omega."

Styx froze at the familiar words.

"The children," he murmured, speaking of the twin babies that had been found by the half-Jinn mongrel, Laylah. She hadn't known that they were the babies mentioned in the prophecies. Or that they'd been created by the Dark Lord so he could use them as vessels for his eventual resurrection. "What about them?"

Roke traced the symbol in the air. "Here they are joined."

Styx nodded. When Laylah had found the children they'd

been wrapped in the same stasis spell and she'd assumed there was only one child.

"Yes."

"And then they were separated." Roke pointed toward the second etching. "The Omega is lost to the mists."

Viper muttered a low curse. Styx didn't blame him.

They'd struggled to protect the children, but while Laylah and Tane had managed to rescue the boy child and named him Maluhia, the girl child had been taken through the barriers between dimensions and used by the Dark Lord in his attempt to return to this world.

Styx shifted his attention to the last symbol. "What's this?"

"The children reunited."

Hissing in disbelief, Styx turned to meet Roke's steady gaze, the pale silver eyes even more eerie than usual. "Reunited?"

"'The Alpha and Omega shall be torn asunder and through the Mists reunited,'" the clan chief of Nevada murmured, quoting the Sylvermyst prophecy.

"Maluhia," Viper breathed, his expression grim. "Cassandra was warning us that the baby is in danger."

"Shit." Styx shoved his hand in his pocket to yank out his cell phone, his sense of furious urgency frustrated by the realization there was no service. He needed to get back to civilization. Now. Grasping the startled Roke by the upper arm, he headed back across the desert at a blinding speed. "You're coming with us."

Three weeks earlier
Las Vegas

The Forum Shops in Caesars Palace were a wonderland for any female, let alone one who had spent the past thirty years secluded from the world.

Beneath the ceilings that were painted to resemble a blue sky, the elegant stores wound their way past fountains that were intended to transport shoppers back to Roman days. Glass display cases were filled with the sort of temptations designed to make a woman drool.

With a wry smile, Caine stepped behind his dazzled companion to wrap his arms around her waist, tugging her back flat against his chest. He could only wish Cassie would look at him with that same wistful longing, he ruefully acknowledged.

Or perhaps not, he swiftly corrected as his body hardened with a familiar, brutal need.

Since discovering Cassie being held prisoner in the cave of a demon lord weeks ago, Caine had done his best to play the role of knight in shining armor.

Although possessing the natural strength of a pure-blooded Were, Cassie had not only been altered in the womb not to shift, but she was as innocent as a babe and twice as vulnerable.

Add in the fact she was the first true prophet born in centuries, and currently being hunted by every demon loyal to the Dark Lord, and she was a disaster waiting to happen.

She desperately needed a protector.

And since Caine, once a mere cur, had died and been resurrected as a pureblooded Were in her arms, he'd assumed that protecting Cassie was the reason the fates had returned him to this world instead of leaving him to rot in his well-deserved hell.

Unfortunately, his miraculous return to life hadn't included a sainthood and he remained a fully functioning male with all the usual weaknesses.

Including a rampaging lust toward the tiny female currently wrapped in his arms.

As always completely impervious to his torment, Cassie breathed a soft sigh of wonder. "Oh . . ."

"Cassie." Bending down, he spoke directly in her ear. "Cassie, listen to me."

She tilted back her head to meet his narrowed gaze and Caine briefly forgot how to breathe.

Holy shit, but she was beautiful.

Her hair was pale, closer to silver than blond, and pulled into a ponytail that fell to her waist. Her skin was a perfect alabaster, smooth and silken. Her eyes were an astonishing green, the color of spring grass and flecked with gold.

Her face was heart-shaped with delicate features that gave her an air of fragility that was only emphasized by her slender body. Of course, beneath her jeans and casual sweatshirt, she possessed the lean muscles of all pureblooded Weres.

"What?" she prompted when he continued to gawk at her in mindless appreciation.

He sucked in a deep breath, savoring the warm scent of lavender that clung to her skin. "You promised me that you would blend."

She wiggled from his grasp and darted toward the nearest store to press her face against the window. "Mmm."

Caine rolled his eyes. "I knew this was a mistake."

"There's so many," she murmured as he moved to stand beside her. "How do you choose?"

"We'll go into a store, pick out a few of your favorite clothes and try them on—"

"Okay."

Without waiting for him to finish, Cassie was darting through the open doorway. Caine was swiftly on her heels, but with immaculate timing a buxom nymph with dark hair and brown eyes pretended to stumble and landed against his chest.

Instinctively, his hands reached to grasp her shoulders, his sapphire blue eyes narrowed with irritation.

Once upon a time he had appreciated beautiful females tossing themselves into his arms. Even though he'd been a mere cur, his short blond hair that fell across his brow and tanned, surfer good looks ensured he had more than his fair share of babes. And it didn't hurt that his body was chiseled muscles beneath the low riding jeans and muscle shirt.

And oh yeah, he'd made an obscene fortune cranking out prescription drugs from his private lab.

Now it took every ounce of willpower to politely set aside the damned nymph and not toss her into the line of sleek metallic mannequins showing off the latest designer swimwear.

"Didn't we meet in . . ." she began, but Caine wasn't listening as he swept past her and headed straight toward the tiny blonde who was fingering a pretty white sundress with black polka dots.

"Cassie."

He had barely reached her side when her hands grasped the bottom of her sweatshirt and began pulling it over her head.

"I want to try it on."

"Holy shit." He grabbed her hands, yanking the sweatshirt back into place. "Wait."

She frowned in confusion. "But you said—"

"Yeah, I know what I said," he muttered. When was he going to learn she took every word quite literally?

"Did I do something wrong?"

"Never." He brushed a finger over her pale cheek. Christ, she was so unbearably innocent. "Why don't you show me what you like and I'll pick out the right size?"

"You can do that just by looking?"

His lips twisted in a dry smile. "It's a gift."

"A well-practiced gift?"

He stilled, regarding her in surprise. Despite the fact they'd been constant companions over the past weeks, Cassie rarely seemed aware of his presence, let alone the fact that he was a red-blooded male.

Not that he took it personally. She was plagued by her visions of the future and too often impervious to the world around her.

"Are you truly interested?" he husked.

She flashed him a dimpled smile. "Perhaps."

He swallowed a growl, his body once again hard and aching. She was going to have a raving lunatic on her hands before this was over.

"Better than nothing." He motioned toward the hovering saleslady, indicating he wanted one of the sundresses, before steering Cassie toward the khaki shorts and pretty summer tops. "Now, let's choose a few sensible outfits before we move on."

Within an hour they had a reasonable pile of clothes for both of them and a bill that would make most men shudder in horror.

Caine, however, didn't so much as flinch as he gathered the packages and headed out of the store. They had left Missouri with nothing more than the clothes on their backs after Cassie had offered her warning to Laylah. Tonight he intended to enjoy a hot shower, clean clothes, good food, and a soft bed. In that order.

In silence they wandered down the wide passageway, occasionally halting for Cassie to peer into the windows. For the moment, Caine was content to allow her to behave as a normal female. It was all too rare that she was able to put aside the burden of her visions.

And as long as he didn't detect any danger lurking . . .

His brain closed down as his searching gaze was snared

by the sight of lace and ribbons and feminine temptation spread in front of a shop window.

Instinct alone had him herding Cassie through the door and into the hushed atmosphere of the exclusive store.

"What are you doing?" she asked in confusion.

"We did your shopping, now it's my turn," he informed her, moving toward a table that held a pile of satin teddies with matching thongs.

Oh . . . hell.

Cassie halted at his side, her expression puzzled. "Here?"

"Absolutely." Dropping his packages, Caine reached for a scarlet teddy, holding up the fragile garment for her inspection. "What do you think?"

"Tiny." There was a faint hint of dimples. "I don't think it will fit you."

Heat blasted through him at the vivid image of Cassie wearing the lacy lingerie and spread across his bed, that same almost-smile teasing at her lips.

"We'll take one of each color," he croaked toward the saleswoman.

"They're not very practical," Cassie protested.

"Practical is the last thing you should be when you're wearing fine lingerie."

Expecting an argument, Caine was caught off guard when she reached to gently stroke a finger over the shimmering fabric.

"I suppose they will be comfortable to sleep in."

Sleep?

Caine's fantasy abruptly altered to reality—a reality in which Cassie slept like a baby in one bed while he tossed and turned in another.

Did he really need to add in a skimpy bit of lace to add to his torture?

"For one of us," he wryly admitted.

Predictably, she didn't have a clue why he was suddenly questioning his own sanity. "What?"

He headed toward the discreet sales desk at the back of the store, pulling his wallet from his pocket.

"I'm an idiot."

Chapter 2

Cassie wandered through the casino, watching the humans as they stood mesmerized by the flashing lights and spinning wheels of the slot machines. The air was filled with their tangled emotions—the hope, the greed, the rare jolt of joy, and the far more common desperation.

She was fascinated, even as she was saddened by their frantic attempts to grasp . . . something.

Money? Sex? Happiness?

Without thought, she reached to grab Caine's hand, needing the steady sense of security he offered. He squeezed her fingers, tugging her closer to his hard body as a group of drunken revelers stumbled past.

"As much as I enjoy civilization, are you going to tell me what we're doing here?" he murmured, the scent of soap and shampoo from his recent shower doing nothing to disguise the warm, wicked tang of his wolf.

For reasons that Cassie didn't understand, a rash of excitement prickled over her skin, making her want to strip off her new sundress and rub against the male at her side.

Of course she didn't give in to the impulse.

She was slowly learning that there were all sorts of stupid

rules and regulations that had to be followed when surrounded by mortals. And taking off her clothing seemed to be at the top of the list.

Instead she turned her thoughts to his question, heaving a faint sigh. "I'll tell you when I know," she said.

"Brilliantly vague."

She shrugged. "It is what it is."

"That doesn't mean I have to like it," he muttered with a grimace.

"No."

She came to an abrupt halt, turning to meet his rueful expression. Despite the chronic distractions that clouded her mind, she knew that she didn't always appreciate this man as she should.

Who else would have saved her from a fate worse than death, and then stayed at her side as she had led him from one random place to another, compelled by the visions that consumed her to the point of oblivion?

No one, that was who, a voice whispered in the back of her mind. No one but Caine.

With a frown of concern, Caine reached to cup her cheek in his hand, his warm touch her only anchor to this world. "Cassie?" he prompted.

"I'm sorry," she said abruptly, her gaze skimming over his lean, finely chiseled features. He truly was a beautiful male with his pale hair shimmering like gold beneath the bright lights and his eyes as brilliant as sapphires. It was no wonder she could smell the desire coming from the numerous women staring at him with hungry eyes. "I haven't been fair to you."

His thumb pressed against her lips as he gave a shake of his head. "Don't."

She grasped his wrist, tugging his hand from her face.

She had to speak now. Who knew how long her brief clarity would last?

"I become . . . lost in my visions and I have never truly stopped to consider what you've sacrificed to keep me safe." Her fingers absently caressed the skin of his inner wrist, feeling the leap of his pulse at her soft touch. "Without you . . ."

His eyes darkened with a heat that Cassie felt to the tips of her toes.

"This isn't necessary," he growled.

Distantly she could hear the clanging noise of the machines and the deafening buzz of a hundred conversations, but in this moment she was aware of nothing beyond the man standing in front of her and the steady sapphire gaze that a woman could drown in.

"No, let me say this," she pleaded.

His lips tightened, but he was smarter than the average Were. He knew better than to try and halt a determined female. "Okay."

"For as long as I can remember I've been a prisoner." She shivered, battling back the grim memory of the past thirty years. "I was not only held hostage by the demon lord, but also my knowledge that I could never survive on my own."

He didn't bother to protest. They both knew that she wouldn't last a day without him. "That's something you're never going to have to worry about," he gruffly promised.

She stepped closer, the sizzling power of his wolf calling to her most primitive instincts. Although she couldn't shift, her beast still crawled beneath her skin, relishing the delectable male who had earned her trust. Something she would never have believed possible just a few weeks ago.

"If it wasn't for you I would still be in that cave."

"Don't make me into a hero, Cassie." He scowled. "We both know I started out as the villain of the piece."

Her lips twitched. She might not be worldly, but she knew that Caine was far more comfortable with his bad-boy image. And from what he'd confessed, he deserved the reputation.

But as far as she was concerned, he'd always be her champion.

"If you were a villain, then you wouldn't be here with me," she pointed out softly.

He snorted, running a searing gaze down her slender curves shown to advantage by the dress. "Have you looked in the mirror?" he demanded. "There isn't a red-blooded male who wouldn't kill to share a hotel room with you."

She ignored his ridiculous words, tilting her head to study him with a curious gaze. "Why do you stay?"

"I just told you."

Her fingers tightened on his wrist, annoyed by his flippant tone. "I'm unfamiliar with the world, but I'm not stupid, Caine."

He arched a golden brow. "I never thought you were."

"I've seen how the females watch you."

"Really?" Something dark and predatory flashed through his eyes. "And how's that?"

She glanced toward the gaggle of women who pretended to watch the roulette table while they were sneaking looks of longing in Caine's direction. For no reason at all, she felt the sudden urge to bare her teeth at them. Or maybe she would yank out a few handfuls of their overbleached hair.

"They would be eager to share their bodies with you," she said, an edge in her voice she'd never heard before. "If all you desired was sex, then you could find a much easier, not to mention a far more experienced, bed partner."

A slow, wicked smile curved his lips as he abruptly wrapped an arm around her waist and hauled her tight against his body. "There's sex and then there's what is going to happen between us."

She trembled, a pleasurable heat exploding in the pit of her stomach. "And what's that?" she husked.

His gaze dipped to her lips, the scent of his wolf filling the air. "Magic."

Entranced by the sensations flowing through her, Cassie tilted back her head to study his beautiful face. "You haven't told me why you stay."

For a long moment she thought he might refuse to answer. Then, threading his fingers in her hair, he heaved a faint sigh. "You could say that I'm trying to even the scales."

"Even the scales?"

His expression became distracted as he allowed his fingers to run through her hair, as if mesmerized by the satin smoothness of the strands. "Because of my bloated ego, the Weres were nearly destroyed," he said, clearly regretting the years he'd devoted to helping Briggs, a crazed Were who'd been in league with the demon lord holding her captive. "It's only fair that I sacrifice to keep their most prized possession safe."

She tensed at his low words, absurdly hurt. "So I'm a duty?"

His head lowered so he could bury his face in the curve of her neck, breathing deeply of her scent. "That's what I tell myself so I can sleep at night."

She laid her hands against his chest, angling her head so he could have easier access to the vulnerable line of her throat.

This was Caine. And she trusted him without question.

"I'm not sure what that means," she breathed.

He went rigid at her unspoken gesture of capitulation, his fingers biting into the curve of her hip before he was abruptly jerking away, a flush staining his cheeks.

"Neither do I, and I intend to keep it that way," he muttered, turning to head across the gaudy carpet of the casino.

"Caine?" She hurried after him, unsure what she'd done wrong. "What is it?"

"Dinner." His step never slowed as he grimly headed for the nearby buffet.

"You're hungry?"

"Christ, you have no freaking idea."

Gaius's lair in the Louisiana wetlands

The Immortal Ones were the stuff of legends.

Centuries ago a clan of vampires had chosen to leave the world behind. Using Nefri's powerful medallion, they'd traveled through the Veil to another dimension where they were secluded from the weaknesses that plagued the less civilized.

Beyond the Veil there was no hunger, no lust, no need for sleep.

Instead, they devoted their nights to studying among the endless libraries or cultivating the gardens that managed to grow despite the lack of sunlight. And their days to meditation.

But it was the rumors that they retained the old powers lost to the vampires of this world that made them feared.

Most of the gossip was exaggerated, but there were still some forgotten talents that could be mastered.

Which, of course, was precisely why Gaius had petitioned to travel through the Veil after the death of his mate. Although most had assumed that he'd been seeking the peace to be found on the other side.

As if meditation and flowers could ease the brutal loss of his beloved Dara.

Stupid bastards.

Forced to stand and watch his mate being burned at the

stake by a rival vampire clan, Gaius would have walked
straight into the sun if it hadn't been for the Dark Lord.

Even as Dara had burned, the powerful deity had appeared as a misty shadow at his side, whispering promises
of Dara's return from the grave, all for the small price of
Gaius's soul.

It was a trade-off that Gaius had made without a second
thought. The return of his mate? Hell yes, he'd sell his soul
a dozen times over. And it was a decision he hadn't regretted,
despite the long years of seclusion beyond the Veil.

Obeying his new lord, he'd avoided attracting attention
while learning the skill of shape-shifting and eventually
using the medallion he'd found hidden beneath one of the
fountains to mist-walk. It was the latter skill that had allowed
him to escape undetected from the Veil to return to the world
he'd left behind so many years ago.

Briefly disoriented by his abrupt journey, Gaius leaned
against the nearest cypress tree and struggled to regain his
balance.

He felt . . .

Yeah. That was it.

He *felt* all the things that were forgotten on the other side.

The weight of his slender body covered by a simple robe.
The summer breeze that stirred the dark strands of his hair,
which he wore short and slicked from his face. Startled, he
lifted a hand to touch the chilled skin of his cheek before
trailing down the strong thrust of his nose, which bore the
proud stamp of his days as a Roman general. Most creatures
would find him handsome, he vaguely recalled, although his
dark eyes remained as bleak and lifeless as the day he'd
watched Dara die.

And then he was struck by less desirable sensations.

With a frown his fingers shifted to the fangs that suddenly
throbbed at the distant scent of human blood.

Hunger.

And not just of the liquid variety, he angrily realized, his body hardening with a nearly forgotten ache of desire.

Shoving away the unpleasant realization, Gaius grimly turned his attention to the secluded house that was located on the edge of the Louisiana swamp.

Built on brick stilts, it was a large structure painted white with black shutters and a screened-in wraparound porch. The front yard was filled with large trees draped in Spanish moss that effectively hid the place from the narrow path that led to the small town.

All in all it was the perfect place for a vampire to remain hidden.

Which was no doubt why the Dark Lord had sent him here to wait for his next orders.

Ignoring the humid heat and swarms of bugs that filled the air, Gaius made his way through the front gate and up the wide staircase. He stepped through the door of the porch, relieved to catch sight of the overhead fan providing a much needed breeze.

Although he'd been on the other side of the Veil, he was well aware of the changes in this world, and after centuries of choosing a spartan existence to concentrate on his studies, he was anxious to enjoy a lair equipped with all the modern technology. Including electricity and a hot shower.

And privacy.

Narrowing his gaze, he belatedly realized the scent of human was coming from inside the house. And that it was drawing closer.

His time away had made him sloppy, he chastised himself, reaching beneath his robe to withdraw the *pugio*—a small Roman dagger—he'd hidden among the satin folds. Then, moving with a silent speed, he shoved open the door and stepped into the shadows of the living room.

"Who is there?" he growled, his gaze skimming over the padded bamboo chairs and couch that were scattered over the wooden floorboards.

There was a faint rustle, then the lights tucked in the high, open-beamed ceiling were flipped on and a young female stepped into the room.

"Me."

Gaius tucked away his dagger. If he decided to kill the human it would be by draining all that sweet, tempting blood.

"Be more precise," he commanded, his speech pattern becoming rigidly formal as his anger overcame his months of secret training to mingle among the natives.

"Sally Grace."

His gaze narrowed as he studied the intruder. She might have been cute in a childish manner, with her dark hair pulled into two braids on each side of her pale, pretty face. But her brown eyes were heavily lined with makeup and her full lips painted a shocking shade of black and pierced with a gold hoop. There was a matching hoop in one brow and a dozen more along the shell of her ear.

Worse was her strange costume.

The scarlet corset was all that covered her tiny bosom and a tiny leather skirt was plastered to her hips. She had on leggings and high-heeled boots, but they did little more than emphasize her slender curves. She clearly had no males in her life to forbid such a shocking display of her body.

"Why are you in my home?"

She propped her shoulder against the doorjamb, looking far too comfortable. "Our master sent me to make sure you had everything you need for your return."

So, she was sent by the Dark Lord.

Not that it made her presence any more welcome.

"You are a housekeeper?"

"Housekeeper?" The female straightened, her hands slapping on her hips in outrage. "Do I look like a freaking housekeeper?"

His jaw tightened at her shrill tone. "Do not test me, female."

She gave a toss of her head. "I happen to be a very powerful witch. One who is favored above all of the Dark Lord's disciples . . ."

"A witch." His power blasted through the air, sending the female slamming into the wall of the attached dining room. He stalked forward, his fangs exposed as he prepared to put an end to the bitch. It had been a witch who had held him powerless as his beloved mate was burned at the stake. "I detest witches."

Reaching the female, he wrapped his fingers around her throat and began to squeeze. He sure as hell wasn't going to soil his tongue with her tainted blood.

Intent on choking the life from his companion, Gaius was unprepared when her dark eyes abruptly flashed with a crimson fire.

"Stop," she commanded, her voice low and filled with a power that made Gaius pause in astonishment.

Staring at her suddenly blank face, Gaius felt alarm flicker down his spine. "What's wrong with your eyes?"

Sally's lips parted, but it wasn't her voice coming out of her mouth. "Gaius."

He frowned, realizing that the power choking the air had nothing to do with the witch and everything to do with the strange being invading her body.

"Who is here?"

"It is your master, my beloved son."

Gaius narrowed his gaze, his fingers maintaining their tight grip on Sally's neck. "Is this a trick?"

"No trick," the deep voice assured him. "Sally is a conduit."

"Conduit?"

"Through her I am capable of speaking directly with my servants."

Was that supposed to be reassuring?

Gaius grimaced. It'd been bad enough to have the Dark Lord whispering in his mind when he was meditating. To have his voice coming out of the witch's lips was . . . what were the words used today?

Freaking him out?

Yeah, that was it.

Totally freaking him out.

Not that he was about to reveal his weakness. The Dark Lord was a pitiless monster who would destroy him the moment he suspected Gaius might not be of use to him.

"I have no love for magic," he rasped.

The black lips twisted in a mocking smile. "Then we will make this swift."

"Very well." Grudgingly loosening his grip on the witch, he hid his shaking hands in the folds of his black robe. "I am here as you wished."

"You have acquired the skills that I requested?"

Gaius gave a dip of his head. "I am capable of altering my shape, although only for short periods of time."

"And the other?"

"I was able to travel through the Veil with the medallion you left hidden on the other side."

"Good." The crimson fire flickered in the female's dark eyes. "The medallion will also allow you to enter the mists where I am trapped."

"Is that what you desire of me?" Gaius demanded, hoping his bland tone disguised his reluctance.

He was willing to do whatever necessary to bring back his dearest Dara, but the thought of joining the Dark Lord in his hell dimension was enough to give anyone the shudders.

"Not yet. I have a duty for you to perform before joining me."

He offered a bow. "I am yours to command."

"Yes, you are," the dark voice purred.

Gaius wisely ignored the taunt. "What would you have of me?"

"A prophet has been discovered."

Gaius widened his eyes in shock. He'd heard the rumors, of course, but he'd dismissed them. It had been centuries since the last prophet had walked the earth.

"A true seer?"

"I want her brought to me," the Dark Lord commanded. "Alive."

"Of course. Is she a human?"

"A Were."

Gaius considered the logistics. He didn't remember his life as a Roman general, but he maintained a rare talent for strategy.

Which, unfortunately, was precisely the reason his clan had been attacked . . .

No. He wrenched his mind from the painful memories. He couldn't go there. Guilt, no matter how well deserved, was a distraction he couldn't afford.

"That will make her capture a trifle more difficult, but I am confident I will be capable of bringing her to you with minimal injury."

"She is being protected by a male Were," the Dark Lord continued. "I want him brought as well."

"Why?" Even as the word left his lips, Gaius knew he'd made a mistake.

On cue, an agonizing pain drilled through his head, sending him to his knees.

"It is not your place to question me."

"No, Master."

"I will provide you with the necessary companions to assist you in your task."

Companions? That was the last thing he needed, or wanted.

"That's not necessary . . ." Once again the pain shot through his brain, briefly blinding him with the sheer anguish. "Gods."

"Gaius." The witch jerkily moved to pat the top of his aching head, her face still blank and her eyes glowing with an eerie power. "Do not make me wish I had chosen another servant for this important task."

Forcing himself back to his feet, Gaius managed a stiff smile. "You will have no reason for regret, Master."

There was a long pause. As if the Dark Lord was debating the pleasure of killing him against the need to capture the prophet. At last the witch gave a nod. "Sally will travel with you as my personal eyes and ears."

Gaius was proud and stubborn and obsessed with his dead mate. But he wasn't stupid.

This time there was no hesitation as he gave a nod of his head. "Of course."

"I will have two others join you."

Another hasty nod.

He would make certain his . . . companions understood who was in charge when they arrived.

"Where will we find the prophet?" he asked.

The crimson eyes flared. "If I knew where she was I would not need you, would I?"

Good point.

Las Vegas

After consuming enough food to feed a small army, or one hungry Were, Caine escorted Cassie back through the casino.

Instinctively, he slowed his pace to match his companion's as she studied the drunken crowds that weaved their way past blinking machines toward the cover band singing at the back of the vast room.

He wanted to be far away from the chaotic blast of sound and light and emotions that beat at his senses. His change to pureblooded Were left him hypersensitive to even the most subtle stimulus and being stuck in the middle of Vegas made him feel as if he were being sandblasted by sensations.

Worse, his most primitive instincts were stirred to a fever pitch by the male gazes that followed Cassie with blatant lust.

But, he wasn't a masochist.

With every passing night it was growing more difficult to keep to his role as protector. Spending any extra time alone with her in a hotel room . . .

A very bad idea.

Especially when she'd just dropped her latest little bombshell on him.

Covertly studying her perfect profile, he kept a possessive hand at her lower back, steering her toward the front lobby. Maybe if they were on the streets he could clear the cobwebs and return his mind to the task of keeping this female safe.

Which was all he should be thinking about.

Busy reminding himself that there wasn't a demon around who wouldn't kill to get their hands on a genuine prophet, Caine was unprepared when Cassie came to an abrupt halt, regarding him with a baffled expression.

"Have I done something wrong?"

He frowned at the unexpected question. "Why do you ask?"

"You keep staring at me."

"I'm not the only one," he muttered, curling his lips into a snarl as a group of men dressed in khakis and polo shirts halted to ogle Cassie's slender body shown in shocking detail by the sundress. "You need more clothes on."

"I'm not going to be distracted. Tell me what's wrong."

Caine heaved a sigh. For once the emerald eyes held a remarkable clarity. The one time he wanted her to be oblivious to him, he wryly acknowledged.

A typical female.

"What you said earlier," he abruptly admitted.

She grimaced. "I'm sorry, I still don't know why I felt compelled to come here," she said, misunderstanding his confession. "I suppose it will eventually come to me."

He shook his head. "No, not that."

"Then what?"

"About you . . ."

"Caine?" she prompted.

Oh hell. He had to know. It had been eating at him for the past two hours. "About you not being as experienced as other women."

"Oh." She tilted her head to the side. "Are you asking if I've ever had sex?"

With a muffled exclamation, Caine tugged Cassie into a shallow alcove. "Shh."

"Why?" She waved a hand toward the passing crowd. "They all talk about sex here. A lot."

He swallowed a moan, his body reacting with predictable enthusiasm to her words. "You haven't answered my question."

Without warning, she lifted her hand to stroke her fingertips lightly down the line of his jaw.

"You don't need to be a prophet to know that a female who has been held in one prison after another doesn't have a great deal of experience with men," she said softly. "There were a few, of course, but not like a normal female would enjoy."

He held her gaze, reaching up to press her fingers against his cheek. "Briggs?" he asked, referring to the demented Were that had helped to hold her hostage.

"What about him?"

"Briggs . . ."—he found it difficult to even utter the question—"never abused you?"

"Of course not." She allowed a small, mysterious smile to curve her lips. "He was terrified of me."

Caine released a shaky breath, savagely relieved that she hadn't been harmed, even though he'd already suspected the truth.

The innocence shimmering in her eyes was more than just a lack of worldly experience.

"So you're a . . ."

"Virgin."

Chapter 3

Caine shuddered.

There . . . She'd said it.

The V word.

"Virgin," he muttered.

She blinked, tugging her hand from his loose grip. "Why do you make it sound like a bad thing?"

"Not bad. Just . . ." He shoved his fingers through his hair. Dammit, how did he explain he wanted her so badly he could barely breathe, but she was depending on him to keep her safe? And to top it off, she was a damned virgin. Only an animal would take advantage of her. "Christ."

"In the books that I used to read the males always seemed to appreciate the privilege of taking their mate's innocence," she mused.

He moaned, wondering if she were deliberately trying to torture him. "Let me guess," he said in a thick voice. "You read romance books?"

"When Briggs would bring them to me. I liked them." She tilted her chin. "In fact, I still do."

Holy hell. Could this get any worse?

"Of course you do," he muttered, regarding her warily.

"But you understand that men aren't really like the heroes in a story?"

"You are," she said with a confidence that had him shaking his head in instant denial.

"No."

"You rescued me from the demon lord."

"Are you kidding me?" He stepped close enough to make sure that not even a vampire could overhear his words. "The only thing I did was stand in front of the bastard long enough to get myself killed and then mysteriously resurrected."

"You led me out of the caves."

"I was saving my own skin."

"And now you have taken the role of my protector," she said, clearly determined to see him as some sort of savior. A pathetic joke. "What is that if not heroic?"

He grasped her shoulders, gazing down at her wide eyes with a rising sense of frustration. "Shit, Cassie, if I was really heroic I would take you to your sisters where you would truly be protected and get the hell out of your life."

She stiffened, clearly not eager to be reunited with her three identical sisters.

Understandable, considering that one was wed to Styx, the King of Vampires, and another wed to Styx's most trusted guard, Jagr. While the third had mated with the King of Weres, Salvatore.

As soon as they managed to get their hands on Cassie she would be locked away for her own good. Even if being caged again would drive her mad.

"But you won't?" she breathed.

"No, I won't," he admitted without hesitation. "But not because I'm a good guy."

"Then why?"

His hands slid up to lightly graze the sides of her neck, relishing the trust she offered him. A Were would never allow anyone but family or their most intimate friends to be near their throat.

"Because I'm a selfish SOB."

Her lips parted, as if to deny his words; then he felt her tense beneath his fingers, her eyes widening.

"Caine."

"What?" He shifted to make certain his body was between her and the lobby. "What is it?"

"Something's happened."

His instincts were on full alert, but with no visible enemy, he was stuck growling at thin air. "I've warned you, I don't speak vague."

"A . . ." Her words died on her lips as the astonishing green of her eyes was clouded by a strange white glow. "Fluctuation," she at last said.

Caine frowned, waiting for the familiar glyph to shimmer in the air, revealing yet another prophecy that only Cassie could decipher.

On this occasion, however, nothing appeared.

"A fluctuation in what?"

"The game. A new player has arrived."

Freaking perfect.

"I don't suppose he or she is batting for our team?" he asked dryly.

"No. His heart is dark." The white faded from her eyes to reveal a sudden flare of horror as she grabbed his arm to keep her knees from buckling. "Pain. So much pain."

Wrapping a steadying arm around her waist, he covertly made sure he could easily palm the dagger he'd hidden at the small of his back as well as the handgun holstered beneath his left arm.

"Is he in Vegas?"

She heaved a sigh of frustration. "I don't know."

"I suppose we'll find out soon enough." He stepped back,

his gaze sweeping over the lobby for any hint of danger. "In the meantime we need to get away from these crowds."

Two days later
Gaius's lair in Louisiana

Gaius brushed a hand down the elegant black suit that was perfectly tailored to his slender body before making sure the pale silver tie was lying smooth against the white silk shirt.

Despite his dislike for the witch, he had to admit that Sally had done a fine job in preparing for his arrival. Not only had she refitted the house with heavy shutters that kept out most of the daylight, and surrounded it with a revulsion spell that would keep out all but the most powerful demons, but she'd ordered an entire closet full of clothing that suited his understated but elegant tastes.

Odd that such a flamboyant little freak could possess such fine taste in men's attire.

He could only hope she was equally talented in fulfilling his most current need.

On cue, he caught the scent of peaches that always seemed to cling to the witch and moments later there was a light knock on the door.

"Commander?" she called softly.

Gaius's lips twitched. After two days in his constant companionship the female had lost most of her smug arrogance. There was nothing quite like being trapped with a lethal predator who hated witches to give a person an attitude adjustment.

"Enter."

He heard her draw in a deep breath before pushing open the door to study him with a brittle bravado that didn't mask her wariness.

Smart little witch.

Hovering in the doorway, Sally looked like a goth rag doll with her pigtails and heavy black eyeliner and matching lipstick. She was wearing some sort of red camisole with a puffy net skirt.

"It's time for the ceremony."

Gaius adjusted the French cuff links, his expression frigidly controlled. There was no way in hell he was going to reveal to the sneaky little bitch just how unnerved he was by the thought of allowing her to perform her magic on him. It was bad enough that he'd gone to his knees to plead for mercy when the Dark Lord had announced that Gaius would be "altered" to better suit the master's needs.

"You have brought what I requested?" he instead demanded.

Her lips thinned, but she offered a ready nod. Good. The witch was learning. Like any good general, he expected complete obedience from his soldiers.

"I did."

"Well?"

"She's in the guest room."

"Show me."

The dark eyes flared with annoyance at his imperious tone but, wise enough to keep her mouth shut, Sally turned to lead him down the hallway.

Gaius followed at a measured pace, on full alert despite the supposed security of the lair. He'd learned a cruel lesson in ever lowering his guard the night his clan was attacked.

A lesson he would never forget.

"Have you heard from our companions?" he demanded as they climbed the steps leading to the upper floor.

"Yes, they should be arriving within a few hours."

His jaw tightened as he glowered at the back of her head. "You still claim to know nothing about them?"

"I know as much as you do."

"So you say."

She flinched as his icy power lashed through the air, but hunching her shoulders, she halted in front of a heavy door and pointed at the small window that revealed the metal-lined cell inside.

"The woman is in there." She waited for Gaius to move to peer through the window. "Is she satisfactory?"

Gaius hissed as his fangs lengthened in primitive hunger. The slender female chained to the wall possessed the long, dark hair that he'd demanded as well as the golden skin and dark, almond eyes that spoke of the Middle East.

She wasn't an exact match for his beloved Dara, of course.

Her features weren't nearly so delicately carved and her body was covered by a pair of cutoff shorts and a tiny halter top that his mate would have considered tacky, but she was close enough to stir the lusts that he'd nearly forgotten on the other side.

"Yes, she is . . . satisfactory," he admitted, his mouth watering as his gaze traced the line of throat. "Where did you find her?"

Sally shrugged. "Where you find everything. The Internet. Lucky for you she makes house calls." She grasped his wrist as Gaius's hand reached for the doorknob. "Not yet."

Gaius tensed, poised and ready to strike. "Remove your hand, witch."

Hastily, the female snatched back her hand, sensing death in the air. But she stubbornly refused to back down.

"First the ceremony and then the girl," she said.

Gaius offered her an icy glare. "You aren't foolish enough to believe you are in a position to give me orders?"

There was a sudden crimson fire in the witch's dark eyes and a warning heat that sizzled through the air.

"The order doesn't come from me."

Gaius shuddered. *Cristo.* He didn't know what was worse. His fear of being at the mercy of the witch's spell or the heavy weight of the Dark Lord's smothering powers.

"Fine," he snapped. "Let us be done with this ridiculous ceremony."

Sally nodded her head toward the end of the hallway. "I have prepared the room."

Still twitchy, Gaius followed the witch into the large room, his gaze landing on the thick line of salt poured into a circle in the center of the wood floor.

"Wait." He turned to regard Sally with a deep scowl. "Explain precisely what you intend to do to me."

She heaved a resigned sigh. "Again?"

He bared his fangs. "You've been remarkably unwilling to reveal the details."

Her eyes widened before she attempted to hide her fear behind a mask of bravado. "With the master's assistance I will conjure a spell that will remove your . . . scent."

"Why?"

"It will not only protect you from being tracked by your enemies, but as a shape-shifter you will be capable of becoming whomever or whatever you want to be without giving away your true identity."

She tried to make it sound oh so simple. Just a flick of her hand and, abracadabra, his scent was gone.

But nothing was ever simple.

For every action there is an equal and opposite reaction. . . .

Especially when it came to magic.

There would be a cost that he was far from certain he wanted to pay.

"I can accomplish the same goal with a disguise amulet," he pointed out in cutting tones.

"Yes, well, this spell will strip you a little . . ."

"What?"

"Deeper."

"Deeper?"

"It will remove more than just your scent."

Gaius narrowed his gaze. "You mean it will take away my very identity."

"Only on a physical level."

Her casual dismissal made his hands clench. It was that or wrapping them around her neck and crushing the life from her.

"And if I choose not to be"—he curled his lip in derision—"stripped?"

"That's something you need to discuss with the master."

Damn the witch. She had him backed in a literal corner and she knew it.

"*Cristo*," he growled, moving to stand in the center of the corner. "Just be done with it."

Sally ignored his command, moving around the room to light the wax candles with a solemn expression. Next she laid several long feathers in a bowl and set them on fire, filling the air with a cloud of smoke.

Then, once satisfied she'd performed the proper ritual, she slipped on a heavy black robe and shifted to stand directly in front of him.

Gaius made a sound of disgust, unimpressed by the elaborate ceremony. "Is this going to take all night?"

She lifted her hands, a slow smile curling her lips. "You might want to brace yourself."

That was the only warning before the spell slammed into him, sending him to his knees. Gods. He bent his head, quivering as the pain ravaged through him.

It felt as if he were being seared from the inside out.

As if the damned witch had ignited a bonfire in the pit of his stomach that was burning its way out of his body.

He groaned, his eyes squeezing shut as he battled back the howls of misery.

The bitch was doing this on purpose, he savagely told himself. She had him at her mercy and was obviously intent on making the most of her brief moment of power.

There was another wave of blazing pain and the sense of his very . . . what? His essence? Yes, his essence, being yanked from deep inside him.

He bent down until his forehead was pressed to the wood planks of the floor. This was no simple spell. This was a soul-deep invasion that was threatening to destroy him.

A sudden fear crawled down his spine as he recalled Sally's reference to the Dark Lord assisting her with the spell. Had the master decided to put an end to his faithful servant? It wouldn't be the first time the evil bastard had killed one of his minions for the sheer pleasure of watching him die.

Then, as quickly as the ruthless pain had struck, it was gone.

Slowly coming back to his senses, Gaius remained kneeling for a long moment. It was shameful enough that the witch had seen him collapse like a spineless sprite beneath her spell. He wasn't going to make it worse by trying to rise to his feet before he was certain he wouldn't end up planting his face into the floor.

When at last he was confident he could stand without embarrassing himself, Gaius flowed to his feet, glaring at the witch.

"You . . . whore," he growled, his hand pressing to his unbeating heart. "Did you take my soul?"

She paled as the candles flared, then were snuffed out

by his icy fury, but grimly held her ground. "You sold that a long time ago, Commander."

Well, wasn't that the god-awful truth?

He shrugged off the dark thought. What was done, was done. There was no going back now.

Instead, he pointed a finger toward the witch, his powers lashing against her with enough force to pin her against the wall.

"Tell me what you did to me."

She licked her lips, the scent of her fear teasing at his senses.

"I . . ."

He took a threatening step closer. "Tell me."

"I removed your existence," she hastily babbled.

Gaius barely resisted the ridiculous urge to glance down and make sure he hadn't simply vanished.

"Explain."

She lifted her hands in a pleading motion. "I don't know how."

"Try," he snapped. "Try very, very hard."

"The spell is designed to purge your identity," she haltingly attempted to clarify. "You have no scent, no . . . presence. Others will know that you're near, but unless they're an extremely powerful demon they won't be able to detect anything about you. Not even the fact you're a vampire."

It was exactly what he expected. So why did he feel as if he'd just been raped? He hissed, wishing he could at least have the satisfaction of killing the witch responsible for his sudden sense of loss.

"Gods."

Easily sensing his desire for death, Sally inched her way along the wall. At last she reached the door and, never allowing her wary gaze to leave his grim expression, she shoved it open. "Go to your female," she husked. "She'll make you all better."

His fury was abruptly forgotten.

Dara.

No. He gave a shake of his head. Not Dara. But a female who would ease his most pressing hungers. Surely he would feel better once he'd taken care of his needs?

Strolling toward the door, he paused long enough to whisper in Sally's ear. "Someday soon, witch," he warned.

He had the pleasure of watching her turn a sickly shade of gray before he was headed back down the hall and entering the lead-lined cell. Closing the door behind him, Gaius halted to savor the moment.

Was there anything sweeter than the rich scent of warm, female blood? Or the sight of his prey struggling in helpless terror?

A smile curved his lips as the female strained against the shackles chaining her to the wall. She turned her head from side to side, able to hear his arrival although the room was too dark for her human eyes to see him.

"Who's there? What do you want with me?" she rasped, the frantic beat of her heart like a siren's call to Gaius. "Talk to me, you perverted freak."

Compelled forward by his sharp-edged hunger, Gaius used his powers to light the lone candle set on a stool in a far corner. The flickering flame was barely noticeable in the vast darkness, but it provided just enough of a glow for the female to see Gaius's approach.

Her lips parted to scream, but cupping her face in his hands, Gaius peered deep into her wide eyes.

"Shhhh. Look at me," he purred, capturing her gaze and easily ensnaring her mind. He wasn't as talented as some vampires in enthralling humans, but the female readily succumbed to his power. In a heartbeat her face became slack and her muscles eased until her arms hung limply at her side, the heavy shackles forgotten.

"What is your name?" he asked softly.

"Farah."

Her voice was too high with a harsh American accent instead of Dara's husky, singsong voice, but Gaius grimly blocked out the reminders that this female could never fill the empty ache in the center of his heart.

"Pretty, but from this night forward you will be known as Dara."

"Dara," the female obediently parroted.

"Yes, and I am Gaius. The man of your deepest fantasy."

Instantly, her eyes darkened with a mindless devotion, her lips parting on a soft sigh. "Gaius," she breathed.

"Very good," he commended, his hands tightening on her face as he guided her down to her knees. "Now you will demonstrate just how pleased you are to be reunited with your beloved mate."

With the obvious skill of a professional, the female had his pants unzipped and her lips wrapped around his erection. Gaius groaned in approval, closing his eyes as he dredged up memories of his beautiful mate.

All too soon he was reaching an intense orgasm that had more to do with physical release than actual pleasure and, shoving one hand into her long hair, he yanked her upright. She made no move to fight him as he angled her head to the side and with one smooth strike had his fangs buried deep into the flesh of her neck.

He heard her low moan of arousal at his bite but, ignoring her writhing body, he drank deeply of her blood. He grimaced as the warm liquid slid down his throat. There was no taint of drugs and alcohol, thank the gods, but the taste was flat on his tongue.

Still, he drank deeply, only halting as he felt her heart

flutter in warning. It had been too long since he'd enjoyed feeding straight from the vein and the sensation was intoxicating.

Later, he would find a surrogate for Dara who was more pleasing to his taste buds. Then he could take full pleasure in draining this one dry.

Catching the sound of approaching footsteps, Gaius extracted his fangs and released his hold on the female. Boneless from her sexual reaction to his bite and her sudden drop in blood pressure, the female sagged against the chains that were all that kept her off the floor.

Not that Gaius noticed.

The woman was forgotten as he straightened his clothing and turned toward the door. He already sensed the reason for the witch's untimely approach.

With a brief rap on the door, Sally pressed it open, her gaze flicking toward the unconscious prostitute before meeting Gaius's sardonic smile.

"Our guests have arrived," she said stiffly.

His nose flared at the stench of dog already tainting his lair. "Curs?"

The witch didn't look any happier than Gaius. But then, why should she? Curs didn't like magic-users any more than vampires did.

"A matched set."

Gaius frowned. "I beg your pardon?"

She rolled her eyes. "You have to see it to believe it."

Not about to play guessing games, Gaius brushed past her to step into the hall. "Bring them to my study."

"What about the whore?"

He glanced back at the female, who hung from her shackles like a broken doll. "She will remain here."

Sally wrinkled her nose. "But . . ."

"If she dies I will see to her removal," he interrupted in

impatient tones. Humans were annoyingly squeamish when it came to corpses.

"Charming," Sally muttered.

Without bothering to reply, Gaius headed down the stairs and into the small library he'd taken as his study.

Not that he would ever consider the long room lined with shelves and furnished with a walnut desk and two matching chairs as more than a temporary place to conduct his business. Once Dara was returned to him, he would take her back to their vast palace hidden among the hills of Italy.

His lavish home possessed a library that was twice the size of this entire house and filled with thousands of precious books that dated back to the invention of the printing press. That did not even include the fragile scrolls that were kept protected in his vault.

Unfortunately, "beggars couldn't be choosers" and until the Dark Lord was satisfied that Gaius had fulfilled his side of the bargain, he was stuck in this backwoods swamp.

And worse, stuck with allies he neither wanted nor needed.

Leaning against the desk, Gaius smoothed back his dark hair and squared his shoulders as the stench of cur filled the air. There was a sharp knock on the door, but he waited for several long minutes before answering.

He was a master tactician who knew that the most subtle power plays were the most effective. Anyone could be a bully. It took cunning and patience to be a leader.

"Enter," he at last commanded.

A young man who looked to be thirty in human years entered first. He was built on muscular lines with a square head that was propped on a thick neck. His hair was blond and buzzed in military fashion that was matched by the green T-shirt and cammo pants.

Behind him was a smaller, female version of him, down to the military buzz and cammo pants.

Cristo. He understood Sally's comment that they were a matched pair.

Strolling forward, the twins halted to stand side by side, their arms folded over their chests.

"Vampire," the male said with a respectful dip of his head.

Gaius slowly straightened from the desk, his expression one of chilly displeasure. "You will call me Commander."

Anger sizzled through the cur's hazel eyes, but he was smart enough to keep his annoyance to himself.

"Whatever floats your boat," he muttered with a shrug. "I'm Dolf and this is my sister—"

"I do not care who you are or about your tedious life stories," Gaius interrupted in crushing tones.

The air prickled with the heat of the cur's mounting frustration.

"And a big fucking hello to you too."

"This is not a social call." Gaius flicked a dismissive gaze over the two. "Tell me why the Dark Lord believes mere curs can be of service to me."

Dolf clenched his jaw. "Because I have powers beyond a *mere* cur."

Gaius ignored the hint of sarcasm in the man's voice. "What powers?"

"This." Lifting his hand, the cur pointed toward the shelves of books, muttering beneath his breath. There was a brief moment when Gaius wondered if the man was demented; then without warning one of the heavy books flew off the shelf to land on the desk with a loud thud.

Gaius hissed in disgust. Magic. Was the Dark Lord deliberately attempting to test his loyalty by surrounding him with creatures he most detested?

"You're a witch?" he spat before he could control his reaction. "How is that possible?"

The cur shrugged, obviously accustomed to the question. Not surprising. He might very well be the only magical cur on the face of the earth.

"I was a fully trained witch before I was turned."

Gaius narrowed his gaze. "Curs hate witches."

"True."

"Then how did you get bitten?"

The cur smiled with a smug arrogance. "I can be very convincing."

Gaius wasn't impressed. "If that is your only skill, then you and your sister can—"

"Wait," the cur rasped.

"What?"

"Ingrid." Dolf glanced toward the silent woman at his side. "Show him."

Reaching into her back pocket, the female cur withdrew a small cell phone and held it up for his inspection.

"You're here to sell me a phone?" he mocked.

Ingrid pressed a button on the phone that brought up the picture of a blond-haired man with pale blue eyes.

"I worked for Caine," she said.

"Caine?" It took Gaius a moment to realize why the name was familiar. "The Were protecting the prophet?"

"Yep." The cur smiled. "This is his direct line."

Chapter 4

Las Vegas

The penthouse suite of the casino consumed most of the top floor. Tastefully decorated in muted shades of brown and tan, it had a large sitting room filled with long sofas and overstuffed chairs arranged around a wet bar and hot tub. On each side were matching bedrooms with their own private bathrooms that were as large as most spas.

Such hushed elegance was a welcomed respite from the crowded gaming rooms, but it was the stunning view from the glass walls that attracted most guests.

Caine included, although it wasn't for the usual reasons, Cassie wryly conceded.

The overprotective Were didn't care that the view at night offered a dazzling display of lights from the nearby casinos, or that during the day there was a breathtaking panorama of the surrounding desert and line of craggy hills.

His only interest was having the best possible view to make sure that nothing could sneak up on them. And of course, being high enough off the ground to keep anything without wings from sneaking through the window.

Cassie appreciated his concern. She truly did. It was just . . .

Pacing from one end of the sitting room to the other, Cassie struggled to pinpoint the source of her dissatisfaction. Not an easy task. Cassie rarely remembered that beyond her visions she was a normal female who should possess normal female emotions. And she most certainly never took them out to examine them.

Not until Caine.

So now she was stuck trying to process the bizarre contradictions that were plaguing her.

The breathtaking tingles of excitement that raced through her whenever Caine happened to touch her, followed by the achy sense of disappointment when he pulled away. The restless inability to concentrate when he was in the same room and the ridiculous fear the moment he left the hotel suite without her.

A growingly common occurrence, she acknowledged, halting to stare out the glass wall, barely noticing the streets baking beneath the fierce summer sun or the wilting tourists jamming their way into the buses that briefly halted before moving on to the next casino.

Over the past four days Caine had spent an inordinate amount of time searching for enemies that he seemed convinced were lurking just outside the door. She sensed it was more than the driving need to protect her that was sending him out the door, but she didn't have interpersonal experience to know what she was doing wrong.

Or more importantly, how to halt him.

She turned, her gaze instinctively searching out the clock set above the entertainment center. It had been three hours since Caine left.

Far longer than he was usually gone.

Her strange sense of abandonment ratcheted up another notch. Had he gone for good this time?

It would be perfectly understandable. Playing babysitter to a female who spent most of her life besieged by glimpses of the future wasn't a role any man would willingly take on. If Caine had grown tired and decided to cut his losses, she wouldn't blame him for a minute.

The brave, noble thought had barely crossed her mind when she ruined it all by breathing a tiny sob of relief as she caught the familiar scent of Caine's approach.

He hadn't abandoned her . . .

Wrapping her arms around her waist, she forced herself not to leap forward and knock the poor man down as he stepped into the hotel suite and closed the door. Unfortunately, she couldn't prevent her shaky sigh of relief or the compulsive words that tumbled from her lips before she could halt them. "You're back."

He appeared weary, with a hint of golden stubble on his jaw and his exquisite sapphire eyes shadowed. His white-blond hair was rumpled, as if he'd been running his fingers through it, and his muscles tightly coiled beneath the tight white T-shirt and faded jeans.

Still, he was on instant alert as he caught sight of her pale face. Moving with liquid speed, he was across the room, grasping her shoulders in a tight grip.

"What is it?" His gaze ran down her slender body, assuring himself that she was unharmed. "Did something happen?"

"No, you were just gone a long time. I thought . . ." She bit her lip, unwilling to burden him with her ridiculous fears.

Of course, he easily read her mind. It was one of his tricks that she didn't particularly appreciate.

"I'm sorry." Stepping back, he scrubbed his face with his hands. "I didn't mean to worry you."

"Where did you go?"

He shrugged. "I made a sweep of the hotel."

She frowned. It didn't take three hours to make a sweep of the hotel. Not unless he was searching room by room.

"Do you sense trouble?" she asked.

"Always."

She caught the dry edge in his voice. It wasn't a sense of trouble that was bothering him. Or at least, not entirely.

"You don't have to make excuses, you know."

"Excuses?"

"For leaving the room." She tried to keep her voice steady. "You clearly dislike being here with me."

"Dislike?" A raw disbelief darkened his eyes. "Is that what you think?"

"I can sense your tension."

"It sure as hell isn't dislike." She could hear his teeth grinding together. "I wish to God it was."

She frowned, realizing that once again she'd gotten it wrong. "Then what's bothering you?"

"I need a shower."

With an abrupt motion, he was spinning on his heel and heading into the bedroom he'd claimed as his own. Minutes later she heard the sound of the shower running.

For a confused moment she was hurt by his sharp retreat. What had she done now to make him so eager to flee from her company?

Then she caught the unmistakable scent of his arousal.

Oh.

Was that why he'd taken off in such a hurry? Because he wanted to make love to her?

The thought was thrilling. Intoxicating.

She shivered as a bolt of desire sliced through her body. Along with a determination to do something about her clawing need. She might not understand why Caine was taking a shower rather than wrapping her in his arms as she longed for him to do, but she knew that she was done waiting for him to make the first move.

Before she could lose her nerve, Cassie headed across the room and into Caine's bedroom. She didn't have experience. But she did have primitive instincts.

What else did she need?

Pausing long enough to strip off her clothes, Cassie entered the bathroom, crossing the mosaic-tiled floor to step into the shower stall that was the size of most apartments.

The air, filled with moist steam laced with the scent of soap and warm male skin, wafted over her like a delicate caress. Cassie trembled, her nipples beading in anticipation as Caine turned to regard her with a wary gaze.

"Cassie." He reached to shut off the water. "What the hell?"

She smiled, slowly advancing even as he backed against the wall, his golden body shimmering with water droplets and his hair slicked from his beautiful face.

"I've come to ease your tension."

He squeezed his eyes shut, as if in pain. "A back rub isn't what I need, pet. Maybe later."

Halting directly in front of him, Cassie skimmed her hands over his broad chest, savoring the sensation of his muscles clenching beneath her soft touch. "Then tell me what you do need."

His eyes snapped open, his hands reaching to grasp her wrists, although he made no effort to pull them away.

Thank the gods.

"I need you out of here before I do something we're both going to regret," he rasped.

"You would regret making love to me?"

His eyes blazed with a compulsive need, even as his face

twisted with an expression of supreme torment. "Are you deliberately trying to drive me crazy?"

She leaned forward, trailing her lips over the silken smoothness of his chest. He tasted of heat and feral animal. Delicious.

"I only wanted to help."

"Help?" he breathed, his heart thundering beneath her lingering kiss and the scent of wolf suddenly filling the air.

Cassie felt her own wolf responding. Just because she couldn't shift she wasn't any less of a Were. Her animal was prowling just below her skin, restlessly seeking the touch of this man. "To relieve your tension."

Unexpectedly, Caine stiffened, his muttered curses warning he wasn't pleased by her explanation. "So you're willing to give away your virginity for a pity fuck?" he growled.

She pulled back, confused by his sudden anger. "I don't know what that means."

He grimaced, instantly regretting his harsh words. "It means that I'm not so desperate for sex that I'm willing to take your innocence."

Ah. Relief surged through her. He was simply protecting her.

Again.

She reached up to brush her lips along the line of his stubborn jaw. "And what if I am?"

She felt him tremble, his muscles coiled so tight it was a wonder he didn't cramp.

"What if you are what?" he managed to husk.

"Desperate," she readily admitted, nipping the lobe of his ear. "Would you give me a pity fu—"

Caine swooped his head down to end her words with a kiss that sent a sizzling jolt of pleasure straight through her body. She gasped, clutching at his shoulders as her toes curled in the warm water pooling at their feet.

"Don't say it," he commanded against her lips.

She allowed her tongue to trace the chiseled lines of his mouth, pleased when he groaned in helpless need.

"You did," she reminded him softly.

"I say a lot of stupid things when I'm—"

"Tense?" she offered when he bit off his explanation, a line of color marking his cheekbones.

"Yes." His voice was hoarse, his eyes glowing with his wolf in the billowing steam. "Cassie, you really need to leave."

In response, she pressed herself against his naked body, her breath catching at the feel of his hard erection pulsing against her lower stomach.

She hadn't expected it to be so large. Not only long, but thick. And hot. It burned against her skin like a branding iron.

Or maybe that was just her fevered imagination. Not because she was nervous. Or uncertain. But because she was so damned hungry for him.

She might be a virgin, but she had zero doubt that she wanted Caine. He was, in fact, the only man she'd *ever* wanted.

All of him.

"You don't want me?" she demanded.

His hands gripped her hips, his fingers digging into her flesh as if he were caught between the urge to yank her closer and shove her away. "So badly that I can barely think straight," he breathed.

She allowed her fingers to skim over his shoulders and then up the curve of his throat. Her touch was tentative. A Were was extremely selective in who was allowed to touch their neck. The fact he made no effort to halt her exploration proved he already accepted her on the most intimate level.

"Then make love to me."

He tensed, his eyes dark with pain. "No."

Stubborn man. Thankfully, she could be just as stubborn.

She threaded her fingers through his damp hair, deliberately rubbing the tight buds of her breasts against his chest, groaning at the tiny darts of sensation that arrowed straight to the pit of her stomach.

Oh . . . my.

"Why not?"

Caine swore, his fingers biting into the flesh of her hips. "I won't take your innocence because you're feeling sorry for me."

She stilled, tilting back her head to study him in confusion. "Is that what you think? That I feel sorry for you?"

"Why else would you be in my shower?"

"Because I want . . ."

He frowned as she struggled to find the words to express the need aching deep inside her. "What?"

"This."

She might not have the words, but she knew what she wanted. Besides, talk was overrated under the best of circumstances. And in this moment, it was completely superfluous.

Cupping his face in her hands, she went up on her tiptoes, pressing her lips to his in a kiss of blatant longing.

Caine froze and Cassie felt her heart sink. So much for her awkward attempt at seduction.

Then, just as she was about to pull back, Caine's arms lashed around her body and he hauled her off her feet so he could deepen the kiss with a satisfying urgency. Unlike her, the male possessed all the experience and skill necessary to turn the fumbling connection of their mouths into pure magic.

Sheets of heat blasted through her as his tongue expertly parted her lips and dipped inside. She trembled.

Sweet heaven. It was just as wonderful as she'd dreamed it would be.

The hungry press of his lips. The enticing stroke of his warm tongue. The arms that held her so tightly she could barely breathe.

But she needed . . .

What?

Hell, she didn't know. Only that Caine still wasn't close enough.

Using her innate strength, Cassie wrapped her legs around his waist and they both moaned as her most sensitive part rubbed against his fully erect shaft.

Oh yes. That's precisely what she needed.

The thought had barely drifted through her fuzzy mind when Caine lifted his head, regarding her flushed face through eyes that glowed with sapphire fire. "Cassie," he groaned, a feverish color staining his high cheekbones. "Christ. You don't know what you're doing."

She licked her tongue up the length of his neck, capturing the droplets of water clinging to his bronzed skin. "Not yet, but you're going to teach me."

He released a shuddering sigh. "I am?"

The heavy scent of his musk wrapped around her, his cock twitching against her.

"Hmm," she husked.

"No." His hand skimmed up her back to cup her nape. "Wait."

She nuzzled at the pulse hammering at the base of his throat, wondering what she was doing wrong. It was never this hard in the romance books to get a man to make love to a woman. They were always ready to get down to business.

"Now what?" she muttered.

He moaned as her teeth lightly bit his neck. "This isn't the time to be making life-altering decisions."

"Life-altering?" she tilted back her head to meet his smoldering gaze. "Isn't that a little melodramatic?"

His gaze skimmed over her flushed face to the small breasts that were begging for his attention.

"Pet, when I make you mine it's going to rock your world," he said, his need making his voice rough.

"I want it to be rocked now," she murmured, not above pleading. "Please, Caine."

His jaw tightened as his gaze skimmed downward, lingering on the small tattoo that marred the skin just beneath her belly button. "You've already been used enough."

Cassie barely resisted the urge to cover the crimson hieroglyphic that flickered with an unsettling shimmer. It wasn't as if Caine hadn't already seen the mark of the demon lord. Or felt the chill that clung to the strange tattoo.

"This isn't about being used," she corrected softly. "It's about sharing something wonderful. I need you, Caine."

There was a charged silence as Caine's savage need visibly battled with his conscience. Cassie held her breath, knowing that she'd already said too much.

The last thing she wanted was for him to do something he might later regret.

Then, with a low growl he moved to the back of the shower, lowering her onto the wet marble bench. Gently, he tugged her legs from around his waist, although he kept them parted so he could kneel between them, his face on level with hers.

Oddly, their new position felt even more intimate, a sensation only emphasized as his gaze ran a searing path over her breasts and down to her feminine core, already damp with her arousal.

"Caine," she breathed, tracing the curve of his noble brow and down the narrow line of his nose.

His eyes were more wolf than human as they lifted to meet her steady gaze. "Christ, you're so beautiful."

She offered a dimpled smile. "No, you're the beautiful one."

He captured her fingers, which had been exploring his face, pressing them to his lips. "I'm an immoral bastard who has no right to paradise," he corrected in harsh tones. "But if you want to offer me heaven, then I'm going to snatch it with both hands."

Cassie's lips parted, but her words went unsaid as he leaned forward to place an openmouthed kiss at the base of her neck. Oh. Her arms instinctively wrapped around his shoulders, her head falling back to offer him greater access.

Stroking his lips up the curve of her throat, he took a minute to trace the line of her jaw before at last finding her mouth to claim it in a kiss of sheer possession. Her wolf growled in satisfaction as her lips were crushed beneath his hungry onslaught, her nails scoring down the smooth skin of his back.

Still surrounded by the thinning steam and the quiet hush of the outrageously expensive suite, they might have been alone in their own world. There was nothing beyond the feel of Caine's kiss and the light touch of his fingers as they tucked her hair behind her ears.

Cassie moaned. The water was turned off, but she felt as if she were drowning beneath the tidal wave of sensations crashing through her.

As if sensing her rising passion, Caine eased his kiss, allowing his lips to sweep over her upturned face. Tenderly, he caressed every line and curve before turning his attention to the sensitive flesh of her neck.

"Yes," she breathed in encouragement, shivering as his hands moved slowly downward, at long last cupping the swollen fullness of her breasts.

"So perfect," he muttered.

She barely heard his soft words as she arched in pleasure, her eyes sliding shut as his fingers lightly teased the puckered tips of her nipples. Who knew her breasts could be so sensitive? Or that his touch could offer such pleasure?

A pleasure that went from sensational to shattering as he dipped his head even lower and sucked one nipple between his lips.

A soft cry tumbled from her lips as she shoved her fingers into the thick strands of his hair, shifting restlessly on the marble bench.

So this was what all the fuss was about, she conceded, trembling as his tongue and teeth sent her up in flames. She never, ever wanted him to stop. And yet . . .

There was an empty ache between her legs that demanded attention.

"Caine," she murmured, trusting he would know what she needed.

"Patience, pet," he countered.

She wanted to protest, but then he turned his attention to her other breast and she decided that patience wasn't such a bad thing. Especially when she felt his clever fingers drift along the curve of her hip and down the length of her leg.

Her head pressed back against the tiles as he suckled her with a growing insistence, his searching fingers drifting up her inner thigh. He was close. So close.

Then suddenly he was there.

"Oh."

Her heart slammed against her chest as his finger swept through her moist heat. Had she been struck by lightning? It seemed impossible that the electric jolt could come from a mere touch.

Then Caine proved that his touch truly could create electricity as his finger returned to find a tiny pearl of pleasure.

"Do you like this, pet?" Caine rasped.

Like? She groaned. She was quite certain that she could become addicted to his skillful caresses.

But as the shimmering excitement began to clench her muscles, she grasped his face in her hands. "I want you, Caine," she husked. "I want you inside me."

The sapphire eyes darkened with feral hunger, but surprisingly he made no move to pull her from the bench and have his wicked way with her. Instead, he returned to brush his lips over her breasts before skimming his mouth slowly down her quivering stomach.

What the devil was he doing?

The answer came when he gently tugged her legs even farther apart and, leaning forward, replaced his seeking finger with his tongue.

Sweet, sweet heaven.

Forgetting her aching need to feel him take her innocence, Cassie moaned, her fingers knotting in his hair as he stroked and nibbled and teased her with unmistakable skill. Not that she minded his obvious experience, she acknowledged as his tongue penetrated her tight channel before returning to lavish attention on that small knot of nerves. Not when she was the recipient of his exquisite talent.

Her breath came in short pants as the pleasure spiraled even higher, her toes curling in anticipation. Oh Lord, it was glorious. So glorious.

Easily sensing she was nearing the peak, Caine clamped his arms around her thighs and sucked her between his lips.

It was all that it took to make Cassie shatter in pure ecstasy.

Crying out, she was barely aware that she was trembling from head to foot. Not until Caine gave her one last sweep of his tongue, then gently tugged her to her feet and wrapped her tightly in his arms.

"Shh," he whispered into her hair, his lips stroking her temple.

She clutched at his shoulders, the tiny quakes of pleasure still shooting through her. "That was . . ."

He chuckled as she struggled to find the words. "Yes?"

"Almost perfect," she breathed.

She felt him tense beneath her hands, his head lifting to regard her with a searching gaze.

"Almost?"

She allowed a smile to curve her lips at his male pique. Clearly, he wasn't pleased by her refusal to admit that what had just happened had been the most spectacular event of her life.

Then, deliberately holding his gaze, she allowed one hand to drift down his chest. His breath caught as she traced the tense muscles of his stomach.

"Cassie?"

"I wanted to share our pleasure."

He groaned, his hand reaching to grasp her wrist. "We will."

"When?"

His jaw clenched, his breath rasping through his gritted teeth. "Once the danger is past and you can think clearly."

Although considerably smaller than Caine, Cassie was a pureblood Were with a strength that always caught others off guard.

With a twist of her arm, her wrist was free of his grasp and her hand was continuing its downward path until it at last reached her goal.

"You might be my protector, but you're not allowed to tell me that I can't decide what I want." She wrapped her fingers around his thick erection. "Or when I want it."

He cursed, but he was wise enough not to try and get into

a tug of war with her hand. Not when she was holding such a tender object.

"I'm not taking your innocence," he growled.

"Fine." Already prepared for his stubborn refusal, Cassie pressed her lips to Caine's chest, just above his pounding heart. "Then I'll find another way for us to share this moment."

"Christ," he breathed as she planted a trail of kisses to his beaded nipple.

She didn't have any idea if it would feel as good for him as it had for her, but she was hoping he would give her a clue. With perfect timing, he gave a low groan, his hand threading through her hair to hold her against him.

It was all the encouragement she needed.

Allowing her wolf out to play, she tasted the nipple with her tongue even as her fingers explored the hard length of his erection. It was astonishingly smooth, and warm. Deliciously warm.

Curious, she skimmed down his shaft, finding the heavy sack at the base. He jerked beneath her touch, and tilting back her head, she met his wild gaze. "I'm sorry, did I hurt you?" she husked.

"I . . ." He clearly struggled to swallow. "No, it didn't hurt."

"Ah."

He'd enjoyed her stroking his arousal. A lot.

With a wicked chuckle, she skimmed her fingers back to the tip of his cock, finding a tiny drop of moisture. She rubbed it lightly, circling the broad head before returning downward.

She repeated the caress twice more before he released an explosive sigh. "For the love of God, Cassie, don't torture me."

Although the thought of making Caine plead for release was tempting, she sympathized with his desperation. They'd been hurtling toward this moment for weeks. Later, she would enjoy the heady power of making him wait for hours before she gave in to his pleas.

She lifted herself on tiptoes to press her lips softly to his mouth.

"Show me."

With a choked groan, Caine reached to wrap his hand over her fingers, pressing them tight against his cock. Then, slowly he urged her to stroke up and down the shaft, his breath hissing through his teeth as his hips surged forward.

Cassie could feel the blood pulsing beneath the velvet skin and smell the rising musk. Instinctively, she quickened her pace, pleased when Caine gave a low growl of approval.

"Yes . . . that's it," he ground out, his hand cupping the back of her head and urging her face toward his neck.

Her wolf knew exactly what he wanted and without hesitation she sank her teeth into the side of his neck, the raw male taste of him on her tongue sending another climax pulsing through her.

At the same time, Caine gave a shout of joy as he pumped his erection in her hand, the warm spray of his seed covering her stomach.

"Hmm. That was nice." Cassie licked the trickle of blood her teeth had drawn. "Can we do it again?"

Several hours later Caine lay with Cassie wrapped in his arms on one of the wide beds. Predictably, she had fallen fast asleep the moment her head hit the pillow, while he'd remained wide awake, watching her in stunned amazement.

He was a fool.

No surprise there, of course. He'd worked so hard to keep his hands off this beautiful, all-too-vulnerable Were. Cold baths, long runs across the desert, hours of patrolling the sixty-story hotel for the least hint of danger.

But one soft touch of Cassie's hand and all his good intentions went flying out the window. Or rather, flying out the shower. He swallowed a harsh groan as he recalled the afternoon in vivid detail. Every kiss, every tentative stroke of her hand, every soft groan.

His only consolation was that while he might have stolen her innocence, he hadn't committed the ultimate sin of taking her virginity.

Why was that so important?

Caine grimaced, not wanting to consider the dangerous question. It was easier to tell himself that he was simply being noble. That he wanted to wait until Cassie was out of danger and capable of considering the consequences with a clear mind.

He didn't want to acknowledge the tiny voice that warned taking her virginity would somehow tie him irrevocably to the beautiful Were. And that once he'd truly made her his lover he would never, ever be willing to let her go.

No matter what she wanted.

Mate . . .

With a low growl, he fiercely squashed the terrifying word.

Nope. Not going to go there. Things were bad enough.

As if to emphasize the point, Cassie turned in her sleep, her slender body snuggling into him with a trust that made his heart shift in his chest.

Hell. He should never have allowed her to climb into bed with him. Not just because he was a full-blooded male not a damned saint, and the feel of her warm curves covered by nothing more than the tiny teddy he'd been stupid enough to buy was destined to keep him hard and aching throughout the long night. But because the sheer intimacy was touching him places he didn't want to be touched.

Of course, it wasn't as if he'd had a choice. One pleading glance from those big emerald eyes and he'd been a lost cause. Pathetic. With a rueful smile, he buried his face in the silken softness of her hair. What was a poor man to do?

Absently running a soothing hand down her back, Caine was near the point of drifting off when he abruptly felt Cassie's muscles tense. He frowned, lifting his head. Was she dreaming or had his slight touch wakened her?

He had his answer the moment her eyes opened to reveal the beautiful green was already veiled by a disturbing white film.

"Cassie." He grasped her shoulders, ridiculously attempting to shake her awake. "Cassie."

Oblivious to his presence, Cassie shrugged off his hands and scooted off the bed. Then, with mechanical movements, she headed out of the bedroom.

"Shit." Leaping to his feet, Caine rapidly pulled on his jeans and a sweatshirt that had been tossed on a nearby chair. A loaded Glock was tucked at his lower back, then, yanking a robe hanging on the back of the bathroom door, he hurried in her wake.

There was no use trying to stop her. Lost in the power of her visions, she wouldn't halt until she'd reached her goal. Whether that goal was standing in the sitting room to weave one of the strange, shimmering glyphs that revealed a foretelling. Or dragging him halfway across the country.

All he could do was keep her from hurting herself. He entered the sitting room only to find it empty with the door standing open. With a curse he jogged into the hallway, at last catching up with her as she stepped into an empty elevator.

"Hold on, baby, I'm with you," he muttered, entering

the small cubicle at the same moment she hit the button for the lobby.

She stared straight ahead, her face blank even when he tucked her into the robe and tied the belt. He grimaced. At least the hotel was nearly silent. Well, if one didn't count the hideous music being pumped into the elevator.

It was that strange hour just before dawn.

The window of time when even the most hardened of gamblers had returned to their beds and the early morning workers were still gulping down their first cup of coffee. He and Cassie wouldn't be bothered by unwelcomed gawkers, and more importantly, there would be no crowds an enemy could use to disguise their approach.

The elevator at last gave a subtle shudder as it slowed, the metal doors sliding open. Without hesitation Cassie stepped into the lobby, her feet moving at a measured pace across the tiled floor and out the glass doors to the street.

Staying at her side, Caine shook his head at the uniformed driver who was leaning against his limo in the off chance of a fare, and captured Cassie's arm as she started to step off the curb, directly in the path of an oncoming taxi.

"Wait," he commanded, refusing to release her until he was certain the coast was clear.

She stood passively beneath his touch, waiting in silence for him to at last release his grip so she could continue across the road and toward the edge of town at a swift jog.

Caine sighed as he followed behind. If the whole knight protector gig crapped out he might just have a career as a crossing guard. Something to consider.

Focusing on the absurd thoughts to keep from panicking as Cassie remained locked deep in her vision, Caine nevertheless was on full guard as they circled the edge of the airport and headed into the desert.

Not that there was much to guard against. A few coyotes,

lizards, snakes . . . Nothing that could harm a pureblooded Were. Thank the gods.

Eventually, the perpetual glow of the city was left behind and all signs of civilization were lost to the barren desert. Still, Cassie continued forward, indifferent to the cool breeze and the thick silence.

Where the hell were they going?

It took another half hour before the question was answered, and even then it didn't make any sense.

Halting in the middle of a flat basin, Cassie stood at rigid attention, her pale hair floating on the breeze. Then, as if she were possessed by a sudden madness, she dropped to her knees. Caine cursed, leaping to the side as she grabbed a sharp stone and began to feverishly draw symbols in the arid ground.

Gritting his teeth, Caine tried to leash his primal instincts that demanded he scoop Cassie off the filthy ground and return her to the safety of the hotel room. He even succeeded for several torturous minutes. But when the scent of Cassie's blood hit his nose, his good intentions were blasted into a million pieces.

Her knees were scraped raw and her hands cut more than once by the stone. Enough was enough.

"Cassie." He managed to take a step forward when a soft voice floated on the air.

"Do not interfere, Were."

The sudden sound combined with the scent of brimstone had him spinning around, the Glock in his hand.

His eyes narrowed at the sight of the small creature standing directly behind him. Shit. How had she managed to sneak up on him?

Not that she looked like much of a threat. She was barely over three feet tall with a tiny body currently covered by a white robe that shimmered in the moonlight. Her heart-shaped face appeared almost childlike, with delicate features that gave the illusion of innocence.

At least until one noticed the razor-sharp teeth and the ancient power that smoldered in the black, almond eyes.

Yeah, this creature was about as helpless as a live grenade. Or a nuclear bomb.

His wolf was on full alert, his hand steady, as he pointed the fully loaded gun at the center of her chest. "Who are you?" he snarled.

She held up tiny hands as if that would convince him to trust her. "Yannah."

His finger found the trigger. "Give me a reason not to put a bullet through your heart."

She tilted her head to the side. "You cannot harm me with human weapons."

He shrugged, not surprised. "Then I'll rip out your throat."

"There's no need for threats. I'm not here to harm your mate."

"She's not—" He bit off his ridiculous denial. "Then why are you here?"

"To offer a warning." The black eyes narrowed at the unmistakable sound of Caine cocking the hammer. "Hell's bells, what's wrong with you? I said I offer a warning, not a threat."

"And I should trust the word of a creature who pops out of thin air to offer mysterious warnings because . . . ?" he mocked, shifting to make sure his body was still blocking Cassie as she frantically continued to dig in the dirt.

The tiny demon wisely kept her gaze trained on Caine. One glance toward the vulnerable Cassie and Caine would rip off her head.

Or at least he would try, he silently corrected, shivering

as Yannah allowed a hint of her terrible power to glow in the black eyes.

"The warning is not mysterious," Yannah assured him. "In fact, it couldn't be more clear."

"Fine, I'll play." Like he had a choice? "What's the warning?"

"In the very near future Cassie is going to demand that you leave her."

Leave her? Caine was instantly furious. "She wouldn't."

Yannah heaved a resigned sigh. "Why do males always make everything so difficult?"

"Are you a prophet?" he managed between clenched teeth.

"No." The demon shook her head, sending her long braid sliding across her back. "Cassie stands alone with her gift."

"Gift?" Caine snarled. "It's a freaking curse."

"Perhaps."

He lowered the gun, afraid in his current mood he might do something stupid. It was his usual modus operandi. Besides, it wasn't going to do him a damned bit of good.

"If you're not a seer, then how do you know what Cassie will or won't do in the future?"

"My mother, Siljar, is an Oracle."

"Shit." The last thing he needed was interference from the Commission, or as he called them, the Pain-in-the-Asses-Who-Ruled-the-Demon-World. "How does she know?"

"She possesses a talent for sensing a principium."

He grimaced, recognizing the term. It meant that Cassie was important enough to the future of the world that her life was written in the stars.

"A thread of destiny," he muttered.

"So you aren't just a pretty face." Yannah flashed her razor teeth. Yikes. "Unusual."

"I try," he said dryly. "I'm still not entirely clear on why you're here."

"The fate of all of us rests upon young Cassie's shoulders."

"Well, as far as I'm concerned, fate can go screw itself," he retorted, knowing he was being childish. But, dammit, he was standing helplessly in the middle of a desert while the female he was obsessed with protecting was crawling through the dirt until she bled. He had a right to think destiny or fate, or whatever a person wanted to call it, totally sucked.

Something that might have been sympathy touched the heart-shaped face. "It's her destiny," she said softly, "but she doesn't have to walk her path alone."

"She's not alone." Caine frowned. "Unless you mean her sisters? Cassie has refused to contact them."

"No, I speak of you. You must never waver."

Waver? Was she freaking kidding? His anger returned. With interest. "Are you questioning my loyalty?"

"No, but like most alpha males you have more pride than sense."

"What the hell is that supposed to mean?"

"I told you." She looked at him as if wondering if he'd always been so stupid. "Cassie will come to a crossroads. In that moment she will try to push you away. You must not allow her to leave you behind."

"She's not going anywhere without me," he snapped. "Not ever."

His fierce words were still ringing through the air when there was a faint groan from behind him. He turned, his heart halting as he watched Cassie collapse onto the desert floor.

"Shit." With one leap he was bending down beside her, knocking the rock out of her hand before tugging her slender body against his chest. No use taking a chance of getting beaned. A distinct possibility if she was still caught in her vision.

He brushed his lips over her forehead, pulling back as her lashes fluttered upward to reveal her eyes. Back to emerald. Thank the gods.

"Caine?" she husked.

"I got you."

She blinked, her dazed eyes taking in the star-spattered sky over his shoulder before shifting to glance over the barren desert. "Where are we?"

He grimaced. "In the middle of freaking nowhere."

Her brow furrowed in bewilderment. "I thought . . ."

"What?"

"I thought I heard voices."

Oh hell. Caine jerked his head up. He'd completely forgotten the strange intruder.

Gone. Thank the gods. He didn't care why Yannah had come. Or how she'd managed to appear and disappear without leaving a trace. All that mattered was that the powerful demon wasn't anywhere near Cassie.

He returned his attention to the woman in his arms. "We're alone," he assured her softly. "Are you okay?"

"I think so." She gently pried herself from his ruthless hold, taking a puzzled inventory of her fading scrapes and bruises. Then, as if seeking the reason for the wounds, her attention shifted to the glyphs she'd carved into the desert floor. "Did I do this?"

"Quite the Picasso," he said, forcing a teasing smile to his lips as he helped her to her feet. He had no intention of burdening her with his fierce fear that one day she would disappear into her visions and never return. She had enough to deal with, thank you very much. "Do you happen to know *why* you did it?"

"No, but I think this is why we were here."

Good news. At least he hoped it was. He was tired of trying to protect Cassie in such a populated area. Of course, there was no guarantee they weren't about to be led someplace even worse.

On that happy thought, he pointed toward the strange symbols. "What does it say?"

"It's a warning." She frowned, shaking her head. "At least I think it's a warning."

He cupped her chin in his hand, tugging her face up so he could study her pale features. His heart faltered. Man, she was so beautiful drenched in moonlight.

"How can you reveal a prophecy and not know what it is?"

"It's not for me," she said as if the simple words weren't a mind-bender.

"Then who . . . ?" He gave a sharp shake of his head as she swayed in weariness. "Never mind," he muttered, scooping her off her feet and cradling her in his arms. "Are we finished here?"

"Yes."

He peered deep into the emerald eyes. "Does that mean we can go home?"

"Home?"

"You have someplace better to be?" he demanded, praying to the gods that she said no.

She frowned. "It's not that."

"Then what?"

"I've never had a home."

That dangerous, intoxicating warmth filled his heart and spilled through his body. Caine didn't care. Bending his head, he touched his lips to hers in a reverent vow.

"You do now."

Chapter 5

Despite the early hour, Caine had them packed up and checked out of the hotel by sunrise.

Not that Cassie was in the mood to argue. She would always harbor fond memories of Vegas.

A smile touched her lips. No, not just *fond*. Stunningly fabulous memories.

Even now she could close her eyes and recall every touch, every kiss, every mind-blowing orgasm. In vivid, X-rated detail.

But she was more than happy to return to Caine's lair outside Chicago. What could be better than having Caine all to herself without the distraction of trying to blend in?

It was exhausting trying to be normal.

With a sigh of contentment, she shifted in her seat, the breeze tugging at her hair. Caine had removed the top of the Jeep and the late afternoon sunlight spilled over her skin left bare by her khaki shorts and stretchy tube top. Lazily, she watched the cornfields of Nebraska whiz pass, breathing deeply of Caine's warm, wolfy musk.

The smell of him . . . grounded her. There was no other way to say it. Even when she was lost in the dark mists of her visions, when she was blind to the world, she could catch his scent nearby and know that nothing could harm her.

Dwelling on the miracle that had brought Caine into her life, Cassie was unprepared for the burst of unease that destroyed her momentary illusion of peace.

She straightened, reaching out to touch Caine's shoulder. "Pull over."

He shot a frowning glance toward the endless miles of corn. "Here?"

"Yes."

With obvious reluctance, he slowed the Jeep and pulled onto the shoulder. He turned his attention to her. "Are you sick?"

Puzzled by the question, she gave a shake of her head. "I'm fine."

"Then you have to pee?"

"No."

"Then what the hell are we doing?"

"The phone."

He scowled. "What . . ." The sound of his ring tone brought his words to an abrupt end. "Shit," he muttered, digging his cell phone out of the front pocket of his jeans. "I'm never going to get used to that." He glanced at the screen, his scowl only deepening. "Ingrid."

"A friend?" she forced herself to ask, squashing the odd stab of aversion toward the unknown female.

This phone call was important. Even if she didn't know why.

"A lifetime ago," he muttered. "Why would she be calling now?"

She slid until she was leaning against the hard muscles of his shoulder. "I don't know everything." She pointed her finger toward the phone. "Maybe if you push that little button and talk with her you'll find out."

He turned his head to nip the end of her nose. "Smart-ass."

She wasn't fooled by his playful manner. There was something troubling him. "Why don't you answer?"

He grimaced. "She's a part of my past I want to forget."

The ringing stopped as the phone sent the caller to voice mail only to start again seconds later.

"I don't think she agrees with being a part of your past." Cassie studied Caine's tight expression, feeling his tension as if it were her own. "Was she your lover?"

"No. But . . ." Regret flashed through his stunning blue eyes as he reached to outline her lips with the tip of his finger. "There were women, Cassie. I don't share your innocence."

She hesitated, realizing that the unpleasant sensation that had been plaguing her since Caine's phone started ringing was jealousy. How . . . astonishing.

"You have a lover now?"

His lips twitched, easily sensing her inner turmoil. "Only one," he assured her, leaning forward to steal a possessive kiss. "The rest are a part of that past I intend to forget."

Cassie nodded, the tightness in her chest easing, although the phone continued its annoying ringing. "She's very persistent," she muttered, her finger moving to point at the top of the phone screen. "What's that blinking light?"

"She sent me a video."

Cassie tensed, her personal emotions smothered beneath the power of her forewarning. "I think you should watch it."

He studied her with a frown. "Are you speaking as a jealous lover or as a prophet?"

She considered a long moment. "Both."

His breath hissed between clenched teeth. "I don't have to be a seer to know I'm not going to like this."

"Play it, Caine," she softly commanded.

He muttered something beneath his breath, but holding

the phone at an angle so they could both easily view the screen, he tapped the blinking light.

Within seconds a young female with hazel eyes and oddly buzzed blond hair flickered to life, her features more striking than pretty as she flashed a cocky smile.

"Long time, no see, *liebling*," she said, her voice low and raspy. "I suppose you don't have time for your old friends now that you're a big bad Were." The female's lips curled in disdain. "Yeah, word's out that you've turned traitor to the curs. So listen closely—you got what you wanted, now I want it. If you can become a Were, so can I. And to make sure you don't blow me off as you have everyone else, I have a little . . . incentive."

The video went blurry as Ingrid swung her phone camera toward the side and downward. For a minute there was nothing but the vague outline of a person, then the camera came back into focus and Cassie gasped in shock.

The tiny female filling the screen was almost an exact replica of herself. Oh, her hair was a few inches shorter and more golden than silver. And her slender body, which was covered in a casual pair of jeans and stretchy blue shirt, was toned by obvious hours spent in a gym. But her heart-shaped face was precisely the same and if her eyes had been opened, Cassie was willing to bet that they would be some shade of green.

It was one of her three sisters. They hadn't yet been formally introduced, but the resemblance was too great for it to be anyone else.

"Harley." Caine answered her unspoken question, his finger pressing the screen to pause the video.

Cassie clutched his arm in horror, frantically studying the image of her sister bound to a chair with silver chains and a heavy silver collar around her neck. She appeared to be unconscious as her head drooped to the side, a thin line of blood trailing down her cheek from a wound to her temple.

"Oh my God, she's hurt," she breathed, turning to find Caine watching her with concern. "Is there more to the video?"

"Yes, but maybe you should let me—"

"Play it," she pleaded. "Please."

She felt his muscles clench beneath her fingers, but with obvious reluctance he at last pressed his thumb to the screen and the image of Harley was joined by Ingrid as she knelt beside the chair.

"If you want her released unharmed . . ." The female cur smirked. "Well, relatively unharmed, then call me so we can set up a meet and greet. You have twenty-four hours. Oh, and if you're thinking about sharing this video with your new allies . . . don't." She leaned sideways so the camera could catch her hand reaching toward the small bulge of Harley's belly. "If I even suspect that I'm being hunted, the first to die will be these sweet, innocent pups." She pressed her lips to the phone. "Call me, *liebling*."

The video went black and Caine clenched the phone until the case threatened to shatter.

"I'm going to kill that bitch."

Cassie nodded, fully onboard with the kill-the-bitch plan, but only after they were certain Harley was safe.

"Would she really hurt the babies?"

The muscle of his jaw knotted as he visibly fought the urge to protect her with a lie.

"Yes."

"We have to rescue her." She frowned as he pressed his thumb against the phone screen to replay the video. "Caine, did you hear me?"

"It's a trap," he muttered.

"What sort of trap?"

He hit pause, his brow furrowed as he studied the

image of Ingrid standing in a dark room with shelves of wine bottles in the background.

"It could be a trick that your sisters dreamed up to lure you back to their protection."

She snorted. It was no secret her sisters were desperate to have her returned to the bosom of her family. But she didn't for a moment think they would go to such extremes. "They wouldn't."

"No, I don't think so either," Caine readily agreed, "but it has to be considered."

"What are your other theories?"

"It could be that Ingrid was telling the truth." His gaze returned to the screen where the female cur was smiling with smug arrogance. "She might genuinely believe I have some magical means to transform her into a pureblooded Were and is trying to force me to give her what she desires."

She studied his perfectly chiseled profile. "But you don't believe that?"

His lips twisted. "There was a time when I was vain enough to assume that the world revolved around me, but I'm not a complete idiot."

She tilted her head to her side. "I don't know what that means."

He reached to give her ponytail a gentle tug. "I'm traveling with the most sought after creature in the entire universe. If someone's trying to capture us, it's all about you, pet."

Cassie grimaced. Being the most sought after creature in the entire universe wasn't nearly so fun as it sounded. In fact, it sucked.

"Even if that's true, I'm not leaving my sister in the hands of that female."

"I know," Caine soothed. "Are you getting any . . ." He waved his hand in vague motion.

"Any what?"

"Vibes."

She blinked in confusion before at last realizing he was referring to her visions. "Oh." She paused, searching for any hint of a foretelling. "No," she at last said. "There's nothing."

He heaved a sigh. "So you get the command to watch the video, but nothing to tell us what to do about it?"

"That's how it works." She shrugged, pointing toward his phone. "You have to call."

His gaze followed her finger, his muscles abruptly tensing as he studied the image of Ingrid still filling the screen. "Not yet."

"Caine . . ." She halted her pleading words, sensing his distraction. "You have a plan?"

"Not so much a plan as a desperate hope that we can spring the trap before it's set and escape with your sister unscathed," he corrected.

"Is that possible?"

He tapped the screen. "I recognize where Ingrid took this video."

"Really?"

"It's Salvatore's wine cellar."

"You were in the wine cellar of the King of Weres?"

"Of course." He turned to meet her expression of disbelief. "Salvatore used to be my enemy. Hell, he still wants to nail my furry ass to the wall."

"So why were you in the wine cellar?"

"When he turned up in America I needed a secret way to enter his lair if I had to take drastic measures to protect myself. There's a tunnel that leads into his wine cellar."

She rolled her eyes. "I suppose I should expect such madness from you. You are far too reckless. But this female . . ." She frowned at the cur's smug confidence that was captured by the video. "Is she insane?"

"I always suspected she came from the shallow end of the gene pool," Caine said. "Why?"

"Who would be stupid enough to hold the mate of the King of Weres hostage in his own wine cellar?"

"Salvatore must be out of state or Ingrid wouldn't have managed to get within a mile of the lair, let alone get her hands on Harley," he explained.

Cassie still thought the female must be a nut bar.

"So you think they're still in the wine cellar?"

"Doubtful, but we should be able to pick up Ingrid's scent and track her from there."

Her nails unconsciously dug into his arm, her wolf eager to be on the hunt even as her heart clenched with fear. "What if she hurts Harley or the babies before we can reach them?"

"We have twenty-four hours. If we don't pick up Ingrid's trail, then I'll make the call." He cupped her cheek in his hand, brushing her lips with a soft kiss. "I promise nothing's going to hurt your sister."

She leaned her forehead against his, taking strength in his familiar scent.

"Let's go," she whispered.

Salvatore's lair in St. Louis

Gaius was fuming as he paced from one end of the wine cellar to the other.

Who could blame him? He was standing in the lair of the King of Weres with two curs who looked like matching G.I. Joe dolls and a goth witch who was wearing a tight leather skirt and spike-heeled boots that were as impractical as they were ridiculous. He'd been forced to shape-shift to look like the Queen of Weres in an attempt to lure the prophet into his clutches. And now he was stuck waiting with his trio of idiots on the off chance the plot would work.

Plus, adding insult to injury, the entire place reeked of dogs. *Che macello*.

Clearly possessing more brawn than brains, the male cur sauntered within striking distance of Gaius, seemingly indifferent to the frigid fury that prickled through the air. "It really is remarkable," Dolf murmured, compounding his stupidity by lifting a hand toward Gaius's long mane of blond hair.

"Touch me and your sister will be dragging you out of here as a corpse."

The cur jerked his hand back, his face flushed at the icy warning. "No need for threats," he protested. "We're all on the same side here."

Gaius curled his lips. "Do not remind me."

The cur grimaced. "What crawled up your ass and died?"

"I beg your pardon?"

"Why are you in such a pissy mood?"

Gaius narrowed his gaze. "Are you trying to be amusing?"

"No, I just—"

"Do you think I want to humiliate myself with this"— Gaius waved a hand to indicate his slender, delicately curved body—"female form?"

The flush drained from Dolf's face to leave him a frightened shade of gray. "Of course not."

"Or to spend hours trespassing in the lair of the King of Weres?" Gaius continued, his voice edged with a bitterness that was capable of flaying the skin off a lesser creature. "Who, by the way, has his full powers returned and would happily kill me on sight."

Dolf lifted his hands in a desperate attempt at damage

control. "I told you, Ingrid's source says that the king and queen are in Chicago for at least two more days."

Gaius wasn't any more impressed now than he'd been when he first heard the reassurance. Not that he was given any choice, he grimly reminded himself. When Ingrid had approached him with the suggestion of using his ability to alter shapes to bait a trap for the prophet, he'd emphatically refused.

He wasn't about to make a fool of himself by prancing around looking like a damned female while lurking in the wine cellar of the King of Weres. He did have *some* pride left. But, of course, the witch had instantly done her wireless communication with the Dark Lord and Gaius discovered himself on his knees, agreeing to travel to St. Louis and pose as Harley.

He didn't, however, agree to like it.

"Her mysterious source could be mistaken," he pointed out in biting tones. "Or hoping to keep us here long enough to become lambs to the slaughter."

"Ingrid knows what she's doing." Dolf sent a glance that was far too intimate toward his sister. Creepy. "She came up with the plan to trick Caine into coming to this wine cellar, didn't she?"

"So she did." Gaius shifted his attention toward the female cur who leaned against the shelves of wine, her muscular arms folded over her chest. "You're certain he will come to this cellar instead of calling as you demanded?"

Ingrid shrugged. "Caine is pathologically suspicious, which makes it almost impossible to ambush him. We have to convince him that he's actually avoiding the trap while we nudge him where we want him to go."

"You're assuming that he watches the video you sent and then ignores your demands to call despite the threat to his queen." Gaius impatiently brushed back his long blond hair, which was proving to be a constant nuisance. *Cristo*, he would be relieved when this stupid charade was done and he could return to his true form. "And that he recognizes this wine cellar."

The cur smiled. "Trust me."

Gaius hissed in disgust. "Never."

Chapter 6

Salvatore's lair in St. Louis

Caine left the Jeep parked several miles away from Salvatore's lair, located in a northern suburb of the city. Then, leading Cassie along the edge of the large lake surrounded by brick mansions set like fine jewels among the manicured lawns and formal gardens, he came to a halt behind a boathouse.

It was late enough that the neighborhood was shrouded in a slumbering darkness, but his night vision easily allowed him to scour his surroundings for any sign of danger. Not that there was any to be found.

He dismissed the incubus currently fulfilling the fantasy of a neglected housewife and the nest of harpies who were hidden on the small island in the middle of the lake. They posed no threat to a pureblooded Were.

Far from reassured, he studied the vast three-story home perched on a hill that overlooked the lake. The back walls, which were made almost entirely of glass, were partly obscured by a large veranda framed by marble columns. Trellised gardens descended the length of the steep slope, coming to a halt at the edge of a stone grotto that not only served as a perfect picnic spot, but a lookout for Salvatore's guards.

Guards that should have been on duty.

So where the hell were they?

He was still searching for an answer when he felt Cassie crouch beside him, her wide gaze trained on the mansion above them.

"Good Lord," she breathed. "That's Harley's house?"

"One of them."

"It's very large."

His lips twisted at the understatement. The place was big enough to lodge a small country. "If you like it I could have one built for you."

She shuddered. "No, I spent too many years in soulless caverns to feel comfortable in such a place," she said. "I prefer your home."

He reached to give her hand a light squeeze. "Our home," he corrected.

"Yes." Her dimples made a brief appearance. "Our home."

Satisfaction seared through him and with a small groan, Caine tugged her close enough to claim her lips in an urgent kiss. *Our* sounded amazingly perfect.

Then, with a curse, he forced himself to pull away. Now wasn't the time to be distracted. No matter what the temptation.

Even if this wasn't a trap, he knew that Salvatore had a bounty out on his head. If the king's pack caught scent of them he would never shake them off their trail.

"Do you sense anything?" he asked, returning his attention to the seemingly abandoned house.

She tilted back her head, sniffing the air. "No."

"Neither do I."

She grimaced. "Is that a good thing or a bad thing?"

That was the question, wasn't it?

"Salvatore would never have left Harley completely alone," he muttered. "If she was kidnapped, his pack should be swarming through the neighborhood searching for her."

Cassie shrugged. "Maybe they don't know she's missing."

"Then they should at least be guarding the house."

"You think it's a trap?"

His jaw tightened. "Absolutely."

She blinked at his blunt honesty. "Then shouldn't we be somewhere that isn't here?"

"Yes."

She tilted her head to the side, regarding him in confusion. "Caine?"

He heaved a sigh. His every instinct screamed to toss Cassie over his shoulder and rush away from Salvatore's lair at top speed. The very air whispered a warning.

But he'd spent enough time with Cassie to know that she wouldn't be satisfied until she was certain that Harley had been rescued and was safely back in the hands of her mate.

"Shit," he muttered. "What?"

"If I'm going to pick up Ingrid's scent I have to get closer."

Without hesitation she pushed herself to her feet, as always completely fearless.

"Then let's go."

"Wait." He straightened, taking her hands in a warning grip. "I want your promise that you won't leave my side. Not even for a second."

Cassie hesitated, chewing her bottom lip. "I'll try," she at last conceded.

"Cassie."

"That's all I can promise."

His lips twisted as he met her candid gaze. "I suppose it is."

He grasped her hand and led her along the lakeshore, ignoring the stone steps leading to the house. Cassie fell into step beside him, a puzzled frown marring her brow.

"Where are we going?"

Caine led her past the boat dock and at last halted at a line of Dumpsters near the gravel service road. "The entrance to the secret tunnel is hidden inside the Dumpster."

"Clever," Cassie said, only to slap a hand over her nose and mouth as Caine broke the lock and threw back the lid on the green metal bin set slightly away from the others. "And pungent," she muttered, taking an instinctive step backward. "Yow."

Prepared for the spell of revulsion, Caine ignored the foul smell billowing from the Dumpster as well as the magical "push" to turn and walk away. "It keeps demons from sniffing close enough to discover the entrance," he said, vaulting into the bin and holding out his hand.

"A very effective deterrent," Cassie gagged out, reluctantly taking his hand and climbing into the Dumpster.

Once they were both through the barrier the spell abruptly vanished to reveal a scrupulously clean container with a trapdoor cut into the metal bottom. Caine bent down, sliding his fingers along the outline of the door until he found the hidden lever. With a faint click the door abruptly swung downward to reveal a tunnel dug into the ground.

Reaching behind him, he grabbed Cassie's hand and tucked her fingers into the waistband of his jeans. "Hold on and don't let go," he commanded.

She wrinkled her nose. "Bossy."

"No. Terrified."

Without giving her time to reply, Caine dropped into the tunnel, landing on the cement floor with Cassie descending lightly behind him.

He paused, searching the darkness with his heightened senses. There was . . . nothing.

No lurking enemies.

No waiting traps.

And no scent of curs.

He growled in frustration. "Ingrid didn't come in or out of the tunnel."

"Then we have to go on," Cassie whispered softly. "We know she was in the wine cellar. We can pick up her scent there."

He shot a glance over his shoulder, meeting her stubborn glare. "And what if this is a trap?"

She managed to look even more stubborn.

Stubboner.

Was that a word? If not, it should be.

"I'm not leaving until we find the trail leading to my sister."

He turned to move down the tunnel, muttering beneath his breath. Man, it had to be the greatest cosmic joke ever. Fate had given him his deepest desire and transformed him into a pureblood Were only to punish him with the constant pressure of keeping the most endangered creature in the entire world safe.

He was supposed to be enjoying a carefree existence at the top of the food chain, surrounded by his adoring harem and collecting hordes of ill-gotten gains. Hadn't that been his fantasy?

Certainly, it hadn't been creeping through the dark, tormented by the fear that he was somehow going to fail the female who'd become an essential part of his life.

Fingers tightened on his waistband, and his bout of self-pity was forgotten as the scent of warm female and lavender wrapped around him.

Cassie.

He wouldn't trade one hour with this female for all the harems and fortunes in the world.

Oh, how the mighty were fallen.

Shaking his head at his foolishness, Caine followed the tunnel that led straight to the cellars beneath Salvatore's lair. Then, as they reached the heavy wood door imbedded with iron spikes, he sucked in a deep breath, not at all comforted by the strange void filling the air.

There should be some odors.

On full alert, he reluctantly shoved the door open, doing his best to keep Cassie behind him as they entered the room, which had a dirt floor and cement walls lined with towering shelves that held hundreds of dusty bottles. In the center of the room sat a collection of aged-wood barrels and across the vast space were a number of arched doorways that led to storage alcoves and high-tech refrigerators.

Focused on searching the nearby shadows for an ambush, Caine nearly missed the slender, blond-haired Were that was sprawled in a chair next to the wine racks, apparently knocked unconscious.

He did, thankfully, sense the moment Cassie prepared to launch herself across the room. Grabbing her arm, he grimly held on. "Wait."

"It's Harley," she hissed, straining against his grip. "We have to help her."

He wrapped an arm around her waist, speaking directly in her ear. "Cassie, there's something missing."

"What?"

"Smell."

"I don't smell . . ." She stiffened as she realized there wasn't any hint of her sister's scent in the air. "Oh."

On the point of shoving her back through the doorway, Caine felt the air stir as one of the shelves swung open to reveal a hidden chamber. He had a brief impression of a small cement-lined cell before his attention turned to the two matching curs and dark-haired witch who spilled out of the cramped space.

"Very good, Caine," the female cur mocked, obviously overhearing their private conversation.

"Ingrid."

Caine's lip curled in derision as his attention shifted to the male cur. The twins looked like Tweedledum and Tweedle-dummer on steroids with their matching buzz cuts and muscular bodies bulging beneath the olive wife-beaters and cammo pants. He'd always been creeped out by Ingrid's overly intimate relationship with her twin, and not just because Dolf was a magic-user.

His opinion of the two hadn't improved when he discovered the male had managed to get turned into a cur.

In fact, he'd been downright homicidal. And it was only because the cur had gone into hiding he hadn't given in to his impulse to rid the world of his perverted presence.

"And Dolf," he sneered. "I should have known there wouldn't be one without the other."

The male shrugged, the crystal hung around his neck glinting in the muted overhead light. "Did you think you could keep me in the closet forever?"

"I should have killed you the minute I realized your sister had managed to get you turned." He covertly shifted to stand between the curs and Cassie. "You're a freak of nature."

"*I'm* a freak of nature?" Dolf mocked, folding his arms over his chest. "Isn't that the pot calling the kettle black, Caine? You're the one who walked into a cave as a cur and walked out as a Were."

"Yeah," Ingrid added. "We're all agog with curiosity at how you performed that little miracle."

"Is that why you lured me here?"

Without warning, the faux Harley rose from the chair, shaking back her long mane of blond hair. "No." The female moved to the side, her gaze seeking Cassie. "You're here because the Dark Lord has requested the presence of the prophet."

Caine heard Cassie suck in a sharp breath. "You aren't my sister," she accused.

"Obviously not," Gaius retorted, grimacing with intense relief.

That was his cue.

With a surge of power, he shifted back to his true form, grabbing the long satin robe he'd left on the nearby shelf to cover his naked body. Then, smoothing back his raven hair, he turned to meet the wary gazes of the intruders.

They didn't look like they should be on the Dark Lord's most wanted list. The tiny, pale-haired female with her green eyes too big for the heart-shaped face and the surfer boy Were who looked like he should be sunbathing on the nearest beach.

How had they managed to elude the most skilled trackers in the demon world?

Then Caine placed a protective arm around the prophet and Gaius caught a glimpse of feral fury smoldering in the blue eyes. The surfer boy would destroy the world to protect the female at his side.

"Shit. Who are you?" Caine muttered in revulsion. "No, scratch that. What the hell are you?"

Insulted by the lack of appreciation for his considerable skill, Gaius smoothed his hands down the black satin of his robe. "I don't know why I'm continually shocked by the Weres' lack of manners," he drawled. "You are dogs, after all."

Caine narrowed his gaze, obviously struggling to accept Gaius's unusual talents. "Leeches can't shape-shift."

"I have powers beyond your imagination."

The Were snorted. "And an ego to match."

Gaius clenched his teeth, waving his hand at the two curs. He wasn't going to bicker with a damned dog. Not when he was standing in the wine cellar of the King of Weres. The sooner they were away from St. Louis and back in his lair, the better.

"Get the seer," he commanded.

Caine growled, his eyes glowing with power as he prepared to shift. "Over my dead body."

Dolf swiftly shed his clothing, his own eyes flashing the crimson of all curs. "That can be arranged."

"No, you idiots, the Dark Lord wants them taken alive," Gaius snarled as the air around Ingrid and Dolf shimmered and with the savage sound of popping muscle and bone they shifted into wolves.

The size of small ponies with pale fur and crimson eyes, they bared their fangs, ignoring Gaius's sharp reprimand as they kept their attention fixated on Caine.

Muscle-bound morons. If their lust for violence ruined this opportunity for him to please the Dark Lord and reap his long overdue reward, he was going to have them skinned and nailed to his wall.

Not that their lack of control seemed to matter. Even as they crouched for an attack, a choking heat filled the cellar and with an explosion of power Caine was shifting. Gaius muttered a curse, watching in horror as the monstrous beast appeared out of the shimmering magic.

Standing as tall as Gaius even on all four legs, the beast's head was the size of an anvil and his chest as wide as a small car. Even more unnerving was the ruthless intelligence burning like sapphire fire in his eyes.

Unlike the curs, Caine wasn't consumed by his bloodlust. Just the opposite.

With a frustrating cunning, the Were used his head to

herd the reluctant prophet into the cement cell, then blocked the narrow doorway with his large body. There would be no getting to Cassandra without going through Caine.

Bastardo.

Gaius took a covert step backward as Ingrid and Dolf charged into the literal jaws of death. He had no intention of getting caught in the fray. Not when he was drained from his shape-shifting, not to mention the effort of mist-walking with two curs and a witch to get to this wine cellar in the first place.

Instead, he waved an imperious hand toward the witch, who tried her best to hide behind a stone column. "Sally."

Her feet visibly dragged as she forced herself to move to his side. "What?"

He scowled at her petulant tone. "Are you just going to stand here gawking?"

She sent a wary glance toward the snarling curs who were trying to use the tag-team offense against the larger Were.

A futile effort.

Even as one managed to dig their fangs into Caine's thick fur, he was savagely ripping into the flesh of the other. Of course, the brutal battle did mean he was temporarily distracted.

"What do you want me to do?" Sally demanded, her nose wrinkling as the potent scent of blood saturated the air. Or maybe it was the howls of pain that echoed through the cellar as Caine managed to rip a chunk out of Dolf's muzzle.

The two curs were managing to wound the Were, but not without taking a dangerous amount of damage.

"You're a witch, aren't you?"

She shrugged. "It's too small a space to risk a spell."

"You were quick enough to use magic when we first arrived."

"That was a harmless masking spell to disguise our

presence in this place," she reminded him, her gaze deliberately skimming down his tense body. "Not all of us have been . . . neutered."

Gaius grasped the bitch by her neck, infuriated by the reminder he'd allowed himself to be stripped of his very essence. Digging his claws into her throat, he yanked her off her feet, holding her so they were eye to eye. "Don't think you can taunt me, witch," he hissed, his voice thickening with an accent as ancient as the Roman Empire.

She grabbed his wrist, her eyes wide with agony. "The Dark Lord—"

"Will accept my most abject apologies for the death of his conduit and swiftly find another," he smoothly interrupted.

"Please," she begged. "No."

Abruptly releasing his hold, he allowed Sally to drop to the ground. Her ridiculous pigtails bobbed around her face, which was painted with black liner and lipstick, as she straightened, wiping the blood from her neck.

"Then make yourself useful and bring me the seer," he snapped.

"Are you mental?"

Gaius watched the witch's fear of him being replaced by a flare of panic at being ordered to wade into the gory battle.

"Even if I could get past her rabid protector, which I couldn't, she's a pureblooded Were."

"She can't shift."

"She can still rip me in half."

He leaned down until they were nose to nose, his power making her flinch. "So can I."

"Crap. I should have just let my mother kill me," she muttered. "She, at least, intended to make it quick."

Clenching her hands at her sides, Sally grudgingly made her way across the floor, abruptly jumping sideways when a bloody Ingrid went sailing past her to slam into the wine barrels and lay unconscious.

Gaius shook his head. Things weren't going well.

Not that he was particularly surprised. He'd suspected from the beginning that the curs' confidence that they could defeat a pureblooded Were was more a product of their mutual arrogance than genuine skill.

But he'd at least hoped they could disable Caine long enough that he could get his hands on the prophet and disappear from the cellar.

Now Ingrid was down and out for the count. Dolf was pinned to the ground with the Were's fangs clamped in a death lock on his throat.

And the witch was trying to wriggle her way into the narrow cell with all the enthusiasm of a prisoner headed to the gallows.

The temptation to simply walk away from the unfolding fiasco screamed through him. He could return to his lair and pretend he'd never been near St. Louis. Unfortunately, he couldn't be certain that Caine and Cassandra would do him the service of actually killing the Three Bumbling Amigos. And if one survived, they were bound to squeal to the Dark Lord.

Then . . .

He shuddered, unwilling to imagine what might happen. No. He couldn't run. But he was still too weak to battle an enraged pureblooded Were. So now what?

Lost in his dark broodings, he was caught off guard when Sally gave a sudden war cry. Or he assumed that's what it was supposed to be. To be honest, it sounded like a bad imitation of Tarzan.

Gaius watched in disbelief as the witch darted toward the female Were and grabbed her by the ponytail, giving it a violent tug.

Had she gone mad?

Clearly as baffled as him, the prophet shoved the female away with more confusion than actual fear. Her protector, however, didn't give a shit what Sally was trying to do and, after giving the unconscious Dolf a toss to land on top of Ingrid, Caine turned his lethal attention to the witch.

Sally screeched as he snapped his bloody fangs directly at her face, and she charged out of the cell with a speed that was considerably faster than the pace she used going in.

Nothing quite like having a Were trying to bite off your head to offer a bounce to your step.

Heading directly toward him, she waved a closed fist in the air. "Get us out of here."

He scowled, silently hoping that the rabid Were managed to strike the killing blow.

Of course, he couldn't be so lucky.

Clearly wounded, the animal refused to give in to his bloodlust. Instead, he remained in the doorway, resolutely protecting his companion rather than yielding to his primitive instincts.

Bastardo.

Cursing in resignation, Gaius moved to stand beside the mangled curs who were neatly piled next to the shelf. Then, wrapping his fingers around the medallion that hung from a chain around his neck, he waited only long enough for Sally to reach his side before muttering a word of power and surrounding them in mist.

A spectacular fuck-up from start to finish.

Caine had a vivid memory of his battle with the two curs. The taste of their blood as he'd ripped out chunks of fur and flesh. The sound of their howls of pain. And the scent of their escalating desperation.

But he hadn't managed to entirely avoid injury. And while none of his wounds were life-threatening, they were all leaking blood at a rate that was rapidly stealing his strength.

Grimly ignoring his increasing weakness, he managed to drive away the human witch before his legs collapsed beneath him. His head hit the cement of the floor with enough force to briefly knock him loopy and when he at last managed to clear the fog, it was to discover he'd shifted back to human form and Cassie was kneeling beside his naked body.

"Caine." She tenderly brushed the hair from his sweaty forehead. "We have to get out of here."

"Yes." His voice was hoarse, but he sensed that most of his wounds had sealed shut during his shift. Unfortunately, it would take time to completely heal. Time he wasn't sure they had.

"Let me help you," Cassie murmured, slipping her arm beneath him as he struggled to stand.

"The vampire?" he rasped, his blurry gaze searching the seemingly empty cellar.

"He disappeared."

Reluctantly allowing Cassie to take the majority of his weight as they stumbled toward the tunnel, he frowned at her vague response. "Which way did he go?"

Her arm snaked around his waist as they entered the tunnel, her lavender warmth wrapping around him. He sucked in the sweet scent, hoping to ease his wolf's rabid fury.

It didn't matter that he logically understood Cassie was unharmed. Or that there didn't appear to be any immediate danger. The beast inside him wasn't going to be satisfied until those who dared attack his female were destroyed.

"No, I mean he disappeared, disappeared," she said. "Poof."

He frowned. Had the witch managed to befuddle Cassie long enough to make it seem as if they'd disappeared?

"That's impossible."

She shrugged. "Then he has made himself and his companions invisible." She sent him a challenging glance. "Is that more possible?"

"The witch . . . ?"

"No, it was the vampire," she stubbornly insisted. "He grabbed an amulet that was hanging around his neck and they all vanished."

Christ. His head throbbed as he tried to accept the nasty leech could not only shape-shift, but could appear and disappear in the blink of an eye.

Just. Freaking. Perfect.

"The entire world has gone mad," he muttered.

Cassie patted his shoulder. "Yes."

"Are you humoring me?"

"Yes."

Caine swallowed a sigh, too weak to conjure the proper outrage. In fact, it was taking everything he had just to put one foot in front of the other.

He clenched his teeth as they slowly made their way to the end of the tunnel, but glancing up at the opening, he was forced to concede defeat. There was no way in hell he was going to be able to leap five feet in the air.

"I can't get out until I rest," he grudgingly admitted.

Cassie moved so he could lean against the side of the tunnel, her expression one of calm determination. "I'll go up first and pull you out."

He scowled. "It's supposed to be the other way around."

"Why? Because you're the male?"

"Exactly."

She rolled her eyes. "Sexist dog."

It was an accusation that had never been thrown Caine's way before. Even when he was a cur he'd preferred women who were strong and independent, with a dangerous edge. Nothing kept a man on his toes like bedding a woman who might rip out your throat if you pissed her off.

But with Cassie . . .

He wanted to become the worse sort of cliché.

He wanted to build a perfect lair where she would be safe and warm and so comfortable she would never leave.

He wanted to hunt for their food and then stand guard, offering protection as she eased her hunger.

He wanted to hold her in his arms as she slept, feeling her soft breath on his neck and her heart beating steadily beneath his hand.

"I like having you depend on me," he muttered.

She smiled, moving to place a gentle kiss on his lips. "Partners depend on each other."

"Partners," he breathed, ignoring just how perilously close the word sounded to mates.

Chapter 7

Cassie had learned a great deal about patience over the past three decades.

Being a hostage to a demon lord meant that she'd spent the majority of her life in dank caves. On occasion, she was allowed a television or books to help pass the time, but for the most part she'd had to endure endless days with nothing but her visions to distract her.

Still, it took all of her skill to urge the testy Caine out of the tunnel, using her strength to boost him up and then over the garbage bin. And then, ignoring his snappish complaints that he wasn't an invalid, she'd managed to wrestle him to the waiting Jeep, loading him into the passenger seat before sliding behind the steering wheel.

Trying to hide the lingering weakness from his injuries, Caine wiped the sweat from his brow and sent her a frustrated glare. "What are you doing?"

She hid her smile. He wouldn't be in such a foul mood if he weren't healing.

When he'd first collapsed at her feet she'd been frantic with fear. What if he'd been killed trying to protect her? The mere thought had been like a brutal punch to her gut.

She couldn't bear the loss.

It was that simple.

Wrenching her thoughts away from the destructive memory, Cassie instead turned to the task at hand. Whether he liked it or not, Caine was still weak and it was going to be up to her to take charge.

"I'm going to get us out of here," she said, nibbling her bottom lip as she concentrated on locating the key that Caine always kept hidden beneath the floor mat and sticking it into the ignition.

"Can you drive?" Caine demanded.

The engine roared to life and she studied the knobby thing that she recalled she had to pull down to allow the vehicle to move forward.

"How hard can it be?"

"Shit," he muttered. "Just wait. I'll be fine in a few minutes."

She managed to get into gear and pressed gently on the gas pedal, holding the steering wheel in a death grip as they eased down the dark, empty street.

"What if we were followed?"

"There was a masking spell that should have dampened our scent," he said, his hand reaching to brace on the glove box as she began to pick up speed. "Besides, whatever is chasing us can't be any more dangerous than you behind the wheel."

"Very funny. I happen to be doing just fine, so sit there and be quiet." She sent him a chiding glare, only to have her moment of victory ruined as the wheels hit the curb and they took out a stop sign. "Oops."

"I guess we're about to find out if I'm truly immortal."

With a sniff, she turned her attention back to the road. "Keep it up and I'll kick your naked butt out. Maybe Ingrid and her creepy twin will stop by and pick you up."

He made a sound of disgust, but obviously accepting he was in no position to complain, he instead pointed toward the side street. "Turn left here."

Cassie followed his direction, keeping her speed slow but steady as they headed out of the fringes of St. Louis. Soon they left all signs of town behind, traveling down a gravel road that was flanked by cornfields.

An hour later Cassie was wondering if she'd bitten off more than she could chew. She hadn't wrecked, thank the gods, but her muscles were cramped from her nervous tension and her fingers were aching from gripping the steering wheel so tightly.

"How much farther?"

"Not far," Caine assured her. "Take a right at that mailbox."

She slowed, turning onto a narrow path that was rough and nearly overgrown with weeds. "Where are we going?"

He straightened in his seat, his power sizzling through the air to assure her that he was nearly fully recovered from his battle. "I have a hidden lair just a few miles north of here."

"How many lairs do you have?"

It spoke of his trust in her that he didn't even hesitate to answer. "A dozen spread across North America and another six in Mexico."

She blinked. That seemed . . . excessive. "Why so many?"

"I always knew that Salvatore would eventually stumble across my trail," he said with a shrug. "I needed to be able to disappear no matter where I was."

Wise, of course. Being hunted by the King of Weres was a lethal sport. Still, she couldn't resist teasing him. "Always prepared?"

"That's my motto. Just like a Boy Scout."

She snorted. "I can't imagine you were ever a Boy Scout."

"No," he readily agreed, "but there was a time when I aspired to become an altar boy."

"An altar boy?" She couldn't disguise her shock. "You?"

"I had a life before I was turned into a cur, you know," he said dryly.

She kept her gaze trained on the narrow path, hoping that nothing darted out of the thick underbrush that had replaced the cornfields. "Tell me."

He tensed at her request. "It was so long ago I barely remember."

Cassie hesitated. She might be socially inept, but not even she could miss the I-don't-want-to-talk-about-this vibe he was sending out. Which, of course, only made her more determined to discover what he was hiding. "Where were you born?"

She heard his faint sigh. "In the gutters of Paris in the year 1787."

"Paris?" She sent him a startled glance. "Really?"

"Eyes on the road, pet," he reprimanded, gently grasping her chin until she was facing straight ahead.

"Sorry," she muttered. "I'm just surprised."

"Why?"

"I'm not certain. You seem very . . ."

"What?"

She considered, trying to find the perfect word for his blond good looks, his hint of swagger, and the devilish charm that sparkled in his sapphire eyes. "American," she at last said.

"Not surprising." She felt him shrug. "I was barely thirteen when I signed on as a deckhand to the first ship that would take me. I foolishly thought nothing could be worse than starving in the streets."

She had read enough about history to suspect that being a young boy on a ship wasn't the dashing adventure that the poor kid no doubt hoped it would be. "But there was?"

His fingers drummed a restless tattoo on the door handle.

"We'd been out to sea less than a month when the ship was taken by pirates."

Oh . . . gods. She slowed the vehicle to a mere crawl. "Did they hurt you?"

"Yes."

And that was all he was going to say on the subject, she ruefully acknowledged. Not that she needed the gory details. A young boy in the hands of brutal, lawless pirates . . . it was all very self-explanatory. "I'm sorry."

The tapping halted as Caine sucked in a slow, deep breath, no doubt battling back the memories of those bleak years of misery. "I survived and eventually they sailed close enough to land for me to risk throwing myself overboard and swimming for shore. I ended up in New Orleans."

"How old were you?"

"By then I'd lost track, but I think I must have been around seventeen."

"So young," she breathed. "How did you survive?"

"I begged or stole. Occasionally, I sold my body." His voice was bland. Too bland. "You can't afford pride or morals when you're hungry."

"I understand," she said softly.

He reached to brush a stray curl from her cheek. "Do you?"

Cassie nodded. She'd never been beaten or starved or raped. But she'd been held against her will by one of the most evil creatures to ever touch the world. She knew the toxic combination of anger and frustration and fear at being at the mercy of others. And the strange sense of guilt at not being strong enough to take control of her own destiny.

"How long were you in New Orleans?"

"For five years." He smoothed the curl behind her ear as she kept her gaze on the path, which was becoming increasingly more difficult to see beneath the weeds. "I might have stayed there until I died, but one day I was caught in bed with the wife of the mayor. The bastard put a bounty out on my head, so I thought it might be a good idea to leave Louisiana for a few years."

She chuckled. It didn't surprise her at all that he'd been run out of town by a cuckolded husband. What female wouldn't try to lure him into her bed?

"Where did you go?"

"St. Louis."

"And?"

His fingers outlined the shell of her ear before trailing along the line of her jaw. Cassie shivered in anticipation. She hoped his lair was near. Once Caine was fully rested, she intended to have her wicked way with him.

"And I had barely stepped foot in the city when I was attacked by a strange animal. I thought it was going to be the end of my sorry life." He paused, his hand cupping her nape in a gesture of pure male possession. "Instead it was just the beginning."

Caine stroked his fingers down the elegant curve of Cassie's neck, his thumb lingering on the steady beat of her pulse. A part of him felt . . . raw at having exposed a past that he'd devoted over two hundred years trying to erase from his mind.

Not that it had ever truly been forgotten, he wryly conceded.

He didn't have to be a shrink to know that his obsessive search for a way to become a pureblooded Were came from an overwhelming need to climb the evolutionary ladder. He'd spent his entire life at the mercy of others. He'd been determined to become the master, not the slave.

But a larger part of him was relieved to have unburdened

his darkest secrets. It was like lancing a wound that had been festering for far too long.

A faint smile touched his lips as he studied Cassie's profile, which was tense with concentration. She'd accepted his confession without judgment or disgust. And for once, he hadn't been insulted by the knowledge he was being pitied. Her sympathy was as pure and untainted as her heart.

At last it was the call of a robin that jerked him out of his dangerous preoccupation with his beautiful companion. He swallowed a curse as he glanced toward the overgrown hedge, realizing his distraction had nearly allowed him to drive right past his lair.

"Stop."

Caught off guard, Cassie stomped on the brake, nearly sending him through the windshield. Wisely, he reached over to shove the gearshift into park and switch off the key.

"Why are we stopping here?" she asked in confusion.

"My lair is just beyond the hedge."

She grimaced. "It's not a cave, is it?"

He gave a soft chuckle. "The house is hidden behind an illusion."

"Oh."

Crawling out of the vehicle, Caine was relieved to discover he was nearly healed. A shower, some food, and a few hours of sleep and he would be as good as new. He stretched, getting the kinks out of his muscles before moving around the hood of the Jeep and pulling open the driver's door. Then, with one smooth motion, he was scooping Cassie out of the seat and cradling her against his naked chest.

"What are you doing?" she asked.

"The hexes that guard the house are specifically cast to recognize me," he warned, halting to place his hand flat against the hedge.

There was a silvery shimmer in the air that revealed a

narrow opening that would be invisible to all but the most powerful demons.

He stepped past the magical barrier, halting to run a searching gaze over the large, wooden cabin set among the thick trees. It wasn't nearly as large as many of his lairs, but the simple structure with the A-frame roof and large windows offered a panoramic view of the small pond in back and was fully equipped with every modern convenience as well as Internet service. There were also sturdy cells beneath the house to hold his prisoners and a dozen escape tunnels.

He continued up the stone pathway, pausing at the foot of the railed porch, placing his hand against the invisible barrier until it briefly parted to allow him to step through.

Cassie leaned her head back to send him a puzzled frown. "There are hexes around the house as well?"

"Yes." He climbed the wide steps and skirted around the hot tub. "They're particularly nasty, so don't leave the porch unless I'm with you."

"Wouldn't it be easier to turn them off?"

He snorted, pulling open the glass door to enter the living room, which was spotlessly clean. The L-shaped room was paneled in a glossy cedar with an open-beamed ceiling and matching wood floors. A huge stone fireplace consumed one wall and at the back of the room was a staircase leading to the open loft above. Traditional leather furnishings were scattered over the handwoven rugs and priceless Turner oil paintings were framed on the walls instead of the usual mounted animal heads.

"I could also send an engraved invitation to every demon hunting you and request them to creep up on us while we sleep, but I'd rather not," he said, crossing the room to enter the kitchen.

"I don't think hexes are going to protect us from the vampire, no matter how nasty."

He set her on a stool next to the breakfast bar and folded his arms over his chest. "No, that's something we need to discuss."

She wrinkled her nose, no doubt sensing what he was going to say. "Dinner first."

"Cassie . . ."

"Or we could shower," she interrupted, the wicked invitation in her eyes making him hard in an instance. "The last one was fun."

"Shit." He turned to yank the frilly apron off the peg near the stove and wrapped it around his waist to cover his thickening erection. "Are all females born knowing how to manipulate men?"

She batted her lashes. "I don't know what you mean."

"Convenient."

Her dimples flashed, stealing any ability for him to be annoyed. "I truly am hungry."

"Fine. Let me check the pantry." He conceded defeat. Or maybe he was just as reluctant as Cassie to discuss what had to come next, he acknowledged as he entered the large pantry and opened the stand-up freezer. He reached for the nearest box. "Pizza?" he called out.

"Sure."

He returned to the kitchen, pulling the pizza out of the box. "I'll get this in the oven, if you'll set the table." He slid the pizza on a cooking tray and popped it in the oven. "The plates are in the cabinet over the sink and the cutlery is in the drawer near the fridge."

He was choosing a bottle of wine from the rack on the marble-top counter when he heard her give a choked laugh. Turning, he discovered she'd pulled open the wrong drawer to reveal the skimpy aprons, maid's uniforms, and edible panties that his playmates enjoyed.

"Do you keep all you lairs so well stocked?" she asked with an overly innocent smile.

He moved to shove the drawer shut and yanked open another to pull out two forks and the corkscrew. "Some better than others," he muttered.

She laughed, moving to collect the plates, and placed them on the breakfast bar along with linen napkins. Then, ignoring his warning growl, she moved to peer into the oven.

"Mmmm." She sucked in a deep breath. "It looks odd but it smells yummy."

In the process of pouring the wine, Caine glanced toward his companion in surprise. "You've never had pizza?"

She smiled, moving to stand in front of him, her hands boldly exploring the bare width of his chest. "There are a lot of things I've never tried," she reminded him, her fingers circling his beaded nipples.

He choked back a groan, his hands gripping her wrists to halt her bewitching seduction. "Keep that up and we'll burn down the house. Literally," he groaned, grimly stepping back to reach for the wineglasses. Christ, this female was going to be the death of him. "Here."

She took the glass he offered, sniffing it with a frown. "What is it?"

"A very fine Château Margaux," he explained, sipping the delicate bouquet with the appreciation of a true connoisseur.

Cassie hesitated, watching his obvious enjoyment. Then, taking a reluctant sip, she grimaced as if he'd shoved a lemon down her throat.

"Bleck."

"Bleck?" He lifted his brows in amusement. "It cost five hundred dollars a bottle."

She wrinkled her nose. "It still is bleck."

"I guess it's an acquired taste." He moved to gather an oven mitt to take the pizza from the oven, swiftly running a knife through it before returning to divvy up the slices.

"Why would you want to acquire a taste for something that costs a fortune?" Cassie asked as he settled on a stool next to her.

He shrugged. "Because it costs a fortune."

"I may have just crawled out of a cave, but even I know that's stupid."

"Maybe." He watched as she picked up a slice, studying the chunks of sausage and mushrooms. "Be careful, it's hot."

She leaned forward, taking a small bite as Caine watched. Her teeth sank into the cheese and sauce, her eyes closing in pleasure. "Mmmm."

He chuckled, attacking his own food with gusto. He'd expended energy at an alarming rate. First to fight off the damned curs and then to heal his wounds. He needed serious calories to regain his full strength.

"I take it that the pizza meets with your approval?" he asked between bites.

She demolished her first slice and chewed her way through another. "Much better than the wine."

"Wait until you taste my famous lava cake."

"Lava?"

"Molten chocolate paradise."

She popped the last of the pizza in her mouth and shoved the plate away. "It sounds delicious, but not tonight."

"Hold still." He leaned sideways to brush his thumb over her lower lip. "You have cheese right . . ."

He forgot what he was going to say. Hell, he forgot how to think as the feel of her lush lip sent a blaze of heat through his body.

Dammit.

He'd struggled so hard to leash his driving lust for this

female. He wanted to be noble. Chivalrous. Cassie was all that mattered, and he wanted to do what was right for her. Even if it meant denying what he desired with every breath, with every beat of his heart.

With every fiber of his being.

Unfortunately, he couldn't get his body on board with the whole Dudley Do-Right plan. It wanted to knock the plates aside and take her right there on the breakfast bar.

Or against the fridge . . .

Or . . .

As if to add to his torment, Cassie parted her lips to suck his thumb into the warm wetness of her mouth. He jerked, feeling like he'd just been struck by lightning.

"Cassie, don't," he breathed.

She nibbled the tip of his thumb, her eyes darkening with a desire that pulsed deep inside him.

"Why not?"

Yeah, why not?

His entire body clenched in agony as he struggled to think past his painful erection.

A tug—just one little tug—and she'd been in his lap, her legs spread wide and her innocence his for the taking.

"We have to talk," he hissed between clenched teeth.

She shook her head, leaning so close he could feel the heat from her skin. A scalding promise of lavender temptation. "I don't want to talk."

"Cassie, listen to me." He reached to grasp her shoulders, hanging on to the last shreds of coherent thought. "I can't protect you from the vampire."

"You already did."

"We both know that was nothing but shithouse luck." His lips twisted with regret. Some hero he was turning out to be. "Christ, I led you straight into the trap."

"We couldn't possibly have known that the vampire could

shape-shift." She lifted her hands to skim them down the bare skin of his arms in a soothing motion. "Or appear and disappear."

"All the more reason for you to be protected by your sister and their mates," he forced himself to admit, trying to disguise his bitterness. What did it matter if he couldn't be the one to protect her? So long as she was safe, he should be satisfied. "They could make sure that you're surrounded by enough guards to keep away any danger."

She shook off his hands, which held her at a crucial distance, leaning forward until they were nose to nose. "No."

He shuddered, becoming lost in the drowning emerald of her eyes. "Dammit, why do you have to be so stubborn?"

"I'm not being stubborn, Caine," she said softly, her hands shifting to frame his face. "I had a foretelling."

And that was that.

He bit back his protest as his heart sank to his toes. Did he want to be the one protecting Cassie? Hell, yeah. Was the future of the world more important than his pride? Hell, yeah.

How was he supposed to keep her safe when he didn't have a clue how to stop the vampire and his trio of doom from attacking whenever they felt the urge?

He leaned his forehead against hers. "Did this foretelling happen to mention some magical means to keep us from becoming leech food?"

She brushed her lips over his mouth. "No. But we have to return to your lair in Chicago."

As far as foretellings went, it could be worse, he wryly conceded. He wouldn't have been surprised if he were expected to haul her to the nearest hell dimension and fight off an entire army of demons.

An unnerving shiver of premonition inched down his spine and with a curse, Caine shoved aside all thoughts of looming foretellings, of vamps with crazy-ass abilities, and traitorous curs.

Just for a few minutes he wanted to be a man alone with the female who set him on fire.

"Now?" he rasped, spanning her waist with his hands.

"No." She gave a small shriek as he lifted her to set her on the edge of the bar. Then a slow smile of anticipation curled her lips. "Soon, but not tonight."

Rising to his feet, he stepped between her legs and skimmed his hands beneath her shirt.

"Good."

Chapter 8

Arriving back at his private lair, Gaius dumped the two unconscious curs on the porch. Then, ignoring the witch's demands that he wait and listen to her babbling, he headed up the stairs and into the cell holding the human female.

Still under his enthrallment, she willingly went into his arms, tilting her head to offer her throat for his hungry fangs.

He drank deeply, desperate to regain his strength. He wasn't going to share his lair with his unwelcomed comrades while he was on the point of collapse. Which, of course, meant that he was forced to drain the female until she was nothing more than an empty shell that would have to be dumped in the swamps.

Damn the idiots.

Dropping the dead female on the floor, Gaius retraced his steps. Someone was going to pay for this screwup. And it wasn't going to be him.

Although dawn was nearing, he followed the scents of the curs to the kitchen. He intended to vent his displeasure before seeking his bed for the day.

Punishment was like a soufflé. If not served immediately, they both fell flat.

He entered the kitchen, taking a moment to glance around the narrow room. At one end the walls were lined with a tiled countertop and white painted cabinets. An ancient fridge hummed in the corner and a matching stove was set under a window that overlooked the dilapidated chicken coop.

At the other end was a small wooden table with matching chairs. Not that there was much to see of the table beneath the huge slab of raw meat the two curs were consuming with gusto. In the corner the witch was perched on a stool, reading from a battered, leather-bound book.

At his entrance the three froze, smart enough to comprehend that their lives hung in the balance.

He concentrated on the dim-witted duo. He would have to take greater care with the witch.

"I trust that the two of you are proud of yourselves?"

Ingrid flinched, lowering her head in a gesture of subservience. "Caine was a lot stronger than we expected him to be."

Gaius moved to stand in the center of the tiled floor. "You knew he'd become a pureblooded Were."

Dolf shifted closer to his sister, his hand lifting to touch the crystal hung around his neck. "Yes, but his power isn't just that of a Were," he tried to bluff. "I doubt there's anyone but Salvatore who could beat him in a head-to-head fight."

"A convenient excuse for your failure," Gaius said, his voice soft. Lethally soft.

"A convenient excuse?" Dolf's fingers tightened on the crystal, no doubt wishing he had the nerve to lob a spell in Gaius's direction. "That bastard almost killed me."

"Hardly a great loss," Gaius drawled.

"Yeah?" Dolf scowled. "Well, where were you during the battle? I didn't see you doing anything to help."

"A good commander directs his troops. He doesn't waste his talent by becoming a foot soldier."

"Talk about convenient," Ingrid muttered beneath her breath.

The bitch was dead.

Her and her perverted brother.

Gaius clenched his fists, his power slamming through the room with enough force to overturn the table and shatter the overhead light.

"Do you dare imply that I—"

"Wait." The witch was abruptly standing directly in front of him, her hands held up in a gesture of peace. "Squabbling among ourselves isn't going to help. What we need is a new plan."

Utterly unaware of how close he came to death, Dolf turned the table upright and continued chewing on the bloody slab of meat. "What kind of plan?" he demanded between bites. "There's no way in hell we're going to be able to lure the seer and her protector into another trap."

Sally shrugged, looking worse for the wear with her black eyeliner smeared and her pigtails drooping. "There's no need for a trap."

"No?" With an effort, Gaius regained command of his temper and regarded the tiny female with a mocking smile. "Do you intend to wiggle your nose and make them appear?"

"Something like that." She reached into her bustier to pull out several golden strands of hair. "Abracadabra."

"Hair?" Gaius rasped.

"Not just hair. The prophet's hair."

Gaius frowned, recalling Sally's insane charge toward Cassandra in the cellar. Was that what she'd been doing? Yanking out the female's hair?

"Am I supposed to be impressed?"

Sally smiled. "I can use this to track her."

Suddenly Dolf was at the witch's side, his face filled with awe. "You can scry?"

"Yes."

Annoyed at being left out of the conversation when he should be in control of it, Gaius pointed a finger toward the witch. "Explain."

She paled, swallowing heavily as his displeasure was focused on her. "Having a part of Cassandra means I can use a spell to locate her."

A portion of Gaius's fury eased. As much as he wanted an excuse to kill his bumbling companions and lay the blame on them for allowing the prophet and her protector to escape, he understood that the Dark Lord might not be in a forgiving frame of mind. In fact, he might just kill Gaius before he could convince him that the fiasco wasn't his fault.

"You can locate her now?" Dolf growled, his eyes glowing crimson.

"Don't be any more of an idiot than you have to be, cur," Gaius snapped.

The stupid creature scowled. "What?"

Gaius waved a hand to slam shut the heavy shutters over the window. "It's nearly dawn."

"So . . ." Realization at last managed to penetrate his thick skull. "Oh."

"Precisely." Dismissing the fool, Gaius turned his attention to the witch, moving with blinding speed to grab her by the throat and lift her off the floor. "You will perform this scrying at nightfall," he commanded, his glare warning that he would rip out her heart if she tried to find the prophet while he was imprisoned by daylight. "Not a moment before, *capisce*?"

She struggled to breathe, her eyes wide with fear. "Of course."

His eyes narrowed. "Oh, and I'll need a new female. Order one off the computer."

"It's not that—" She squeaked as his fingers tightened, a fraction from crushing her windpipe. "Yes, fine. I'll have one here by dusk."

"Good." He released his grip, watching her crumple on the floor before turning back to the curs. "Dolf."

The cur lowered his head, flinching as if he expected a blow. "Yes, Commander?"

"Get rid of the body upstairs."

"Yeah." The cur hissed a sigh of relief. "No problem."

Feeling the heavy press of dawn begin to sap what little energy he had left, Gaius turned to leave the room. The night had been a debacle. For now he just wanted to lock himself in his private rooms and drift into oblivion. He'd reached the doorway when Ingrid foolishly halted his retreat.

"What about me?"

Gaius threw a jaundiced glare over his shoulder. "Try not to burn down the house while I'm sleeping."

Caine stood between Cassie's legs, gliding his fingers up and down her throat as he studied the faint color that stained her cheeks. The wolf inside him remained edgy, needing the comfort of holding this woman in his arms to reassure himself that she was safe. The man . . .

He needed something far more primitive.

"You are so beautiful," he breathed.

She brushed the hair from his brow, her smile oddly uncertain. "Do you truly think so?"

He frowned. Was it possible she didn't realize she was the

most gorgeous creature ever to walk the earth? "You've looked in a mirror, haven't you?"

"Not often. My appearance has never mattered to me." She shrugged. "Not until now."

His thumbs slid beneath her chin, tilting back her head to meet his curious gaze. "Why should it matter now?"

"I want you to find me attractive."

He growled, his hands cupping her face as his body ached to show her just how damned attractive he found her.

"You are exquisite," he assured her, his voice thick with the need pulsing through his veins. "But it's not the shimmer of silver in your hair, or the stunning emerald of your eyes that has bewitched me." His gaze slid downward. "It's not even your hot little body, although that has given me more than one sleepless night."

She leaned forward to nip the lobe of his ear. "Then what?"

Pleasure jolted through him at the tiny bite, his erection so hard that the mere brush of the ridiculous apron was painful. Christ, he felt like he was going to explode.

Don't pounce, Caine. Do. Not. Pounce.

Gritting his teeth, he instead lowered his hand to press his palm over her rapidly beating heart. "This."

Her brows lifted. "My heart?"

"Yes."

"Oh." Her arms wrapped around his neck as her eyes melted into pools of emerald. "I don't know much about these things, but I believe that was the perfect thing to say."

He flashed a smug smile. "Was it?"

She stroked her lips along the line of his jaw. "Hmmm."

Caine went rigid, a groan wrenched from his throat. "I try."

"Yes." She found a particularly erotic spot just below his jaw, using her tongue to drive him mad with need. "You certainly do."

He muttered a curse, reaching his breaking point. There was more than one way of sharing pleasure.

"I could try better if you had on fewer clothes."

Without missing a beat, Cassie leaned back to hook her hands beneath the bottom of her top and peel it off. "Like this?"

His breath escaped him on a hiss as she tossed the shirt on the floor, his gaze locked on the sight of her mouthwatering breasts barely concealed by the black lace bra. "It's a start," he managed to choke out.

"More?"

Oh. He wanted so much more.

"Let me help," he rasped, reaching to pop the button and unzip her jeans before dropping to his knees.

Ignoring her protests, he gently removed her tennis shoes and tugged off her socks. He lifted her foot to stroke his lips along the line of her arch.

She gasped, the scent of her arousal spicing the air. "That tickles."

He chuckled, nipping the tips of her toes. "Such sweet little toes."

"Oh . . . Lord."

Grasping the hem of her jeans, he pulled them ruthlessly downward. They dropped on the tiled floor as his hands lifted to worship the pale alabaster skin of her calves.

"And these legs." His voice was rough with the power of his wolf. "They were surely made to wrap around me."

Her breathy chuckle filled the air. "And here I thought they were made to take me from one place to another."

"They are far too lovely for such a mundane task."

His kissed a path up the inside of her leg, tilting back his head to savor the sight of her poised above him.

Wearing nothing more than her lacy bra and matching panties, she perched on the edge of the breakfast bar like a statue of feminine temptation. Her fragile features were flushed with passion and her hair a satin curtain of pale silver that tumbled over her shoulders. But it was the musky scent of her wolf that made his heart slam against his ribs.

Cassie might not be able to shift, but her beast was telling him that she was ready and eager.

He swallowed a pained groan, continuing to kiss a path up her leg, taking time to explore the sensitive back of her knee before performing the same service to her other leg. She shivered beneath his light caresses, her fingers gripping the marble top of the bar as he found the sensitive skin of her inner thigh.

"Caine," she pleaded.

"Patience, pet." He used his tongue to outline the edge of her panties, breathing deeply of her sweet scent. "There's so much to explore. And I intend to taste every . . ." He kissed the icy tattoo just below her belly button. "Satin . . ." He grasped her hips to keep her from squirming as he continued up her flat stomach until he was able to slice through the bow holding her bra together with a sharpened fang. "Inch."

"I want to explore," she protested.

"Later." His tone was distracted as the bra fell away to expose the tender curves of her breasts.

They were delectable, he decided. Perfectly shaped to fit his palms and tipped by rosy nipples that tightened beneath his heated gaze.

"And I can do whatever I want?"

"Whatever you want," he agreed, his head dipping toward the waiting bounty.

"Do you promise?"

"Mmm." He abruptly paused, sensing he'd just stepped into a trap. Lifting his head, he studied her with a narrowed eye. "Wait."

She blinked, her eyes glazed with need. "Why?"

"What did I just promise?"

"That I could do whatever I want."

"Maybe you should be more specific."

A slow, teasing smile curved her lips. "Scared?"

"Wary," he admitted. "I've told you I won't take your innocence." He watched as her expression tightened into stubborn lines.

"You can't *take* something that I give you willingly."

His gut twisted. What the hell was she trying to do to him? He was hanging on to his nobility by a thread. A very thin, very fragile thread.

"Dammit, Cassie."

"What?"

"You don't know what you're doing."

Her eyes glowed with an emerald fire. His wolf was on instant alert, sensing the sudden danger in the air.

"Are you saying I'm too stupid to decide what I want?"

Okay, so his words hadn't come out right. He was lucky he could still form a full sentence when his brain had relocated considerably lower in his body.

"I'm saying that you don't have enough experience to know what you want. That's not your fault."

She looked spectacularly unimpressed with his logic. "So you'd make love to me if I wasn't a virgin?"

"It's not just that."

"Then what?"

He struggled to express his fear that he was taking advantage of her naivete. It was easy for her to become convinced that he was some sort of Prince Charming when she didn't have a comparison.

"How many men have you known in your life?"

"I told you, there were a few."

He cupped her chin, forcing her to meet his piercing gaze. "Briggs and the demon lord don't count."

"You weren't Briggs's only accomplice."

He snorted. "I can just imagine the kind of scum who would work with the bastard."

She poked her finger into the center of his chest, seemingly annoyed by his dismissal of her potential lovers. "Some were scum, but there were others who were like you."

He frowned, offended by her comparison to Briggs's nasty servants. "Me?"

"Yes." She gave him another poke. "They were decent men who were simply desperate and willing to believe Briggs's promise he could give them what they most desired."

In a heartbeat, Caine catapulted from *who-the-hell-cares* about the males in her past to insane jealousy. "And you spent time with these men?"

"A few." A reminiscent smile curved her lips, making his wolf snarl in possessive outrage. "There was a very handsome fairy who used to sneak me chocolate when he visited." She sighed. "I adore chocolate."

"A fairy," he muttered. He hated fairies.

"And then there was a charming vampire."

"Charming vampire is an oxymoron," he snapped, deciding he hated leeches even more than he hated fairies.

She shrugged. "He swore he could release me from the demon lord."

Lying bastard. The only way to release her from the demon lord was to cut off the creature's connection to this world. And she still wasn't completely free if the tattoo on her stomach was any indication. But she must have been tempted.

"Why didn't you go with him?"

"Because I knew I had to wait."

"For what?"

She planted her hand directly over his heart, her gaze holding his captive. "For you."

"Oh, shit." His eyes slid shut as he leaned forward to rest

his forehead against hers. The warm scent of lavender filled his senses, his entire body trembling with the driving need to claim this female in the most basic way possible. "You're killing me."

Her arms wrapped around his neck, her lips brushing against his ear. "Take me to the bedroom, Caine."

His nobility died a swift, unmourned death as he plucked her off the breakfast bar and headed out of the kitchen.

"Yes."

Chapter 9

Caine registered Cassie's soft chuckle as he charged with lightning speed through the living room and up the stairs to the loft. The soft sound brushed over his sensitized skin like a tangible caress, winding him impossibly tighter.

He was on fire. The desire he'd kept leashed for so long threatening to burn out of control.

Belatedly realizing the danger, Caine forced himself to slow his pace as he reached the loft. No matter what his instinct, he wasn't going to take Cassie like an animal in heat.

If she was willing to offer him the gift of her innocence, then he would offer her the respect she deserved.

Crossing the polished wood floor, he gently laid her on the bed, which had been hand-carved by the finest craftsmen and matched the armoire tucked in a far corner. The ceiling was open-beamed with a skylight built into the sloping roof that allowed the early morning sunlight to pour over her nearly naked body.

His heart went crazy, skipping beats and then pounding at a frantic pace, as if trying to catch up for lost time. She was just so stunning. An exquisite work of art made of alabaster and gold and shimmering emerald.

He ripped off the ridiculous apron, his aching arousal twitching as he felt her gaze examining the hard length. He paused, searching her expression for any sign of hesitation. Then she smiled, holding out her arms in welcome, and he was lost.

With a leap he landed on top of her, pressing her slender body into the mattress covered by a hand-stitched quilt. "Last chance, pet," he warned, his voice a low rumble.

She rubbed against him, her hands clutching at his shoulders. "Enough talking," she protested, lifting her head to nip his bottom lip.

A growl rumbled in his throat. "You want action?"

Her tongue peeked out to soothe the tiny wound she'd made. "I want you."

Caine didn't need any further urging. Swooping down his head, he was kissing her, a forceful demand that hinted at the endless nights he'd spent tormented by his need for her.

Later there would be time for soft seduction and hours of foreplay. For now he allowed the delicious sensations to flood through him, drowning any lingering concern.

Gently parting her soft lips with the tip of his tongue, he plunged into the moist temptation of her mouth, groaning at her sweet taste. He heard Cassie give a small sound between a gasp and a moan, her nails biting into his skin.

The tiny pain made his back arch in response, his erection pressing against the soft skin of her stomach. On some level he was aware of the small tattoo that radiated a brutal chill just below her belly button, but that was a worry for another time.

In this moment he was far more interested in the exquisite heat blasting through him. He eased his kiss, moving to trace a soft trail down the line of her jaw. "I should have brought the wine with us," he whispered.

She brushed her hands down his back. "Why?"

"It would be intoxicating to lick it off your beautiful body."

"My body?"

He chuckled at her puzzled tone. "Here." He nuzzled the hollow at the base of her throat. "And here." He kissed down the line of her collarbone, his hands cupping her breasts. Her skin quivered beneath his light touch, her breath coming out in a small explosion as his lips found the tip of her tight nipples. "Yeah, especially here."

She shifted beneath him, one leg wrapping around his hips to allow him to settle more firmly against her feminine core. They groaned in unison.

"I feel intoxicated enough without the wine."

"Tell me what you like, Cassie," he rasped, teasing her nipple with the tip of his tongue. "Tell me what feels good."

"That," she moaned. "That feels so good."

He captured the nipple between his teeth, biting it just hard enough to have her gasping in pleasure, her hips pressing up in a silent plea for release.

Oh yes. No matter how vivid his fantasies, nothing could compare to the sensation of her slender body spread beneath him, her hands cupping his ass as her soft pants filled the air.

Continuing to caress her breasts, Caine allowed his fingers to trail downward, following the curve of her waist. He took time to appreciate the delicate flare of her hips before moving to the soft skin of her inner thigh.

He felt her tremble as he stroked tiny circles that brushed near her clit without touching her most sensitive flesh. Up and down he moved, smiling as she gave a choked curse.

"Caine, please."

Her harsh plea sent a shudder of need through him. Giving her nipple a last lick, he surged up to bury his face in her neck.

"Are you sure you're ready?" he whispered, his body trembling as his canine fangs erupted from his gums at the scent of her arousal. "My hunger for you is too great. I'm not sure how gentle I can be."

Without warning, she reached between them to press his hand to the wet slit between her legs. "Do I feel ready to you?"

Caine hissed, his finger sliding into her body as his thumb sought out the source of her pleasure. Slowly, he stroked his finger deeper and deeper, listening to her short gasps as she spiraled toward release.

"No more teasing," she moaned in a strangled voice, her hands grasping his hips.

He quivered, his hunger so intense it filled the air with pulses of heat.

"Cassie," he growled, his voice oddly strained.

"Now, Caine," she commanded, her other leg shifting to wrap around his hips, blatantly demanding his penetration.

Pulling back far enough to meet her gaze, which glowed with the hunger of her wolf, Caine grabbed her fingers, wrapping them around his hard shaft to guide him to the entrance to her body.

His teeth clenched at the feel of her slender fingers circling his cock, his balls tightening as she gave him a slow, destructive stroke.

Christ. He was close.

Too close.

Gently tugging her hand away, he pushed his hips forward, breeching her with the head of his shaft. He paused one last time, giving her the opportunity to protest. Even if it killed him.

When she lifted her head to sink her teeth into his neck, Caine lost all ability to think.

With a choked howl, he grasped her hands and jerked

them over her head, pressing them against the quilt as he slowly forged a path into her tight body, breaking through her virginity with barely a hesitation.

"Yes," she breathed against his neck, her legs tightening around his waist. "Oh, God, Caine."

His eyes squeezed shut as he struggled to rein his savage desire. He wasn't going to pound his way to paradise. Not when slow and steady was so much sweeter.

With care he pulled back, bending his head to the side. "Your teeth, Cassie," he managed to rasp. "I want to feel them on my neck."

She didn't hesitate as she sank her teeth back into the base of his throat, sending a jolt of pure adrenaline through his system.

"Cassie. Gods."

He surged back into her slick heat, his harsh groans matching her soft sighs as he found a steady pace, his hips rolling upward with each thrust.

Her teeth clenched harder on his neck as she lifted to meet his quickening onslaught, her nails raking across his back.

He forgot to breathe, his heart thundering in his chest. Deep inside, his wolf howled in primitive satisfaction.

This was more than sex. More than a passing hookup with a female who stirred his lust.

This was soul-deep and forever.

The terrifying thought barely had time to form when he felt Cassie stiffen and then shiver beneath the force of her orgasm. The sensation of her convulsing around his erection toppling him over the edge.

With a shout of release, Caine gave one last thrust, his eyes squeezing shut as the profound bliss exploded through his body.

* * *

Cassie slowly drifted awake, heaving a sigh of contentment at the sensation of Caine's warm arms wrapped around her and the steady beat of his heart beneath her ear.

Mmm. This was how every day should start. A warm bed, a delectable male wrapped around her, and not one demon lord, vampire-on-steroids, or crazed cur in sight.

Or at least she was assuming there were no lurking enemies. Just to make sure, she forced open her eyes to cast a quick glance around the room. Nope. She was all alone with her delicious, delectable, divine lover.

Yes, lover.

Finally.

A smug smile curved her lips as the memories from the previous night flooded through her. Once she'd managed to convince the stubborn Were that she wasn't some fragile treasure he had to protect, even from herself, he'd taught her the true meaning of desire.

Several times.

Breathing in the rich scent of his musk, Cassie tilted back her head. She wasn't surprised to find Caine studying her with a slumberous gaze. She'd already sensed he was awake. What surprised her was the excited flutter of her heart even after hours of decadent sex.

"Good morning," he murmured, his attention shifting over her shoulder to glance at the clock on the dresser. "Or I suppose I should say good afternoon."

She stretched, too lazy to turn her head. "What time is it?"

"Just past two."

She'd been out nearly five hours? Amazing.

About to admit she never slept so well alone, Cassie belatedly noticed Caine's recently shaved face and the scent of soap that clung to his bronzed skin. He'd recently showered?

The sudden knowledge made her eyes narrow in suspicion. "Did you sleep?"

"I rested."

She sighed, her expression one of guilt. "You were keeping guard, weren't you?"

He smiled, angling his head down to kiss the tip of her nose. "I was enjoying the view."

"I wish . . ."

"Shh." His lips drifted lower, teasing the edge of her mouth. "How are you feeling?"

Her guilt was forgotten beneath the warm tide of pleasure. "Deliciously sated."

He pulled back, his expression almost . . . sheepish. "I didn't hurt you, did I?"

She frowned in confusion. Hurt her? "Of course not."

"I wasn't always gentle."

"Oh." A faint blush touched her cheeks. Not at the memory of his aggressive lovemaking. They were pureblooded Weres. Rough and ready was part of their natures. But at the recollection of her wild response. "We both know my screams weren't from pain."

A growl rumbled in his chest, his eyes darkening with a ready heat. "Don't give me encouragement unless you plan on spending the next several hours in this bed."

With a wicked smile, she lifted her hand to brush the pale hair off his forehead. "Is that a promise?" Cassie felt his body tense at her husky words, the scent of his musk laced through the air.

"You, Cassandra, are a very dangerous female."

Her smile widened as she inwardly gloated. She liked knowing how easily she could rouse his desire. "Dangerous is good," she admitted. "It's much better than loony."

His brows snapped together, as if he were angered by her confession. "Don't ever say that."

"I don't say it, other people do."

"Not if they want to avoid a nasty death," he rasped.

She blinked at his vehemence. He truly was upset. Then, with a wistful smile, she allowed her fingers to smooth down the angular line of his cheekbone. "My protector."

"For all eternity."

They both froze as his words seemed to hang in the air. Like a live grenade that might explode if anyone moved.

Did he say eternity?

Only mates stayed together for an eternity. Or at least that's what she'd always believed.

So was he implying they were more than temporary lovers?

"Caine?"

With one fluid movement, Caine was tossing aside the quilt and sliding off the bed. As if he was hoping to distract her.

And it worked.

No big shocker, of course. What female could think clearly when she was offered such a tempting view?

Caine was naked male perfection.

Lean, flawlessly chiseled muscles. A wide chest and wider shoulders. Smooth, bronzed skin. And a fully erect arousal that would make any man proud.

And any woman sigh in anticipation.

Ignoring her appreciative glance, Caine leaned down to tuck her hair behind her ear in a tender gesture. "Are you hungry?"

Cassie pressed her hand to her stomach as it growled on cue. "Starving," she admitted.

"Understandable." He smiled with sinful amusement, his fingers trailing down her jaw. "You expended a lot of energy."

"I did, didn't I?"

He chuckled, turning to cross the floor and pull a pair of faded jeans and white T-shirt from the dresser. "Have a shower while I make us some breakfast," he said, quickly dressing. "There are clean clothes that should fit you in the closet."

Sitting up, Cassie regarded him with a narrowed gaze. "Female clothes?"

The sapphire eyes twinkled and Cassie abruptly realized that the edge in her voice must be jealousy.

How odd.

"Most of them have never been worn."

"Hmm."

He shoved his feet in a pair of sneakers and then moved to place a lingering kiss on her forehead. "Later, I'll go to the Jeep and get your suitcase," he promised.

The disturbing sensation eased at his soothing touch. "Fine."

"Come down to the kitchen when you're ready."

She watched him stroll out of the loft, a smile of satisfaction curving her lips. Who would ever have believed it? After thirty years of being crapped on by fate, she'd at last hit the jackpot.

And what a jackpot he was.

A pity she couldn't halt time. She couldn't imagine anything better than spending the rest of eternity alone with Caine in this isolated cabin.

Taking a few minutes to wallow in her rare sense of happiness, Cassie at last forced her lethargic body out of bed and into the shower. She truly was hungry. And besides, she didn't want to spend one unnecessary minute away from Caine.

Once clean, she dried off in front of the window that overlooked the pond. The sun was shimmering on the water and the wildflowers danced in the breeze. A perfect invitation for a picnic, she decided.

With a smile of anticipation, Cassie pulled on a pair of khaki shorts and a scoop-neck white shirt. She shoved her feet into her own sneakers and combed her hair into a ponytail. Once presentable, she headed for the stairs.

A step away from the door, however, she staggered to a halt, her balance precarious as a vision slammed through her with shocking force.

She hissed in shock.

Usually, the visions flowed through her to appear as a floating hieroglyphic that she could decipher later. Sometimes she understood them. Sometimes she didn't. But only rarely did she actually see her predictions in full-fledged living color as they seared through her mind.

Pressing her palms to her aching temples, she watched in confusion as the vision of herself came into focus. She was standing alone in the middle of a white fog that was so thick she couldn't see through it. She sensed there was something lurking in the fog. Something so powerful that its mere presence was flaying the skin from her body.

Oh, Lord. She whimpered in pain. She wanted to curl into a tiny ball and pray the lurking thing wouldn't notice her. But she couldn't. The scent of Caine was drifting through the air and she knew she had to reach him.

He was in trouble.

Deep trouble.

Then, as if on cue, the fog slowly parted.

She cried out in shock as she caught sight of Caine. Oh, please blessed mother, no.

He was lying in the mist, his body twisted and deformed as if he'd been caught midshift, trapped between human and wolf. Impulsively she stepped toward him, only to come to a halt as he bared his fangs in warning.

Only then did she notice the sapphire eyes were filled with a feral insanity.

He didn't recognize her.

The thought had barely flashed through her mind when he was awkwardly shoving himself upright, his savage howl echoing through the creepy fog. Frightened, Cassie backed away.

Precisely the wrong thing to do.

Lost in the savage instincts of his wolf, Caine tracked her movements with the cunning of a predator. In this moment she was his prey.

And he was preparing to attack.

Cassie didn't fear for herself. She'd always assumed she was destined for an early grave. She was, after all, the only known prophet. The most desired and feared creature in the world.

No. She'd prepared for years to die. But if Caine came to his senses and realized what he'd done . . .

A gut-wrenching dread lodged in her heart. He would never, ever be able to forgive himself.

Or worse, what if he was stuck in that hideous state between wolf and man? What if he was forever trapped as a monster?

As if sensing her fear, Caine crouched, no doubt excited by the scent of her panic. But even as she braced for the impact, the vision vanished as abruptly as it had arrived.

Reeling in reaction, Cassie fell to her knees, her head bowed with the sheer horror of what she'd been shown.

Oh, gods, she had to stop this.

But how?

She didn't know where the two of them had been, or how they'd been taken, or even what evil had been lurking just out of sight.

"Think, Cassie, think," she muttered, wiping away the useless tears.

Though she didn't know where they'd been, she sensed that it would happen soon. And if they were both in the strange fog, then they'd obviously been together when they were taken.

So . . . she had to make sure they weren't together.

Ever.

She ignored the brutal pain that sliced through her at the mere thought of spending the rest of her life without Caine. It would be a barren, lonely existence, but she could survive if she knew that Caine was alive and well.

And more importantly, she ignored the whispered warning that she'd never been able to alter the future. No matter how often she tried.

This time it would be different.

It *had* to be different.

With an effort she forced herself to straighten, her knees still weak and her head aching. She would worry about the future later. For now, she had to get away from Caine.

Something that was easier said than done.

She was under no illusion that she could simply give him a kiss good-bye and stroll away. Caine had declared himself her protector and nothing short of death was going to pry him from her side.

Which meant she would have to slip away.

Her gaze turned toward the window. Although she couldn't shift, she was still as strong and as fast as other Weres. If she jumped out the window and took off at top speed there was a fifty/fifty shot she could reach the Jeep before Caine realized she was trying to escape.

Of course, she'd only have one shot.

Caine would chain her to the wall if she failed.

Sucking in a deep breath, she was actually in the process

of crossing the floor when she was struck by a sudden thought.

Crap. She couldn't just leave. The hexes surrounding the cabin would fry her if she left the house alone.

Which meant she'd have to find a way to have Caine escort her past the barriers and *then* escape.

She squeezed her eyes shut in frustration. Yeah. No problem.

"Cassie?"

The sound of Caine's voice calling from the kitchen jerked Cassie out of her dark broodings. First things first. She had to convince Caine to leave the house. She would worry about escaping later.

"I'm coming," she called, heading reluctantly down the stairs and stepping into the kitchen.

She was greeted by the scent of waffles fresh from the toaster and warm syrup. Her stomach rumbled in approval, even as her heart sank to her toes at the sight of Caine mixing frozen orange juice into a pitcher.

It all looked so wondrously homey. Like a scene from her deepest fantasies.

Caine turned at her entrance, instantly sensing her distress despite her forced smile. Setting aside the pitcher, he moved across the tiled floor, grasping her hands in a tight grip. "What's wrong?"

She hesitated. She might be the world's worse liar, but this was for Caine. It was her turn to step up to the plate and do whatever was necessary to protect him. Just as he'd always protected her.

"I had a vision," she admitted, sticking to the truth for as long as possible.

"Damn," he muttered, the contentment leeching from his magnificent eyes. "Now what?"

"We have to leave."

"Okay." Her heart nearly shattered at his ready nod. He was prepared to follow her no matter what new disaster she was leading him into. Without question, without hesitation. How had she ever earned such steadfast loyalty? "Do you know where we're headed?"

She forced her eyes to meet his searching gaze, fiercely reminding herself that Caine's life hung in the balance.

"West."

"That's it?" His brows lifted, but he looked more confused than suspicious. Thank the gods. "Just west?"

"For now."

"Do we at least have time for breakfast?"

Say no, a voice whispered in the back of her head.

The sooner she was away from Caine, the sooner she could hope she'd managed to avoid his fate. But, the need to spend just a few extra moments in his company overcame her common sense.

Surely a half an hour wouldn't make any difference?

"Yes."

"Breakfast in bed?" he murmured, his fingers brushing over her cheek. Then, noting her strained expression, he gently tapped the end of her nose. "Come on, your waffles are getting cold."

Squashing her prick of guilt at her selfish need to savor just one meal with the man who'd rescued her from hell and filled her heart with joy, Cassie joined him at the breakfast table.

They ate in near silence, but Cassie was content to absorb the pleasure of his leg pressed against hers, and the delicious musk of his wolf that spiced the air. These memories were going to have to last her a lifetime and she intended to enjoy every moment.

All too swiftly they were finished with the waffles and Caine had cleared away their dishes.

With an effort, Cassie crushed the urge to find some excuse to linger and instead allowed herself to be carried out the front door and down the walk to the waiting Jeep. She had already dared fate enough. She had to get away from Caine before destiny took matters out of her hands.

Settling her in the seat, Caine moved to take his place behind the wheel. Then, with an ease that made her shake her head in rueful resignation, he had the vehicle shifted into gear and they were hurtling down the dirt path with a steady speed.

Her lips parted to tease that he would have to give her driving lessons so the next time she had to save his butt she wouldn't embarrass herself, only to snap shut as she remembered there would be no next time.

She clenched her hands, something deep in her heart slowly withering and dying.

Was it hope?

Stoically, she watched the overgrown meadows being replaced by well-manicured fields, the road widening to a paved street that eventually became a four-lane highway.

Beside her she felt Caine's concerned glances, while inside she was increasingly tormented by the urgent need to travel north to Caine's lair outside of Chicago. She'd known for weeks she would eventually have to return to the farmhouse. Now it was an imperative demand she wasn't going to be able to fight for much longer.

Still, she'd hoped to lead Caine as far west as possible. Once she managed to escape him, she wanted him convinced that she would be fleeing toward Kansas City. It would hopefully give her the necessary time to disappear before he could pick up her scent.

"You're quiet." Caine at last broke the thick silence.

She turned to meet his worried gaze, pasting a fake smile to her face. "I'm distracted."

"And that's all?"

She pressed her lips together, trembling with the effort to deny the powerful compulsion to leap from the Jeep and head north.

"Can we pull off here?" she rasped, pointing toward the narrow road just ahead.

He automatically exited, his brow furrowed as he studied the empty parking lot that framed a small park with public bathrooms and a handful of picnic tables.

He pulled to a halt beneath a shade tree, his eyes skimming the park in confusion. "A rest stop?"

"There's something in the woods." She pointed toward the distant line of trees. "Something you need to see."

He jerked his gaze toward her, his jaw clenching as if sensing he wasn't going to like what she had to say. "Me?"

She drank in the bronzed beauty of his face, memorizing every angle, every line and curve until it was branded on her heart.

"Yes."

"What about you?"

"I need to stay here."

He shook his head, returning his gaze to the empty countryside. "I don't like this."

"I'll be fine," she assured him.

"If something attacks I'll be too far away to protect you."

"Nothing will attack. It's daylight."

He didn't look reassured. In fact, he looked downright pissy. "There are more dangers than just leeches."

She trembled, struck by another urgent need to be traveling north. "Please, Caine."

Clearly sensing her distress, Caine muttered a curse and reached beneath his seat to pull out a small handgun. "Here."

He pressed the weapon into her hand and wrapped her fingers around the grip. "Shoot anything that moves."

Knowing that this was most likely her last moments with the man who would haunt her for the rest of eternity, she leaned forward to brush her lips softly over his mouth.

"Take care of yourself," she whispered.

He nipped her bottom lip before pulling back with a rueful smile. "I'd rather take care of you."

Oh . . . Lord.

She battled back the tears as she pushed him away. "You have to go."

"Fine," he sighed.

With one last scan to make sure the park was empty, Caine crawled out of the Jeep and took off at a swift trot. She waited until he reached the edge of the woods, knowing he would glance back before disappearing from view.

Once certain he wasn't going to come charging back, Cassie hastily clambered into his seat and put the Jeep into neutral. She clutched the steering wheel, gnawing her bottom lip as she resisted the urge to stomp on the gas. Caine would hear the change in the engine even from such a distance.

Refusing to glance back, Cassie concentrated on keeping a straight line as the Jeep rolled with excruciating sluggishness across the parking lot and back onto the access road. Only when she was near the interstate did she offer a silent plea for the fates to keep Caine safe, and shoved the gearshift into drive, taking off with enough force to lay rubber.

Chapter 10

Despite being shifted into his wolf form, Caine could feel the panic claw through him as he reached the end of Cassie's trail and realized that it had doubled back.

God dammit. He'd wasted nearly an hour running along the highway, desperate to catch up with the Jeep and massacre the bastards who'd kidnapped his female.

Now he was forced to halt and reassess his limited choices. With a snarl of impatience, he padded behind a hay bale and shifted, careful to remain hidden from the passing cars. For whatever stupid reason, humans were far more shocked to catch sight of a naked man standing in a field than a massive wolf.

Sucking in deep, shuddering breaths, he wiped the sweat from his brow and tried to think through his mind-numbing fear.

When he'd first heard the squeal of tires he'd been terrified that Cassie had accidentally knocked the Jeep out of gear. He'd burst out of the woods expecting to see her driving in circles around the parking lot or, gods forbid, crashed into a tree.

What he hadn't expected was to find she was gone.

Just . . . gone.

The parking lot was empty, with no scent of any intruders and no sign of a struggle.

For long minutes he'd stood in the center of the parking lot, baffled.

If Cassie had been attacked, why hadn't she fired the gun? Or at least screamed for help?

And why couldn't he catch their scent?

Then, with a growl of sheer fury he'd shifted and gone in pursuit of Cassie's rapidly fading trail.

What the hell did it matter who or how or why Cassie had been kidnapped? All that mattered was finding her before she could be hurt.

Now he had to wonder if he'd been deliberately led on a wild-goose chase.

And if he had, what now?

He was debating the question when there was a faint rustle directly behind him. With a snarl he whirled around, his teeth bared in warning.

The sight of the tiny demon with oblong black eyes and fair hair pulled into a tight braid standing in the hay field did nothing to soothe his desire for blood.

"You."

"Yes, me." Yannah smoothed her hands down her pristine white robe, her lips pinched in disapproval. "Although I don't know why I bother. I specifically warned you not to be separated from the prophet. And yet, here you are with Cassie nowhere in sight."

Why the aggravating . . . bitch.

Caine clenched his hands, too infuriated to care he was completely nude. Or that the hay bale was poking his bare ass.

Instead, he was savagely reminding himself this demon had enough power to destroy him with a thought. And as much as he might want to shake the tiny creature until her pointed teeth rattled, he couldn't rescue Cassie if he was rotting in hell.

"Do you think I deliberately left her?" he demanded. "She disappeared."

Yannah snorted. "It doesn't matter how you were separated, only that you find her."

"What the hell do you think I'm trying to do?"

Yannah shrugged. "It looks to me like you're running in circles."

Caine tensed. How the hell had she known he was running in circles? Unless . . .

"Have you been spying on us? Do you know where she is?" He stepped forward, glaring down at the tiny heart-shaped face. "Has she been kidnapped? Is she hurt?"

"No and no and no and no."

He trembled, his wolf straining to be released to return to his hunt. With every passing second Cassie's scent faded a little more and the beast didn't give a shit that this demon might or might not hold information that could help them find their female.

"Then what happened to her?"

The black eyes widened. "It would seem that she dumped you."

"Dumped?"

"Isn't that how you say getting rid of an unwanted partner?" she asked with faux innocence. "Dump, chuck, give the ol' heave-ho?"

"Yeah, I got the meaning," he ground out. "I just don't know why you think Cassie would dump me."

"She drove off and left you at a rest stop in the middle of nowhere."

Caine hissed, refusing to allow the smallest suspicion to taint his mind.

It would kill something inside him if he thought Cassie deliberately abandoned him.

"She must have been kidnapped," he said with more force than necessary, reminding himself of their passionate night together.

There was no way a woman would so eagerly give her innocence to a man she intended to discard at the first opportunity. Hell, they'd still be in that bed if it hadn't been for the damned vision.

Caine sucked in a sharp breath, realizing he could pinpoint the precise moment that Cassie had changed from his sweetly generous lover to a distant stranger who could barely look him in the face.

Clearly sensing his revelation, Yannah narrowed her dark eyes. "What is it?"

"The vision."

"A prophecy?"

"Yes." With a muttered curse he shoved his fingers through his tangled hair. "I knew something was wrong. Gods. I should have forced her to tell me."

"Hey." Yannah snapped impatient fingers. "You can wallow in self-pity later."

His low growl rumbled through the air. "You are—"

"Charmingly blunt?" she interrupted with a hint of warning. He was nearing her line in the sand. They both knew he didn't want to step over it.

With an effort, he leashed his frustration. "Do you know where Cassie is going?"

"No, but you do."

"Me?" He scowled at the ridiculous accusation. "If I knew, I wouldn't be running in circles."

"I knew you were all brawn and no brain." Yannah shook her head with profound disappointment. "You're lucky you're so pretty."

His hand dropped, his fingers curling into a tight fist. He wanted to hit something. Or better yet, kill something.

"God dammit, we're wasting time," he rasped. "Why can't you just tell me?"

"Because I don't know." She held up a hand as his lips parted with an angry protest. "I only know that you know."

"Crap," he muttered. "You're making my head ache."

"She must have said something," Yannah said, utterly unapologetic. "Think."

Caine bit back his angry words and forced himself to recall what Cassie had said about her vision. For all he knew this Yannah was a crazy-ass demon who was following him around to make his life hell. But if there was even the slightest chance she could help him locate Cassie, then he'd jump through hoops and dance the mambo if that's what she wanted.

"All she said was that she had a vision and we had to travel west."

"Just west?" Yannah appeared troubled. "That's a little vague."

"You think?"

A choking power filled the air, wrapping around Caine with enough strength to warn Yannah could easily crush his every bone.

"Careful, Were."

He waited until the power had receded enough he could draw in a breath. Only when he was reasonably confident he wasn't about to become a mangled corpse did he speak. "She'd obviously decided to take off before . . ." He lost track of his words as he actually considered the time line. "Wait."

"What?"

He stared blindly over the recently mowed field, mentally

walking through the morning from the moment that Cassie woke in his arms.

"She started acting strange after her vision."

"And?"

"The vision must have convinced her that she had some task she had to deal with alone."

"Yes, yes." Yannah waved an impatient hand. "Quite possibly."

"So when she said we had to travel west she must have been trying to throw me off her trail." He frowned, not entirely satisfied with his logical conclusion. "But why the elaborate scheme? Why not sneak away from me while I was cooking breakfast?" He sorted through his chaotic thoughts, brutally ignoring his snarling wolf, which was nearing the edge of a meltdown. "Oh, I'm so stupid," he at last muttered.

Yannah flashed her pointed teeth. "You'll get no argument from me."

He ignored the insult. "She had to get past the hexes."

The demon blinked in confusion. "What hexes?"

"The ones I had placed around my lair."

"You were holding her prisoner?"

His brow furrowed in outrage. "No, I damned well was not holding her prisoner. I was trying to protect her. In case you haven't noticed she has more than a few demons desperate to get their hands on her."

"I'm all too aware of her danger. Which is why you must find her." The demon poked a finger into his belly. "Soon."

Caine froze in fear, detecting the worry that Yannah was attempting to disguise. "You know something," he accused. "What is it?"

"I only sense that she's being hunted." She gave him another poke. "Think, Caine. Where did she go?"

"Dammit, I don't know," he roared.

Pacing in a tight circle, he wracked his mind for any clue

he might have overlooked. Cassie rarely spoke of the future. Who could blame her? Her visions were a crippling burden that she wanted to forget, not dwell on.

But a niggling voice in the back of his mind whispered that she had said . . . what?

Something he should remember.

He continued his pacing, ignoring Yannah's dark glare and the distant sound of passing cars as he fiercely tried to recall his every conversation with Cassie over the past week.

Then suddenly he had a vivid image of Cassie perched on the edge of the breakfast bar as the scent of pizza filled the air.

"Did this foretelling happen to mention some magical means to keep us from becoming leech food?"

"No. But we have to return to your lair in Chicago."

"Now?"

"No. Soon, but not tonight."

"That's it," he muttered.

"You know?" Yannah demanded.

"I know."

"Where?"

"She's going to my lair near Chicago."

The demon studied him with a frown, as if trying to decide whether or not he could be trusted. "You're sure?"

"Yes."

"Fine." Without warning, she reached out to clamp her fingers around his wrist, her grip shockingly strong. "Then let's go."

"Go?"

Her smile sent a sizzle of alarm down his spine. "Hang on."

"Wait." Caine tried to pull free of the nutty female. Who knew what she was plotting? But it was too late. Before his eyes the world simply melted away, leaving him surrounded by a black sense of nothingness. "Oh, shit."

Caine's lair outside Chicago

Dusk was painting the sky in vibrant shades of violet and amber as Cassie pulled to a halt near the two-story brick farmhouse. With a shaky sigh, she turned off the engine and allowed her trembling hands to fall into her lap.

It'd been a hellacious trip.

Not only because she'd spent the past six hours struggling not to kill hapless motorists as she'd driven to this remote location, but she'd been on constant edge that Caine might somehow manage to pick up her trail and follow her.

Now that she was here, however, with no sign of the Were who'd become a vital part of her life, she felt . . . what? Hollow. As if she was a mere shell that was going through the motions.

Where was Caine? Was he still searching for her? Perhaps tormenting himself with blame that she'd disappeared?

Or had he at last decided he'd had enough of her craziness?

He certainly had every right to walk away in disgust. After he'd sacrificed everything to become her guardian, she'd just disappeared with no warning, no explanation. What man in his right mind wouldn't decide she was more trouble than she was worth?

She clenched her teeth against the pain that sliced through her heart. Dang it. So what if she felt like she'd lost a part of her very soul? As long as Caine was safe, nothing else mattered. Nothing.

Forcing her stiff muscles to move, she stepped out of the Jeep and started cautiously toward the house. The last time she'd visited the lair, Caine had altered the hexes to recognize her. But it had been weeks since she'd last been there. Would they remember her?

One way to find out.

Sucking in a deep breath, Cassie moved through the hedge and followed the narrow pathway. When she wasn't zapped or skewered or turned into a newt, she continued forward, climbing the steps of the wraparound porch.

She paused, taking a last glance around the empty yard, which was surrounded by a heavy line of trees, before pulling open the heavy oak door and stepping into the living room.

It was a plain room with rustic furniture and towering bookshelves that were stuffed with leather-bound chemistry books. A wistful smile touched her lips. The house was a painful reminder of Caine.

Gods, the very air smelled of him.

The thought had barely crossed her mind when the door was slammed shut behind her and she whirled to discover a blond-haired Were leaning against the wall, his arms folded over his chest and a mocking smile on his lips.

"Hello, pet. Miss me?"

Her mouth literally dropped open.

Caine.

But . . . it wasn't possible, was it?

He couldn't be here when she'd left him miles behind.

"Are you a trick?"

"No trick." He shoved away from the wall and prowled toward her stiff form, wearing a casual pair of jeans and white T-shirt. "Surprised?"

She gave a shake of her head, struggling to come to terms with the fact he was really there and not just a figment of her imagination.

"How?"

He arched a brow. "How?"

She cleared her throat and tried again. "How did you get here?"

Without warning, he grabbed her upper arms and spun her around so he could press her against the wall. Only then did she realize that beneath his sardonic composure he was seething with fury.

"That's not the question."

The heat of his anger seared over her skin, his grip careful not to bruise, but tight enough to warn she wasn't getting away.

"Caine."

The sapphire eyes glittered in the gathering gloom. "The question is why the hell you took off without me."

His words seared away the stunned shock fogging her mind. He was right. It didn't matter how he'd found her. Or even how he'd managed to know where she was going and get here ahead of her.

All that mattered was getting rid of him before it was too late.

She turned her head to stare at the rolltop desk set near the window, desperate to hide her all too expressive face. "I would think that would be self-explanatory."

"Do you?"

"Yes."

He snorted, his hands cupping her chin and forcing her face back to meet his narrowed glare. "Obviously I'm particularly dense because I don't find anything self-explanatory about being abandoned at a rest stop by my lover."

She licked her lips, floundering beneath his penetrating gaze. Who knew that lying would be such a vital skill? Or that sucking at it might very well get Caine trapped in hell.

Crap. She had to do this. And she had to do it well enough to make sure Caine walked away and never returned.

With an effort, she plastered something she hoped resembled a smile to her lips. "I decided that I'd had enough."

"Enough of what?"

"Enough of us."

"No."

"What?"

"Try again."

She frowned. "I don't understand."

"A woman doesn't give her innocence to a man when she's 'had enough,'" he challenged.

"I don't know why you're making such a big deal about my virginity," she muttered.

His simmering anger that she'd hope to provoke into a *don't-call-me-I'll-call-you* rage abruptly faded to be replaced with a heart-melting tenderness.

"Because it was a big deal to me." His thumb traced her lower lip, a ready passion darkening his eyes. "It's a gift I'll always cherish."

She swallowed a sigh of frustration. What was wrong with the man?

"Well, it was nothing more than a burden to me," she said, adamantly refusing to shiver at the exquisite sensation of his thumb tracing the curve of her lip. "Now it's gone I can move on to . . ."

Something that might have been amusement glinted in his eyes. "To what?"

"To someone else."

That should have been it. What man could stand to be told his female was leaving his bed and going to another? Instead, that annoying amusement only deepened.

"And you thought you would find this mysterious someone else in my lair?" he drawled. "That doesn't really make any sense, does it, pet?"

"Of course not," she snapped. "I needed somewhere to stay until I can find a lair of my own."

His gaze lowered to where his thumb continued to stroke over her mouth. "Surely, your next lover will provide you with a lair? Or at least a bed."

"That's none of your business."

"It is if you intend to use my private lair for your orgies." A wicked smile curved his lips. "I should at least be allowed to participate."

She shivered, a deep yearning threatening to undermine her noble intentions. "Stop that," she hissed, batting away his tormenting hand and reminding herself the cost of failure.

His amusement vanished as he slammed his hands against the wall on each side of her shoulders, caging her with his body. "Tell me why you're here."

She turned her head, frightened by the grim resolve etched on his beautiful face. "Because I wanted to get away from you and I thought this would be the last place that you would look for me."

"It has nothing to do with your vision?"

"No, now go away."

"Never."

"Then I'll leave." She grabbed his arm, frantically trying to push it aside. "Dammit, let me go."

There was a tense silence and she could feel Caine's gaze searing over her rigid profile. Then, without warning, he dropped his arm and stepped back.

"Fine. You're free to go." He said nothing as she stood there, trembling from head to foot. Finally, he reached to brush a gentle hand down her cheek. "You can't, can you?"

She dropped her head, her hands covering her face as her eyes filled with tears. "Please, Caine."

She felt him wrap his arms around her shivering body, pulling her against him and pressing his lips to her temple.

"What?" he pleaded. "Talk to me, Cassie. I need to know what's going on."

"I can't."

"Was it the vision?"

She resisted for another long moment, before conceding defeat. There was no way she was getting rid of the stubborn Were. At least not unless she could prove to him it was too dangerous for him to stay.

Something that was as likely as her sprouting wings and flying.

She heaved a resigned sigh, resting her head against the welcome strength of his chest. "Yes."

His hands glided up and down her stiff back in a comforting motion. "Can you tell me?"

"It's you."

"Me?" He stiffened, obviously shocked by her confession. "Do I do something wrong?"

"No, you're captured." She shuddered, the memory of her vision painfully vivid. "We both were."

"Captured by whom?"

"I don't know."

"Where were we being held?"

"I don't know." She gave another shudder. "We were surrounded by a white fog."

There was a long pause.

"So you took off because a vision revealed I'm going to be captured?" he asked softly.

"Yes."

She heard his low growl a mere heartbeat before he was roughly pulling away, his jaw clenched and his eyes glowing with the power of his wolf. "God dammit, Cassie," he barked. "What the hell were you thinking?"

Caught off guard by his unexpected attack, she blinked in confusion. "I was trying to protect you."

"No." He pointed a finger toward her, the veins on his neck visible as he struggled to contain his outrage. "That's not allowed."

"Not allowed?"

"It's not your job."

She scowled. "But it's fine for you to protect me?"

"Yes."

His blunt response left her tongue-tied. How did you argue with someone who didn't bother to be reasonable? "How is that even logical?" she finally managed to inquire.

"You're the prophet." His tone was hard, unapologetic. "And whether you like it or not, you're number one on the most wanted list right now."

"I don't like it."

He ignored her childish outburst. "And for whatever twisted reason, fate has chosen me as your protector. That's just how it is."

She stepped forward, desperate to make him understand the danger he was in. "I couldn't bear it, Caine." She framed his face in her hands, her voice thick with fear. "You were . . ."

He swooped down to capture her lips in a fierce kiss that stole her words.

"Hush," he commanded softly, pulling back to regard her with a somber expression. "I don't care if I was dead, you will never again try to leave me."

She shook her head, her fingers tightening on his face. "I won't let you be hurt."

"Think, Cassie. You said yourself it's too dangerous to try and alter fate." He peered deep into her wide eyes, his hands lightly encircling her wrists and his thumbs rubbing over her unsteady pulse. "What if your misguided attempt to keep me safe has tilted the balance of power to the Dark Lord?"

"I don't care."

He went still at her harsh words. "You would sacrifice the world for me?"

She didn't hesitate. "Yes."

"Cassie." With a groan, he leaned forward, resting his forehead against hers. "Gods, you never fail to astonish me."

She made a sound of exasperation. She didn't want to astonish him. She wanted to make him flee in fear.

"Please, please go, Caine."

His jaw jutted. "No way in hell."

"Which is quite likely where we're going," she snapped.

"I always knew it was inevitable."

She hissed at his flippant retort. "This isn't funny."

"Actually, I would say that it's the greatest cosmic joke in the history of the world," he added, a humorless smile twisting his lips.

"What does that mean?"

"Those visions of yours are bigger than both of us." He turned his head so he could plant a kiss in the center of her palm. "And right now I'm all you've got to guard you from the bad guys." He gave a sharp laugh. "The gods help us."

Chapter 11

Gaius's lair in Louisiana

The female wasn't as adequate as the last. Her dark hair was too short and her skin too pale, while her curves were on the wrong side of lush. But beggars couldn't be choosers, and shuddering to a climax beneath the skilled stroke of her mouth, Gaius grasped her by the hair and jerked her upright.

Her dark eyes were drenched with adoration as she rubbed her naked body against him. "Was it good, baby?"

Gaius grimaced, roughly turning her around as he straightened his black slacks that he'd matched with a crisp white shirt. Then, pressing her against the paneling of his private bedroom, he tilted her head to strike deep into the flesh of her throat.

"Oh yeah," she groaned, writhing in pleasure as he drank deeply of her blood. "More."

He continued his meal even as he heard the sound of approaching footsteps. It was only when the sharp knock rattled his door that he at last pulled out his fangs and licked shut the female's tiny wounds.

"Wait," he commanded, stepping back to smooth down his hair and adjust his black silk tie.

Without warning the female turned to toss herself against him, wrapping her arms around his neck. "No, don't stop."

He hissed, his lips curling in disgust. "Release me."

The dark eyes were filled with mindless need. "Please, fuck me."

"Watch your language." Raising his hand, he slapped her hard enough to slam her head against the wall. With a low groan she crumpled to the floor and Gaius turned toward the door. "Enter."

The door was pushed open to reveal Sally dressed in her usual uniform of tight black leather skirt and red bustier with her hair in pigtails. Instead of heels, however, she was wearing black combat boots that laced up to her knees, with spiderweb stockings peeking between the top of the boots and the hem of her too-short skirt.

Her heavily lined eyes widened as she stepped into the room to discover the unconscious female sprawled at his feet. "Did you kill another one?"

"She lives," Gaius said with utter indifference. "Why have you interrupted?"

The witch licked her black lips. "You said that you wanted to know when I was ready to scry for Cassandra."

Gaius paused, making certain he was at his full strength before he gave a short nod. There was no way in hell he was agreeing to go after the prophet unless he was confident he could keep himself protected.

"Fine." He waved a dismissive hand. "Get the curs in place and I'll join you in a few minutes."

With a last glance at the motionless whore, Sally left the room, pulling the door shut behind her.

Once alone, Gaius reached beneath his jacket to pull out

an antique gold locket. Pressing the hidden lever, the locket sprang open, revealing the miniature portrait of Dara.

His unbeating heart warmed at the sight of his mate. Her pretty features. Her satin-smooth hair. The proud tilt of her head. And the piercing sweetness of her smile.

His fingers tightened on the locket, the aching void in his soul so large he thought at times he would fall in and never crawl back out.

"I know you wouldn't approve of my methods, my love, but I do these things for you. For us," he whispered. "I can't bear this life without you and since I'm too much a sinner to join you in heaven I must return you to my hell. Please, my love, forgive me." He pressed the locket to his lips. "Forgive me."

Reluctantly replacing the locket, Gaius headed toward the door, allowing his anguish to transform back to the frigid anger that kept him from sinking into complete madness.

Soon Dara would be returned from the grave, he reassured himself. And he would forget the vile cost of having her back in his arms.

As if to remind him that the vile costs weren't over yet, the scent of fairy blood filled the air. With a hiss, he moved with fluid speed to enter the kitchen, not at all surprised to discover a circle of flickering candles on the floor with a wooden bowl set in the center filled with thick blood.

Black magic always demanded a sacrifice.

The greater the magic, the greater the sacrifice.

Without hesitation he charged around the circle to grab the witch by her neck. "I told you to wait."

"Hey, it's not me," she squeaked, her eyes wide with panic. "Do you think I could kill and drain a full-grown fairy?"

His fangs burst from his gums as he dropped the female

and whirled to prowl toward Dolf, who tried to scramble backward. "What the hell are you doing?"

"Preparing a spell." He gave a yip of pain as Gaius slammed him against the wall. "Shit."

Keeping the cur pinned to the wall with one hand, Gaius lifted the other to point a finger directly into Dolf's flushed face. "You've obviously forgotten the first rule of this household."

"What rule?"

"No magic without my permission."

"I wasn't going to cast it," Dolf hastily assured him. "At least not yet."

"No. Magic." His power was a tangible force that blasted through the room. "Is that clear enough?"

Blood trickled from Dolf's ear from the explosive burst of power, but with a dogged determination, he refused to back down. "Let me explain." He grimaced as Gaius's hand pressed against his chest with enough pressure to crack a rib. "Please, it's important."

Dio. Gaius dropped his hand and stepped back. Obviously the stupid dog wasn't going to be satisfied until he'd pleaded for his cause. "Make it quick," he snarled.

Dolf sucked in a shallow breath, his expression wary. "We have to assume that Caine will be protecting Cassandra."

"And?"

"And unless you plan to get your hands dirty, we're going to need a weapon to keep him out of the fight."

The bastard had a point. If Gaius was forced to use the medallion to take them to the prophet, he would be weakened and not about to risk a battle with a pureblooded Were.

That didn't mean he had to like it.

"A spell?" he managed to spit out.

Dolf fumbled to grab the crystal hung around his neck. The clear stone glowed with a disturbing green light. "Yes."

Gaius stepped back, his nose flaring in revulsion. "What does it do?"

"Once the magic is released it will hold Caine in stasis."

"Explain."

Dolf furrowed his brow. "It's like a magical coma," he struggled to explain. Thinking always proved to be a chore for the cur. "He'll be suspended in a place between life and death."

Gaius abruptly narrowed his eyes, struck by a sudden inspiration. "He'll be completely incapacitated?"

"Completely."

"How long can you hold it?"

Dolf nodded toward Ingrid, who stood in a corner with a duffel bag that matched her cammo pants and T-shirt. "Long enough for Ingrid to put him in a pair of silver shackles."

Absently smoothing his tie, Gaius paced across the floor, weighing his options. "Can you put the prophet in the same spell?"

There was a startled silence before Dolf nervously cleared his throat. Did he sense that Gaius was plotting to betray their twisted little Justice League?

"I can only cast it once, but if she was standing close enough to Caine, then it should work on both of them."

"Good." Gaius turned back to meet the cur's guarded gaze. "I want them both incapacitated."

"There's no guarantee—" Dolf bit off his words as Gaius took a step forward. "Of course. No problem."

Confident the cur would obey, Gaius snapped his fingers in Sally's direction. "Witch."

The female moved toward him with a sulky pout. "I have a name."

He dismissed her complaint with a wave of his hand. "Do

whatever it is you have to do to find the prophet so we can be done with this."

"I'm a witch, not a miracle worker. It'll take a few minutes."

He bared his fangs. "Then stop wasting time."

"Okay." Stomping toward the counter, she dropped Cassandra's hair into a shallow bowl. "Don't get your panties in a twist."

"Someday you will learn your place," he warned. "Let's hope you survive the process."

Seeming to sense he wasn't joking, Sally hastily bent over the bowl and muttered low words of magic. As she'd warned, it took several moments before she at last lifted her head, a layer of sweat coating her face.

"I found her."

Gaius strolled to stand at her side while the matching curs crowded behind her. He peered into the bowl, uncertain what to expect. Then, as he studied the thin layer of water, he realized that there were pictures flickering over the silver surface.

Leaning closer, he watched in fascination as the image of a pretty young female with long, blond hair and emerald eyes came into focus.

Cassandra.

The debacle of his last encounter with the prophet was forgotten as renewed hope flared in his frozen heart.

This time there won't be any mistakes, he silently swore.

"Where is she?"

"Hold on."

The witch waved her hand over the bowl and the picture shifted. Or more precisely it expanded, like a camera zooming back to reveal a wider angle. He saw a farmhouse surrounded by trees and acres of rolling cornfields. Then the cluster of lights that marked a small town.

"Fascinating, but nothing helps to pinpoint the location," he said dryly. "This could be anyplace in the Midwest."

The image widened even farther and Sally made a sound of satisfaction. "There's a city."

"It's Chicago," Dolf abruptly announced.

Gaius sent him a warning glance. "You're certain?"

"Absolutely. I recognize the skyline."

"Fine." Gaius pointed toward the bowl. "Return to the prophet."

There was a blur of movement as the image condensed to focus on the female Were, who was standing in the center of a book-lined room with Caine holding her in protective arms.

"Is that what you wanted?" Sally demanded.

"I need to know if she's alone with the Were."

The witch concentrated as she shifted the images to search the farmhouse and outlying buildings.

"Looks like it."

It did, indeed. Which did nothing to reassure Gaius.

"Why?" he muttered.

Dolf sent him a baffled frown. "What do you mean?"

"Why are they always alone?" he clarified in icy tones. Was he the only one with a brain? "They could surround themselves with the most powerful Were guardians. Or even vampires. Why leave themselves so vulnerable to attack?"

Dolf shrugged. "Caine has hated the King of Weres and his people for centuries. There's no way in hell he'd turn his honeypot over to that megalomaniac," he said, clearly indifferent to any fear they might be walking into a trap. "And he isn't stupid. He would never trust the leeches. To be honest, I don't think Caine has ever truly trusted anyone."

"And they're not unprotected," Sally added, pointing toward the edge of the yard. "The entire house is surrounded by layers of hexes and cloaking spells. There's no way we'll get through that barrier without some serious magical mojo."

Gaius was not entirely satisfied, but he wasn't stupid enough to believe the Dark Lord's patience was infinite. Any moment he was going to demand results.

And the gods have pity on all of them if the evil bastard was disappointed.

"I'll get us in," he grimly promised, stabbing Dolf with a warning glare. "You make sure you have your spell ready."

The cur smiled. "Whatever you say, boss."

Caine kept Cassie locked tight in his arms, his wolf needing the intimate contact to reassure the beast that she was unharmed and back where she belonged.

The past few hours had been . . .

He shuddered, unwilling to relive the torturous wait for Cassie to arrive.

Logically, he'd been convinced that the aggravating female was headed to this isolated lair. But after his hair-raising journey with Yannah that had defied the basic laws of physics, he'd had far too many hours to pace the floors and dwell on the numerous ways this could all go to hell.

What if she'd had another vision that led her in a completely different direction?

What if she'd been attacked or kidnapped on the way?

What if she'd wrecked the damned Jeep and was even now lying hurt alongside the road?

What if she was simply lost?

The worrisome thoughts had looped through his mind, gnawing at him until he felt like climbing the walls.

Then, at last, he'd heard the sound of the approaching vehicle and watched as she made her way to the lair, clearly unhurt. From one beat of his heart to another, his savage fear had mutated to fury.

A fury that had gone ballistic when she admitted that she'd left herself vulnerable because she wanted to protect him. Dammit, his entire life had been an empty struggle for survival and even after he'd made his deal with the devil to try and alter curs into Weres, he'd known that there was something vital missing.

Then he'd stumbled across Cassie in the caves of the demon lord and he'd realized with crystal clarity that she was his reason for existing.

There had been no trumpets or angels singing or freaking rainbows and unicorns. Just an acceptance that he had been created to protect the prophet in a world gone mad.

Now, his burst of outrage faded and he just wanted to hold the female who meant more to him than life itself and savor the lavender scent that soothed his wolf as nothing else could.

"Are you hungry?" he at last asked.

She shook her head, her hands wrapped around his waist and her head resting on his chest.

"No."

"Are you sure?" He brushed his lips over her temple. "I have chocolate."

She pulled back, her eyes filled with a sudden glow of anticipation. "Chocolate?"

With a smile, he led her through the large, airy kitchen decorated with blue and white tiles and gingham curtains and up the stairs to the second floor. Then, with a tug he had her in the bedroom that was dominated by a carved walnut bed. Leaving her standing next to the armoire, he entered the closet and returned with a slim black and gold box.

"Straight from Godiva in Brussels." He crossed to stand beside Cassie, pulling the lid off to reveal the truffle temptations. "It's so decadently good it will spoil you for any other chocolate."

"Really?" She reached to take one of the small chocolates, popping it into her mouth.

Caine waited, a low growl rumbling in his throat as her eyes slid shut in sensuous pleasure and her tongue peeked out to capture the tiny crumb on her bottom lip. He bent down, stealing the speck of chocolate with a swipe of his tongue.

"Just as I've spoiled you for any other man," he whispered against her mouth.

She shivered, her hands lifting to smooth over the hard muscles of his chest. "Arrogant."

He nibbled down the line of her jaw. "Confident in a manly man sort of way."

"Hmmm." She angled her head to offer her throat in a gesture that sent an explosion of heat through his body. "You haven't told me how you got here ahead of me."

He found the tender spot at the base of her neck that always made her heart beat faster. "A story for later," he murmured, his tongue stroking over her racing pulse.

She pressed her slender curves tight against him, but she refused to be completely distracted. "You're hiding something from me."

"Nothing important." He'd be damned if he allowed the thought of Yannah to spoil the mood. "Right now I don't want to think about anything but you."

Just for a second she held herself rigid, as if wanting to press for an answer. Then, with a soft sigh, she melted against him. No doubt she understood better than he did that their time together was limited.

Stroking his hands up and down her spine, Caine buried his face in the curve of her throat, soaking in the rare moment of peace.

He lost track of time, but his senses remained on full alert. Which meant Cassie was unable to hide the sudden change in her heartbeats.

"What is it?" he demanded.

"They're coming," she whispered.

"Who, Cassie?" He pulled back, his heart squeezed in a painful vice at the sight of her eyes shrouded in white. He gripped her beautiful face in his hands. "Cassie, stay with me. We have to get out of here."

"It's too late."

Even as the words tumbled from her lips, Caine felt the unmistakable change in air pressure. Whirling toward the doorway, he reached back to make sure Cassie was hidden behind him as there was a shimmer in the air.

The shimmer solidified into four distinct shapes and Caine struggled to rein in his wolf as he recognized the vampire and his Three Stooges from the wine cellar.

"Leech." He curled his lips in open disdain. There was no point in trying to be diplomatic. They'd come to take Cassie and he would either kill them or die trying. Nothing diplomatic about that. "And his stray mutts. Did you come to get your asses kicked?" He sent the male cur a taunting glance. A cur's downfall was always his temper. "Again."

"The master wants the prophet, Were," the vampire stated the obvious in a frigid voice. "This time you won't be allowed to stand in my way."

"Not in this lifetime," he snarled, already shifting when Dolf stepped forward, his eyes sparking with crimson light.

"Bring it on," the cur challenged.

But even as Dolf took another step forward the leech was grabbing him by the arm, the cold prickle of his power like shards of ice piercing Caine's skin.

"The spell, you idiot," he hissed.

Lost in his transformation to wolf, Caine barely heard the

words, but he caught the flash of green fire as the cur lifted a crystal. Then, trying his best to protect Cassie with his half-turned body, he braced for the explosion of magic.

Gaius would never change his opinion of magic. Or magic-users. If he had his way, they would all be burned at the stake, just like they were in the good old days.

But he had to admit that the cur's spell had achieved results.

Spectacular, if gruesome, results.

Taking a cautious step forward, Gaius studied the male Were who had been frozen in midchange. The face had elongated, but retained human characteristics, while his body was oddly twisted and covered in patchy fur.

It was . . . unnerving, to say the least.

With a shake of his head, he turned his attention to the female lying on the floor beside the contorted Were, obviously caught in the same spell. She looked incredibly young and fragile as she sprawled unconscious on the hardwood, but Gaius understood that the visions she carried in her head made her the most powerful weapon on the face of the earth.

Which made her a potent bargaining tool.

"It worked," Dolf muttered at his side, seeming as surprised as anyone at the success of his spell.

"So it did." Gaius snapped impatient fingers toward the silent Ingrid. "What are you waiting for? Get the restraints on them."

With a visible shudder the female cur crept forward, tugging on leather gloves before removing the silver shackles from her bag. "Holy shit," she breathed, snapping the cuffs around Caine's distorted wrists. "That's nasty."

Gaius watched as the cur efficiently placed matching cuffs around the Were's ankles before she moved to perform the same service on Cassandra. Instantly, the stench of searing flesh filled the air.

The silver would keep the prisoners incapacitated even if they did manage to wake from the spell.

Once she was finished she moved back to stand at Dolf's side, her hand running an intimate caress along the bulging muscles of his bare arm.

Gaius didn't bother to disguise his grimace. He had more important things to hide.

"Take your sister and search the rest of the house," he commanded of the male cur. "Start in the cellars."

"Why? We already know that—"

"I gave you a command, dog."

Both twins flinched at the icy warning in his voice.

"Fine," Dolf muttered, grabbing his sister by the hand and pulling her out of the room.

Waiting until he could hear their footsteps descending the staircase, Gaius pointed toward the witch, who hovered near the door, as if ready for a quick retreat. "You."

"Sally," she reminded him in sullen tones. "It's not hard to remember."

He ignored her complaint. "Go outside and make sure the spells are still intact."

Predictably, the witch narrowed her gaze in suspicion. Unlike the curs, she had a functioning brain. Unfortunate, but nothing that was going to spoil his plans.

"What are you plotting?"

"I'm plotting to keep us from being ambushed. Do you have a problem with that?"

"No problem."

"Then go."

She studied him for a long minute, then with a shrug, she turned to head out the door. "Whatever."

Gaius remained frozen in place until the door had shut

behind the witch and he could sense her moving down the staircase and out of the house. Only then did he cross to kneel beside the unconscious Weres, making certain they remained locked in the spell before he tugged the medallion from beneath his sweater, clutching it in a white-knuckled grip.

The strange amulet allowed him to mist-walk. That much he'd already proven by leaving behind the Veil. And the Dark Lord had said that it could be used to travel to the prison where he was being held.

But the question was, just how close would the medallion take him to his master?

A hell dimension, after all, could consume a considerable amount of territory. He could waste hours, days . . . hell, centuries.

Still, he had no choice but to take the risk. It was the only way to be certain he could claim full credit for fulfilling the Dark Lord's command.

Closing his eyes, Gaius sorted through his mind with a clinical precision, at last locating the faint bond that led from the medallion to the distant sense of power.

Evil, pulsing, insidious power.

He shuddered in revulsion, but grimly reminding himself of all he'd already sacrificed, he closed his eyes and allowed the world to dissolve around him.

Chapter 12

Mere seconds later he wrenched open his eyes to discover he was surrounded by a thick white fog. Disoriented, it took him a second to realize he was still on his knees with the unconscious Weres stretched out beside him.

Slowly he rose to his feet, scanning the strange mist with a wary frown. Where the hell was he?

"Master?" he called softly, puzzled by the emptiness that surrounded him. He'd been expecting fire and brimstone. Instead, it felt as if he were standing alone in the middle of a snow globe. "Hello?"

Then, just when he was debating whether or not to chalk it up to a failed experiment and return to the farmhouse, Gaius was sent back to his knees as an annihilating pain slammed through him.

"How terribly odd," a deep, disembodied voice mocked. "I do not recall inviting you into my lair, vampire."

Gaius pressed his head to the ground covered by mist, his muscles trembling beneath the brutal pressure of the Dark Lord's power.

Be careful what you wish for, he wryly told himself.

"I have come to show you that I have captured the prophet

and her protector as you commanded," he managed to grit between clenched teeth.

"And you assume that your gifts will allow me to forgive your intrusion?"

"I thought you would wish to have them in your hands as soon as possible, my lord."

"I see." There was a long, excruciating pause. "And where are your companions?"

"They were unnecessary baggage once the Weres had been incapacitated."

The power pulsing in the air altered, the pressure easing to become a sharp-edged punishment that threatened to flay the skin from his body.

"And you hoped to be granted the full reward for their capture?"

Hell, yes.

Why would he share the rewards with the damned curs and witch if he could claim full benefits? Honor was the first thing he'd sacrificed after the death of his mate.

Unfortunately, the Dark Lord didn't seem to be as pleased by his surprise appearance as Gaius had hoped. Perhaps it was time for some damage control.

"I only seek to be given what I was promised," he carefully admitted.

"I have not forgotten our bargain." The fog stirred, as if reacting to the Dark Lord's flare of impatience. "Nor the fact that you pledged fealty to me until I deemed you had earned the return of your mate."

"The prophet . . ."

"Is a mere down payment on the debt owed."

The razor-sharp words sent a shiver of anxiety down Gaius's spine. Cautiously he lifted his head, unable to see anything beyond the choking fog.

"Down payment?"

There was a sneering laugh. "Surely you don't hold the value of your beloved mate so cheap as to think you could earn her return so easily?"

Easily?

Cristo. He'd betrayed his son, his clan, and his own soul to become a servant of darkness.

A spike of loss pierced his heart, giving him the foolish courage to slowly rise to his feet. "I have served you loyally for centuries, my lord."

"And what have I asked of you?" The force of the angry question sent Gaius reeling backward. "To acquire skills that have only made you more formidable? To be prepared for the day of my return? Hardly onerous tasks."

Gaius bowed his head, but his growing desperation overcame his claim to sanity. "Perhaps not, but I have missed Dara so badly that each day is a torture," he confessed, unashamed of the edge of pleading in his voice. "I ache to hold her in my arms again."

"While I have been trapped in this hell between worlds, stripped of my form and all but my most primitive powers." The fog suddenly boiled with a searing heat, threatening to toast Gaius into a tiny pile of ash. "Do not speak to me of torture."

Gaius fell to his knees, his head bowed. "Forgive me, Master."

"I don't want your pathetic apologies."

"Then what do you want?"

"Your obedience."

"I am your servant, as always."

"Then prove your loyalty."

Gaius didn't dare to so much as twitch as the blast of heat slowly began to dissipate. Inwardly, he fiercely struggled to obliterate the niggle of suspicion that was beginning to worm its way through his mind.

He couldn't allow himself to question whether or not the Dark Lord intended to fulfill his end of the bargain.

The doubt would destroy him.

"What do you want from me?" he instead asked.

"Return to the servants I have given you."

Gaius glanced toward the Weres nearly hidden in the fog. "What of the prophet and her companion?"

"She's now mine." The voice purred with satisfaction. "Which means her gift is mine. At last."

Gaius struggled to disguise his impatience. If the Dark Lord was so pleased, why wasn't he showing a little more gratitude?

"So I just return and await my reward?"

"No." The Dark Lord crushed his brief hope and Gaius struggled to rise to his feet. "You will lead your allies to protect my disciple, Rafael."

Yet another disciple?

Merda. Was he expected to babysit every damned demon who claimed allegiance to the Dark Lord?

"I am, of course, anxious to do as you command."

There was a chuckle that made Gaius's flesh crawl. "You don't sound anxious."

"I'm not sure I have the necessary strength to use the medallion to transport two curs and a witch without an opportunity to rest and feed," he improvised.

Although he had no memory of his years as a Roman general, he retained all the cunning that had led him to such a position of power.

"There will be no need to shadow-walk," the voice informed him. "It's a short distance from Caine's lair to where Rafael is hidden."

Before Gaius could contrive another excuse there was a sudden explosion in his head. With a sharp cry, he pressed his hands to his temples, unprepared for the vision—a gaunt spirit with crimson fire burning in his sunken eyes—that was branded into his brain. As the Dark Lord had promised, the creature was hidden in a spiderweb of tunnels only miles away from Caine's farmhouse. That didn't, however, make him any happier.

"You want me to protect a dead wizard?" he hissed, shaking his head in an effort to ease the pain of his brain being used as the Dark Lord's personal GPS.

"You'll do as I command," the master snapped. "I have no interest in your prejudice toward magic-users."

"Of course," Gaius readily agreed, dropping his hands. "I just wonder why such a powerful spirit can't protect himself."

"Not that I need to explain my orders to you, Gaius, but the wizard is currently protecting my child."

Gaius made a sound of shock, abruptly understanding the Dark Lord's vehemence that the wizard be protected.

The babes had been created centuries ago and, if rumors were to be believed, they were intended to be used as a means of resurrecting the Dark Lord if all other efforts failed to return him to the world.

"The Alpha and Omega," he muttered.

"Only one." An anger as vast and merciless as the pits of hell pulsed through the fog. "The other babe is in the hands of the leeches. They can't be allowed to interfere again. Is that understood?"

"Yes."

"Then you will lead the curs and the witch to this meadow." There was another painful intrusion into his mind. This time the image was of a slender fey male with long chestnut hair and oddly metallic bronze eyes. At his side was a slender female vampire with dark hair and blue eyes. They both stood in the center of a meadow not far from the tunnels where the wizard was hidden. "The Sylvermyst and the vampire must not be allowed to reach Rafael while he is finishing his preparations to bring me my child."

Gaius nodded. Did he have a choice? "Fine."

"Once the child has been brought to me, I want you and Dolf to return here." There was a kiss of pain. "Understood?"

"Completely."

"And, Gaius."

"My lord?"

"The next time you arrive without invitation I will assume that you're here to challenge me," the Dark Lord warned in soft, lethal tones. "You won't like my punishment."

Gaius offered a deep bow, wryly conceding he'd miscalculated. Badly.

He'd hauled the prophet and her protector to this dimension in the futile hope that the Dark Lord would be so pleased that he would return Dara in effusive gratitude. Instead, the Dark Lord had barely acknowledged his offering and, rather than being pleased, he'd threatened grim reprisals if Gaius ever approached without permission.

To make matters worse, he had to return to the damned curs and witch to save yet another magic-user.

Not his finest night.

Wrapping his fingers around the medallion, he closed his eyes and disappeared.

The Dark Lord's prison
Two weeks later

Cassie opened her eyes to discover she was shrouded in a thick mist.

She wasn't surprised.

Despite being held unconscious in the cur's spell, she'd been distantly aware of being transported to another dimension and the passage of time.

There had also been dreams. Strange dreams where she'd sensed a female vampire and Sylvermyst creeping through the fog in search of a mage carrying an unconscious child.

And then there had been a terrifying power struggle that had made the very air shudder in fear.

And speaking of shuddering in fear . . .

Shoving herself to her feet, Cassie absently rubbed her wrists, feeling the uncharacteristic smoothness. New skin. Which meant she'd been injured while she slept. No doubt silver handcuffs, she hazarded a guess.

Not that she gave a damn. Not when she was desperate to find Caine.

With shaky steps, she moved through the clinging fog, her senses so muted she nearly stumbled over his unconscious form hidden by the swirling white mist.

Her heart halted as she realized he was still trapped in his mutated form, caught between wolf and man.

"Caine." She squatted beside him, her hand reaching to touch the silver manacles that had seared to the bones of his wrists. "No, no, no." Closing her eyes, she concentrated on the bonds of awareness that connected them, only to find . . . emptiness. As if there was nothing left of the man she'd come to love so desperately.

"Oh, gods," she whispered on a sob. "Why did you have to come after me, you stubborn, stupid wolf?"

"How terribly touching."

Caught off guard by the mocking voice, Cassie jerked upright, spinning around to discover a slender young woman standing just a few feet away.

Her first thought was that she was an astonishingly beautiful human teenager. In the strange glow, her naked skin was tinted a rich honey with long, dark hair that spilled down her back. Her eyes were a stunning blue and when she smiled a pair of disarming dimples danced next to her mouth.

Then the force of her power lashed through the air and Cassie nearly fell to her knees as her skin was nearly flayed from her body.

Yikes.

Only the Dark Lord could pack that sort of punch.

Which meant that her dreams had been real. The Dark Lord had managed to get his hands on the babe and turn it into his vessel.

Now he was a "she" with a physical body to replace the one he'd lost when he'd been banished from the world.

The words of the prophecy whispered through her mind as she met the eyes that flickered from blue to crimson.

Flesh of flesh, blood of blood, bound in darkness.
The Alpha and Omega shall be torn asunder
and through the Mists reunited.
Pathways that have been hidden will be found
and the Veil parted to the faithful.
The Gemini will rise
and chaos shall rule for all eternity.

"The Omega," she whispered.

"Yes, my servants managed to resurrect me." With a preening smile, the Dark Lord ran a hand down her slender stomach. "Do you like my new form?"

Cassie took a cautious step to the side, trying to draw attention away from Caine's unmoving body. If she was going to get fried, then she didn't intend for Caine to get caught in the crossfire.

"If you were resurrected why are you still here?"

The crimson fires consumed the blue of her eyes. "The

vampire bitch destroyed this body. She'll pay for that. They all will."

Cassie could only surmise that the battle she'd sensed while held in the spell hadn't gone well for the Dark Lord. Not that she could see any physical damage to the slender form. Still, there was no way the powerful creature would be wasting her time chatting with Cassie if she could return to the world.

"So you're trapped?"

The air thickened, making it nearly impossible to breathe. Then, with an obvious effort, the Dark Lord managed to rein in her temper. Her eyes even returned to blue, although there were a few embers burning deep in the center.

"I merely await the arrival of the other child. Once the two have been reunited I will be invincible."

Cassie didn't miss the implication. The two babies had been hidden for centuries, but recently they'd reemerged. One was rumored to be in the hands of the vampires, while the other was now standing in front of her in the guise of the Dark Lord.

If the two were reunited . . .

"*The Gemini will rise.*" Cassie quoted the prophecy with a shiver.

"*And chaos shall rule for all eternity,*" the Dark Lord completed.

A stab of sheer terror arrowed down her spine.

She didn't need an ancient prophecy to warn her of the hell awaiting the world if the Dark Lord was allowed to destroy the barriers between dimensions.

Or that it was her duty to do whatever necessary to prevent such a hideous fate.

Not that she had a clue what she could do.

The Dark Lord could squash her like a bug if she tried

to attack. And she didn't have the talent to travel between dimensions.

All she could do was discover how the evil minions intended to steal the child and try to pass along a warning.

"Your minions will never get close to the child," she deliberately prodded the dangerous creature. "He's being guarded by the vampires."

As hoped, the creature couldn't help but share just how clever she was. "Then who better to slip past them than another vampire?"

She frowned. "Gaius?"

The female shrugged, not refuting or confirming Cassie's guess. "He is but one of many vampires who worship me."

Well, that wasn't overly reassuring. And worse, it was too vague to be of any help.

"Only those most trusted by the king will be allowed near the child," she pointed out.

"Not a problem." The female stroked her fingers through the dark satin of her hair. "Gaius can be anyone he chooses to be, after all. Even the King of Vampires."

Damn. She'd forgotten about that unfortunate trick.

"Maybe, but his lack of scent will alert the Ravens long before he can get to the babe."

A secretive smile made the Dark Lord's dimples dance. Cassie grimaced. The contrast of such innocent beauty housing such pure evil was creepy as hell.

"Never trust the shadows," she taunted.

Cassie blinked. "What does that mean?"

"I am the Dark Lord. Nothing can stand in the path of my destiny."

Well, the resurrection certainly hadn't done a thing to diminish the creature's arrogance.

She took another step away from Caine, a raw pain festering deep inside her as he remained so frighteningly still.

"I don't understand what shadows have to do with getting your hands on the child."

"Enough," the Dark Lord commanded, allowing a thin ribbon of her power to slice through Cassie's upper arm. "My plans for the child are none of your concern."

Cassie ignored the blood dripping down her arm, but she wasn't stupid enough to press for more information. The Dark Lord had always been rumored to have an impulse control problem, often killing trusted servants in a fit of temper. She didn't want to be added to the very long list.

Instead, she silently concentrated on trying to send the warning to the one mind she could still sense through the mists. Only then did she return her thoughts to the female who continued to punish her with those razor-thin strikes.

"Why have you brought us here?"

As hoped, the creature was distracted by the abrupt question, her sweet face lighting with a sudden anticipation. "You, my dear, have something I want."

Cassie stiffened. That didn't sound good. "What?"

"The future."

"I don't understand."

There was another disarming flash of those dimples as the Dark Lord moved to brush her fingers over Cassie's cheek. "Those pretty, pretty visions."

It was, no doubt, what Cassie should have expected, but she still found herself reeling in confusion. "I thought you massacred prophets because you didn't like the visions?"

"I was perhaps a bit hasty." The female gave a tiny pout, as if the wholesale slaughter of dozens of seers was a mere inconvenience. "I had hoped that by ridding the world of the prophets I could alter my fate."

"And now?"

The fingers shifted to cup Cassie's chin in a punishing grip. "Now I accept that the future cannot be changed."

A bleak sense of failure raced through Cassie at the aching emptiness in the sacred center of her heart.

Caine.

"No," she breathed. "It can't."

"So I intend to use it to my advantage."

She forced herself to meet the unnerving blue gaze flecked with crimson. "How?"

"You will show me my future so I will know precisely what to expect." The fingers tightened until Cassie felt her chin fracture beneath the force. "There will be no more unpleasant surprises."

She hissed in pain, struggling to concentrate. "It doesn't work like that. I have no control over the visions or what they show me."

Loosening her brutal grip, the Dark Lord patted Cassie's cheek.

Bitch.

"Because you've never had the necessary encouragement to train your abilities."

"Necessary encouragement?" Cassie echoed. "I suppose you mean torture?"

"Semantics."

Yeah, easy for the one not being tortured to say.

She tilted her battered chin, refusing to show fear. "If pain could give me control over the prophecies, then the demon lord who held me prisoner would have been torturing me for the past thirty years."

The creature shrugged. "Oh, I don't doubt that you would endure any amount of suffering to cling to your annoying morals."

"It has nothing to do with morals."

"That might be what you believe, but I suspect that the block is unconscious." Dropping her hand, the Dark Lord stepped back to regard Cassie with a confidence that made her stomach clench. "Once we break it down we will be able to tap into those visions. The future will belong to me."

Cassie shook her head, baffled by the female's assurance that the visions could be controlled. As far as Cassie knew there'd never been a seer capable of focusing her prophecies so they showed a particular person or event.

Had her latest failure driven the Dark Lord—or whatever she was supposed to be called now—over the edge? The thought wasn't particularly reassuring.

"You can torture me all you want, but it won't change anything."

"True."

Cassie scowled in confusion. "But you just said . . ."

"I know that you would allow yourself to die before giving me what I need." The female overrode her words, a hint of disdain in her voice. "Wolves are so stupidly stubborn. But there is more than one way to skin a cat." She deliberately paused, her wide blue eyes turning toward the unconscious Caine. "Or in this case, a wolf."

Realization hit a split second too late. Diving toward Caine, Cassie could do nothing to halt the Dark Lord as she pointed her finger in his direction and a bolt of power slammed into his helpless body.

"No." Landing on her knees, Cassie cradled his head in her arms, feeling his body tremble beneath the force of the attack.

"Only you can halt the pain, prophet," the Dark Lord warned. "Give me what I want."

Chapter 13

Styx's lair in Chicago

The Anasso's private study in his vast mansion wasn't what most people expected.

Far from the dank dungeon with torture devices of the previous King of Vampires, or even the high-tech office that was wired better than the Pentagon that Viper preferred, Styx had chosen a book-lined room with polished mahogany furniture and a delicate Persian carpet.

It was all very civilized. Well, as long as a person didn't count the dozen spells and hexes that were wrapped around the room. Or the entire horde of vampires patrolling the hallway just outside the door.

Nothing was coming in or out without Styx's say-so.

Perched on the edge of the massive desk, Styx was in his usual garb. Leather pants, shit-kicker boots, and T-shirt stretched tight over his heavily muscled chest. His hair hung down in a long braid threaded with turquoise ornaments.

A complete opposite of Viper, who stepped into the study, his ivory silk shirt ruffled at the neck and cuffs and his black velvet pants as flamboyant as Styx's were stark.

"All quiet?" the clan chief of Chicago demanded, his silver hair shimmering in the light from the overhead chandelier.

Styx grimaced. "So far."

Viper halted in the center of the room, his dark gaze all too perceptive. "You don't sound as pleased as you should."

"I hate this waiting."

"You still have your Ravens guarding the child?"

Styx gave a sharp nod. He'd insisted that Tane and Laylah remain in his lair with their child, Maluhia. It had become even more vital that the babe be protected after Jaelyn and Ariyal had escaped from the hell dimension to reveal that the female twin of Maluhia had already been used to resurrect the Dark Lord. It'd only been because Jaelyn had drained the blood of the creature during their battle that the Dark Lord hadn't been able to return to this world.

Now the bastard, or rather the bitch, would be more determined than ever to get her hands on Maluhia. And if the prophecy was to be believed, the reunion of the two children behind the Mists would be nothing less than . . . chaos.

Not only would the Dark Lord return to this world, but the barriers between dimensions would be destroyed.

Hell would quite literally spew into the streets.

Which was why he had his most trusted guards on duty around the clock.

"Yes, but they can only be asked to be trapped on babysitting duty for so long before they'll go stir-crazy."

Viper folded his arms over his chest. "I know you're a control freak, Styx, but I have trusted soldiers who can help fill in rotations. That will give the Ravens a chance to rest and feed. You only have to ask."

Styx allowed a small smile to touch his lips. He was a control freak, but he wasn't stupid. His men were getting as twitchy as hell.

"Thank you. Send them to Jagr. I put him in charge of protecting Maluhia."

"Consider it done," Viper assured him. "How is Tane holding up?"

Styx abruptly straightened, restlessly pacing from one end of the office to the other. "He isn't thrilled to have so many feral males around his mate and child, but he understands that nothing is more important than keeping them out of the hands of the Dark Lord."

"And talking about feral males," Viper murmured.

Styx turned back toward his friend with a scowl. "What?"

"Your Ravens aren't the only ones going stir-crazy."

"You sound like Darcy."

Viper arched a brow. "Has she been fussing over you like a devoted mate?"

"No, she kicked me out of the bedroom and told me not to return until I got the 'ants out of my pants.' Her words, not mine."

"She's not wrong." The dark eyes narrowed. "Your temper tantrum last night took out half of Chicago's power grid."

Ah, so that's why Viper had taken time from his heavy duties as chief to visit. In the past few days the streets of Chicago had become a free-for-all as demons had turned on one another. Even the most peaceful creatures had become violent as the heavy sense of doom continued to build.

It had kept Viper struggling to prevent a bloodbath.

"I'm the King of Vampires," he countered, not about to admit he'd lost control of his temper when Salvatore had accused him of not doing enough to locate Cassandra and Caine. As if he had the power to travel between dimensions. Annoying dog. "I don't have temper tantrums."

Viper looked unimpressed. "Call them whatever you want, they're threatening to destroy my city."

Styx released a low growl of frustration. "I hate being forced to sit on my ass and twiddle my thumbs."

"For now there's nothing else you can do." Viper studied him with a somber expression. "Have you heard from Santiago?"

Santiago was one of Viper's most trusted soldiers and had gone on a futile mission to find Cassandra when he'd instead stumbled across Nefri—the mysterious and powerful female clan chief who lived beyond the Veil.

It'd been Santiago who'd learned that the vampire who had sold his soul to the Dark Lord and betrayed them was one of her clansmen.

And unbelievably, Santiago's missing sire.

"Yes, he's assisting Nefri in her search for Gaius."

"According to Jaelyn, he has a medallion similar to Nefri's that he can use to travel. Can't she use hers to track him?"

"She's still trying to discover where his medallion came from. As far as she knew, she had the only one ever created."

Viper frowned, his slender fingers adjusting his ruffled cuff. "I don't like this."

Styx stepped forward, sensing his companion's genuine concern. "Why?"

"Santiago is very skilled in pretending he wasn't affected when his sire abandoned him to travel through the Veil, but he carries wounds that have never fully healed," Viper explained. "I'm not sure he can think clearly when it comes to Gaius."

"If the vampire has betrayed us, then I don't care if Santiago is thinking clearly," Styx said in hard tones. He was running empty on compassion these days. "I want the bastard dead."

"It's not always so easy to kill those we consider our family, even when we know it's for the greater good."

Styx hissed at the reminder that he'd nearly condemned

the vampire race to the insane brutality of the former Anasso out of misplaced loyalty. "Point taken."

Viper reached into his pocket to remove a slim cell phone. "Do you want me to call him home?"

He shook off the unwelcome memories, his lips twisting in a wry smile. "You can try."

Viper lowered the phone, his expression suspicious. "Is there something I should know?"

"Darcy claims I have the social sensitivity of a slug demon, but even I've noticed how Santiago watches Nefri when he thinks no one is looking."

"And how's that?"

"Like he's longing to devour her."

Viper made a sound of shock. "Nefri?"

"Why not? She's a very beautiful woman."

"Stunningly beautiful," the clan chief agreed. "And dangerous."

"True." Styx couldn't argue. She was the only vampire he'd met who could match him in strength. Actually, in a head-to-head battle he wasn't sure who would win. "Her power is off the charts. Not every man is capable of accepting a female who possesses such strength."

"That's not it." Viper gave an impatient wave of his hand. "Santiago has always chosen women of power."

"Then what's the problem?"

"If the rumors are to be believed, Nefri deliberately turned her back on this world to live like a cloistered nun," he said. "I don't want her manipulating Santiago with her beauty to get what she needs from him and then disappearing behind the Veil. He has enough abandonment issues without her screwing with his head."

"He's a big boy, Viper." Styx moved forward to clap his companion on the shoulder. "I think he can handle his private affairs."

They both froze as the unmistakable stench of granite wafted through the air.

Viper rolled his eyes. "Were you expecting company?"

"Shit," Styx muttered as the gargoyle waddled through the door.

Not that he was much of a gargoyle. Granted, he possessed the conventional grotesque features, covered by a thick gray skin. His gray eyes were reptilian, his horns stunted and his hoofs cloven. He even had a long tail he polished and pampered with great pride.

But his fearsome appearance was ruined by his stunted size and the pair of delicate, gossamer wings that should have been on the back of a sprite. And worse, his magic was as unpredictable as the Midwest weather.

Who could blame the Gargoyle Guild for voting him out? He was a three-foot pain in the ass who'd latched onto Viper's and Styx's mates and refused to be dislodged.

"Levet," he muttered.

Oblivious to the distinct lack of welcome, Levet blew them both kisses. "Ah, *mes amis*, have you missed me?"

Styx snorted. He'd missed the gargoyle like he missed a hot poker shoved in his eye. "What are you doing here?"

Levet's delicate wings, shimmering in shades of crimson and blue and gold, fluttered in confusion. "Where else would I be?"

"I thought you were searching for Yannah?" he reminded the beast, referring to the peculiar demon who had a habit of appearing and disappearing without warning.

"Bah." Levet rubbed his stunted horn. "She is making me nutmeg."

"Nutmeg?"

"I think he means nutty," Viper said dryly.

"She pops here. She pops there." Levet waved his hands.

"Pop, pop, pop, pop. How can I catch her if she will not stand still?"

Viper snorted. "Females rarely make the chase easy. In fact, I'm beginning to suspect they're born to make men utterly and completely nutmeg."

There was a brief silence as the three males nodded in rare agreement. Then, with a sharp shake of his head, Styx pointed toward the door. "Go keep Darcy and Shay company," he commanded. "I have business to discuss with Viper."

"As much as I prefer the company of your charming mates, I need to speak with you."

"Later."

"*Non*." Levet stubbornly held his ground. "This is important."

Styx clenched his hands. As much fun as it would be to mount the damned creature over the marble fireplace, he knew Darcy would never forgive him. Dammit.

"Fine." His lips curled back to display his massive fangs. "Spit it out."

The gargoyle's tail twitched, but he wasn't so stupid as to challenge Styx's patience. Not tonight.

"You know that I keep in contact with Darcy and her sisters?"

"Yes, you use some sort of telepathy."

"Not exactly telepathy. It's more a portal that I form inside their mind. . . ."

"Do you have a point?" Styx interrupted, not giving a shit how the creature managed to speak mind to mind with his mate.

Levet sniffed. "Darcy asked me to try and contact Cassie using my powers."

"Clever," Styx murmured, his pride in his wife swelling through his heart.

"Clever, but, unfortunately, my efforts did nothing but give me the aching head," Levet admitted.

"So you failed?"

"Not so much a failure as a . . . misfire."

Levet wasn't the only one with the aching head, Styx silently conceded. "What the hell does that mean?"

"I could not contact her, but she did manage to contact me."

A sudden tension filled the air as both vampires stared at the tiny demon in astonishment.

"You spoke with her?" Styx bit out.

Levet gave a lift of one shoulder. "Only a brief moment."

Viper stepped forward. "What did she say?"

"Nothing, but she sent this."

Levet held out his hand to reveal a small piece of paper. Styx leaned forward, taking the paper and unfolding it to study the squiggle of odd lines.

"What is it?" Viper demanded.

"A prophecy." Styx lifted his head to stab his friend with a worried frown. "Get Roke."

Gaius's lair in Louisiana

Gaius sat in a leather wing chair in his office, holding a history book that glorified his battles as a Roman general. He might not remember his human days, but he took pleasure in the knowledge he had been a brilliant commander feared by all. Usually, it was his favorite way to spend a quiet evening in his lair.

Tonight, however, he found no peace.

Not even several hours of rough sex followed by a deep feeding had eased the sense of foreboding that had haunted him for the past two weeks. Tossing aside the book, Gaius surged to his feet and paced toward the window, his brocade dressing gown brushing the floor.

He knew what was troubling him.

After following the Dark Lord's commands to protect the wizard spirit, he'd then returned to the mists along with Dolf. He perhaps shouldn't have been surprised to discover the master had been resurrected into the child. But he'd been frankly unnerved by the sight of the powerful deity in the body of a teenage girl.

Thankfully, he'd concealed his growing apprehension—unlike Dolf, who had managed to incur the anger of the Dark Lord—long enough to escape out of the mists.

There was no way he was going to hang around to bear the brunt of the Dark Lord's frustration when he couldn't use his new body to return to the world. Drained or not, she was still powerful enough to turn Gaius into a puddle of screaming pain.

Now he was left to stew in his own doubts, caught between the urgent need to hear from the Dark Lord so they could finish their deal and he could demand the return of his beloved mate, and a growing desire to be forgotten by the evil bastard. Or rather . . . the evil bitch.

Sensing the approach of a male cur, Gaius was careful to mask his emotions as he slowly turned to watch Dolf step into the room. In the candlelight the dog was looking distinctly worse for the wear.

In the past two weeks his hair had grown past the buzz cut and had acquired several streaks of gray. Worse, he'd dropped nearly fifty pounds, leaving his face gaunt and his stomach sunken.

Not at all the cocky mutt that Gaius had first met just a month ago. But then again, they'd all lost a bit of their cock.

"You disposed of the body?" he demanded.

Dolf nodded, his eyes glittering with a hectic light. The cur was hanging on to his sanity by a thread. A thin thread.

"It's rotting deep in the swamp with all the others." His lips curved in a gruesome imitation of a smile. "You have quite a collection out there. Thirteen, isn't it?"

Gaius stiffened. He didn't like being reminded of the whores that he'd killed over the past few nights. Not because of his conscience. That had died along with Dara. But it was a nasty reminder of his loss of control.

It was happening far too frequently.

"Don't presume to judge me." His words were coated in ice. "My hungers are instinct, not a perversion of nature like some I could name."

Dolf snorted, indifferent to Gaius's disdain. "Hell, I don't care if you drain every whore from here to Timbuktu, but the locals are starting to get itchy about the girls who've gone missing. Unless you want an angry mob, complete with torches and pitchforks, on our doorstep, you might want to dial back on your feedings." He paced to study the books that lined the shelves. "Or at least import your meals from farther away."

Gaius narrowed his gaze. "Is there a reason you've intruded into my privacy?"

There was a long silence, as if Dolf was considering his words. Never a good thing. Then slowly he turned to meet Gaius's rigid expression. "Do you think it's odd we haven't heard from the master?"

Gaius hissed. The question had, of course, been nagging at the edge of his mind. But he was smart enough to know it was too dangerous to speak aloud.

"She will contact us when she needs our services," he said stiffly.

"Are you so certain?"

"Why wouldn't I be?"

Dolf's humorless laugh echoed through the silent house. "Our last mission was yet another epic failure."

Gaius shrugged. "The wizard was to blame for bringing the Hunter and Sylvermyst into the master's lair. It wasn't our fault."

Dolf shuddered, still obviously traumatized by their time spent in the master's company. "Yeah, well, the wizard is dead and the Dark Lord is still trapped," the cur unnecessarily pointed out. "She might have decided to spread the blame around."

"We would know if she'd decided to punish us for the latest disaster," Gaius said with a grimace. "She's never subtle."

Dolf nodded, but his brow remained furrowed. "If you say."

Gaius rolled his eyes. He could send the cur away, but Dolf would only return until he'd said whatever was on his tiny mind. "Now what's bothering you?"

The cur hunched his shoulders. "To be honest, I preferred the thought that we're being punished."

Gaius frowned. "As opposed to what?"

"Have you considered the possibility that the Dark Lord hasn't contacted us because . . ."

His words trailed away and Gaius made a sound of impatience. "*Cristo*, just say it."

"Because she can't."

Gaius cursed, instinctively glancing around the seemingly empty room. Even if the Dark Lord was trapped in another dimension, he—or rather she—had spies everywhere.

"You are a fool," he hissed.

"Perhaps, but I would be even more of a fool to spend the next century waiting in this godforsaken swamp for a master who has already lost the war," Dolf grimly pressed, too far gone in his growing madness to consider the danger.

"What do you suggest?" Gaius asked, the ice in his voice warning he wouldn't be coaxed into an indiscretion. His growing doubts would go with him to the grave. "That we abandon the Dark Lord and pray she doesn't manage to escape her prison?"

Without warning, the nearest bookshelf slid outward to reveal a hidden passageway.

Gaius tensed in shock, his fangs lengthening in preparation for an attack. Instead, Sally stepped into the room, her hair hanging around her face, which was amazingly devoid of her ridiculous black makeup, and her slender body covered by a flannel nightgown.

She looked like a child. As long as you didn't look into the eyes, which were glowing with a crimson fire.

"Yes, Dolf, please enlighten me on how you intend to betray me?"

The cur fell to his knees, his head pressed to the floor at the sudden blast of power that had nothing to do with Sally and everything to do with the Dark Lord. "Mistress."

Sally moved forward, her expression slack as she was piloted by the evil deity to stand directly next to the cringing cur. "I have made allowances for you because you are young and impetuous, but my patience has run its course." The voice was female, but not Sally's.

"No, please," Dolf whined, the stench of his fear filling the air. "I swear I will never again question your powers."

"No, you will not."

Leaning down, Sally placed her hand on the back of Dolf's head, her touch almost gentle. But even as the cur's violent shudders began to ease, a dark mist formed around his body.

At first nothing happened and Gaius wondered if it was simply a spell to keep him trapped on the floor. Then, instinctively, Gaius stepped back, watching in horror as the blackness began to boil and churn, consuming Dolf's body with a silent swiftness.

There was no other way to explain it. Wherever the mist touched Dolf, his body just . . . vanished. There was no sound, no scent, no sense of anything but death claiming its latest trophy.

A ball of dread lodged in the pit of his stomach.

What the hell?

Sally was only supposed to be a conduit for the Dark Lord, but it was obvious she was able to call on some hefty magic. The thought should have been reassuring. It surely meant that the Dark Lord still maintained a large portion of her powers and was capable of returning Dara from the grave.

Instead, Gaius could only watch Dolf being efficiently destroyed and wonder if the cur had been given the preferable fate.

It was the distant howls of Ingrid who had been driven to her wolf form as she sensed the loss of her brother that at last snapped Gaius out of his dangerous sense of unreality.

Lifting his head, he found Sally regarding him with those eyes that burned with crimson fire.

"A shame, but he had outlived his usefulness." Stepping over Dolf's disintegrating body, Sally walked to stand directly in front of Gaius. "What of you?"

Gaius swiftly bowed. "I am yours to command."

"So I have your loyalty?"

"Without question."

"And what of your faith?"

Gaius warily straightened, praying the creature was incapable of reading his mind. "My faith?"

"It's simple, vampire." She reached to run a nail down his

cheek. "Do you still believe we can achieve your glorious future together?"

Gaius suppressed his shudder, holding himself motionless beneath her light touch. No use provoking the crazy creature. "Of course."

"Hmmm." The nail dug deep enough to draw blood. "Not the ringing endorsement I might have hoped for from one of my most devoted disciples."

Gaius desperately sought a distraction. "What would you have of me?"

The crimson eyes narrowed before she dropped her hand and stepped back. "I need you to travel to Chicago."

"Again?" Caught off guard, Gaius spoke without thinking. "Did the prophet escape?"

The air hummed with a surge of power and Gaius silently cursed his stupid question. What the hell had happened to his frigid discipline?

"You agree with Dolf?" Sally asked in a lethally soft voice. "You suspect that I'm incompetent?"

"I . . . of course not."

"But you suspect I'm incapable of holding on to my prisoners?"

"No." Gaius sought to minimize the danger. "I was just curious why you would want me to return to Chicago."

The punishing pressure eased, although the crimson gaze regarded him with an unwavering intensity that warned his brush with death was far from over.

"The child I need is being held there."

Child? There was only one child that the Dark Lord could be interested in, and yet, Gaius paused, certain that he must have misunderstood.

"You mean the babe that's being protected in the King of Vampire's lair?"

Crimson eyes flared with hunger. "Yes."

"That is . . ." This time Gaius managed to swallow his impulsive words.

"There's something you want to share?" the Dark Lord mocked.

Hell yes, there was something he wanted to share. He wanted to share that it was sheer madness to try and battle his way into the most highly guarded lair in the entire world.

He would be dead before he ever reached the front gates.

"No matter what my powers, I can't possibly bluff my way past the Anasso and his Ravens," he cautiously pointed out. "And I certainly can't overpower them."

Sally shrugged. "You won't be alone."

Gaius glanced toward the flakes of black dust that was all that remained of Dolf. "I doubt my remaining companions would offer the firepower I would need."

"The curs are no longer necessary to my plans." Sally gave a wave of her hand. "I have a new servant to assist you."

Gaius didn't know whether to be relieved or terrified. "May I ask who it is?"

"A vampire named Kostas."

Kostas. The name wasn't familiar to Gaius, but that wasn't surprising considering that he'd spent the past few centuries beyond the Veil. But he did know that the vampire wasn't one of Styx's Ravens or one of his trusted allies, which made him wonder what kind of help he could provide.

"He has access to the babe?"

"He assures me that he is capable of sneaking in and out of the lair unnoticed."

Gaius frowned. "Then why do you need me?"

"You will provide the distraction so no one will notice the absence of the child until he is well away from the lair."

Which meant he would be the one the infuriated vampires,

and perhaps even a few pureblooded Weres, would be chasing. "Perfect," he muttered beneath his breath.

Sally put a hand on his shoulder, her palm searing a painful heat through the fabric of Gaius's dressing gown. "Once you're away from the vampires, you will bring me the child. This time there will be no mistakes. Understood?"

Gaius nodded. The mistakes had been made the moment he'd allowed the Dark Lord to whisper in his ear.

The only question was whether or not it was too late to correct them.

Chapter 14

Styx's lair in Chicago

Styx and Viper stood in rigid silence as Roke studied the piece of paper Levet had given them. The Las Vegas clan chief was wearing his usual attire of a pair of faded jeans, with his dark hair left loose and his chest exposed to reveal the dragon tattoo that marked his position as chief.

So far as Styx knew, Roke had rarely left the rooms that he'd been given after his arrival in Chicago. No big surprise. The taciturn vampire had never been the life of the party, and being forced to remain so far from his people hadn't improved his temperament.

Unfortunately for him, Styx had no intention of allowing him to leave. Not until the latest danger from the Dark Lord had passed.

"Is it a prophecy?" Viper demanded, his impatience adding a sharp chill to the air.

Slowly, Roke lifted his head, his lean face hard with concern. "Not so much a prophecy as a warning."

Styx stepped forward. "What does it say?"

"Beware the shadows."

"That's it?" Viper snapped. "Beware the shadows?"

"Yes."

Viper hissed, clearly not pleased by the vague forewarning. "What the hell is that supposed to mean?"

Roke moved until he was nose to nose with the Chicago clan chief, his smoky eyes shimmering with power. "You asked me to decipher the glyph and I did. It's not my fault you don't like what it says."

"He's right, Viper." Styx smoothly stepped between the two. Tensions were riding high and the last thing he needed was two of his most powerful brothers at each other's throats. Literally. He kept his gaze on Roke. "Is that all you can give us?"

There was a tense moment when Styx prepared for violence. Then, with a tight smile, the younger vampire stepped back, his gaze lowering to the paper still clutched in his fingers.

"I sense the child when I touch the glyph, as if the prophet was thinking of Maluhia when she sent this message."

Viper was already headed toward the door by the time Roke finished speaking. "I'll have the guards doubled," he said.

"Viper."

The silver-haired vampire turned to regard him with an impatient scowl. "Yes?"

"Tell them . . ." Styx grimaced.

"Tell them what?"

"To look for shadows."

"They're going to think I've lost my mind," Viper growled.

Styx shrugged. "They assumed that centuries ago."

"Thanks." With a flash of fangs, Viper turned and disappeared down the hall.

At the same time, Roke moved to stand at his side. "Is that all you need from me?"

Styx folded his arms over his chest. "Are you in a hurry to be somewhere?"

"Home," Roke said, a muscle in his jaw knotted with a seething resentment at being away from those he'd taken as his family. "My clan needs me."

Styx shook his head. As much as he sympathized with Roke's fierce loyalty, he needed his talents. Hard times called for hard decisions. "I understand your urgency to be with your people, but for now your duty is here."

Roke hissed, waving a slender hand toward the glass cases that contained some of Styx's most treasured artifacts. "So I can sit on my ass, surrounded by your collection of froufrou, just on the off chance you need me to transcribe a prophecy?"

Styx lifted his brows. "First, my collection isn't froufrou, it's chichi," he informed the younger vampire. "Second, you're here to stop the end of the world. I think that might be worth a few days of boredom, don't you?"

Roke stiffened, his pride offended. "I understand my duty."

"But?"

"But that doesn't mean I have to like it."

"Trust me, Roke, none of us like the waiting." Styx laid a comforting hand on his companion's shoulder. "But then I doubt we're going to like what comes next any better."

Outside Styx's lair

Gaius circled the brick walls that surrounded the Anasso's vast mansion, careful to remain out of sight of the security systems. Both demon security and the more high-tech kind.

On his third trip around the estate, he halted in a small patch of trees, his hands clenched in frustration.

"*Dio*," he muttered. "Where is the fool?"

There was a stir of air before the thick shadows near the brick wall suddenly dissipated to reveal an overly muscular male body covered in black fatigues. Gaius's gaze lifted to the square face that reminded him eerily of his own.

Dark, finely hewed features and black hair that was currently pulled into a tail at his nape had a distinct hint of Roman ancestors. But it was the soulless black eyes that captured Gaius's attention.

Psychopath.

Always the most dangerous creature.

"You really should pay better attention, Gaius," the large vampire mocked, strutting forward with the confidence of a demon who thought he was cock-of-the-walk. "Who knows what might be lurking beneath your nose?"

Gaius managed to crush his instinctive urge to teach the arrogant bastard just who was in charge. He could prove who had bigger balls once they had managed to steal the child. And if he didn't, the Dark Lord certainly would.

Instead, he concentrated on the man standing before him. Just because he was a blustering idiot, not to mention a supposed partner in crime, didn't make him any less dangerous.

"A Hunter," he said. He'd never met one of the elite vampires who were as secretive as they were lethal, but he knew that there wasn't any other vampire who could cloak themselves so thoroughly.

"Not just a Hunter," the vampire corrected, his tone harsh and his dark eyes flashing with a fury that he could barely contain. "My name is Kostas." He waited as if expecting Gaius to recognize the name. "I was the Ruah. The ultimate leader of the Addonexus and commander of all Hunters."

Gaius wasn't nearly as impressed as the man no doubt expected him to be. "Was?" He deliberately latched onto the revealing word. "I assume you were demoted?"

Kostas's growl echoed through the trees. "My position was stolen from me by the King of Vampires."

"Ah." Gaius smiled without humor. "And now you want your revenge?"

"I want the bastard to suffer." The man's anger swept through the trees, snapping off several branches. "And I want that suffering to last for an eternity."

"And I thought the cur was unbalanced," Gaius muttered, irritated by the thought of being saddled with yet another moron who was clearly at the mercy of his emotions.

Kostas moved with shocking speed to clamp his fingers around Gaius's arm. "Don't mistake me for a pathetic dog."

With a sharp blow to the vampire's chest, Gaius sent Kostas's large body crashing into a nearby tree. He waited for the man to rise back to his feet before pointing a finger in his direction and allowing his power to sear over Kostas's flesh.

"Don't think the Dark Lord can save you if I decide I want you dead," he warned.

Kostas lifted a pleading hand. "Stop."

Gaius allowed the pain to continue for longer than necessary before he lowered his hand and regarded his companion with an imperious smile. "Tell me your plan."

Kostas's eyes smoldered with the desire to rip out Gaius's throat, but proving he wasn't a complete idiot, he managed to leash his bloodthirsty urges. "As you have seen for yourself, I'm capable of shrouding myself in impenetrable shadows," he said between clenched fangs.

Gaius studied him in suspicion. "Then why do you need a distraction?"

"I can't walk through walls. The guards are bound to notice the doors opening, unless they have something else to occupy their minds." There was a moment of silence, as if the vampire was weighing how much he had to reveal to pacify Gaius. "Besides, I can maintain my shadows for a considerable length of time if I'm standing still, but when I'm forced to move it becomes more draining on my powers. And once I'm carrying the child it becomes even more difficult."

"How long?" Gaius pressed.

"Ten, maybe fifteen minutes," Kostas grudgingly answered.

"That's not very long." With a frown Gaius glanced toward the sprawling mansion, easily sensing the labyrinth of tunnels that ran beneath the grounds. "What if you have trouble locating the child?"

"Trouble?" The man's conceit returned with a vengeance. "I'm a Hunter. There's nothing I can't track."

"And this is the Anasso's lair," Gaius pointed out. "Who knows what sort of spells and hexes he's placed around the nursery?"

"I'm trained to avoid such traps."

"Fine." Let the bastard have his heart carved out by the King of Vampires. And, if by some miracle he did survive and escape with the baby, Gaius would be happy to claim the rewards from the Dark Lord. "Where will we meet after you've escaped with the babe?"

"I'll contact you . . ."

"No." Gaius pointed a warning finger. "We'll arrange a meeting place before you enter the house and you will be there waiting for me with the child. Is that clear enough?"

"You don't trust me?" Kostas sneered.

"I don't trust anyone."

"Neither do I. How do I know you won't double cross me?" Kostas tilted his chin to a belligerent angle. "And believe me, I'll know if you're lying."

Oh, Gaius believed him.

The same rumors that whispered of a Hunter's ability to

cloak himself in shadows, also hinted that they could smell
a lie a mile off. Not that it mattered. If it came to the point
he had to lie to the miserable SOB he would just kill him.

"My command is to take the babe to the Dark Lord," he
said. "Do you truly think I would defy our master?"

Kostas didn't look happy, but he knew this was a battle he
wasn't going to win.

"We'll meet at my current lair," he muttered. "It's fifty
miles west of here in a small town called Platte. The entrance
is at the back of the old quarry. Knock before you enter or
you might find yourself in a nasty trap."

"I'll be there before dawn." Gaius grimaced, his gaze returning to the mansion where he could sense over a dozen
powerful demons. "Always assuming I survive."

"And Styx?" Kostas demanded.

"What about him?"

"I was promised he would be given to me."

Gaius shrugged. "That's between you and the Dark Lord."

"I'd better not be disappointed," Kostas warned, abruptly
disappearing in a shroud of shadows.

"That, my friend, is almost guaranteed," Gaius muttered,
clutching his medallion as he studied the best place to make
his grand appearance in the Anasso's lair.

Styx was pacing the carpet in his study, wishing he was
upstairs in bed with his mate, when the intercom buzzed.

Crossing the room, he frowned at the sight of his finest
Raven glaring into the camera near the nursery. Jagr was a
six-foot-three vampire who had once been a Visigoth chief.
He had pale gold hair that was braided to fall to his waist and
a pair of ice-blue eyes that were as hard and unforgiving as
his stark features.

If he'd ever been civilized, three hundred years of relentless torture had stripped it away. His recent mating with Darcy's sister, however, had managed to at least house-train him.

"Jagr, what's happened?" he demanded, knowing the vampire would never have bothered him if it wasn't serious.

"Are you in your study?"

"Yes?" Styx frowned in confusion. "Why?"

"DeAngelo's watching the monitors and he just caught sight of you entering the house from a side door and heading toward Tane and Laylah's room."

"Gaius," he growled, silently thanking Nefri for her warning of her clan brother's peculiar talents. "Send the Ravens to capture him—I'm on my way."

Jagr nodded. "You got it."

"And Jagr."

"Yes?"

"Don't leave the nursery unguarded," he commanded. "This might be an attempt to distract us."

Jagr wisely didn't point out he didn't need anyone telling him how to do his job. "I won't."

"Oh, and don't kill the intruder." A cruel smile touched Styx's mouth. "I want the honors."

With a blurring speed, Styx was out of his study and headed down to the lower levels of his lair. As he moved, his power spread before him, shattering lightbulbs and toppling marble statues.

At last reaching the private rooms he'd given to Tane and Laylah, Styx slowed his pace, nodding toward the Ravens standing guard in front of the nursery. Then, with his fangs fully exposed, he moved deeper down the corridor, away from the living quarters toward the narrow stairs that led to his dungeons.

Rounding a corner, he discovered Jagr standing in front of a silver door that had a small window cut at eye level. The one-time Visigoth turned at Styx's approach, his always grim expression more bleak than usual and a massive sword held in his hand.

"Well?" Styx prompted.

"We caught him before he could reach Tane's private rooms and brought him here," Jagr answered, his ice-blue eyes hard with disgust. "Take a look."

Styx moved to peek through the window, hissing in shock as he caught sight of the vampire standing in the center of the lined cell.

Even prepared, Styx found himself reeling at the image of himself on another vampire.

The same long, dark hair pulled into a braid, the same large body covered in leather, and distinctly Aztec features. Christ. It was like looking in a mirror.

Or at least, how he supposed it would be to look in a mirror. Without a reflection, he could only assume the bastard had gotten the features right.

Which begged the question . . . *how* had he gotten them right?

Had they met before? After so many centuries it was impossible to remember every vampire he'd crossed paths with.

"Damn." He shook off the inane thoughts, concentrating on what was to come next. "What gave him away?"

"He was too pretty."

Styx snorted. "Very funny. Now the truth."

Jagr gave a lift of one massive shoulder. "He had to search for the hidden door leading to the lower floors."

Styx shook his head as the faux Styx folded his arms over his chest in a manner eerily familiar.

"That's just . . ."

"Creepy as hell," Jagr finished for him.

"Yes." Styx reached for the doorknob. "Stay here."

Jagr frowned, clearly not pleased. "Are you sure? We don't know the full extent of his powers."

"Which is why I'm going in alone." Styx held Jagr's gaze, knowing his loyal guard's first instinct would be to try and defend him. "For now, nothing's more important than protecting the child. If something happens to me I want you to get Maluhia to the Commission."

"The Commission?" Jagr looked like he'd chewed on a lemon. "They haven't done a damn thing to help so far. Why would they protect the child now?"

Styx thought back to his recent encounter with Siljar, one of the Oracles who sat on the Commission. She hadn't revealed much, but it was enough to make him suspect that they weren't nearly so indifferent to the future of the world as they pretended.

"I would guess they've done far more behind the scenes than we've suspected," he murmured.

"If you say."

Styx laid his hand on his companion's shoulder. "I have your word?"

There was a brief hesitation before Jagr gave a sharp nod. Once the vampire gave his promise, it was unbreakable. "Yes."

Confident the child would be kept safe, Styx opened the door and stepped into the cell. Lifting his sword he'd grabbed on the way out of his office, he pointed it toward the intruder.

"Gaius, I presume?"

A smile. "I see my reputation precedes me. Should I be flattered?"

Styx snorted. "You can drop the disguise."

"You have to admit it's very good," the creature smirked before there was a shimmer around his body and the image of Styx melted to become a vampire built on slighter lines, with lean features and dark eyes. He was naked now that he'd shifted to his natural form, except for the heavy medallion that rested against his bare chest.

"Not good enough."

The vampire shrugged, appearing far too resigned for Styx's peace of mind. "It was worth a try."

"It was a dangerous gamble, which makes me think that there's more to your plan." He resisted the urge to take a step forward. As Jagr pointed out, they didn't yet know the full extent of the bastard's powers and the last thing he wanted was to get within arm's length. "Are you the bait?"

Gaius gave a lift of his hands. "The Dark Lord is growing impatient to get her hands on the child. She doesn't particularly care how many servants she has to sacrifice to achieve her goal."

Styx shuddered. It was hard to remember that the Dark Lord had been resurrected into the body of a young female. "That I believe. You, however, I don't." He pointed his sword toward the center of the vampire's chest. "Hand over your medallion."

"This?" Gaius covered the heavy metal necklace with his hand, a faint smile curving his lips. "It's nothing but a trinket."

"You truly must think I'm stupid."

Gaius pretended to ponder his answer. "To be honest, I haven't given it a lot of thought one way or another."

Styx wasn't amused. "Even if I didn't sense its power, I have seen Nefri's. It's remarkably similar."

Something flashed through the man's dark eyes even as he took a step backward, his fingers clutching the medallion. "So, the frigid bitch has left the Veil," he growled. "Astonishing."

Styx allowed his power to fill the room, even as he debated the wisdom of attacking the vampire to get his hands on the medallion. He was fairly certain he could overpower the vampire, but he couldn't stop him from disappearing before he could get his hands on him. For now, it seemed his only hope was to provoke him in the hopes he could discover what game he was playing.

"You will show respect to your clan chief." He allowed his power to shove the vampire against the silver-lined wall. "She offered you sanctuary when you were at your most vulnerable and you repaid her trust with betrayal."

Gaius cursed, struggling away from the wall as he glared at Styx. "I had no choice."

Styx rolled his eyes. He'd heard the same excuse used thousands upon thousands of times over the centuries. Hell, there'd been once or twice he'd used it himself. And it was always a cop-out.

"Try again."

Genuine anger tightened Gaius's expression. "It's so easy to be noble when you have your mate safely tucked in your bed." Gaius tilted his chin, his gaze defiant. "But tell me, Anasso, how far would you go to keep her there? Is any betrayal too great to have her back in your arms?"

Chapter 15

Styx shut out the accusing words. He couldn't afford to feel sympathy for the traitor. Not when the future of the world hung in the balance.

"None of us can comprehend the loss you suffered, but Dara was not the only one to depend upon you," he said, trying to stir the vampire's ancient loyalties. Just perhaps it wasn't too late to remind the once honorable clan chief of his sense of duty.

"My clan was better off without me."

"And what about your son?"

Gaius stiffened, his eyes dark with a vast sense of loss. The sort of loss that destroyed a man.

"Santiago?"

"So you haven't completely forgotten about him."

"Of course not." Gaius clutched the medallion so tightly his knuckles turned white. "He is my child. He will always be my child."

Styx didn't have to fake his contempt. Not when he'd personally witnessed what had happened to Santiago after Gaius's abrupt departure behind the Veil.

"A father doesn't abandon his child."

Gaius frowned, visibly disturbed by the memory of leaving behind the child he'd sired. "I couldn't allow him to be tainted by my bargain with the Dark Lord."

"So instead you allowed him to become a slave to one of the most vicious vampires it has ever been my misfortune to meet?" Styx rasped, recalling Santiago's broken and bleeding body he'd found in the fighting pits beneath Barcelona. "He made him into a Gladiator. Santiago was forced to fight every night in the blood pits just to stay alive."

"I suppose you slayed his dragon and became his hero?" Gaius attempted to mock.

"Would you rather I had discarded him like you did?"

Gaius flinched, his gaze shifting away from Styx's accusing expression. "No."

Styx lowered his sword, but he wasn't foolish enough to approach the skittish vampire. "Gaius, it's not too late to redeem yourself," he urged.

Gaius shuddered. "It's later than you can even imagine."

On cue, the door behind Styx was shoved open and a female with short, spiky strands of red hair and black eyes rushed into the cell. Laylah, the Jinn mongrel and mother to Maluhia.

"The baby's gone," she announced, her face white with a combination of shock and fear.

God dammit.

He'd known that Gaius was merely a distraction.

"How?" Styx didn't bother with platitudes. People didn't come to him for comfort. They came to him for results.

"I don't know." Laylah struggled to contain her panic. "I was holding Maluhia in my arms when he was suddenly snatched away. He"—she gave a helpless lift of her hands—"disappeared."

"Magic?"

"I don't think so." Laylah shook her head, turning to reach out a hand to the male vampire with Polynesian features and a dark mohawk who rushed into the room.

Behind Tane was another vampire, this one a slender female with long dark hair and tilted blue eyes.

"I could feel the hands as they grabbed Maluhia," Laylah continued, her voice breaking. "And I'm certain something stirred the air when I raced through the door."

Tane tucked his mate tight against him, his expression warning that when he got his hands on the evil bastard who had taken his son, he was going to rip them limb from limb. Then he was going to stitch them back together and do it again.

"The kidnapper was invisible?" he demanded.

There was a minute of silence as they all pondered the strange turn of events.

Then, Jaelyn growled low in her throat. "Kostas," she said.

Laylah sent the one-time Hunter a puzzled frown. "How can you know?"

Jaelyn shuddered. She had never fully revealed what had happened to her in the hands of the Addonexus, and in particular Kostas, but what little Styx had discovered had been enough for him to make a clean sweep. He wouldn't have his people terrorized by tyrants.

"There's no one else who is capable of cloaking themselves so deeply in shadows," Jaelyn pointed out, her gaze turning toward Styx. "And he's been crazed with the need for revenge since you removed him as Ruah."

Shadows.

Styx felt the urge to ram his thick head into the wall.

"Beware the shadows," he snarled. "Dammit, we were warned and I still failed."

"No, the failure was mine," Laylah said softly, her voice filled with such heartbreak that it filled the air with sorrow.

"We will get him back, Laylah," Styx said, his gaze shifting to Tane. "I swear."

"It's too late, Anasso," a voice said from behind him. "Concede defeat and bow to the Dark Lord."

With a snarl, Styx spun on his heel and prowled toward the forgotten Gaius, delighted as hell to have something to stab with his big-ass sword. It was obvious the vampire had deliberately distracted them to give Kostas the opportunity to steal the child.

Now he would pay the price.

"Never."

Gaius smiled with unmistakable bitterness. "Then die."

His words were still hanging in the air when he abruptly vanished from the cell.

"Shit." Coming to a halt, Styx lifted his eyes toward the ceiling. "Could this day get any worse?"

"Don't tempt fate," Tane muttered.

Leashing his fury, Styx forced himself to concentrate on the best means of tracking Maluhia. Then, turning back to his companions, he took command.

"Jaelyn, see if you can pick up the bastard's track."

The Hunter gave a swift nod. "Of course."

"I'm going with her," Laylah abruptly announced.

Styx frowned. The half-Jinn was powerful, but no one was certain if she was truly immortal.

"Laylah."

The hint of lightning prickled through the air. "I'm going."

"Fine." He glanced toward the silent vampire at her side. "I suppose you intend to go as well?"

There was no compromise in the eyes the precise shade of honey. "Yes."

"Take Jagr," Styx said, reluctantly realizing his place was here, organizing additional search parties to look for the babe. "He's the best tracker we have."

"We'll also need the gargoyle," Jaelyn startled them all by announcing.

"Levet?" Styx scowled. The tiny demon was a walking disaster.

"He can see through illusions," Jaelyn said.

Tane's growl trickled through the room. "Then why didn't he sense Kostas when he entered the lair?"

The Hunter shrugged. "I think he has to be searching for the illusion to actually see it."

Styx rolled his eyes. It was a sad day when the damned gargoyle was their best hope for halting the end of the world. "Fine, take him."

"What about Gaius?" Jagr demanded from the doorway.

Styx slammed his sword back into its sheath. "He's mine."

Kostas's lair

Once again fully dressed, Gaius easily found the opening to Kostas's lair, and with an impatient knock on the heavy metal door, he waited for the surly vampire to lead him down the stairs and through a series of cement tunnels. Eventually, they entered an eight-by-eight box of a room with a chair in one corner that was surrounded by a pile of sharp weapons. Nearer at hand was a shelf of tattered books that were focused on the histories of various demon species. No doubt they revealed all the strengths and weaknesses that a Hunter would need to know.

"All the better to kill you with, my dear . . ."

He grimaced. Not so much at the barren lack of comfort. He'd lived as sparsely as a monk beyond the Veil. But rather at the heavy sense of impending death that filled the room.

Was it because Kostas had devoted his existence to killing? Or a premonition?

"This is your lair?" he demanded.

Kostas glanced around the cement box. "Why?"

"It's . . ."

"It's functional."

"I suppose." Gaius shook his head, dismissing his strange imaginings. He had enough troubles without inventing new ones. "Where's the child?"

Kostas planted his hands on his hips, his bulky body consuming a large chunk of the room. "What about my reward?"

Gaius made a sound of impatience. "I told you, that's between you and the Dark Lord."

"Not good enough," the Hunter snapped. "No reward, no child."

Gaius clenched his hands. It wasn't that he didn't sympathize with the man's need to get his payment up front. *Merda*, he was desperate to be given his own rewards. But he wasn't in the mood to play the role of diplomat.

Not only had he seen up close and in person just what happened to a servant who questioned the Dark Lord's ability to fulfill her promises. But, he was still raw from his encounter with the King of Vampires and the reminder of his duty to Santiago.

He never allowed himself to think of the son he'd been forced to abandon.

Never.

"Don't be an idiot," he warned his companion. "The last creature to challenge the Dark Lord was eaten alive by a black mist. Do you think you'll fare any better?"

"I won't be denied my revenge."

Gaius rolled his eyes, wondering how a man could sell his soul for mere revenge. "Once the Dark Lord has returned, you will be able to torture and torment whoever you want," he promised dryly.

"And if he doesn't return?"

"Then we're both screwed."

The blunt words hung in the air as they both considered the heinous consequences of failure. Then, with an angry shake of his head, Kostas turned to kick aside the chair, revealing a small lever built in the floor.

Gaius watched as the vampire tripped the lever and stood back while the hidden door slid open to reveal a small room beyond. Instantly, the sound of a crying baby filled the air.

"In there." Kostas waved a beefy hand toward the dark room. "How do you intend to get it to the Dark Lord?"

Gaius pointed for the Hunter to enter the room ahead of him. Not only because he feared a hidden spell, but because he didn't want the powerful demon at his back.

"I'm a vampire of many talents."

Kostas glanced over his shoulder, a sudden cunning in his dark eyes. "I've heard the Immortal Ones have weird powers."

"Weird?"

"Shape-shifting, mist-walking," he named them off. "Enthralling other vampires."

Gaius would never have answered if Kostas was still the leader of the Hunters. Whatever Styx's accusation, he wasn't indifferent to the debt he owed Nefri and her clan for taking him in.

But Kostas had been tossed out of the Addonexus. And more importantly, it was highly unlikely the brash idiot would survive his current tenure with the Dark Lord. Why not give him the answers he wanted?

"Shape-shifting is a talent that only a rare few vampires

possess," he admitted. "Although it's impossible to fully develop the skill without traveling beyond the Veil."

"And the others?" the man pressed.

"Nefri, the clan chief, has a medallion like mine that allows her to mist-walk and also to part the Veil so vampires can travel back and forth. And as far as enthralling other vampires . . ." Gaius shrugged. "There are those who can seize control of lesser minds."

The dark eyes narrowed. "Are you one of them?"

"If I were, we wouldn't be having this ridiculous conversation."

Kostas stiffly moved to stand beside the narrow bed where the baby continued to cry, its tiny body wrapped in a blanket and his face scrunched and red with distress. "I don't like this," Kostas growled, scooping the baby off the mattress.

"You don't have to like it, you just have to obey."

With a warning glare, Kostas shoved the squalling baby into Gaius's arms. Astonishingly, the child abruptly halted its crying, regarding Gaius with a pair of wide blue eyes that held an innocence that pierced him straight in his dead heart.

"You stiff me and there's nowhere you can hide that I won't track you down," Kostas muttered.

Wrenching his gaze away from the sweet purity that was bundled in his arms, Gaius instead glared at his companion as he grasped the medallion.

"Stand back, you buffoon."

The Dark Lord's prison

Cassie was lost in a choking darkness. There were no sounds, no smells, no sense of touch. Just a vast emptiness that defied even the passage of time.

It was almost a relief when she distantly felt a sharp slap on her cheek.

"Wakey, wakey," a female said in her ear.

Cassie struggled to wade out of the clinging fog, flinching as the slaps became more painful.

"Caine," she breathed, slowly opening her eyes to discover a pretty young face hovering directly over her. "You."

A pair of dimples flashed. "Yes, me."

With a hiss of fear, Cassie scooted away from the evil deity.

And the bitch was evil.

Only a truly black heart would have taken such pleasure in torturing a helpless Caine while Cassie pleaded on her knees for mercy.

She had tried, over and over, to conjure the visions the Dark Lord wanted, but she wasn't a sideshow freak. She couldn't force the visions to appear.

At last she'd been sucked into the black hole of unconsciousness, her mind forced to relive every agonizing moment of Caine's torture for what had seemed to be an eternity.

Now she could only imagine what new hell was awaiting her.

"Where's Caine?" she managed to demand, her voice a mere croak.

The female straightened, smoothing her hands down the pretty white sundress she'd somehow managed to create to cover her naked body. "Don't worry. Your devoted dog is nearby."

The Dark Lord gave a wave of her hand and the swirling fog parted to reveal Caine, who was still trapped between wolf and human, lying motionless.

Cassie warily rose to her feet, her hands pressed to her aching heart. "What have you done to him?"

"He's in stasis." The blue eyes flickered with a sinister crimson. "At least for now."

Cassie understood the warning. The temporary reprieve was over. "What do you want?"

The female reached to grasp Cassie by the hair, pulling hard enough to bring tears to her eyes. "You know what I want."

Cassie didn't try to fight. What was the point? The creature would simply break her neck. Or worse, she'd continue her torture of Caine.

Instead, she sent her captor a pleading gaze. "Please, I can't give it to you."

The Dark Lord gave her an infuriated shake, rattling Cassie's teeth. "You're just not trying hard enough."

"I am," Cassie cried out. "I swear."

The female pointed her finger toward the unconscious Caine. "Do you need a reminder of the cost of failure?"

"No, I beg you . . ."

No big shocker—the evil bitch ignored Cassie's pleas. With a small gesture the Dark Lord sent her invisible power slamming into Caine with enough force to wrench him from the spell and make him howl in brutal agony.

"I need to know the future, seer." She glared at Cassie, frustration making crimson fire nearly consume the blue of her eyes. "You will give it to me."

Cassie cried out, feeling Caine's pain as if it was her own. "You're killing him."

The female gave Cassie another violent shake. "It's up to you to save him."

"Stop . . ."

Cassie's words were lost as a familiar sensation seized her mind, driving out all thoughts of the Dark Lord and even Caine.

This power was bigger than all of them.

With violent force, the prophecy raced through her, searing a path from the great unknown to leave her shaken and disoriented. Like she'd been run over by a cement truck.

Slowly opening her eyes, she found herself befuddled and unable to remember why she was surrounded by white fog. Or why her head was throbbing. Visions weren't usually painful.

Then, her gaze landed on a female who was bent over to study the shimmering glyph that hung in midair. What the hell?

"At last," the stranger straightened, turning to grab Cassie by the throat. "What does it say?" Her fingers tightened as Cassie struggled to clear her mind of the lingering confusion. "Are you listening to me?"

"Leave me alone," Cassie rasped.

"Tell me what it says," the female roared.

"What?"

"The prophecy." The fingers dug into Cassie's flesh, branding her skin with a scorching heat. "What does it say?"

Cassie blinked, forcing her mind to focus on her surroundings. Fog. So much fog. And some strange monster who was shuddering in obvious pain.

Oh, gods. She was trapped in this hellish white mist with a crazy Dark Lord and Caine.

"I remember," she whispered.

"Then tell me." The Dark Lord shifted her hand to crush Cassie's chin in a brutal grip, forcing her face toward the shimmering glyph. "Give me my future."

Cassie grudgingly allowed her gaze to settle on the floating prophecy. The last thing she wanted was to give the Dark Lord the advantage in their ongoing war. But then again, did she have a choice? One way or another, the Dark Lord was going to force her to translate the vision.

She focused on the glyph, her brows drawing together as the words slid across her mind.

"Well?" the Dark Lord prompted, her nails slicing through Cassie's skin.

Cassie bent her head, allowing her hair to cover the smile that suddenly curved her lips.

"*The tides of chaos break upon an impenetrable wall.*"

"No." Abruptly loosening her hold on Cassie, the Dark Lord waited until she'd landed on her knees before she gave Cassie a vicious kick to the side. "A lie."

Cassie lifted a hand to cover her shattered ribs, sensing that at least one of them had punctured her lung.

"The prophecies don't lie," she said.

"Then you lie." The Dark Lord grabbed another handful of Cassie's hair, yanking her head back to meet the crimson flames that had engulfed her eyes. "You hope to save your mate."

Cassie frowned, failing to follow the logic. "If I wanted to save him, then I would have told you the key to your success is to release him."

"No, this is a trick." The female paced a circle around Cassie, her expression as petulant as if she were a teenage girl. "It has to be."

Cassie kept a wary eye on the infuriated deity, knowing that it was quite likely she wasn't going to survive the next blow. "I gave you what you wanted."

"So you did." Coming to an abrupt halt, the Dark Lord glared down at Cassie with all-consuming hatred. "Now it is my turn."

Cassie tensed, knowing this was going to be bad. "What do you mean?"

"You wanted your mate, didn't you?" The Dark Lord turned to smile toward Caine, who twitched in continued agony in the mists, his entire body rigid with the pain that was shooting through him. "Now you can have him."

The female gave a twist of her hand and Caine jerkily rose to his feet, as if he were a marionette on strings. Then, with another wave of her hand the Dark Lord forced open Caine's eyes, revealing the madness that had claimed him.

With a humorless laugh, the Dark Lord patted Cassie's cheek. "Enjoy your reunion."

Cassie didn't bother to watch the bitch disappear into the fog, her attention entirely focused on the savage beast that was stalking toward her with lethal intent.

Sorrow filled her heart as she edged backward. "Caine."

Chapter 16

Kostas's lair in Platte

It was almost three a.m. when Styx got the call he was waiting for. Leaving Viper to deal with any emergencies, he took off for the small town of Platte, easily following Jagr's direction to Kostas's hidden lair.

Once there, he moved through the starkly barren bunker to the cramped cell where Jaelyn was waiting.

The Hunter was nearly invisible in black spandex that covered her from neck to ankle. Even the sawed-off shotgun strapped around her waist was made of a dull, unreflective metal. Currently, she was running her hands along the cement walls, clearly seeking a trapdoor. At his entrance, she turned to regard him with a somber expression that warned Styx the news wasn't good.

"Kostas was here." He stated the obvious, catching the scent of the vampire along with a sour hint of growing madness.

Damn. He had known the Ruah was furious at being demoted. He'd even expected the bastard to plot revenge.

Kostas's bloated pride would demand nothing less. But he hadn't expected him to sell his soul to the Dark Lord.

Yet another mistake to add to his very long list.

Jaelyn nodded. "Yes, along with Maluhia."

"Do you know when he left?"

"Less than an hour ago."

An hour. Had the traitor known they were on his trail? Or was it just another example of Styx's piss-poor luck that Kostas had taken off just before they could corner him?

"You can't follow his scent?"

"Not yet." Jaelyn nodded her head toward the open door. "Levet is searching."

Perfect. Freaking perfect.

"Anything else?"

"He wasn't alone."

Styx didn't have to be a mind reader to know who Kostas would be meeting. "Gaius."

The Hunter grimaced. "Yes."

"Damn." Styx clenched his hands at his side, frustration pouring like hot acid through him. "Then he's already taken the child to the Dark Lord."

At his low words Tane stepped into the room, his expression bleak in the glow from the fluorescent lights. "It's not too late," he said, his tone defying anyone to tell him otherwise. "Where's Nefri?"

"I'm not sure." Styx moved to stand directly in front of his brother, easily sensing the vampire was about to snap. The one-time Charon's fear for his son had made him a seething rampage just waiting to happen. "Why?"

"She has the same pendant as Gaius. She can follow him and—"

"No, Tane," Styx gently interrupted. "I'm sorry, but Nefri has already tried to use her medallion to locate the Dark

Lord, without success. She thinks it's because Gaius's medallion is directly connected to the evil pain in the ass."

Tane shoved unsteady fingers through his mohawk. "Damn."

Styx placed a comforting hand on Tane's shoulder. "We'll find a way to reach your son."

The honey eyes blazed with a sense of furious helplessness. "Laylah will demand to use her powers to shadow-walk."

Styx grimaced, although he wasn't surprised. Laylah didn't have the power of a full Jinn who could move between worlds, but she could enter the mists that traveled between the dimensions. It was only to be expected she would try to use that talent to reach her child. No matter how dangerous it might be.

"You want me to forbid her?"

Tane snorted at the ridiculous question. "It wouldn't help."

True. Styx might be king, but that didn't mean jack-squat to a female who was desperate to reach her child. "You're afraid she'll be captured by the Dark Lord?" he instead asked.

"No, I'm afraid she'll be disappointed," Tane admitted, his low voice harsh with pain. "She's never sensed the entrance to the Dark Lord's prison during her previous travels. I doubt it will make a magical appearance now that we need it. She'll be devastated if she fails."

Styx squeezed the younger vampire's shoulder, offering his unspoken sympathy. "Will you go with her?"

Tane arched a brow. "Is that a joke?"

"Just be careful," Styx commanded. "There are more dangers than just the Dark Lord."

"This isn't my first rodeo," Tane reminded him.

Styx nodded, wise enough not to point out that both Tane

and Laylah were emotionally compromised and hardly capable of making rational decisions.

At the moment they were all emotionally compromised.

"And stay in contact."

"I will."

Tane gave a faint nod before whirling on his heel and disappearing from the room. Jaelyn followed behind him, leaving Styx alone in the barren cell.

Powerless to do anything to assist Tane in finding his son, let alone halting the return of the Dark Lord as the all-powerful Gemini, Styx turned to ram his fist into the cement wall. A shower of rubble and dust filled the air, along with his blistering curses.

"God dammit," he roared. "I'm tired of constantly being one step behind."

There was a faint stir of air before a slender woman with short, spiky, blond hair and green eyes that looked too large for her heart-shaped faced stepped into the room.

"It's not your fault, my love."

Styx instinctively reached for his tiny Were mate, pulling her into his arms and allowing her presence to ease his need for destruction. "I'm the Anasso," he said, leaning his cheek against the top of her head. "It's my duty to protect my people."

Darcy wrapped her arms around his waist. "Now is not the time to dwell on failure. We must concentrate on what comes next."

Styx's growl rumbled through the room. "Chaos comes next," he told her. "The Dark Lord has both of the children. The prophecy has been fulfilled."

She gave a click of her tongue, tilting back her head to regard him with a chiding frown. "We don't fully know what the words of the prophecy mean," she said. "But I do know that the easiest way for the Dark Lord to defeat us is for us to simply give up."

Ever the optimist, he wryly acknowledged. Which worked out just fine, considering he gave the definition of pessimist a whole new meaning. His gaze skimmed over her delicate face. This female was the light to his dark. Tenderness to his brutality.

The heart to his brawn.

Which made her a treasure beyond price. And specifically why he'd refused her request to join him.

"I thought I told you to stay at home."

She snorted at his reproach. "And you know how well I obey orders."

He brushed her lips with a rueful kiss. "Troublemaker."

"You wouldn't have it any other way."

"No," he instantly agreed, pressing her head back to his chest and returning his cheek to the top of her head. "I'm afraid, my angel."

"I know," she whispered, her hands running up and down his back in a soothing caress. "We all are."

"If we can't stop—"

"Shh," she interrupted his dark words. "We'll find a way."

"How can you be so certain?"

"We're the good guys."

His short laugh bounced off the cement walls. No one had ever called him one of the "good guys."

"I doubt you could find many who would agree with that rather prejudiced claim." Styx abruptly stiffened, lifting his head to glare at the miniature gargoyle who waddled through the door. "Get out."

Levet stuck out his tongue, as always impervious to the fact that Styx could crush him with one hand. "Is that any way to speak to a demon who is attempting to save your sausage?" the aggravating demon mocked.

Styx scowled. "What the—"

"Bacon," Darcy explained, pulling away to send a brilliant smile toward the walking, talking chunk of granite. "Save your bacon."

Styx rolled his eyes. "What do you want?"

"I picked up his scent."

"Kostas?"

"*Oui*. He used a tunnel hidden behind a spell of illusion." The gossamer wings fluttered. "A very good spell. I nearly missed it."

"I never thought I'd say this." Grudgingly, Styx pulled his sword and pointed toward the door. "Lead on."

Using his medallion to travel to the Dark Lord's prison, Gaius placed the child in the swirling mists and lowered himself to his knees. Bending his head, he waited for his presence to be noticed.

He sensed time passing, although it was impossible to judge the exact length in the strange fog, and in truth, he didn't really care. Since his last *tête-à-tête* with the Dark Lord he'd become . . . what? Not indifferent. Not even numb.

It was more a sensation of being resigned. As if the last thread of hope he'd clung to since the death of Dara had snapped, leaving him to float in a sea of defeat.

He would do as he was commanded, quite simply because he had no choice. But his fierce belief that he would soon be reunited with his mate was fading with every passing hour, leaving behind an empty void.

Eventually, he felt the crushing power that warned of the Dark Lord's steady approach. He shuddered at the sensation of his skin being flayed from his flesh, but he wisely kept his head lowered.

"Ah, Gaius." A girlish giggle sliced through the fog. "So you have learned discretion."

"Yes . . ." He struggled for a suitable title. "Mistress."

"Mistress, hmmm. I suppose that will do."

Gaius kept his head down. "I have brought you the child."

"So you have." He felt a stir of air, the punishing pain easing. "Bring him to me."

Reluctantly glancing up, Gaius discovered the Dark Lord had created a throne out of the swirling mist and was perched on it, wearing a white sundress. *Cristo*. She looked like a Homecoming Queen, not the ultimate of all evil. Then the crimson fires of hell flared in the guileless blue eyes, ruining the image of purity.

"Gaius?" she snapped with impatience. "I'm waiting."

"Yes, Mistress."

Rising to his feet, Gaius scooped the child into his arms, refusing to glance down. The baby had always been destined to be sacrificed. There was nothing he could do to alter fate, was there? Shoving the warm bundle into the female's outstretched arms, he backed away and stoically waited for her next commands.

The Dark Lord gave a lift of her brow. "Don't you intend to demand your payment?"

Gaius shrugged. "Would it do any good?"

"There's no need to pout, vampire," the lethal female chided. "You shall soon be given your just rewards."

Just rewards.

Gaius shuddered, recalling Dolf being consumed by black mist. At this moment the only reward he dared hope for was escaping the encounter without some hideous torture.

"Shall I return to my lair and await your next command?" he asked.

"Surely you want to witness my glorious resurrection as the Gemini?" The evil creature sounded truly shocked that

Gaius wasn't begging for the opportunity to bask in her transformation.

"I'm only your humble servant," Gaius reminded her. "There are others much more worthy for such a blessing."

"Why, Gaius." The blue eyes shimmered with crimson fire, the pain returning to slam him to his knees. "If I didn't know better, I might think you were anxious to leave me."

Careful, a voice whispered in the back of his mind. This female was a god. Which meant her vanity was as inflated as her powers. Just the implication that he might prefer to be somewhere else would be enough to earn him punishment.

"Not anxious, but I do need to feed."

"That can wait."

It was a command, not a suggestion. Gaius nodded in defeat. "Very well."

Confident that Gaius was playing the dutiful audience, the female turned her attention to the child squirming in her arms. Her expression was one of clinical curiosity, as if making sure there weren't any defects in her creation.

"A charming baby, don't you think?"

Gaius frowned. Was this a trick question? It was well known that children were an Achilles' heel to vampires. They instinctively refused to harm a baby of any species. Or even a pregnant female.

"Yes. Charming."

"I've never understood the fuss made over offspring. Slaves are easier to control and less inclined to be a disappointment." The Dark Lord wrinkled her nose, sniffing the baby's diaper. "They also smell better."

"Most creatures feel the urge to procreate."

The Dark Lord lifted her head, the blue eyes flickering with crimson. "Did you?"

Gaius flinched. He didn't believe in coincidences. So why was he being forced to think of Santiago yet again?

A warning?

"Yes. I have—" He halted, grimacing as he corrected his words. "I had a son."

"He's dead?"

Gaius shook his head. "No, but he's lost to me."

"Lost?" The Dark Lord frowned. "You make no sense."

"It no longer matters." Anxious to turn the conversation away from Santiago, Gaius pointed toward the baby. "What will you do with the child?"

There was a long, tense moment as the female no doubt considered the pleasure of tormenting Gaius with the loss of his son. Then, abruptly losing interest, the female instead returned her attention to the babe.

"He will become a part of me as it was always destined to be. But first . . ."

The words trailed away and Gaius stiffened. Now what? He'd captured the prophet and her protector, as well as the baby. Two impossible tasks. He'd gone beyond the call of duty, hadn't he?

It would seem not, he silently accepted as the Dark Lord sent him a frown, clearly waiting for him to react.

"Yes?"

Her dimples flashed. "A sacrifice must be made."

He hissed in sharp surprise. "Me?"

Her smile widened at his sharp flare of fear. "Are you offering?"

He grimly fought back his panic. "I doubt I would be suitable."

"Are you certain?"

"Mistress, please . . ."

"Don't worry, Gaius. As you said, you don't have the blood I need," she mocked in cruel tones, her eyes nearly consumed by flames. "Not quite so impervious to the thought of death as you wanted to believe, are you, Gaius?"

He stiffened in humiliation. It wasn't surprising the Dark Lord had sensed his growing apathy. Or that she'd managed to shatter his illusion that it no longer mattered whether he lived or died.

Bitch.

"Do you want me to return to the world and acquire what you need?" he demanded in careful tones.

"Actually, I have what I need close at hand."

Gaius glanced around the thick fog. It couldn't be too close. "Who is to be the sacrifice?"

"Caine should have destroyed the prophet by now."

"Caine? Impossible," Gaius muttered, too shocked to guard his tongue. He'd seen Caine defending the prophet. The Were had been willing to die to protect the female. Then sharp shards of pain stabbed into his body, reminding him the danger of speaking without thinking. "I mean, Caine is devoted to the prophet. He would never harm her."

"Thanks to Dolf's spell Caine wasn't in his right mind," she reminded him, a coy smile touching her lips. "And, of course, I might have encouraged his madness."

Gaius thrust aside his disbelief, instead concentrating on the more important question. "But why?" He slowly rose to his feet. "You were desperate to capture Cassandra."

The Dark Lord glanced down at the child, the air filled with a searing anger before the creature managed to regain her composure. "She proved to be a severe disappointment."

Gaius felt the hairs on his nape stand upright. Disappointment could have any number of meanings.

Maybe Cassandra refused to cooperate. Or maybe she hadn't had a vision since her capture. Or maybe the visions had been impossible to decipher.

But Gaius didn't think it was any of those things.

If the Dark Lord was willing to destroy the seer, it was because she gave a prophecy that she didn't like.

Which could only mean bad news for Gaius.

Cristo. He was growngly convinced that he would never be reunited with his mate. Now he had to face the possibility the deity who had purchased his soul was destined to fail, dragging Gaius into the pits of hell with her. "A pity," he rasped.

The Dark Lord jerked her head up, regarding him with a fiery glare. "Retrieve the dog and bring him to me."

"At once."

With a deep bow, Gaius turned to disappear in the swirling mist, following the distant scent of Were.

Chapter 17

Cassie didn't know how long she ran through the disorienting mist. Or which direction she was going. Her only thought was to try and evade Caine as he chased her with a crazed bloodlust.

At last accepting there was no place to hide and no way to shake off her pursuer, she came to a weary halt. Turning, she held up a pleading hand. "Stop."

Astonishingly the Were slowed, pacing around her as he sniffed the air, as if searching for a hidden trap. Or maybe he was savoring the scent of dinner, she wryly conceded, waiting for him to stand directly in front of her, his blue eyes glowing with the power of his wolf.

She forced herself to hold that hungry gaze, desperate to reach the man who was buried beneath the rabid animal.

"Please, Caine, listen to me," she urged softly. "You have to remember. Look deep inside, you know me."

The creature curled back his lips to expose his massive fangs, his mutated features lacking any hint of recognition.

So this was it.

The end.

Accepting that she was on the brink of death, Cassie squared her shoulders and waited for the killing blow.

A blow that never came.

Instead, Caine turned his head to glance over her shoulder, his half-formed paws lifting to expose his razor-sharp claws.

Now what? Cassie cautiously moved so she could keep an eye on Caine as well as the stirring fog behind her. Whatever was coming was enough of a threat to make Caine crouch in preparation of battle.

Then she caught the distant scent of vampire. A vampire she recognized.

Perfect.

Just freaking perfect.

There was another swirl of fog before the thick shroud parted to reveal the dark-haired leech who had brought them to this hellhole.

"Gaius," she breathed, the word a curse.

Coming to a halt, the vampire offered a small dip of his head. "Seer."

"You bastard." She fisted her hands, wishing she had the strength to rip out his unbeating heart. "This is all your fault."

A dark brow arched at the accusation. "It was Dolf's spell that turned your protector into that"—he waved a hand toward the watchful Caine—"monstrosity."

"On your command."

"Not mine," the vampire denied, his pale face oddly stripped of its previous arrogance. "And you will be happy to know that Dolf's been suitably punished." He took a step forward. "He suffered one of the most gruesome deaths I've ever witnessed."

Caine growled, his fierce gaze shifting between Cassie

and Gaius. No doubt deciding which one of them he wanted to kill first.

"Stay back," Cassie snapped, covertly angling herself to stand between Gaius and Caine.

Ridiculous, of course. One or the other was bound to kill her, but she'd be damned if she let the vampire hurt Caine.

The vampire obviously found her protective urges equally incongruous. "Isn't there a human saying about being between a rock and a hard place?" he asked with a sneer, giving a wave of his hand toward the growling Caine.

Cassie hissed as the air shimmered with a curtain of power that hung between her and the suddenly infuriated Were.

"What have you done?" she demanded, flinching as Caine charged the nearly invisible obstruction only to bounce backward with a startled snarl.

Clearly pissed off, Caine shook off his pain and attempted to break through once again. And again. And again.

Cassie pressed her hand to her lips as he crashed into the impenetrable wall over and over, his patchy fur becoming coated with blood, and his face contorted with frustration. At last, maddened by his inability to reach his prey, he tilted back his head to howl with the promise of death.

"It's a temporary barrier," Gaius said with a grimace, instinctively stepping away from the deranged beast. "It will only last a few minutes so we must speak quickly."

Cassie turned to glare at the vampire. "You have nothing to say that I want to hear."

"Don't be so certain."

Something in his icy voice made Cassie swallow her words of searing hatred, regarding him with a wary suspicion. "What do you want?"

"The Dark Lord sent me."

She rolled her eyes. Was that supposed to be a big shocker? "No doubt to kill me?" she muttered.

Gaius shrugged. "Actually, you're supposed to be dead already."

"Sorry to disappoint."

"I'm not the one you disappointed."

Cassie frowned. "I don't know what you mean."

The vampire smoothed a hand down his once elegant suit jacket now coated in dust and torn in several places. "I assume you were foolish enough to share a prophecy that annoyed the Dark Lord?"

Like she had a choice?

She hunched her shoulder. "I have no control over the visions."

"What did you see?"

"Hope."

He made a choked sound, wise enough to comprehend the power of that one word. "Ah. A dangerous viewing." An expression of aching despair touched his pale face before his frigid composure was slammed back into place. "No wonder the Dark Lord was anxious to be rid of you."

She studied the vampire with a growing confusion. What did he want from her?

A promise the Dark Lord would be successful in returning to the world? A vision of his own?

An opportunity to torment her before she was killed?

"My death won't alter the future."

"Alter? Perhaps not." He seemed to consider his words. "But it might tilt the balance."

Cassie waved aside his words. The future was in the future. She was far more concerned with the present. "Is that why the Dark Lord wants me dead?"

A humorless smile touched his lips. "The mistress doesn't

need a reason to want you dead. It's enough that you no longer serve a purpose."

True enough. So why hadn't he struck the killing blow? Was it possible his commitment to his evil mistress was fading? And if it was, why?

No. It didn't matter why. All that mattered was how she could exploit his wavering loyalty.

"And what about you?"

"Me?"

"Do you still serve a purpose?"

The lean face was closed, unreadable. "My command is to bring the Were to the Dark Lord."

Oh, gods. Cassie glanced over her shoulder at Caine, who paced with obvious agitation behind the barrier, his eyes smoldering with a mindless violence. If the Dark Lord wanted him, it couldn't be for any good reason.

"Why?"

"She has the child."

Lost in her fear for Caine, it took Cassie a second to realize the full extent of the vampire's words.

The Alpha.

It was here even after her attempt to send a warning to Styx. Did that mean all was lost?

"'*And through the mist reunited . . .*'" she quoted in numb tones.

Gaius nodded. "Precisely."

Cassie struggled not to panic. It couldn't be too late. She refused to concede defeat.

At last she forced her stiff lips to move. "She's become the Gemini?"

Gaius gave a lift of his shoulder, his gaze returning to Caine. "The ceremony will be completed once she has a suitable sacrifice."

Cassie tensed. No. No. No. Shifting until she stood directly between the vampire and Caine, she prepared to fight to the death.

There was no way in hell the Dark Lord was going to use Caine to unleash her perverted hordes on the world.

"No."

Gaius returned his attention to her, the dark gaze studying her resolute expression. "The choice is not yours."

"Maybe not, but do you think you can defeat both of us?" she bluffed.

"I'm not powerless."

She spread her legs, her body poised for attack. "Neither am I."

The vampire looked more curious than angered by her defiance. "You intend to protect him even though he just tried to kill you?"

Cassie didn't hesitate. "Of course. What would you do to protect your mate?"

That bleak despair returned to the dark eyes as Gaius seemed to be overwhelmed by some unwelcomed memory. "Sell my soul."

Cassie took a hesitant step forward, the vague hope returning at the vampire's hint of emotion. A creature who felt that deeply couldn't be completely evil.

"I'm not the only one between a rock and a hard place, am I?" she asked softly.

He stiffened, belatedly realizing that he'd revealed more than he intended. "It's too late."

"It's never too late." She took another step forward, her expression unabashedly pleading. What did she care about pride? She'd crawl on her knees and kiss the damned vampire's feet if he could use his powers to get them out of the fog. "Help us."

He gave a short, humorless laugh. "You believe I can be reformed after all these centuries?"

Did she?

Cassie grimaced. Why hadn't she honed her lying skills? It seemed every time she turned around she needed to tell one fib or another.

Now she could only shrug and hedge around the truth. "My vision offered hope. For all of us." She held out a slender hand, a sudden shiver inching down her spine. "Please."

There was a long silence and Cassie was forced to bite her tongue as the sense of urgency pulsed through her. Something was coming. Something bad.

But Gaius was skittish enough without her pressing him.

After what felt like an eternity, he at last muttered a low curse. "I am bound to regret this."

Cassie didn't have time to feel relief. Not when the heavy sense of approaching doom was thickening the air until she couldn't breathe.

"Can you get us out of here?" she rasped.

The vampire clutched the pendant hung around his neck. "Yes."

He closed his eyes, as if concentrating on his powers, at the same moment a singsong voice sliced through the air.

"Gaius." The approaching female purred, a searing heat blasting against Cassie and nearly sending her to her feet. "Where are you, you naughty vampire?"

Caine tilted back his head to howl, whether in fury or fear it was impossible to say. Gaius, on the other hand, kept his eyes tightly shut, a shaken expression on his pale face.

"*Cristo*," he muttered. "We are out of time."

"Concentrate," Cassie urged, gritting her teeth as blisters began to form on her skin and Caine whined in sudden pain.

In answer, Gaius grasped her arm in a punishing grip.

Cassie flinched before she realized that the world was beginning to fade to black.

"No . . ." She struggled to break from his grasp. "I won't leave without Caine."

Gaius scowled, refusing to release her. "Are you insane? He'll kill you. If the Dark Lord doesn't manage to do it for him."

"I don't care." She grimly yanked herself free, immediately returning to the fog and searing hot agony. "I won't leave without him."

"Stupid dogs," Gaius muttered, giving a wave of his hand.

The barrier was removed, but the pulsing heat had driven Caine to his knees, making his animal cower in pain.

Thank the gods.

Moving to crouch at his side, she held out her hand toward Gaius.

"She's coming," she warned the vampire as he appeared to hesitate.

Like he couldn't feel the jagged shards of power for himself.

Then, with a resigned shake of his head, he grasped her outstretched hand and the darkness once again began to form like a bubble around them.

In the distance, Cassie heard a shriek that nearly shattered her eardrums.

"No. What are you doing, you fool?" The fog parted to reveal the slender young female with eyes that glowed with a fiery crimson. "You will not escape me."

The darkness continued to thicken, but not swiftly enough. Cassie quivered as the female was flowing through the mists, her pretty face twisted with an unholy fury.

With a speed that was nearly too swift to follow, she was

at their side, shoving her arm into the rift that Gaius was forming and grabbing the vampire by his hair.

"Gaius," Cassie breathed in terror, feeling the bubble begin to falter.

The vampire's dark eyes widened with a bone-deep fear, but surprisingly, he gave her a shove toward the center of the rift.

"Go," he commanded.

Cassie wavered, realizing in astonishment that the vampire intended to sacrifice himself to save them.

But why? Hadn't he been the one to hunt them down, torture Caine with the cur's hideous spell, and then haul them to this mysterious dimension so he could offer them to the Dark Lord?

Why would he betray his mistress now?

The question had barely formed when it was crushed beneath a powerful vision that blasted through her mind. She groaned. The vivid image was there and gone before she could fully process it, but she did comprehend enough to know that it was a warning.

Not for her. But for the vampire who was being yanked out of the rift by the infuriated Dark Lord.

"Gaius, listen to me," she shouted over the evil deity's screams of frustration. "A face, no matter how familiar, can be a lie."

His head was bent backward, blood running down his forehead, but he managed to send her a puzzled frown. "What?"

"Don't trust your eyes."

Still regarding her with confusion, Gaius was sharply jerked out of the bubble and tossed aside. Cassie caught a glimpse of him lying in an unconscious heap before the arm was shoved back into the contracting darkness, reaching toward Caine.

"I will not be denied my sacrifice," the Dark Lord snarled.

Clearly sensing the danger, Caine growled low in his throat, his teeth bared. The female ignored the threat, grabbing Caine by the scruff of his contorted neck.

Cassie wasn't certain if the Dark Lord assumed Caine was incapable of hurting her, or if she thought she was the big-bad scary and nothing had the courage to fight back.

Whatever her logic, she grossly underestimated the level of Caine's crazy. Even as her fingers dug into his fur, the frantic Were turned his head to sink his teeth deep into her forearm.

Cassie wasn't foolish enough to believe that Caine could truly hurt the powerful creature, but he did provide a distraction. No doubt the only one they were going to get. Which meant escape was now or never.

Without giving herself time to think, Cassie rushed forward, taking full advantage of the element of surprise as she slammed her body straight into Caine.

Her intention had merely been to knock him away from the Dark Lord. After that . . . well, the truth was that she didn't really have a plan.

But her unexpected attack made Caine stumble awkwardly, his teeth ripping deep gouges in the Dark Lord's arm as he fell backward. In the same motion, he wrapped a thickly muscled arm around Cassie's waist, pulling her down with him.

There was another screech from the Dark Lord as the darkness flowed around them, sucking them through the still open rift.

Cassie groaned as Caine's claws dug into her back, but there was no breaking away from his ruthless grip as they fell through the empty space. Besides, she didn't want to get free.

For the moment they were falling farther and farther from the infuriated Dark Lord.

She didn't care where they were going.

It had to be better than where they were.

The middle of nowhere, Illinois

After running nonstop for the past two hours, Styx came to a sharp halt in the center of the narrow road, which was rapidly being overtaken by weeds. In silence, he studied the empty factory that was shrouded in shadows.

It took a minute to realize why the dilapidated building had caught his attention. There was no blinking arrow pointing to it with the words "Evil Minion Lair." Or nasty creatures peering out the shattered windows, wearing bad-guy uniforms.

Just the opposite.

At a glance, it would be easy to assume that nothing had disturbed the crumbling pile of brick and steel for years. There were no footprints, no animal droppings, not even a spiderweb.

But to Styx it was the very lack of trespassers, both human and animal, that proved there was something very powerful that lurked in the area.

"Wait, Levet," he commanded.

The stunted gargoyle came to a grudging halt, turning to glare at him with obvious impatience. "*Pourquoi?* We are finally gaining on him."

"Kostas is near."

"*Non.*" The tiny demon shook his head, pointed down the isolated road that headed toward the distant lights of St. Louis. "His trail continues into town."

Styx pointed toward the silent warehouse. "He doubled back."

Darcy moved to stand next to him, her head tilted to

the side as she studied his stubborn expression. "How can you know?"

"It's what I would do."

Levet's wings fluttered as he stomped back toward Styx. "And that is all the evidence you have?"

Styx ignored the aggravating pest, lifting his hand to bring Jagr and Jaelyn from the shadows where they were standing guard.

"Jagr, circle to the back of the building. Make sure nothing escapes."

"You got it."

The massive Goth disappeared in a blur of speed, his sword already drawn and his fangs flashing in the moonlight.

"Jaelyn."

"Yes?" The tiny Hunter stroked the stock of her sawed-off shotgun, her eyes shimmering with anticipation. She more than anyone had suffered beneath Kostas's arrogant harassment. Hell, the bastard had wanted to execute her. It was no wonder she was anxious to get her hands on the ex-Ruah.

"On the roof."

She was off with the same blinding speed as Jagr, blending into the darkness. Still Styx remained at the edge of the road, forcing himself to wait until his soldiers were in place.

Restlessly his gaze skimmed over the two-story building. The bricks had faded to a dull shade of rust with occasional rods of rebar sticking out like thorns. The roof was sagging and the window frames were rotted beyond repair. Closer at hand, the parking lot was cracked with large clumps of grass growing wild.

There was, however, a new lock on the double steel doors and the faint hint of fairy that lingered in the air. Kostas had no doubt brought dinner with him.

On the point of heading into the warehouse, Styx was halted as Levet waddled to stand directly in his path.

"What of me?"

He bit back a curse of impatience. "Keep an eye on the road. I don't want anything or anyone sneaking up on me."

"Bah." Levet's tail twitched. "My talents are wasted out here."

Styx scowled. "What talents?"

"I believe he's referring to his magic," Darcy gently reminded him, a faint smile curving her lips.

"Exactly." Levet pointed a claw toward Styx. "You are just trying to be rid of me."

"Fine." Styx folded his arms over his chest. "If you want to fight one of the most powerful vampires to walk the earth, who has not only trained for the past millennium to become the ultimate assassin, but has recently sold his soul to the Dark Lord, then you can take the lead."

"Ah." The gargoyle cleared his throat, scratching one horn as he glanced toward the deserted road. "Perhaps it would be best if I keep guard out here."

"Good choice," Styx said dryly. Then, knowing the next battle wasn't going to be so easily won, he turned to study his stubborn mate with a warning glare. "You," he growled, cupping her chin in his hand. "Stay here."

Any other creature would have fainted in sheer terror. Styx was a demon who put the bad in badass.

Darcy, of course, rose on her tiptoes and poked her finger into the center of his chest. As badass as Styx might be, he was no match for this tiny Were.

"And let you go in there alone?" Her eyes sparked with emerald embers. "No. Way."

"Darcy."

"Don't you Darcy me." Poke, poke, poke. Her finger nearly drilled a hole through his chest.

He grabbed her hand to lift it to his lips, as much to end her painful prodding as to offer her comfort. "Angel, we both know that Kostas is foaming at the mouth to get his hands on me after I demoted him."

"Which is precisely why you shouldn't be the one to confront him," she pointed out through clenched teeth. "He's obviously gone over the edge."

Styx shrugged. "He's also involved with the plot to return the Dark Lord. It's my duty to stop him."

"Hasn't he already done his part?" Darcy demanded with a scowl.

Styx growled at the unwelcomed reminder. His fangs ached for blood. Kostas's blood. The bastard had snuck into his lair and stolen the precious baby who had become as beloved to him as if he were his own son. And why? Because his bloated pride had been dented at being removed as the head of the Addonexus.

"One part. At least, that we know about," he said. "I need to know if there's more. And just as importantly, I need to know if I have more traitors among my people."

Darcy froze, their bond allowing her to fully feel the sense of unbearable failure that pulsed through him. "You think he'll confess the truth to you?" she asked softly.

"He believes he's beaten me. He's too arrogant not to boast."

"And if he doesn't?"

"I'll kill him."

She heaved a resigned sigh, her beautiful features somber as she stepped forward to lay her head over his unbeating heart.

"Be careful."

Styx pressed his lips to the top of her head, savoring the feel of her warmth seep into his chilled blood. How the hell had he ever survived without this astonishing female?

"Aren't I always?"

She harrumphed, pulling back to reveal her frown. "Being immortal doesn't mean you're immune to death."

"Don't worry, angel." He brushed his lips over her forehead. "You're not getting rid of me that easily."

"Styx," she muttered, needing to be reassured that he wouldn't allow his desire for revenge to overcome his common sense.

"I will take the greatest care, I promise," he swore, stroking another kiss over her forehead before shifting his gaze toward the hovering gargoyle. "Take care of her."

Levet gave a solemn dip of his head. "Always."

Pulling away from his mate, Styx turned to cross the empty parking lot. It was too late for a stealth approach. Thank the gods. Six-foot-five Aztec warriors didn't do sneaky. At least not very well.

Of course, they did do destruction quite well, he consoled himself, slamming his foot against the steel doors. With an ear-piercing screech the doors were wrenched off their hinges and flying across the narrow lobby.

Styx didn't hesitate. Jogging across the peeling linoleum, he ignored the doors that opened into the warehouse floor and instead headed for the stairs that led to the basement. The air was edged with a distinct chill as he descended into the darkness, and pulling his sword from its scabbard, Styx followed the thickening scent of fairy.

The traitor was near.

Pressing his back against the wall, Styx inched his way down the narrow corridor, slowly entering the room at the end.

A swift glance revealed that it was little more than a six-by-six cement box that had been stripped of everything but a long wooden table that was stained with blood.

An altar?

It would explain why Kostas had run to this location. He no doubt hoped his new mistress would protect him from Styx's wrath. Where else would he go to seek her assistance, but to the shrine where he worshipped her?

Curling his lips in disgust, Styx stepped through the doorway, briefly glancing toward the fairy who was cowering in the corner. The poor creature was shivering in obvious terror, her deep red hair hanging in tangles around her tear-stained face and her arms wrapped around her naked body. It was her wide gaze, however, that captured Styx's attention.

Following the direction where she stared in obvious terror, Styx moved to stand directly beside the altar.

"You can drop the shadows, Kostas," he commanded. "I know you're here. I smell your worthless ass."

The musty air stirred, and then the darkness in front of him faded to reveal Kostas.

Wearing a too-tight T-shirt that matched his cammo pants, the vampire gripped a large dagger in his hands. Another dagger was strapped to his waist with two guns holstered on each side of his chest. He looked like a paranoid Rambo on steroids.

With a snort, Styx move forward, his lips twisting with amusement as the large Hunter took a hasty step backward, his hands curled into tight fists. Then, realizing what he'd revealed, the vampire squared his broad shoulders and glared at Styx.

"Did your nasty little pet rock manage to lead you here?" he mocked.

Styx shrugged. "Does it matter?"

"You should be ashamed," Kostas sneered. "No self-respecting Anasso would need the talents of lesser demons to fulfill his duties. Especially not a stunted gargoyle that has been banned by his own guild. You are a disgrace to vampires."

Styx flashed his fangs. The savage desire to slash open the bastard's throat pulsed through him.

It was only the knowledge that he couldn't afford to destroy the traitor until he was convinced he didn't have any information that could help to rescue Maluhia that kept him from striking the killing blow.

Then . . . oh then, the bastard was going to become up close and personal with a whole world of hurt.

"You dare to claim that I've disgraced myself when you are one who has betrayed your own people?" he accused with frigid disdain. "And for what?" He pointed his sword toward the center of the barren room. "This?"

"You will soon discover." The dark eyes glittered with a feral hatred. "The child has been delivered and nothing can halt the return of the Dark Lord."

Styx hissed in pain despite having suspected that Maluhia was in the hands of the evil bitch. Someday very soon he intended to obliterate everyone responsible for the kidnapping. For now, however, he could only try to provoke the traitor into revealing what information he might possess.

"Then shouldn't you be out celebrating instead of lurking in this filthy basement?" he drawled.

"In good time."

"Are you sure you haven't been tossed aside now that you've served your purpose?"

Kostas's grip tightened on the dagger, but he wasn't stupid enough to try and attack. They both knew that in a fair fight Styx would kick his ass.

"I shall soon have my rewards."

"When?" Styx continued to prod. "Why the delay?"

"Do you truly believe I would be idiotic enough to reveal the Dark Lord's plans to you?" the Hunter snarled.

Styx's scornful laugh filled the room. "No, because you don't know his—" He stopped with a grimace, silently reminding himself that the Dark Lord was no longer a he. "Her plans. At least no more than any other bottom-feeder might have picked up."

Kostas puffed out his chest, but Styx sensed his taunting words had hit a nerve. The vampire wasn't nearly as confident in his new mistress as he wanted Styx to believe.

"A bottom-feeder wouldn't have been able to steal the babe from beneath your nose." He deliberately reminded Styx of his failure. "You and those Ravens who think they're better than the rest of us. Arrogant SOBs."

The vampire's jealousy of Styx and his Ravens was a tangible force in the air. Christ, it was no wonder that his festering bitterness had driven him into the service of the Dark Lord. The only surprise was that it took so long.

"But that's it, isn't it? You've been used and discarded. Not a surprise." Styx flicked a dismissive gaze down the man's stiff body, lingering on the weapons before returning to meet the dark, resentful glare. "You have always had an overly bloated opinion of your worth."

"You know nothing," the vampire blustered. "The mistress has favored me above all others."

Styx shook his head as he heard the desperation in the man's voice. He was wasting his time. This idiot was nothing but another meaningless minion that had believed the promises whispered by the Dark Lord. Pathetic.

"You're the one who knows nothing," he growled, lifting his sword. "Which means I have no reason to keep you alive."

Realizing that Styx had every intention of chopping off

his head, Kostas backed up until he hit the corner of the table. "You can't do this."

"Actually, I'm pretty sure I can. Do you want me to demonstrate?"

"No."

Styx smiled with anticipation. "It was more of a rhetorical question."

With a futile effort to halt his inevitable death, the Hunter vaulted over the table, his gaze lifted heavenward. "Hear me, blessed mistress."

Styx rolled his eyes. Idiot. "You don't actually think—"

His mocking words were interrupted as a sizzling heat seared through the room.

With a grunt of surprise, Styx gripped his sword, sensing the approach of something . . . big.

Something big and bad and evil.

Had the bastard actually managed to call the Dark Lord? It would be just his luck that of all the pathetic pleas, the treacherous bitch would choose to hear Kostas. If only to screw with Styx.

He took an instinctive step backward, warily watching the shimmering line that formed directly over the table. The long, thin streak didn't look like a portal, although he was no expert.

Actually, it looked like the air had been sliced open.

Kostas continued his crazy babble, but Styx kept his attention pinned to the wavering line. Slowly it began to widen, as if the air was being ripped open by a profound power. Gods, was this it? Was this the moment of the Dark Lord's return?

He briefly considered yelling for Jagr and Jaelyn, only to squash the impulse. What was the point until he could be certain he wasn't calling them to certain death?

The heat intensified, bringing with it the stench of burned

sulfur. Styx shuddered, but he refused to budge another step. The time to run was gone.

He would take a stand and pray for the best.

As if mocking his spurt of bravado, the heat that seared against his skin became laced with electric jolts of pain. As if he was being skewered by unseen lightning.

Holy . . . shit.

He felt like a shish kebab being grilled over an open flame.

The rift spread wider and with a low moan, Kostas fell to his knees. "Mistress, you have heard the pleas of your most loyal servant."

The stench of burning sulfur thickened, nearly making Styx gag. Kostas, however, had an expression of euphoria as a light spilled through the rip in space to spill over him.

"The sacrifice," a voice pulsed through the air, nearly driving Styx to his knees.

"What?" Kostas appeared momentarily confused. Then, his puzzled gaze shifted to the fairy who had been wise enough to faint. "Yes, of course."

Scrambling to his feet, Kostas darted across the room and scooped the limp female in his arms. Styx took a step forward, his first thought to protect the fairy from the evil that blanketed the room. But even as he moved, the blazing light flared toward him, driving him backward.

Blinded, Styx lifted his sword, hearing Kostas cross the room and the sound of the fairy being dumped on the table.

"Here," the vampire said. "My offering for you."

Styx's eyes cleared in time to see a glowing hand reach through the rift to grasp the fairy by her hair, yanking her into the black mist that swirled on the other side of the opening.

"You have served me well, Kostas." There was a low laugh that sent shards of agony shooting through Styx's brain. "A pity you shall not survive to appreciate your efforts."

"No." Belatedly realizing he was about to be abandoned by his faithless mistress, Kostas leaped onto the table, his hand reaching through the opening. "Wait."

Styx had only a moment to appreciate the sight of the once-smug vampire's groveling before the black mist boiled from the rift. In the blink of an eye the darkness was crawling over the screaming Kostas, consuming him on a cellular level.

"Christ." Styx leaped backward, watching in horror as the powerful vampire became nothing more than a stain on the table.

He half expected the mist to continue pouring into the room, destroying everything in its path. Instead, it retreated back through the opening.

Styx had a brief second of relief. Just enough time to believe he'd dodged a bullet, he wryly conceded as all hell broke loose.

Quite literally.

Even as the black mist receded, Styx caught a glimpse of a crimson-tinted landscape with black, razor-sharp rocks that were dissected by rivers of flowing lava. The opening had shifted from the Dark Lord's prison to a hell dimension— whether by accident or intent, he didn't know. All he was certain of was that a creature that looked something like a troll with a large, muscular body covered in a thick, hairless hide and a large head with beady crimson eyes and a snout with protruding fangs was crawling through the opening.

The creature smashed the table, his clenched fists the size of a sledgehammer. And no doubt they would cause as much damage if they happened to be aimed at Styx's face.

Something he didn't intend to find out.

"Jagr," he roared, his feet spread wide and his sword lifted to strike. "Jaelyn."

Chapter 18

Cassie cursed as the portal that Gaius had created abruptly collapsed, leaving them trapped in the white mist.

Although . . . She frowned, scanning the swirling fog. It didn't feel as if it were the *same* white mist. She couldn't see more than a few inches in front of her face, but the scalding pain from the Dark Lord had faded and the sense of endless space had narrowed to the sensation they were in a long corridor.

Odd.

Equally confused by their surroundings, Caine released his bruising hold on Cassie to rise to his feet with a low growl.

Swift to take advantage of his momentary distraction, Cassie scooted away, warily straightening as she considered her extremely limited options.

She could run, but Caine would swiftly catch her. And rousing his predator instincts seemed like a bad thing right now.

She could try to overpower him, but it would be a wasted effort. His strength had been increasing at an accelerated pace since he'd been turned into a Were. She would be no match for him now.

And in his current state he was beyond trying to reason with. Which left what?

She didn't have an answer, but even as Caine started to turn back toward her, the unmistakable scent of vampire filled the air.

Cassie froze, scanning the thick mist. Could it be Gaius? No. Not Gaius. But the scent was familiar.

Caine growled, preparing to attack as the mists stirred to reveal a large vampire with a black mohawk and honey brown eyes. Tane. The vampire Charon that she'd met a few weeks before. And behind him was his mate, Laylah, the tiny half-Jinn with short, spiky red hair and black eyes.

"Stop," she warned, knowing that Caine was on a razor edge. The least provocation and he would strike. "Don't come any closer."

"Harley?" Laylah asked in shock, then her eyes widened with comprehension. "No. Cassandra. And . . ." The female grimaced as she caught sight of the hulking beast nearly hidden by the fog. "Caine?"

Cassie nodded, not entirely certain whether to be relieved or concerned. The Dark Lord had already implied that there was more than one vampire willing to betray their people.

"How did you get here?"

"I'm half-Jinn. I can shadow-walk," Laylah explained. "How did you . . ."

Her words broke off in a scream as Caine suddenly charged toward Cassie, perhaps fearing that the two intruders were about to steal away his prize.

Cassie braced herself as Caine grabbed her in a punishing grip, yanking her against his chest as he howled in warning. At the same time, Cassie heard Laylah commanding her mate.

"Tane, do something."

Cassie hissed as she felt her ribs crack beneath Caine's tight grasp, but she held up a hand as Tane moved to rescue her. "Don't hurt him."

The vampire faltered in confusion. "Are you kidding me?"

She struggled to breathe. "Don't. Hurt. Him."

"Dammit." Tane stalked forward, and then with shocking speed he lifted his arm and slammed his fist into Caine's elongated jaw. The crazed Were gave a grunt of pain, and then tumbled backward as he was knocked senseless.

Cassie was thrown from Caine's arms, but swallowing her groan of pain, she crawled back to his side, her hand reaching to wipe the blood from his mutated face. "What have you done?" she breathed.

Tane folded his arms over his bare chest. He was wearing nothing more than a loose pair of khaki shorts. Well, unless you counted the humongous sword strapped to his back.

"It was that or kill him."

Logically, Cassie knew he was right. Caine might very well have squeezed her to death if the vampire hadn't interfered. But that didn't make it any easier to see Caine lying injured on the ground.

She felt a hand lightly touch her shoulder and she glanced up to discover Laylah standing next to her, an aching loss in the black eyes.

"Cassandra."

"What?"

The half-Jinn hesitated, as if afraid to ask the question hovering on her lips. "My baby," she at last breathed.

"Maluhia."

Laylah pressed a hand to her heart as her mate moved to wrap a protective arm around her shoulders. "Have you seen him?" she asked.

Cassie gave a reluctant nod. "Yes."

"Where?" Laylah's eyes filled with tears as she read the regret that was etched on Cassie's face. "The Dark Lord has him?"

"I'm afraid so."

Laylah leaned heavily against her mate, but her face hardened with a grim determination that only a mother could claim. It warned she would move heaven and earth to get her child. And kill anything that stood in her way. "I have to get to him."

Cassie bit her lip as she debated the wisdom of concealing the brutal truth from the poor woman. Then accepting it would be worse to give false hope, she slowly straightened. "The mists are impossible to penetrate without Gaius's magic necklace."

"Gaius." Tane muttered the name as if it were a curse. "Where is he?"

"The Dark Lord has him." Cassie frowned, thinking back to the vampire who had opened the portal. "He sacrificed himself so we could escape."

Tane scowled at the confession. "Why would he do that?"

"I don't know. I doubt we'll ever know." Cassie shrugged, not prepared to care what had prompted the vampire to help them. Gaius may have opened the portal, but he was responsible for Caine's hideous transformation. Not to mention, forcing them to the Dark Lord's prison. No. She didn't give a damn why he'd helped or what he might be suffering for his betrayal. "We have to get Caine to Salvatore."

Tane gave a sharp nod, turning to glance at his mate. "Laylah?"

The half-Jinn closed her eyes in concentration. "He's at Styx's lair in Chicago."

Cassie didn't take time to wonder why the King of Weres would be in the lair of the Anasso. "Can you take me there?"

Laylah gave a slow nod. "As near as possible, but I must continue my search for Maluhia."

Cassie squeezed Laylah's hand, her expression filled with sympathy. "Of course." She glanced toward Tane. "Will you help me with Caine?"

Tane moved to bend over the still unconscious Were, pausing to send Cassie a troubled glance. "Cassandra."

"No." She knew what he was going to say. He was going to tell her that Caine was beyond the point of help. That he'd been lost between the worlds of animal and human without hope of returning to either. "Don't say it."

With a grimace, the vampire grabbed Caine and tossed him over his shoulder. Then, balancing the considerable weight, he rose to his feet and nodded for Laylah to lead them through the mists.

They walked in silence for several long minutes before Tane spoke the question that had no doubt been on his mind since crossing paths with Cassie. "I don't suppose you have any clue at how we're supposed to halt the Dark Lord."

Cassie gave a helpless lift of her hand. "We must be united."

"United?"

"A wall must have no cracks."

"That's . . ." Tane struggled for the proper word. "Vague."

Laylah glanced over her shoulder with a frown. "Tane."

"I'm sorry," the powerful demon muttered. "I just hate being constantly one step behind the evil bitch."

A bitter smile touched Cassie's lips as her gaze lingered on Caine. "Knowing the future doesn't help prevent it."

Her soft assurance brought an end to the conversation and they continued through the mists without talking. None of them were in the mood for chitchat. Not when they were each desperate to save the ones they loved.

At long last Laylah came to a halt. "Here."

Cassie gave a lift of her brows. All she could see was mist and mist and more mist. Certainly, there was nothing to indicate they'd arrived at a specific location. "How can you be certain?"

"It's a feeling." Laylah wrinkled her nose. "I really can't explain how it works."

"Oh." Cassie offered an understanding smile. "I get that."

Lifting her hand, Laylah formed a doorway in the swirling fog. Cassie took a step forward, only to halt when Tane shouldered his way past her.

"Wait," he commanded. "Let me go through first."

As if she had a choice?

Cassie shared a glance of feminine exasperation with Laylah before she leaned forward to place a gentle kiss on the female's cheek. "Don't lose hope," she urged. "Sometimes it's all we have."

She stepped through the shimmering opening, giving the manicured parkland and nearby mansion a cursory glance before turning her attention to Tane as he lowered Caine to the ground.

The vampire studied the unconscious Were with a frown. "You need to get him locked up ASAP." He turned to meet her mutinous expression. "It's the only way to protect him."

"Don't worry," she promised. "I will do whatever necessary to keep him safe."

"That's my worry." He grabbed her chin to force her to meet his honey gaze. "You're the prophet. You can't put yourself at risk."

She made a sound of disgust. Right now she didn't care if she was the prophet, or that she was expected to save the world. All that mattered was that Caine was in trouble and she would sacrifice everything to help him.

"Return to your mate," she said. "She needs your strength."

"And we all need you and your gift," he persisted. "Don't do anything foolish."

She gave a weary shake of her head. "Go."

Realizing she'd made up her mind, he gave a solemn dip of his head and swiftly disappeared back through the portal.

She felt the air pressure shift as the doorway was closed, but even as she turned toward Caine there was a blast of frigid air and a pair of matching vampires stood less than a foot away.

And what a pair they were. Cassie blinked, wondering if they were a mirage. Certainly, they looked too magnificent to be real.

Identical twins, they were tall with skin polished gold by a long-forgotten sun. Their faces were chiseled perfection with features that were a gift from their Egyptian ancestors. High cheekbones that you could cut paper on. Hawkish noses. And noble brows.

Their almond black eyes were outlined in heavy kohl and their full lips were touched with color. Long, ebony hair was pulled into a braid that hung down their backs.

And their insanely beautiful bodies were covered by . . .

Good god, were those loincloths?

One of the two stepped closer, a gun in his hand. "Don't move."

Cassie held up her hands. "Please, I need to speak with the King of Weres. Is he here?"

The almond eyes widened as the vampire took a closer look at Cassie's face, belatedly realizing she had a few twins of her own.

One of which was the Queen of Vampires.

"God almighty," vampire one muttered, glancing over his shoulder at vampire two. "Get Salvatore. Now."

The warehouse

Styx had killed two of the troll-like demons and was watching a third crawl through the rift when Jagr dashed into the room. Thankfully, the opening had remained narrow enough that only one creature could crawl through at a time, but Styx was suffering from a dozen small wounds and it wouldn't take long for him to become too weakened to hold back the slow tide of evil.

"What the hell?" the vampire muttered.

Styx swung his sword at the demon's thick neck, having discovered after several futile attempts that their hearts were covered by a layer of bone armor that was impossible to penetrate.

"A rift has been opened," Styx growled, lopping off the head of the demon and kicking its body back through the opening. The things were not only ugly, but they reeked.

There was a momentary silence as the rift remained empty, although he could catch glimpses of various creatures that prowled through the hell dimension. He didn't doubt that once they discovered there was an open doorway they would eagerly try to enter this world.

Jagr moved to his side, grimacing at the gaping rip in space. "Can you close it?"

Styx snorted. If he was as omnipotent as people expected him to be, he'd be wearing a cape and leaping over tall buildings. "No. We're going to need backup." He grimaced, barely able to form the words. "Get Levet."

Jagr blinked. Then blinked again. No doubt wondering if Styx had taken a blow to the head. "I hate to question your decisions," he said cautiously, "but I don't think the gargoyle has the magic to deal with this."

"No, but my power has no doubt drained our phones," he admitted, all too familiar with his effect on modern technology. Usually, he was happy as hell to do without the constant buzz and intrusion of electronic devices, but right now he'd give his right nut for a working phone. "And he's the only one who can contact the lair so they'll send out the troops."

Jagr pulled out his phone to glance at the black screen with a grimace. "Fine. I'll have him contact Regan. She'll be able to organize things from Chicago."

Styx nodded. Regan was Jagr's mate and his own mate's sister. The female Were was proving to possess a talent for detailed organization. She'd already rearranged Jagr's massive library so a covey of harpies—who were astonishingly brilliant when they weren't in mating season—could sift through them in search of any prophecies that might have been overlooked, as well as set up safe houses for children and those too weak to protect themselves.

Jagr was torn between undiluted pride in his mate and a resigned acceptance that his life would never be the same.

There was a blast of frigid air as Jaelyn skidded into the room at the same moment a demon with jagged horns, skin the color of puce, and a long snout that made him look like a perverted anteater climbed through the rift.

"What the hell?" the female vampire hissed in shock.

"Yeah, my words exactly," Jagr muttered, stepping forward to swing his sword at the creature.

Styx motioned Jaelyn forward. "I'm going to need you, Hunter."

"Of course. I haven't had a good fight in days." She smiled, revealing her razor-sharp fangs in a smile of anticipation. "Move out of the way, Goth-boy."

Pulling out her sawed-off shotgun, Jaelyn began firing silver bullets into the creature as Jagr muttered a curse and leaped to the side.

"You're a menace," he informed his fellow vampire.

Jaelyn shrugged, kicking the demon back through the rift. "You should see me when I'm pissed off."

Both men shuddered. Jaelyn pissed off was a sight neither wanted to experience.

Then, as there was the sound of nearing growls through the rift, Jagr turned to head for the door. "I'll return as soon as Levet has contacted Regan."

"Jagr," Styx called out.

"Yes?"

"Have Salvatore send some of his Weres, but tell him to remain at my lair. This could be yet another distraction."

Jagr nodded. "Is that all?"

"Make sure my mate returns to Chicago."

The large vampire snorted as he continued out the door. "I'm not a miracle worker."

Styx grimaced. He knew better than to hope his mate would return to the safety of his lair. But then, he wouldn't leave her behind. Why should he expect anything different from her?

Poised for attack, Jaelyn glanced over her shoulder. "Did Kostas create this?"

"No." Styx's expression was grim. "The Dark Lord."

"Shit." The blue eyes darkened as she instantly comprehended the danger. "The ceremony has been completed?"

"I'm sure it has by now." His jaw tightened beneath the tide of frustrated fury. "She has the child as well as a sacrifice."

Unexpectedly, Jaelyn frowned. "But she hasn't come through?"

"Not yet." He was struck by a sudden, hideous thought. "Or at least not here."

"You think there's other rifts?"

"'*Pathways that have been hidden will be found and the Veil parted to the faithful,*'" he quoted in harsh tones.

"Oh hell." Jaelyn glanced toward the swarms of distant shapes that crawled on the other side of the opening. "That can't be good."

No it wasn't good.

In fact, things were going in the toilet at hyperspeed.

And all he could do was try and hold back the tidal wave of disaster. Like Hans Brinker sticking his finger in the dyke.

"We have to get the warning out."

The Dark Lord's prison

Gaius remained on his knees, his head pressed to the ground, which was cloaked by white. He'd been in the same position since his abortive attempt to flee with the prophet, simply waiting for the torture to begin.

Why fight the inevitable? He'd rolled the dice and lost. Now it was time to pay his debts.

Barely aware of the passing time, he remained kneeling, praying for a swift, painless death even as he accepted it was going to be slow and bloody and quite likely to stretch over centuries, if not longer.

After what might have been minutes or an eternity, the punishing pain that warned of the Dark Lord's approach slammed into him.

"Ah, my faithless Gaius," she purred, her low voice nearly peeling the skin off his flesh.

His teeth clenched in agony. "Mistress."

Without warning, he was grasped by his hair and yanked to his feet.

"Do you think that groveling will save you?" the Dark Lord demanded, her eyes smoldering with crimson fire.

He hung loosely in the painful grip, his gaze shifting to the unconscious fairy that the Dark Lord had dropped at her feet.

How . . . odd.

The powerful bitch gave him a violent shake, reminding Gaius that he hadn't answered her question.

"No, Mistress."

"Ah." Fingers grasped his chin, forcing his head up to meet the fiery glare. "So you are pretending to be resigned to your fate."

Her gaze blazed through him like a blowtorch, making Gaius flinch despite his numbing sense of defeat.

"As you say."

"Don't be such a . . ." The burning eyes returned to blue as the Dark Lord considered her words. "What is the saying? A wet blanket?"

With a casual flick of her hand she sent Gaius flying backward. He landed awkwardly on his side, breaking at least two ribs, but with an effort he forced himself to his feet and walked back to stand before her.

"Forgive me, Mistress."

She sniffed, not entirely pacified. "Certainly you shall be punished for your betrayal, but for now you're in for a special treat."

He hid his shudder. The Dark Lord's idea of a "special treat" would make any sane man cringe in horror.

"Am I?"

"Yes, I have my sacrifice." Reaching down, the Dark Lord grabbed the fairy by the throat and dangled her like a trophy. "Isn't she a beauty?"

"Very beautiful," he dutifully agreed, despite the fact the poor fairy looked like she'd been pulled out of a cesspit.

"I do wish she was awake," the Dark Lord pouted. "Sacrifices are so much more fun when they scream, don't you think?"

Gaius grimaced, the unwelcomed reminder of his twisted pleasure in causing females pain slicing through him. He tried to tell himself that it had been his driving sense of guilt at betraying his mate, even if she was dead, that had caused the violence. And that he'd always known deep inside him that he was allowing himself to drown in the evil temptation the Dark Lord offered because it was the only way to ignore his faltering sense of honor.

But there was no excuse.

None.

"I do," he admitted bleakly.

The blue eyes narrowed as the Dark Lord easily sensed his pulsing regret. "Really, Gaius, you have proven to be a serious disappointment," she snapped, her power slashing against Gaius like a thousand knives. Only when blood was dripping from his wounds and his knees barely capable of holding him upright did she return her attention to the fairy dangling from her hand. "But no matter. Soon enough I shall be able to have my pick of worshippers."

Thank the gods, Gaius silently celebrated. The sooner the bitch had her worshippers, the sooner she would put an end to his misery.

Then his dark thoughts were interrupted by the unmistakable scent of vampire. Testing the air, he realized the odor was coming from the fairy.

"She smells of Kostas," he muttered in confusion.

"Yes." The female deity smiled with a cruel satisfaction. "He was kind enough to have her waiting at his altar."

"And Kostas?" He glanced over her shoulder, seeing nothing but swirling fog. "Is he here?"

"Of course not. He used his talents to kidnap the child.

He was no longer needed." The Dark Lord frowned at Gaius's sharp burst of laughter. "What is so funny?"

Gaius shook his head, unable to mourn the arrogant vampire. He'd warned the bastard, hadn't he? "Nothing."

The Dark Lord stabbed him with a suspicious glare before giving a wave of her hand to part the mists, revealing the baby she'd left hidden.

"Bring me the child," she commanded.

Reluctantly, Gaius moved to scoop Maluhia into his arms, a strange ache in the center of his chest as he gazed down at the wide blue eyes.

Innocent. So horribly innocent.

"He's awake," he said, his voice unsteady. A warning prickle of heat crawled over his skin.

"Don't even think of doing anything foolish."

Gaius's lips twisted. He'd already tried foolish. What else did you call helping the prophet and her protector to escape?

It didn't work out any better than his blind faith in evil.

"I've accepted my destiny," he assured his companion, crossing to stand directly before her.

"As have I," the Dark Lord murmured, bending the fairy over her arm and casually ripping out her throat. She chuckled in gruesome pleasure as the blood gushed over both of them, her eyes once again filled with crimson fire. "And it is to be glorious."

Gaius stumbled backward as the Dark Lord dropped the dead fairy and reached to take the baby into her arms, the mists abruptly thickening around her.

A suffocating power crackled through the fog and Gaius groaned. *Cristo*, the very air was crushing him beneath its force.

He considered fleeing, but where would he go? And what would happen when the Dark Lord came looking for him?

He'd earned enough punishment for one lifetime.

Besides, if he stayed close enough, maybe the backlash of her transformation would rip him apart. Not a bad way to go, all things considered.

The defeatist thought had barely been formed when there was the sensation of trembling beneath his feet. He frowned, glancing down. What was that? An earthquake? A tsunami?

Or was the very fabric of the world about to be split apart?

At this point, nothing would surprise him.

Or at least, that's what he was arrogant enough to assume.

Until a blinding flash of light pierced through the fog surrounding the Dark Lord.

Gaius hissed, throwing up his arm to protect his eyes. It was like being in the middle of a nuclear blast. No, worse, he corrected as an abrupt wind seared past him, melting his flesh from his bones.

He was being cooked alive with no promise of death.

Sinking to his knees as the ground beneath his feet heaved and rolled with a growing violence, Gaius screamed until he had no voice left.

And still the brutal wind continued to pummel him, stripping him to his very bones as a female laugh echoed in the distance.

"Tremble before me."

Chapter 19

Outside Styx's lair in Chicago

Cassie kneeled beside Caine, keeping guard despite the knowledge she would be no match against the powerful vampires and Weres and a dozen other demons she could sense in the massive brick home.

A fact that was only reinforced as a male Were crossed the manicured lawn with long strides, the glow of his golden eyes visible even from a distance. She shuddered, her muscles rigid with shock.

Holy crap. The very air sizzled with his power. The kind of power only a king could command.

She instinctively moved to stand between Caine and the approaching intruder, something in her expression making him halt a few feet away, his hand lifted in a gesture of peace.

"Cassandra?"

She allowed her gaze to skim over the lean, hard body that was emphasized by the tailored pinstripe suit before rising to the handsome face. With his dark hair slicked back into a neat tail, and his bronzed skin recently shaved, he should have looked like a civilized businessman.

Instead he looked . . . lethal.

A predator that would kill without mercy.

"You're Salvatore?" she demanded, her voice husky with weariness.

"Yes." He lowered his hand. "May I approach?"

She hesitated. She hadn't forgotten that not so long ago Salvatore and Caine had been mortal enemies. Or that the king had sworn to have Caine's head on a platter.

But what choice did she have?

She didn't know precisely what had been done to Caine, but she did know their best hope was Salvatore. Only a king could call back a Were once they'd gone feral. It had something to do with their connection to the pack.

If anyone could reach Caine, it would be this man.

Hesitantly she moved back, glancing toward the Were who lay unconscious on the ground, his mutilated body bathed in moonlight.

"Caine's been hurt."

"So I see," he said gently, moving to study Caine. "Was it a spell?"

"Yes."

"Do you know who cast it?"

"A cur named Dolf."

His golden gaze snapped in her direction, the scent of his wolf thick in the air "The cur traveling with Gaius?" He muttered a curse at her nod. "Bastard. Do you know where he is now?"

She didn't have time to wonder how the king knew about Dolf. "Dead."

"You're certain?"

"That's what Gaius claimed." She frowned at the urgency in his tone. "Why?"

He schooled his features into an unreadable mask. "It's always easier for the caster to remove the spell."

She heaved a frustrated sigh. She had celebrated the thought of Dolf's painful demise and now it seemed he was the one person she needed alive.

Such perfect irony.

"You can help him, can't you?"

"I . . ." Salvatore abruptly cut off his words as Caine shifted on the ground, clearly starting to shake off Tane's savage punch. "We need to get him inside."

Cassie leaped forward to place a restraining hand on Salvatore's arm. "Wait."

The king frowned, clearly unaccustomed to having his decisions challenged.

Typical alpha.

"We don't have much time before he wakes."

"I need your promise that you won't hurt him."

He held her steady gaze, his expression hardening. "You know I can't make that promise, Cassandra." He held up a hand to halt her impulsive words. "But I do swear that I will do everything in my power to call him back."

She scowled at his bleak promise. "That's not good enough."

"It's all I have."

Before she could continue the argument, Salvatore bent down to grasp Caine around the waist. Then, with an impressive display of raw strength, he had the still-unconscious Were slung over one broad shoulder and was heading toward the looming mansion.

"Crap," Cassie breathed, forced to concede defeat as she rushed to catch up to his long strides.

She had no choice but to trust that Salvatore would do everything possible to rescue Caine from his feral madness. And if he couldn't . . . She grimly squared her shoulders. She would make sure that Caine was protected.

She kept that thought in the forefront of her mind as they reached the mansion and the matching Pharaoh twins appeared to open the French doors.

They passed through a sitting room with a blue and silver decor and she had a brief impression of delicately carved furniture along with a large crystal chandelier that was reflected in ornately framed mirrors before they were entering a long marble hallway that held an unmistakable scent of female Weres.

"Are my sisters here?"

"Darcy is currently with Styx, but Harley and Regan are here." Salvatore sent her a searching gaze. "They're anxious to meet you."

Cassie understood their desire. She truly did. There was a part of her that would never be complete until she was reunited with her twins.

But there was another part, a weak, cowardly part, that wasn't prepared for the emotional meeting.

"Perhaps after Caine is recovered," she hedged.

Salvatore shifted Caine on his shoulder as they passed by Grecian statues set in shallow alcoves and high, arched windows that overlooked the vast parkland.

"There's no need to be afraid," he assured her. "They already love you."

She hunched a defensive shoulder. They might love her, but would they be able to accept her?

She wasn't . . . normal. Okay, with Caine's constant encouragement she was becoming more comfortable with the baffling rules of society. But she would never be able to easily mix with others. Not when she was plagued by her visions.

Besides, being a seer was a dangerous business. She'd

been hunted from the day she was born. She would never willingly place her family in such constant danger.

"I've been alone a very long time," she said, her gaze lingering on Caine's limp body, her heart twisting with a savage fear. "Until Caine."

Salvatore nodded, almost as if he understood. "Caine found you in the caves?"

"He did more than find me," she corrected. "He gave his life to rescue me from the demon lord."

A dark brow arched. "So he truly did die?"

She gave a somber nod. How many times would Caine be forced to suffer for her?

"Yes."

As if sensing her surge of raw regret, Salvatore reached out to lightly touch her cheek, his power a soothing force as it flowed through her.

"I'm going to take good care of him, *cara*, I promise."

She gave a small nod, but before she could respond there was the unmistakable sound of running footsteps and, with a dizzying speed, two female Weres pounced out of a side hallway and wrapped her in a fierce embrace.

"I'm Harley," one of the females said, her heart-shaped face as delicately carved as Cassie's but with large hazel eyes that were thickly lashed. Her golden blond hair was left free to tumble down her shoulders and her petite frame covered by a loose kimono that hinted at her growing baby bump.

"And I'm Regan." The other claimed Cassie's attention. She looked remarkably similar to Harley, except her golden blond hair was longer and pulled into a tight braid and her eyes were more green than hazel. She was casually dressed in a stretchy T-shirt and yoga pants, and there was a sheen of sweat on her delicate face, as if she'd been in the middle of exercising.

The two were laughing and crying at the same time as they bombarded a dazed Cassie with overlapping questions.

"How did you get here?"

"Are you hungry?"

"How long will you stay?"

"What about a shower? Do you need—"

"Wait." Cassie battled her way free of the clinging arms, her focus trained on Salvatore as he attempted to slip away unnoticed. "Where are you taking him?"

Busted, Salvatore had no choice but to halt and meet her suspicious glare. "I have to get him locked in a room before he wakes up."

"Fine." She planted her hands on her hips. "I want to be with him."

"No."

Moving to his side, Harley sent her mate a chiding frown. "Salvatore."

The king heaved a rasping sigh, his golden gaze remaining trained on Cassie. "I'll try to use my powers as king to connect with Caine, but since he's never truly been a part of a pack I don't know if I can control him."

"And if you can't?" Cassie pressed.

"My methods will have to become . . ." He broke off with a grimace.

Cassie tilted her chin. "Tell me."

"Messier."

She sucked in a sharp breath. She wasn't stupid. Messier meant bloodier. "No. Absolutely not."

The golden eyes flared with a drowning power. "Do you want him back or not?"

"Please, Cassandra," Harley softly pleaded. "You can trust Salvatore. I swear that Caine is in good hands."

Cassie reached out a helpless hand, her heart breaking. "He needs me."

Harley wrapped an arm around her shoulders while Regan wrapped another around her waist.

"And you'll be there for him once he's conscious," Regan assured her.

"But . . ."

"What would Caine want you to do, Cassandra?" Salvatore overrode her in stern tones. "Watch him while he is at his weakest or go with your sisters and regain your strength?"

Her jaw clenched at his devious cunning. They all knew precisely what Caine would want and Salvatore was using that knowledge as a weapon against her. Unfortunately, his Machiavellian tactics worked.

"Fine," she grudgingly muttered. "I will give you until dawn. Not a minute longer."

The golden eyes narrowed, but before Salvatore could remind her that he was not only her brother-in-law, but her king as well, her sisters were herding her down the marble staircase.

"Come with us," Harley muttered.

The Dark Lord's prison

Gaius assumed his prayer that the merciless light and heat would put an end to his misery had been miraculously answered.

He had, after all, been burned to a crisp. Quite literally.

Not even a vampire could come back from such utter ruin.

But like a damned Phoenix rising from the ashes, his body began to regenerate, the slow process nearly as painful as the original destruction.

Merda.

Would this never end?

It seemed not, he decided, rolling onto his back and at last forcing open his newly healed eyes.

Only to see . . . what?

Baffled, he studied the sickly yellow sky spread above him. Where were the choking white mists that had surrounded him? The impenetrable fog?

Had he actually died and resurrected in a hell dimension?

The vague hope lasted only long enough for a massive power to smash into him, the scent of burning sulfur filling the air.

"Gaius, rise," an all-too-familiar voice commanded.

He didn't try and fight the compulsion to push himself to his feet. Why bother? If he didn't do as he was ordered, then he'd be forced to obey.

In the most painful way possible.

Still weakened from his intimate brush with death and the effort of regenerating, it took Gaius several tries before he was able to stand upright. Once certain his knees would hold his weight, he took a brief glance around, astonished by the dramatic change to his surroundings.

With the mists seared away, presumably by the same nuclear energy that had melted him into a puddle of goo, the landscape was revealed in all its bleak glory. Drenched in the same sickly yellow as the sky, the flat ground stretched toward the distant horizon, occasionally dotted with the skeletal remains of dead trees and small pools of noxious water.

He shuddered. Not long ago he would have sworn that nothing could be worse than the nasty fog.

Yet another example of "being careful what you wish for," he wryly accepted.

Speaking of which . . .

Unable to put off the inevitable any longer, Gaius at last turned his reluctant gaze toward the source of the pulsing power that seemed to be strengthening with every passing moment.

He wasn't sure what he expected. A column of pure, searing light. Or a towering ten-foot monster with massive fangs. Perhaps a creature beyond his comprehension.

Instead, he discovered that the delicate female body remained, currently covered by a black satin robe, as did the long, raven hair that floated on the faint breeze and the guileless blue eyes that held hints of crimson fire.

It was only when the Dark Lord took a step forward that he realized there was a translucent outline that flickered around the human form. He frowned, studying the odd halo. The head looked vaguely like a lion, although larger and far more terrifying than the real beast. And the body was a muscular human shape that was neither male nor female.

Was that the Gemini?

And if it was, why was it still no more than a shadow?

The questions were driven from his mind as the Dark Lord lifted a hand and her blistering power wrapped around him.

He clenched his teeth against the pain. "Mistress."

"Come forward."

The voice rang through the air like a massive bell, sending his feet moving forward. "I am your servant," he muttered, shuddering beneath the force of her coercion.

He was a puppet.

A weak, spineless puppet.

"Yes, you are." To emphasize his defeatist thoughts, the Dark Lord ran a mocking glance down his naked body before reaching out to wrap her fingers around his neck. "Pretty, pretty leech. What shall we do first?"

"You promised to return my mate."

Nails sliced into his flesh as the flickering lion's head briefly merged with the pretty female face. "You are so eager to join your mate?"

Gaius shuddered. He had no desire to be around when that hovering specter joined its power with the Dark Lord.

"Yes."

"No." A petulant expression settled on the deity's pretty features. She didn't like that Gaius wasn't eager to play the devoted worshipper. "Not yet."

"What do you want from me?" he managed to choke out.

There was a long pause, as if his captor was inwardly weighing the pleasure of ripping out his throat against her mysterious need of him.

At last he was shoved away and the Dark Lord smoothed a hand down her robe, turning it to a pale shade of peach. The color emphasized the absurd innocence of her youthful appearance even as the strange shadow loomed behind her in a silent threat.

"For now, you will offer me your military expertise."

Gaius blinked. His military expertise? Was this yet another trick?

"You intend to lead an army into battle?" he demanded.

The female smiled with cruel anticipation. "No, but I do intend to release my hordes on the world."

Gaius stilled, his mind racing. It wasn't that he gave a damn what happened once the Dark Lord unleashed her minions. Hadn't he turned his back on the world that had allowed the brutal death of his beloved mate? No, of course he didn't care. But after being deceived and manipulated by this evil bitch, he wasn't opposed to witnessing her downfall.

Or even helping it along.

"You don't need a general to release hordes," he pointed out in cautious tones.

She shrugged. "I want to be certain they are released where they can cause the most harm. The sooner they deal with my enemies, the sooner I can make my return."

"Why wait?" Gaius lifted his brows. "Surely you want

the satisfaction of personally destroying those who stood in your path?"

"It would certainly be pleasurable to witness the slaughter," the Dark Lord admitted, "but I'm not foolish enough to take the risk." The blue eyes narrowed with suspicion. "And as my devoted worshipper, I'm disappointed you would not be more concerned for my safety."

"Safety?" Gaius pretended confusion. "Aren't you omnipotent now that you've become the Gemini?"

Something that might have been frustration rippled over the delicate features. "My powers are still . . . fluid."

Gaius's gaze shifted to the flickering outline of the beast. "I don't understand. Didn't the transformation work?"

Crimson fire consumed the blue eyes as the Dark Lord's power wrapped around Gaius with a punishing grip.

"Focus your energy on finding the quickest path to victory, Gaius, unless you desire to find out firsthand the extent of my transformation."

Styx's lair in Chicago

Cassie had a fuzzy impression of being led into an enormous dining room with wood-paneled walls and then being seated at a table long enough to accommodate an entire clan of ogres. She ate what was put in front of her and answered the endless stream of questions without being conscious of the words leaving her lips.

Distantly, she was aware when Regan was abruptly called from the room, her cell phone pressed to her ear and servants scurrying around her as she barked out a series of orders. And then again when she returned to the room to whisper in Harley's ear. There was even a part of her mind that understood something had happened, no doubt something to do with the Dark Lord, but she could concentrate on nothing but the thought of Caine and the relentlessly slow passing of minutes.

How long had Salvatore been with him?

She glanced toward the clock on the ornately carved sideboard. Two hours? Three? Surely long enough for the king to have discovered whether or not his powers were enough to return Caine to his humanity?

At last reaching the end of her patience, Cassie was at the point of demanding that her sisters take her to Caine when the scent of approaching Were had her rising to her feet and turning toward the door.

Her heart sank at the sight of Salvatore's weary expression as he beckoned for his mate to join him.

"Excuse me," Harley murmured, pausing to give Cassie a sympathetic hug before hurrying across the room.

Cassie took a step forward. "What's happened?"

"We'll speak later, Cassandra," Salvatore promised, wrapping his arm around Harley's shoulders and tugging her into the hallway.

"Wait."

She was heading toward the door when Regan abruptly stepped in her path, grasping her shoulders with a grip that warned she wasn't going to let Cassie pass. Not without a fight.

"Cassandra, I'm sure he'll come speak with you when he's ready."

Cassie's brows snapped together. Logically, she didn't doubt that her sister was simply attempting to help. The two female Weres had fussed and fluttered about her with an obvious devotion.

But at the moment Cassie was in no mood to be logical.

Nothing was going to keep her from finding Caine. Not even the love of a sister.

Meeting Regan's wary gaze, Cassie dismissed her instinctive urge to simply thrust her sister out of her way. Even if she could match her sister's strength, something that wasn't at all certain, she wouldn't get out of the room before Regan could have half a dozen servants running to help her.

No. If she wanted to be with Caine, she would have to get rid of her family first.

Which meant managing to tell a convincing lie.

She used her heavy sigh to her advantage, allowing her shoulders to wilt and her head to lower, as if in resignation. "Yes, I suppose you're right."

"Cassandra, it really is for the best—" Regan's reassuring words were abruptly interrupted by the buzz of her cell phone. Releasing her grip on Cassie, she pulled the phone from her pocket to read the name flashing across the screen. "Shoot."

"What is it?"

"Jagr, just returned," Regan said, speaking of her mate. "I need to update him."

Ah. Saved by the bell. Or rather the buzzer. Cassie, however, was careful to keep her expression resigned. "Go, Regan. I'll be fine."

"Are you certain?" Her sister bit her bottom lip in a gesture that was endearingly similar to Cassie's own habit. "I hate to leave you on your own."

Cassie refused to acknowledge the stab of guilt as she managed a stiff smile. "Don't worry. I'm dead on my feet," she assured Regan. "I think I'll try to get a little sleep."

The phone buzzed again and Regan gave a grudging nod. "There are plenty of empty bedrooms upstairs. Take one that you want." She headed slowly toward the door, clearly torn between her duty to her mate and her newly discovered sister. "You'll come find me if you need me?"

"Yes, of course."

Watching her sister disappear through the door, Cassie forced herself to count to one hundred. Only when she was certain Regan wasn't going to pop back into the room did she make her way to the marble hallway and slip silently through the shadows.

She didn't like the feeling she was sneaking behind her sisters' backs, but what choice had they given her? All right, maybe they thought they were protecting her, but they didn't understand. She *had* to be with Caine. It was a ruthless, driving force that was making her stomach clench and a cold sweat break out on her skin.

He needed her.

She knew it to the very depths of her soul.

Tracing Salvatore's scent, she followed it to a narrow staircase that led down to the basement level. Her foot was on the top step when she heard the sound of Salvatore's voice coming from the ceiling.

What the heck?

She glanced up, at last spotting the vent hidden in the ceiling.

Obviously, the king and Harley were in a room above her, unaware that their conversation could be overheard.

"So there's no hope?" Harley was softly demanding.

"I'm afraid not," Salvatore said, unaware his bleak words were slicing through Cassie with a savage pain. "He's too far gone."

Harley made a sound of distress. "What if we call for a witch? If the spell could be removed, then maybe you could reach him."

She heard Salvatore heave a harsh sigh. "There's nothing left of the spell."

Cassie frowned as Harley asked the question that was on her own lips.

"How's that possible?"

"Cassandra said that the cur who cast the spell is dead. I would guess the spell died with him."

"Salvatore, we have to do something," Harley pleaded.

"He needs to be put out of his misery."

Cassie slapped a hand over her mouth to hold back her shattered cry of denial at Salvatore's ruthless confession. What did it matter what the king wanted? There wasn't a chance in hell that she was going to let anyone hurt Caine.

Not now. Not ever.

"No," Harley said, her voice shaky.

"I don't intend to make a decision tonight," Salvatore assured his mate, although Cassie didn't miss the grim edge in his voice. He would do what he thought best for his people. Even if it meant destroying a feral Were. "There are too many other pressing concerns."

"True," Harley grudgingly conceded. "Styx and Jagr have returned."

"I must speak with them."

"What should I tell Cassandra?"

"Nothing tonight," Salvatore said in weary tones. "Let her have a few hours of rest. We'll break the news in the morning."

Harley sniffed, as if she were trying to hold back tears. "This is going to destroy her."

"Not if she has us to give her the support she needs," Salvatore comforted his distraught mate. "Are you coming with me?"

"Yes, I need to warn Darcy what's happened."

Chapter 20

It took Cassie several deep breaths before she could force her shaky legs to continue down the stairs.

She had no intention of accepting defeat, no matter what the king might say, but she couldn't deny a piercing sense of disappointment. She'd desperately hoped that Salvatore could force his way through Caine's feral insanity. To reach the man, or even the wolf, beneath the madness.

Now she had no one to depend on except herself.

Not a particularly reassuring thought.

Reaching the bottom of the stairs, she was forced to a halt, not surprised by the confusing maze of cement tunnels that sprawled beneath the vast estate. The lair belonged to the King of Vampires. The only surprising thing would be if there weren't a hundred passageways for Styx's sun-challenged clan to travel around Chicago.

A tiny chill inched down her spine. Gods, but she hated being below ground.

Even with the high ceilings that were lined with fluorescent lights and the well-ventilated air, the tunnels were enough to make her have flashbacks to those long, dark years she'd been trapped in the demon lord's lair.

She needed Caine, she acknowledged with a smile of pure irony. If he were with her, she wouldn't be afraid.

He was her courage.

Reminding herself that she was wasting precious time, Cassie squared her shoulders and followed Caine's fading scent down the nearest tunnel.

She was forced to double back twice when she caught the scent of an approaching vamp, but at last she reached the narrow passage that led to Caine's cell. Her steps were halted, however, by the distinct scent of granite that teased at her nose.

Granite?

She slowly turned, her brows rising at the sight of the tiny gargoyle who waddled around the corner, his wings shimmering in a dazzling display of crimson and blue with veins of gold.

"*Ma chérie?* Where are you going?"

Cassie frowned; then the brief memory of seeing the small creature in the company of Tane and Jaelyn several weeks before teased at the edge of her mind. "Oh. I remember you."

"Levet." The gargoyle performed a deep bow. "At your service."

At any other time, Cassie might have been charmed by the odd little creature. Right now, she just wanted him gone. "I'm sorry, I don't mean to be rude, but I don't have time now."

Turning back to the passageway, she cautiously made her way down the cement floor, trying to ignore the gargoyle, who hurried to keep pace at her side.

"I received your message," he said, his voice carrying a lilting French accent.

"My message?" Cassie furrowed her brow before she abruptly recalled her futile attempt to send the warning that Maluhia was in danger. "Oh. It wasn't enough." She grimaced, her gaze trained on the heavy metal door at the end of the hall. "It's never enough."

"We are all simply trying to do our best in very difficult circumstances," Levet assured her.

"Yes," she muttered in distracted tones, far more concerned with the imposing door and whether or not it was locked. "I suppose."

There were a few seconds of blessed silence before the gargoyle was tugging on the hem of her new khaki shorts, which Regan had insisted she borrow along with a jade green shirt.

"Darcy is here."

She heaved a sigh, her steps never slowing. "So I heard."

"I am certain she would desire an opportunity to meet you."

"Later."

With a flutter of his wings, Levet moved to stand directly in her path, a worried expression on his ugly little features. "I really think it would be better if you went now."

Forced to halt, she glared at her unwanted companion. Had he been sent by one of her sisters? She couldn't imagine the arrogant Salvatore depending on this demon to guard his prisoners.

"Please, Levet," she pleaded in husky tones. "Just leave me alone."

He lifted his hands in a helpless motion, his long tail twitching. "I cannot."

"Why?"

"I've seen that expression before." He pointed toward her face. "On warriors."

She blinked in confusion. Was that one of those things she was supposed to understand? She instinctively turned her head, knowing that Caine would know, only to have her heart miss a painful beat. She pressed a hand to the aching void in the center of her chest.

"I don't know what you mean."

"You look like you're marching into a battle you don't intend to survive."

Oh. She flinched at his shocking perception. Was he an empath? She'd never heard that was a talent of gargoyles, but then Levet was obviously not the usual run-of-the-mill sort of gargoyle.

Wary of what other powers he might possess, she cautiously considered her words. "I'm no warrior."

"*Non*, you are the prophet. *Our* prophet," he insisted, the gray eyes holding a hint of chastisement. "And we need you."

She continued to rub her chest, the emptiness becoming a physical pain. "I can't do this without Caine."

"But, *ma chérie*, sacrificing yourself will not bring him back."

"I have to try," she stubbornly insisted. Why couldn't people understand that Caine was as essential to her as her visions were to the world? Besides, she'd already shared what little information she had of the future. A wall could hold back chaos. They had to be united. Blah, blah, blah. What more did they . . . United. Her breath tangled in her throat. "Oh my God."

Levet took a step forward, his scent of concern drenching the air. "Cassandra?"

"We must be united," she breathed.

"I agree," the gargoyle said, watching her with a suspicious frown. "This is a time we must all stand together. Which is why I cannot allow you to do this."

A slow, determined smile curved her lips. "I'm sorry, but nothing is going to stop me."

"Cassandra." He grasped her shorts as she stepped past him. "Cassie, wait." His claws scraped against the cement as she forged a path to the door, dragging him along. Two steps from the door he lost his grip and she heard him muttering in frustration as he headed in the opposite direction. "*Sacre-bleu*, where is that mangy dog when I have need of him?"

Cassie ignored the retreating demon, reaching out to turn the handle of the door. Stark relief blazed through her as it swung inward, although she didn't doubt that once it slammed shut behind her it wouldn't be nearly so easy to open.

Not that she cared. She knew once she entered the room there was only one way she was getting out.

Taking a cautious step forward, Cassie allowed her gaze to inspect the barren cell, which was lined in lead. Heavy silver shackles hung from the low ceiling and there was a drain in the center of the floor that she assumed was to get rid of the blood.

Salvatore's words whispered in the back of her mind. . . . Messier.

She swallowed her urge to cry. She couldn't think about what Caine had been forced to endure. What she had allowed him to endure in the hopes of saving him, she reminded herself with a stab of self-disgust.

The future was all that mattered. Their future together.

Gathering her courage, she turned her gaze to the large, twisted body that lay in a corner, the fur caked with dried blood and his ankles seared by the silver manacles around them.

Her heart twisted, but with a fierce resolve she moved to crouch at his side. Reaching out, she laid her hand on his neck, reassured by the steady beat of his heart even as a frown touched her brow.

She knew what she wanted—no *needed*—to do. But she didn't have a damned clue how to go about it. And for once, she couldn't blame her years of isolation for her lack of knowledge.

True matings between purebloaded Weres had become nothing more than a distant legend until Salvatore had driven the demon lord back to his hell.

Now she could only hope that the primitive instincts that had been buried deep inside her would take over and complete the mating ceremony that had begun the moment Caine had rescued her.

Or at least it had begun for her, she was forced to concede.

She had no actual proof that Caine felt the same connection.

In fact, it was just the opposite.

What little she read of the ancient matings said that they usually drained the power of the males. The theory was that the female would always have the last say on whether or not to complete the mating. But Caine's strength had been steadily increasing.

Of course, he wasn't a traditional pureblood and his powers had been fluctuating since he'd been transformed from a cur to a Were, she hastily reassured herself.

Oh, and he hadn't yet marked her with his musk. Wasn't that a part of the whole mating thing?

Damn.

Refusing to consider failure, she closed her eyes and concentrated on her connection to Caine. Or at least on the painful void in the center of her heart where she'd come to depend on feeling his presence.

It was still there, she grimly assured herself. Just . . . muted. As if his current transformation was suppressing the signal.

For long, stressful minutes she focused everything she had on the tenuous bond. He was there, she could feel him, but every time she tried to hold on to his presence he would slither away.

Slippery as an eel. The stupid cliché teased at her mind even as she clenched her teeth and dug her fingers into his patchy fur.

No. He wasn't going to elude her.

Ignoring the simmering fear, she again concentrated on the thin connection, releasing her power until the entire cell was flooded with the thick heat of her desperation. And still she couldn't reach him. Couldn't force . . .

Her eyes abruptly flew open.

Of course she couldn't force him. Any more than he could force her into the mating.

All she could do was try and offer her heart and hope that he could battle through his madness to accept it.

Yeah, one hell of a plan.

Sucking in a deep breath, she thrust aside her rising panic and released her fragile connection with Caine. Then, returning her focus inward, she concentrated not on the void in her heart, but the warm, boundless love that spilled through her like a rich, intoxicating nectar.

She didn't know when it had started.

Perhaps when Caine had stepped in front of her to protect her from the demon lord. Or when he'd taken her to his lair and badgered her to eat because she'd forgotten.

Or when she opened her eyes after yet another vision to find him patiently waiting at her side.

Or maybe she'd been fated to love this man before she'd ever been born.

The *when* didn't matter.

Only the fact that it filled every particle of her being.

Not allowing herself time to marvel at the strength of her emotion, which had become so familiar she took it for granted, Cassie regained command of her connection to Caine. This time, however, she didn't attempt to bludgeon him with her power.

He didn't need more strength to battle back from the edge of madness. He needed a reason.

Releasing the tidal wave of love, she stroked her hand softly over his head, her wolf impatiently prowling beneath her skin. Her beast had been oddly passive since Caine's transformation, as if patiently waiting for his return. Now it was anxiously straining to reach something just out of touch.

A low growl stirred the air and, opening her eyes, she met Caine's glowing gaze.

Her heart briefly halted at the glitter of feral insanity that remained in the astonishing blue depths. Gods, had she failed? Was he too far gone to accept the mating she was offering?

Or had she mistaken the instinctive need of a male alpha to protect her for something more . . . eternal?

She was pulling back in raw disappointment when she belatedly caught the scent of his musk. His wolf. She leaned closer, fiercely concentrating on the faint sense of his wolf that strained to reach her.

"Caine," she breathed, leaning down to bury her face in his neck. "I'm yours. Bond with me."

He growled again, but there was no threat in the sound. She pressed herself closer to his trembling body, feeling his power brushing over her skin and the familiar heat of him cloaking around her.

Then, as if a leash had suddenly snapped, she could feel the essence of his wolf slamming into her, filling the void in her aching heart with an intoxicating combination of wild animal and human male.

Reeling beneath the impact, she made a sound of shock. Oh . . . gods. It felt as if she'd been run over by a truck.

Was this the mating?

The question lasted only long enough for her own wolf to surge up to meet the charging assault, a stunning joy exploding through her.

Caine.

He was a part of her.

In every beat of her heart. And in every breath.

They were one.

Complete.

Slowly pulling back, she shuddered, still trying to adjust to the new sensations racing through her.

And the power.

Not just her power. Or Caine's power.

But an astonishing new melding of the two that sizzled through her like a bolt of lightning.

Her gaze encountered the blue eyes that still glowed with a feral wildness, but deep in her heart Caine was firmly entrenched.

"Just hold on, Caine," she rasped. "Hold on."

Styx's study

Dawn was approaching, pressing on Styx with a ruthless heaviness. He needed to shower, to feed, to spend several hours in the arms of his mate, and at least a week of uninterrupted sleep.

Unfortunately, he wasn't going to be getting any of those things. At least, not any time soon.

Instead, he was closeted with Salvatore and Roke as they poured over the maps he'd spread across the desk. Regan had done a good job getting reinforcements to Kostas's warehouse, but now they needed a full-out strategy. Which meant coordinating with Salvatore.

The King of Weres didn't look any better than Styx. His elegant suit was gone and replaced with a pair of dojo pants and a loose sweatshirt. And his lean face lined with a tension that was echoed in all of them.

Roke was standing silently on the other side of the desk. The younger vampire possessed a talent not only for reading prophecies, but for speaking demon dialects. He would be needed if they had to contact the leaders of other species.

Styx pointed to a spot on the map south of Chicago, speaking directly to the King of Weres.

"Viper has his clan stationed where the rift is opened, as well as several of your Weres outside the warehouse to protect them from any enemies that might be sent to stop them." He brought Salvatore up to speed. "Ariyal should be arriving with several of his tribesmen within the hour."

Salvatore nodded. The Sylvermyst were the most powerful of the fey and as their prince, Ariyal was the most talented at creating portals. If anyone could find a way to shut the rift it would be him.

"Does he think he can close the opening?"

"No one knows," Styx conceded with a shrug. "If he can't close it they intend to try and block it."

"If they can't?"

"I'm still working on plan B."

They grimaced in unison.

"What about the Chalice?" Salvatore at last asked.

Styx stroked the amulet at his neck, grateful that he hadn't been forced to inform Abby that she was going to be spending the next few weeks hidden from the oncoming war.

As the Phoenix—the mortal chalice who held the Goddess of Light—she had the ability to scorch demons into tiny piles of ash. A wise man didn't like to annoy her.

"Dante has taken her to a secret lair." Even Styx wasn't sure where they'd gone. "She's not happy to be taken out of the fight, but we have to protect the goddess she carries inside her. If we can somehow strip the Dark Lord of her newest powers, then we'll need the Phoenix to keep her trapped in her current prison."

"Good." Assured that the goddess was properly protected, the Were turned his attention to the looming fight. "Where's Jagr?"

"With Regan for now. Tomorrow at nightfall he will lead Troy in the search for other rifts that the Dark Lord might have opened."

Salvatore arched his brows at the mention of Troy, the Prince of Imps. "Poor schmuck," he muttered.

Styx couldn't argue. The tall, crimson-haired fey who strutted around in spandex and flirted with anything that crossed his path was a pain in the ass, but war truly did make strange bedfellows.

"Troy is eccentric, but there's no one who possesses a greater talent in sensing the dimensions that separate worlds," he said. "Even Ariyal admitted the imp was superior to his Sylvermysts in predicting where the veils are thinning. He should be able to detect a rift long before any of us could."

"Fine. I'll send Hess with them," the Were agreed. "He can help coordinate with any packs in the area if a rift is found."

Styx smiled with wry amusement at the thought of the barely house-trained cur and the nearly feral vampire trying to work together. "That should make an interesting partnership."

"No more than ours," Salvatore pointed out dryly.

"True." Lifting his head, Styx glanced at the vampire who stood in motionless silence. The younger man hadn't spoken a word since the meeting started, but Styx had been well aware of his growing disapproval. "Roke?"

The odd, silver eyes shimmered in the light of the overhead chandelier. "Yes?"

"Do you have something to add?"

The lean face remained unreadable. "Not really."

"There's something on your mind," he insisted, knowing that the younger vampire would refuse to express his doubts unless directly confronted.

There was the slightest hesitation before Roke pointed toward the map. "It's all defensive."

Styx frowned. "What is?"

"Your strategy," he explained. "It's all about defense, not offense."

Styx made a sound of disgust. Did the younger vampire think that Styx wanted to play the game of whack-a-mole with the Dark Lord? That he didn't realize how futile it was to be constantly reacting to trouble that popped out of thin air instead of staging an attack on his ground and on his terms?

"Until someone finds me a way to get into the evil bitch's prison, I don't have a hell of a lot of choices."

"No choices," Roke slowly agreed, his gaze never wavering. "Unless you draw her out."

Salvatore planted his hands on the desk and leaned forward, his expression one of curiosity. "Explain."

Roke held his ground despite the Were's choking power thickening the air. Styx hid a small smile. The Nevada clan chief was as cold-blooded and fearless as the rattlesnakes that populated his territory.

"As long as the Dark Lord is able to hide in the mists while she empties hell into our world, she'll be impossible to destroy," Roke clarified. "Our only hope is to lure her to this dimension before we're completely overwhelmed."

"And how are we supposed to lure her to this world?" the King of Weres demanded.

"I don't know."

Salvatore made a sound of disgust. "A helluva lot of help that is."

"I'm just a humble soldier." Roke's eyes flashed with silver fire. "You're the king. Both of you."

"You want the crown?" Styx mocked. "You can have it."

Roke squared his shoulders, not amused. "All I want is to return to my people."

"Fine." Styx held the younger vampire's annoyed gaze. "Figure out how to entice the Dark Lord out of the mists and you'll be free to go."

Roke scowled. "You keep changing the rules."

"I'm the king. It's my prerogative."

Salvatore abruptly straightened, glancing toward the open door. "Gargoyle."

"Shit." Styx rubbed the back of his neck, already prepared for the tiny creature to piss him off. "Like this night hasn't been bad enough?"

On cue, the miniature gargoyle waddled into the room, his wings twitching and tail as stiff as a board. A sure sign he wasn't rushing in with good news. But then, who did have good news these days?

"Salvatore, you must come," Levet commanded.

Ah, he wanted the dog. Styx gave a sharp laugh at the sour expression on Salvatore's face. "Things are looking up," he murmured softly.

The King of Weres gave a warning growl before turning to glare at the gargoyle, who was nearly dancing with impatience.

"Actually, whether I come or not is very much up to debate," Salvatore corrected, his wolf prowling close to the surface. "What do you want?"

"It's Cassandra."

All three men stiffened at the mention of the prophet. Shit. They'd just managed to get her back. They couldn't lose her now. Not when she might hold the key to the future.

"What about her?" Salvatore growled.

"She's with Caine."

"Damn," Salvatore breathed, exchanging a horrified glance with Styx.

The Were had already revealed that Caine was trapped in his feral insanity with no hope of being salvaged. If Cassie had gone into his cell, then . . . Styx shuddered at the mere thought.

"Why didn't you stop her?" Salvatore rasped, his infuriated gaze snapping back to Levet.

The tiny demon lifted his hands in a helpless motion. "I tried. She refused to listen to me."

Salvatore clenched his teeth. "Is she dead?"

"I don't know."

Styx felt a small flare of relief. At least there was still a chance she might be alive.

"I have to go," Salvatore said.

"I'm coming with you," Styx growled, sparing an impatient glance for the vampire still standing beside the desk. "Roke."

"Yes?"

"Cezar is waiting for me in the library. Get with him and find a way to draw the Dark Lord into this world." He gestured toward the gargoyle. "Levet will assist you."

Roke widened his eyes at the unreasonable command. "But—"

Styx lifted a hand to halt the outraged protest. "Just do it." He turned his narrowed gaze toward the gargoyle. "Both of you."

Roke hissed in frustration. "Damn you."

Assured the vampire would do everything in his power to find a method of luring the Dark Lord from her lair, Styx fell into step with Salvatore as he headed out of the study and down the hall.

One disaster at a time.

"Damn. I thought I was a bastard," the Were muttered.

"You are," Styx assured him.

Chapter 21

Styx grimaced at the sound of scurrying guards as they wisely fled the tunnels.

He didn't blame them for their hasty retreat.

He and Salvatore were powerful alphas. Perhaps the most powerful in the world. Just being in the same room with them was enough to make most demons cringe in fear. But when they were both in hunter mode, the very air trembled in fear.

Struggling to leash his power, which was shattering the overhead lights, Styx was caught off guard when Salvatore came to a sudden halt.

"Shit," the wolf muttered, his eyes glowing gold.

"What is it?"

"My weapons." He glanced down at his sweatpants in disgust. "I left them in my rooms."

"Here." Styx pulled a gun from the holster at the small of his back, his expression somber. "If you want, I can take care of this."

"No, Caine belongs to me." He reached to take the gun, loaded with silver bullets. "It's my duty."

Styx understood. Being a leader not only meant making

the hard decisions, but also carrying them through. "Evil times," he murmured.

Salvatore nodded. "*Sí.*"

The Were jerked back into motion, leading Styx down a corridor to the isolated cell. The true dungeons were a level below. These rooms were for vampires awaiting sentencing from the Anasso, or for the nonmagical demons who could be held by conventional means.

They had taken less than two steps when they caught the sound of a muffled female voice.

"Caine, can you hear me?"

"Cassandra?" Styx demanded.

"Yes."

Pure relief flowed through Styx. "Alive."

"At least for now," Salvatore said, racing toward the end of the corridor and throwing open the heavy steel door.

Styx entered the cell directly behind the King of Weres, his fangs lengthening as he caught sight of the mutated beast that rose up in fury at their entrance.

Holy . . . shit.

Even after Salvatore's warning, he was shaken. He'd seen any number of creatures, some so grotesque they could turn the stomach, but this was . . . wrong.

Perverted.

Distracted, Styx nearly overlooked the tiny female until she darted in front of the beast, her arms spread wide.

"No, stay back," she cried, her delicate features so like Darcy that it made Styx's heart clench in fear.

She had to be kept safe. His beautiful mate would be devastated if she were to lose her sister.

Not to mention the danger to the world at the loss of their prophet.

"Salvatore," he muttered in low tones. "Do something or I will."

The Were ignored his threat, focusing his power on the stubborn female who stood between them and the feral beast who could kill her with one blow.

"Cassandra, come to me."

The force of his words crashed through the small cell, sizzling through the air with enough power to make Styx hiss in annoyance and Caine whine in pain.

Cassandra, however, stood without flinching, her eyes flashing emerald fire and the fine strands of her blond hair floating in the sudden breeze. "No. I won't let you hurt him."

"He'll kill you," Salvatore muttered, taking a step forward. "Now come to me."

She scowled as the beast behind her growled in warning, his eyes glowing with madness and his large body poised to attack, despite the heavy silver manacles wrapped around his ankles.

"He won't hurt me," she ridiculously tried to convince them. "He only wants to protect me."

"I'm sorry, Cassandra, more sorry than I can say, but he isn't trying to protect you," Salvatore said, lifting the gun. "He doesn't even recognize you. He's too far gone."

Her eyes widened, the scent of her agitation making Caine howl in fury. "You're wrong," she hissed, her hands lifted in a pleading motion. "I reached him."

Salvatore shook his head. "It's impossible."

"Not for his mate."

Styx heard the King of Weres suck in a startled breath. "Mate?"

"He . . . no." The prophet waved a frantic hand as Salvatore took a step forward when the feral beast wrapped a clawed hand around her arm. "Stay back."

"Cassandra, it doesn't matter." Salvatore slowly continued forward, his gun aimed at the center of Caine's chest. "I have to get you out of there."

Cassandra winced as the beast dug his claws into her arm, his glowing gaze watching Salvatore with a growing fury, but still she tried to keep her body between her approaching king and the creature who had once been her mate.

"Listen to me. We're connected," she said in desperate tones. "He's part of my family now."

The words had barely left her lips when Caine thrust her behind his large body. The rough shove sent the much smaller female sailing through the air, her head hitting the lead wall with a sickening thud.

"Shit," Styx rasped, watching Cassandra crumple to the ground before he turned to glare at the Were standing silently at his side. "What are you waiting for?"

A muscle in Salvatore's jaw knotted, as if he were battling back his wolf. "She said family," he replied, his voice harsh.

"So what?" Styx snapped, his attention shifting to the beast, who was pacing as far as the silver chains would allow him, his fangs bared in warning. The only good thing in this most recent debacle was that he seemed to have forgotten the unconscious woman behind him. "She's desperate to save her mate. She would say anything to prevent the inevitable."

"*Sí*. Her mate."

Assuming that the King of Weres was regretting the need to sacrifice one of his pack, even if he had more than once desired Caine's death, Styx held out a hand. "Salvatore, allow me to deal with this."

"No." The Were shook his head. "They weren't mated before."

Styx grimaced. "She completed the mating even knowing his madness is irreversible? Foolish female."

"Not foolish," Salvatore said in low tones, turning to meet Styx's frustrated gaze. "Actually, she's been very, very clever."

"Why?"

"I couldn't reach Caine because he was transformed into a pureblood by the demon lord. He'd never been a part of a pack."

Styx didn't know the ins and outs of the mangy mutt society, but Salvatore's words made sense. "And now?"

"Now he's bound to Cassandra."

Styx glanced toward the unconscious female. "But wasn't she raised in isolation with the demon lord?"

"She was."

"So she isn't a part of a pack either."

"Her connection was formed in the womb with her sisters, as well as through her mother, Sophia, to me."

"What does that mean?"

"That there's a chance I can call him back."

Their gazes clashed, a silent battle between Salvatore's grim determination and Styx's fierce refusal to endanger the prophet.

At last, Styx reached to pluck the gun from Salvatore's hand, conceding with ill grace to the Were's need to try and salvage his newest pack mate. "Here, give me that."

Salvatore narrowed his gaze in warning. "Styx."

"You concentrate on doing your thing and I'll make sure the rabid wolf doesn't kill us all."

Salvatore arched a brow. "Doing my thing?"

"Just get on with it."

Convinced that Styx wasn't going to go Tony Montana the minute his attention was diverted, Salvatore turned back toward the crazed beast and lifted a hand.

At first, nothing seemed to happen.

Caine continued his frantic pacing, his eyes wild with his desire to sink his massive teeth into the two male intruders. Styx lifted the gun, willing to give Salvatore a chance to reach the rabid dog, but only as long as the creature didn't so much as glance in Cassandra's direction.

The minutes ticked past, Salvatore's hand still raised and the air beginning to heat with his power. Then the King of Weres was abruptly striding forward, his wolf so thick in the air that Styx could taste fur on his tongue.

Caine tossed back his head, howling beneath the force of Salvatore's will. Salvatore never faltered, reaching up to grasp the creature's chin and force him to meet his ruthless gaze.

Styx hissed. The crazy-assed King of Weres was going to get himself killed. Something he wouldn't tolerate.

Not when he'd promised himself the pleasure.

Placing his finger on the trigger, he aimed between Caine's eyes. But before he could fire there was a sudden flurry of magic surrounding the one-time cur. At the same time, Salvatore fell heavily to his knees, his head bent in exhaustion.

"Shit." Shoving the gun back into the holster at his lower back, Styx darted forward to grasp Salvatore by the shoulders and towed him away from the shower of sparks that were swirling around Caine. Then, halting in the doorway, he watched as the sparks died away to reveal that Caine's mutated form had been altered into his wolf form.

The beast that came to Styx's chest gave himself a shake before he lowered his head to study the unconscious woman at his feet. Styx tensed, but the animal gave a low whine, gently nuzzling her cheek.

"Amazing," Styx muttered. "I think it worked."

Rising to his feet, Salvatore ran a weary hand over his face. "*Sí.*"

"Unfortunately, he doesn't look any happier."

Salvatore snorted as the large wolf stepped out of the manacles that no longer held him captive and bared his teeth, clearly prepared to pounce.

"How happy would you be to have two males near your unconscious mate?"

"Fair enough, but you can't leave her in there with him."

"No, but only Cassandra can calm his beast."

"So the only one who can call off the enraged wolf is the unconscious woman?" Styx rolled his eyes. "Why am I not surprised?"

Ignoring Styx, the King of Weres once again raised his hand, pointing a finger at the motionless prophet.

"Cassandra," he commanded, his voice echoing through the small cell. "Cassandra, open your eyes."

Cassie was perfectly comfortable as she floated in a state of unconsciousness.

Why not? Here in the darkness there were no cares, no worries, and best of all, no bothersome visions.

Well, there was that nagging voice that kept calling her name, she ruefully conceded, wishing it would go away. Of course it didn't. In fact, it became so compelling that it wrenched her out of her soothing cocoon with a merciless jerk.

Vaguely realizing she was lying on a hard floor, she lifted her head, only to give a low moan. Crap. It felt like someone was trying to drive a spike through her brain. "Ow," she breathed.

"Cassandra." The damn voice refused to leave her in peace. "Can you hear me?"

"Please, do you have to shout?" she complained, her hand lifting to the large bump on her temple. "My head is killing me."

"That's because it was recently smacked into the wall," a familiar voice informed her.

Salvatore.

Yes, he was the aggravating pest who kept interfering in

her attempt to return to the darkness. And he was saying that her head hurt because she'd smacked it into the wall.

Odd.

"Why would I—"

Cassie gave a small gasp as her memories rushed back with shattering force.

Caine.

Shaking off the lingering fog in her brain, she surged to her knees and sent a frantic glance toward the looming presence she could feel beside her.

"Oh." A lump formed in her throat, her heart nearly shattering at the sight of the large wolf standing protectively in front of her. She'd hoped her mad plan would work, of course. She'd even prayed. But she hadn't believed. Not really, truly believed. Now she burst into tears as she threw her arms around Caine's neck and buried her face in his thick fur. "Caine. Caine."

She didn't know how long she wept, lost in the tidal wave of relief. At last it was the sound of Salvatore clearing his throat that brought her head up to meet his golden gaze.

"Cassandra, I rejoice in your reunion, but we need to get you out of here."

She leaned her head against Caine's neck, her fingers stroking through his fur. The rich scent of his musk wrapped around her, seeping into her skin. "You reached him."

The king gave a nod of his head, a smile on his lips despite the weariness that was etched onto his handsome face. "With your help."

She allowed her eyes to briefly flick toward the towering Aztec vampire at Salvatore's side before hastily returning them to the Were. She wasn't sure she was ready to deal with both the King of Weres and the Anasso. Not at the same time. Either one was overwhelming. Together . . . well, they were more than any poor female should have to confront.

"Why is he still in animal form?"

"Because he's protecting his mate," Salvatore said. "Until you convince him that we aren't a threat to you he won't shift back to human."

Oh. Of course. Caine had been uberprotective from the moment they'd met. Now that they were mated he was bound to be an over the top, pain in the ass fanatic.

"Caine." She grabbed his muzzle with both hands, gazing deep in the glowing blue eyes that were no longer crazed, but still plenty feral. "Caine, listen to me. I'm fine. The danger has passed. No one's going to hurt me."

She said the words slowly, not because the wolf was stupid—Caine was as frighteningly cunning in his animal form as in his human—but because he kept glancing over her shoulder and growling at the two demons near the door.

"Down, boy," Styx muttered.

Salvatore breathed a low curse. "You're not helping, leech."

"Actually, it would be easier if you both would leave," Cassie pointed out dryly.

"No way in hell," Salvatore snapped, the prickles of his power causing Caine to growl in agitation.

Cassie heaved a resigned sigh, glancing over her shoulder. "Well, that answers a question that has been bothering me."

Salvatore scowled. "What question?"

"Whether Caine's irrational stubbornness was a personality trait or if it was a character flaw shared by all men." Her glance encompassed both kings before returning to Caine. "Now I know."

"I think we were just insulted," Styx drawled.

Salvatore snorted. "It wouldn't be the first time."

"Speak for yourself."

"Just ignore Shaggy and Scooby-Doo and concentrate on me," Cassie told her mate, leaning forward to kiss the tip of his nose. "You've done your job. You protected me. Now it's time to rest." She settled on the floor as the dangerous blue gaze took a last, cautious survey of the two males standing near the door before slowly sinking down on his haunches. "That's right, my love," she crooned softly, urging his massive head into her lap as she stroked his fur. "Just rest."

She felt the massive body shudder beneath her hand, and continuing her gentle strokes, she waited patiently until the ancient magic filled the air. There was the sound of popping bones and the snapping of muscles as Caine shifted back to human, his head still in her lap as he sank into a deep, healing sleep.

Her heart swelled with an emotion so big it couldn't possibly be contained in such a small space, exploding through her as her trembling fingers stroked through the pale blond hair that fell over his forehead and down the narrow line of his nose.

Her mate . . .

The other half of her soul.

She forgot the darkness that still waited to consume the world. And her duty as the prophet to try and halt the approaching doomsday.

She forgot everything but this man who had sacrificed all to protect her.

Eventually there was the sound of approaching footsteps and Salvatore squatted beside her.

"Let me take him upstairs," he coaxed, wise enough not to reach for Caine until she gave a hesitant nod.

"Be gentle."

The golden gaze slammed deep into her worried gaze, offering her a silent promise of safety. "He's a member of my pack. As you are, Cassandra." His lips twitched. "Even if you did call me Scooby-Doo. You have nothing to fear from me."

She believed him. She could feel his presence flowing

through her and into Caine, offering his strength without hesitation.

With another nod she rose to her feet, turning her head as a chill wrapped around her. Not surprising, she discovered that Styx had silently moved to stand beside her, his gaze on Salvatore.

"I'm going to take a shower and then share breakfast with my mate," the vampire said. "Unless a rift opens in the front room I don't want to be disturbed."

Salvatore scooped Caine into his arms and with one fluid motion straightened to regard the Anasso with a mocking smile. "Your wish is my command, oh mighty majesty."

The King of Vampires rolled his eyes, his stunningly beautiful face softening as he turned to offer her a small bow of his head. "Cassandra, welcome to my lair. I hope you will consider it your home."

"Thank you," she murmured, still wary of the large predator who looked like he might eat small children for breakfast.

"I also hope you'll make time for Darcy," he continued, his words more a command than a request. "She's anxious to meet you."

"I will try once Caine is healed."

The vampire nodded, his expression warning he would come fetch her if she didn't make the required appearance to meet her sister. Then, with a last glance toward Salvatore, he was turning to move out the door with a fluid grace that was unnerving for such a large man.

Salvatore was swiftly following in Styx's path, cradling the naked man in his arms with an ease only a Were could achieve. "There are rooms upstairs," he said. "You'll be more comfortable there."

She hurried to catch up to his swift pace, a faint frown

marring her brow as she unexpectedly recalled Styx's parting words. "What did he mean by rifts?"

"The Dark Lord has managed to rip open a doorway between dimensions," Salvatore said.

She sucked in a shocked breath. "She's here?"

"Not yet, but her minions are eager to cross over."

Cassie never faltered as she followed Salvatore out of the tunnels and up the stairs, but her mind was . . . empty.

Frighteningly empty.

The question was, why?

If the Dark Lord had truly managed to rip open doorways to the world, then surely that meant they were hurtling toward a turning point in time.

She should be inundated with visions. The gods knew that previous moments of upheaval had nearly drowned her in a confused avalanche of prophecies.

So why wasn't she seeing them now?

Had the Dark Lord done something to steal them from her?

Or had her mating to Caine altered her on some fundamental level?

"Crap."

She wasn't aware that she'd spoken aloud until Salvatore snapped his head in her direction, his expression concerned.

"Is something wrong? Did you have a vision?"

"No." She wrapped her arms around her waist as a trickle of alarm inched down her spine. "It's dark."

"What is dark?"

"The future."

Chapter 22

Caine woke in an unfamiliar room, stretched naked on a bed the size of Utah.

Usually the sign of a great night of partying, he wryly acknowledged, having spent more than a few nights indulging in the sort of decadent sins that would shock the most dedicated hedonist.

But not on this occasion.

At the moment, his only hope was that this was the end of a nightmare. A shudder wracked his body, wrenching a groan from his throat. Most of his memories were hazy, thank the gods, although not hazy enough to allow him to forget how close he'd come to doing the unthinkable.

Regret seared through him as he jerked upright, his gaze skimming over the opulent ivory and gold furnishings. Not that he gave a crap about the antique dressing tables, or armoires, or matching wing chairs. Or even the overhead chandelier that caught the sunlight that spilled through the bay window.

He had one thing, and one thing only, on his mind.

"Cassie," he growled, pushing toward the edge of the acre-wide mattress.

"No, don't move," Cassie commanded, appearing in the doorway of the connected bathroom wearing nothing more than a short silk robe. "I'm here."

A melting tenderness flowed through him as he took in her tousled blond hair and the pillow marks on her cheek that revealed she'd just woken. With her wide emerald eyes and perfectly formed body she was as beautiful as an angel.

His angel.

The mating bond pulsed through him, as potent and intoxicating as any drug he'd created in his former life.

"Why aren't you here?" he questioned, patting the mattress in invitation.

She blinked, as always taking his words quite literally. "I was going to take a shower while you slept."

"Can it wait?"

She smiled, and Caine felt as if the sun had settled in his heart. Then, with a natural grace, she was moving across the polished floor to perch on the mattress next to him.

He lowered his head to brush his lips over her cheek, his muscles tensing as he caught an unmistakable scent clinging to her skin. A low growl trickled from his throat. "Why do you smell of another man?"

She pulled back with a startled laugh. "After everything we've been through your first thought is that you can smell another man?"

He nipped the tip of her ear. "You're mine."

"Yeah, I was there when it happened," she said, her voice husky.

His annoyance was abruptly replaced by a jagged burst of guilt. What should have been the most beautiful moment in Cassie's life had instead been a stark necessity performed in the cramped cell of a vampire's lair. And, oh yeah, he'd been crazed out of his freaking mind.

He brushed an unsteady finger over her cheek in a soft caress. "Cassie, I—"

"No," she snapped.

He arched a brow at her uncharacteristic outburst. "No?"

She stabbed her finger to the center of his chest. "You're about to make a big production out of your lack of control despite the fact you were under the influence of magic."

Lack of control? He'd become a monster. And if Cassie hadn't managed to stop him, he would have killed her.

"It wasn't a spell that made me attack you," he said gruffly, his voice thick with self-disgust.

"You're right." Her expression was grim. "It was entirely my fault. I led you directly into a trap."

He shook his head. "Cassie."

"You can't use your guilt to alter the truth." She gave him another poke. "I have put you into danger over and over and even when I knew you were going to be hurt I allowed you to remain with me. I put my dependence on you above your own life."

He grasped her finger and lifted it to his lips, nibbling at the tip. "I don't remember giving you a choice."

Her eyes darkened with an aching remorse. "The choice has always been mine, but I was so selfish I was willing to risk your life just so I could have you with me." Caine felt her violent shudder. "Gods, I came so close to losing you."

With one motion, Caine tugged his mate into his lap and wrapped his arms around her trembling body. "Shh." He buried his face in the fragrant silk of her hair. "I'm not so easy to get rid of."

She snuggled into his chest, but she wasn't done with her self-flagellation. "And then I forced a mating on you when you were in no condition to make such a decision."

"Forced?" Had she lost her mind? With a frown he wrapped his hand around her throat, then pressed his thumb to the underside of her chin, tilting back her head to study her pale face. "Why would you even suggest something so idiotic? A mating can't be forced."

She met his outraged glare without flinching. "You were in no state of mind to decide whether or not you wanted to complete the bond, but I didn't know any other way to give Salvatore the connection to reach you." She gave a small squeak as he abruptly tossed her to the center of the mattress, using his larger body to pin her in place. "Caine."

He ruthlessly arranged her slender body beneath him, settling between her legs and propping himself on his elbows to gaze down at her startled expression. "Let's get two things straight," he growled.

She remained silent a long minute, no doubt trying to decide whether she wanted to hear what he had to say or punch him in the nose for behaving like a caveman.

At last, curiosity won out. "What?"

"I was born to become your mate." He placed a hand over her mouth when she would have protested. "Just listen."

She rolled her eyes, waiting for him to remove his hand before muttering her opinion of males and their deficient DNA. But thankfully she made no effort to escape. "Fine, I'm listening," she at last conceded.

"My destiny has always been to protect you. Always." He caught and held her gaze, laying bare his heart without hesitation. "And if you ever try to take that away it will destroy me." He heard her breath catch at his blunt honesty, a startled tenderness flowing through their mating bond.

But, lifting a hand to brush his hair from his forehead, she managed a faux chiding expression. "Okay, but if I'm not allowed to feel guilty, then neither are you."

"Touché," he muttered dryly, well aware that he'd been outmaneuvered.

He'd intended to spend hours, if not days, wallowing in

his self-reproach. Instead, his mate had cleverly snatched the rug from beneath his feet.

Clever, dangerous wolf.

He leaned down to nuzzle the curve of her neck, a smile touching his lips as she shivered in ready response.

"You said there were two things," she said in a breathy voice.

He didn't need her reminder as he trailed his lips to give the lobe of her ear a punishing nip. "You're now my mate."

Her hands lifted to stroke through his hair. "And?"

He lifted his head to stab her with a gaze that was only partially teasing. "And I don't want you to mention another man's name when you stink of him."

Sensing his wolf was genuinely ruffled, she furrowed her brow in puzzlement. "You mean Salvatore?"

"I warned you." Angling his head, he sank his teeth into the flesh of her throat, his musk filling the air to brand the woman beneath him. It was the most primitive sort of marking, but the mating bond was still raw and in need of proclaiming her as off-limits to other males.

Cassie moaned, the spice of her arousal teasing at Caine's nose as her fingers tangled in the short strands of his hair.

"He carried you to this room and I walked beside him," she said to comfort his beast. "Nothing else."

"I know." He nuzzled a path along the line of her jaw. "But I'm finding it hard to be civilized right now."

"Caine." Her fingers tightened in his hair as he covered her lips with slow, drugging kisses.

"Hmm?"

"You need to rest."

His sucked her bottom lip, pressing his fully erect cock against her inner thigh. They groaned in unison, the mating bond only intensifying the potent desire that flowed between them.

"What I need is my mate," he assured her, stealing another deep kiss before seeking the scented pulse at the base of her throat.

"Mate." She shivered as his tongue stroked her skin, his fingers tugging at the belt of her robe. "It feels . . ."

"Yes?"

She heaved a satisfied sigh. "Astonishing."

Caine was in full agreement.

It was astonishing.

Astonishing and magical and entrancing.

Leaning back, he peeled open her robe, savoring the sight of her small breasts tipped with rosy nipples already hard with need.

She was exquisite.

A masterpiece of ivory and gold that perfectly matched the decor.

With a low growl, he swooped down to circle one of the tempting peaks with the tip of his tongue, chuckling at her soft gasp of pleasure. "And how does this feel?"

Her fingers slid down his neck to trace the line of his shoulders. "Mmm . . . nice enough, I suppose," she teased.

"Nice?" The heat of his desire sizzled through him, nearly setting the air on fire. "You shouldn't provoke a hungry wolf, pet."

Her hands moved to explore the bare width of his chest, a smoldering invitation in her emerald eyes. "Ah, but he's my hungry wolf."

For all eternity, he silently swore, refusing to contemplate the world outside the bedroom door. In this rare moment of peace he was just a wolf with the woman who filled his heart with a joy he'd never dreamed possible.

"Your wolf needs a kiss," he coaxed softly.

A slow smile curved her lips. "Such a demanding beast."

"Ravenous." He gave her nipple a slow lick before turning

to share equal pleasure with her neglected breast. "Greedy." He caught the nipple with the edge of his teeth, biting just hard enough to make her arch in encouragement. "Insatiable."

She trailed her foot up and down the back of his leg, the movement brushing her thigh against his straining erection. At the same time, her lips nibbled a line of searing kisses along his collarbone.

"Just how I like you," she assured him, giving his own nipple a wicked lick.

Carnal bliss jolted through him, and with a shaky groan he rested his forehead between her breasts. "Careful, pet. I'm a breath away from early combustion."

She stilled. "That's one of those strange exaggerations, isn't it? You're not truly going to combust?"

"It all depends on your definition of combustion," he muttered, grasping her wrists and tugging her hands over her head.

He caught a brief glimpse of emerald eyes dark with need before he was claiming her lips in a kiss of blatant hunger. Over and over he devoured her mouth, his hips gently rocking against her in time with her soft sounds of growing need.

"I think I'm beginning to understand," she rasped, shivering as he released her lips and stroked his lips down the curve of her neck and then kissed the tip of each nipple.

Not entirely convinced she was as close to combustion as he wanted her to be, Caine continued his seductive path down the flat plane of her stomach, taking a minute to tease her tiny belly button before he was sliding off the edge of the bed and tugging her legs apart.

His wolf strained at the leash, eager to claim the woman who was now bound to him. The man, thankfully, didn't intend to pounce.

At least not yet.

With a tender thoroughness he nibbled down her slender leg to the tips of her toes, breathing deeply of her delectable scent. Silk and lavender. Pure bewitchment. He made a similar path along her other leg before he pulled back to simply admire the sight of her stretched out before him.

"You are so beautiful," he murmured, his fingers tracing a light path along the inside of her thighs.

She trembled, her soft pants like music to his ears. "Why are you waiting?"

He allowed his fingers to drift upward, brushing close, so very close, to her damp heat. "Anticipation is half the fun."

Cassie muttered something beneath her breath, glancing down where he was poised between her legs.

"Caine?"

He hid his smile of satisfaction at her flushed cheeks and the hectic glitter in her eyes. "Yes, my love?"

"Are you deliberately tormenting me?"

He pretended to consider. "Yes, I believe I am."

Her eyes narrowed. "I can combust alone, you know."

He made a choked sound of disbelief before he tilted back his head to laugh with rich enjoyment. "Ah, Cassie. You're truly an original."

Her lips parted, but before she could continue her chastisement, he leaned forward to discover the very heart of her pleasure.

Whatever she was about to say was lost on a low groan and she flopped back onto the mattress as he used his tongue and teeth until her hips were lifting up in a silent plea for release.

Scooting her back to the center of the bed, he moved to cover her, giving a startled grunt when Cassie reached to wrap her fingers around his aching cock.

"Shit," he breathed as she stroked down to his heavy sack

before moving back to tease at the sensitive tip. "You're killing me."

She arched a mocking brow, her eyes dark with a smoldering desire. "Anticipation is half the fun."

He lowered his head to brush his mouth over her lips. "Cassie, are you tormenting me?"

Her smile was as ancient as Eve. "Yes, I believe I am."

He allowed her another stroke before he gave a low growl and, sliding his hands beneath her hips, entered her with one smooth motion.

Cassie dug her nails into his shoulders, her legs wrapping around his hips as he began a slow, steady pace.

"My mate," she whispered, her words settling deep in his heart. "At last."

He leaned down to capture her lips in a kiss that spoke of his unwavering commitment.

"Forever."

Six hours later, Cassie still hadn't managed to get to the shower. Not that she was complaining.

Laying in a tangle of rumpled sheets and sweaty male Were, she rested her head on the wide width of his chest, listening to the steady beat of his heart as her fingers drew aimless patterns on his skin.

Having Caine as a lover had been magical from his first kiss. Their chemistry had nothing to do with fate or mystic bonds, and everything to do with old-fashioned lust. But there was no denying that their mating had amped up the intensity of her pleasure to almost unbearable heights.

Now she was exhausted in all the right ways. Well, mostly, she ruefully corrected. Her body was so limp with pleasure the mere thought of moving made her groan. But her mind . . .

The stupid thing refused to float in the same sated bliss as the rest of her. It kept churning, searching for answers to the question that refused to leave her peace.

Assuming that Caine had fallen back to sleep, Cassie was unprepared when he slid a finger beneath her chin and tilted back her head to study her pale face.

"There's something troubling you."

She had to concentrate not to be distracted by his masculine beauty. Good . . . Lord. With the dying rays of sunlight shimmering like the finest gold in his pale hair and his eyes glowing like flawless sapphires, he could easily have rivaled Adonis.

"These are troubling times," she managed to hedge.

His jaw hardened with an unexpected flare of annoyance. "Don't bother," he warned in flat tones.

She blinked. "I'm sorry?"

"You're, without doubt, the worst liar I've ever met."

She lifted herself to a sitting position, glaring down at his ruthless expression. "Hey."

"Trust me, that's a compliment, pet," he said, folding his arms beneath his head. "But it does mean that you can't fool me. Besides, I can feel you worry through our bond."

Oh.

She'd been so enchanted by the obvious benefits of their mating bond, she'd never considered the possibility there might be a downside. A sigh escaped between her parted lips. It was too late to regret that she'd forever chained this magnificent Were to her crazy existence.

It was no doubt inevitable.

"I suppose it's a good thing that I don't have a ton of secrets I want to keep hidden."

Without warning, he reached out to cup his hand behind her head, tugging her down to kiss her with blatant possession.

"I don't need a mating bond to discover your secrets," he murmured against her lips.

A shiver of heat raced through her, stirring the passions that she would have sworn were too weary to be stirred. "No?" she breathed.

He nipped her bottom lip, the scent of his musk filling her senses, imprinting his claim on her skin. "I have more creative methods of making you talk."

Catching a glimpse of his smug pleasure at her tremors of need, Cassie boldly trailed her hand downward, rubbing her hardened nipples against his chest as her fingers curled around the thickening length of his erection. "Do your worse."

He groaned, his eyes squeezing shut as she explored the hard shaft with a bold touch. "Ah, how the mighty are fallen," he ground out.

She tilted back her head as his lips branded a path down her jaw before finding the sensitive curve of her throat.

"What do you mean?"

He bit the flesh at the base of her neck, making her arch in a jolt of shocking bliss. Then, releasing his teeth, he soothed the tingling flesh with tiny kisses.

"My creative methods appear to backfire when it comes to you."

"And that's a bad thing?"

Reaching down, Caine grasped her wrist and gently tugged her fingers away from his throbbing cock.

"Cassie."

"Yes?"

His gaze narrowed at her small smile, and he abruptly twisted to the side so he could pin her to the mattress. Tugging her hands over her head, he regarded her with a determined expression. "I'm not going to be distracted," he warned. "Tell me what's bothering you."

She grimaced, accepting playtime was over. The real world was about to intrude whether they wanted it or not.

"Nothing."

His brows snapped together. "Cassandra."

He never used the full name they'd chosen only weeks before, revealing he was nearing the end of his patience. As if his annoyance wasn't sizzling through their mating bond.

"I mean 'nothing' quite literally," she hastily corrected.

He stilled. "You're going to have to be a little more specific."

"If the Dark Lord is truly on the brink of returning . . ."

"Wait," he interrupted, his voice harsh. "I need you to back up, pet. Why do you think the Dark Lord is on the brink of returning?"

Cassie felt a sharp pang of remorse. How had she forgotten he'd been in no condition to comprehend what was happening during the past few days?

"She has Maluhia."

His breath hissed through clenched teeth. "I was hoping that was just a nightmare," he muttered. "Has she become the Gemini?"

Cassie shrugged. "I didn't see it happen, but she must have completed the transformation if she's able to open rifts to this world."

"Rifts?" His eyes abruptly held the power of his wolf. Hunter. "Where?"

"I don't know. I only heard Styx mention them to Salvatore."

"Is the Dark Lord attempting to come through?"

Cassie shook her head. "I think she intends to empty out the bowels of hell first."

Caine considered her words before giving a slow nod of agreement. "That would make sense. Why would she risk her neck when she could send her minions to do her dirty work?" His lips curled in pure hatred. "Bitch."

"Agreed."

His thumbs absently rubbed the skin of her inner wrists, his gaze sweeping over her pale face. "Are you worried we won't be able to stop her?"

She hesitated. "In part."

"Cassie, talk to me," he growled.

Stubborn wolf. He wasn't going to let this go. Not until he was convinced he'd wrung out her entire confession.

"There haven't been any visions."

He seemed more puzzled than frightened by her revelation. "Since when?"

She licked her dry lips. Just talking about her lack of prophecies made her stomach cramp. "Since we escaped from the Dark Lord."

"Surely that should make you happy?" he asked cautiously. "You hate the visions."

"My preference doesn't matter." She shivered at the cost of losing her visions when she needed them the most. "They might make the difference between our survival and the end of the world."

He tensed at her blunt words, belatedly understanding why she was so distressed. "You've never been able to conjure them on command," he tried to soothe. "They might simply . . ."

"Yes?" she prompted.

"Be on hiatus." He clearly reached for the first excuse that came to mind. "It's been a stressful few days, after all."

She smiled wryly, appreciating his effort, even if she didn't believe for a minute that it was a temporary glitch. "Trust me, I've had more than a few stressful days over the years," she said dryly. "But there's never been a time I haven't had visions. And when the future is in chaos, like it is now, I have hundreds of them. It doesn't make sense they would suddenly disappear."

Caine went rigid above her, his face draining of color. "'*The Gemini will rise and chaos shall rule for all eternity,*'" he quoted in his husky tones.

She gave a slow nod. "Exactly."

Their gazes locked as the full implication of her words sank in, Caine's eyes darkening with unease.

"You think . . . ?"

"Maybe I'm not having visions because the Gemini has already won."

Chapter 23

Styx's study

Although he'd managed time for a shower and a few blessed hours in the arms of his mate, Styx was still in a foul mood as he entered his study to find Viper waiting for him.

The Chicago clan chief had only minutes before returned from the rift, and as Styx watched him pace the floor, he wasn't surprised to discover that the younger vampire looked as fatigued as Styx felt.

His silver-blond hair was hanging loose down his back and his usually immaculate velvet jacket and black slacks were wrinkled and coated with dust. Even the pale features were lined with a weariness he couldn't disguise.

Crossing to lean against his desk, Styx folded his arms over his chest, which was covered by a black T-shirt that matched his black jeans.

"Well?"

Coming to a halt in the center of the room, Viper met his questioning gaze with a grimace. "Ariyal's tribe has managed to block the rift, but it's taking all of them to do it." He shrugged a shoulder. "They're only a temporary solution."

Styx gave a nod. It was as much as he could hope for. "They've given us time."

"True." Viper's lips twisted. "Now what the hell are we going to do with it?"

Styx snorted. That was a hell of a question. "I'm open to ideas."

Without answers, Viper instead turned the conversation. "Has Jagr taken off?"

"Yes." Styx had seen his Raven off less than an hour before. "He's promised to report in with Regan."

There was a sudden chime and Viper reached beneath his jacket to remove his cell phone. "Speaking of checking in," the clan chief muttered, swiftly reading his message. "It's Santiago."

Styx lifted his brows in surprise. Not that the powerful warrior wouldn't be a welcomed addition. "He's here?"

"No, he's still with Nefri. They're traveling to the rift."

"Why?"

"To see if her medallion can close it."

Styx hissed in self-disgust. "Clever. I should have considered the possibility myself."

"You can't think of everything."

"I have to if we're going to survive."

With a sharp movement, Viper crossed to the sidebar, pouring two shots of the finest whiskey in Chicago before returning to shove one of the balloon glasses into Styx's hand.

"You aren't fighting this battle alone," Viper said.

"No." With a wry smile, Styx took a sip of the whiskey, enjoying the expensive burn as it slid down his throat. His companion was right. The demon world was coming together as it never had before to face the evil confronting it. "Thank the gods."

Viper emptied his drink with one swallow, setting the glass on a nearby shelf. "What about the prophet?"

"She's still in her rooms, although that damned guard dog of hers finally let Darcy in to see her."

"She hasn't had a vision?"

Styx set aside his own glass, his brows lowering in an annoyed scowl as he recalled his earlier attempt to speak with Cassandra. "Not that I know of, but Caine won't allow me close enough to ask."

Viper rolled his eyes. "Newly mated Weres are a pain in the ass."

"Yes." Styx abruptly chuckled. "You on the other hand were the very essence of a civilized gentleman during your pursuit of Shay."

The younger vampire's lips twitched. They both knew that Viper had become an obsessed predator the moment he'd found Shay being held captive by a coven of witches.

Their courtship had been the stuff of legends.

"There might have been an occasional glimpse of my more primitive side," he ruefully conceded.

"You were a raving lunatic."

Viper sent him a speaking glance. "It takes one to know one."

Styx thought back to his pursuit of Darcy with an unexpected pang of bittersweet longing. At the time, his battle had been with Salvatore. A tangible enemy with enough honor to understand the rules of warfare.

Now . . .

He shook his head. "It all seems like a very long time ago."

"I feel you," Viper muttered.

They shared a glance of mutual regret at the loss of simpler times before the moment was interrupted by the sound of footsteps.

Styx glanced toward the open doorway, already sensing the identity of the approaching vampire. "Roke."

Viper scowled. "Why is he still here?"

"We can use all the help we can get." Styx pointed a finger at the younger vampire. "Behave yourself."

Viper pressed a hand to his chest, his fallen-angel beauty emphasized by his overly innocent expression as he quoted back Styx's own words. "I promise to be the very essence of a civilized gentleman."

Styx snapped his fangs toward his companion. "You're a pain in the ass."

"At least we can agree on one thing," Roke drawled as he stepped into the room.

Viper stepped forward, but Styx grabbed his arm before they could come to blows. If the world managed to survive the looming apocalypse, he was going to lock the two clan chiefs into a room and not let them out until they could play nice.

"Have you completed your task?" he demanded of Roke.

"Task?" The Nevada clan chief narrowed his gaze, his strange silver eyes shimmering with a dangerous glow. "You make it sound like you asked me to rotate your tires, not find a way to tempt the ultimate evil into this world."

"If I wanted my tires rotated I would call a mechanic," Styx informed him without apology. "I expect my clan chiefs to perform miracles."

"No shit," Roke muttered.

Styx waved an impatient hand. He could feel the relentless ticking of the clock beating against him. "Well?"

Roke stood with a quiet confidence that went deeper than his position as vampire or clan chief. He was a lethal predator to the very bones. "We can't force her out of her lair."

Viper pulled away from Styx's grip, his expression mocking. "Genius."

Roke curled his lips to expose his fangs. "At least one of us has brains."

Styx muttered a foul curse, giving another wave of his hand. "Continue."

Roke returned his attention to Styx, although he looked like he would rather continue bantering with his fellow clan chief.

Not a good sign.

"So we have to offer her a temptation too great to resist," Roke said.

There was an empty silence as Styx waited for more, swiftly followed by Viper's sound of disgust.

"That's it?"

"Viper," Styx growled, more to prevent yet another headache-inducing squabble than to protest his skepticism. He wasn't too enthused about the vague solution either.

"Fine," Viper snapped, lifting his hands in a gesture of peace. "What temptation would lure the psycho bastard . . . wait, the psycho bitch, from her bat cave?"

"The person who locked her in her bat cave in the first place," Roke smoothly retorted.

Viper frowned. "The Phoenix?"

"No." Styx's voice filled the air with a frigid power that shattered the overhead chandelier and coated the marble figurines with ice. "No way."

Roke stood unflinching, his raven hair blowing around his lean face as the power rushed over him. "You asked for a suggestion, I gave you one."

Styx clutched his hands. The Phoenix was too vital to the future of the world to risk her in such a dangerous gamble.

"Not one that's feasible," he rasped. "Return to Cezar and—"

"Wait, Styx," Viper interrupted, his expression grim.

"What?"

"As much as I hate to agree with Roke on anything, I

have to admit his suggestion has merit. We should at least discuss the idea."

Styx hissed in shock. Was Viper suggesting that they offer up Abby like a sacrificial lamb?

"Before or after Dante chops off your head?" he snarled.

Viper glanced toward the vampire standing silently near the door.

"Roke, will you give us a minute?" Viper's words were more a command than a request.

The clan chief paused, then with a glance toward Styx's dangerously composed expression, he gave a sharp nod. "I'll be in the library."

Viper waited until Roke was out of the room and headed down the hallway before he stepped toward Styx.

"No," Styx growled, holding up a warning hand. "I don't want to hear it."

The younger vampire planted his hands on his hips, his expression warning it was going to take violence to halt him from sharing his opinion. "Styx, you are without a doubt the finest Anasso to ever lead the vampires."

"You think you can sway me with flattery?"

"I'm not done."

Styx snorted. "Don't let me stop you."

"I was about to say that what makes you such a great leader is also your greatest weakness."

"And what's that?"

"Loyalty."

Styx froze, catapulted back in time to when he was the trusted servant of the previous Anasso. He'd been a savage until the master had recruited him to become his soldier in the fight to pull the vampires out of the dark ages.

It hadn't been pretty. Nefri had led her clan beyond the Veil to create peace among her people; Styx's master, on the other hand, had used brute force and intimidation.

But it had worked. At least marginally. They were, after all, feral creatures.

Unfortunately, at some point the ancient vampire had become infected by the blood of human drug addicts. Styx had tried his best to save his master from his own weakness, even to the point of hiding the Anasso's growing madness from others, but in the end there had been no choice but to put him out of his misery.

"This isn't the same."

"Isn't it?" Viper demanded. The Chicago clan chief had been witness to Styx's conflicted battle between allegiance and duty. "Your heart was convinced that protecting your mentor was what was best for the vampires even though your head understood what had to be done."

Styx narrowed his gaze. Nothing was ever black-and-white. A good leader understood that he had to make decisions among the various shades of gray.

"And if we were speaking of using Shay as bait," he bit out.

Viper's midnight eyes flared with an instinctive fury, but with an obvious effort, he refused to be swayed. "I would try to kill you," he admitted in cold tones. "But your duty isn't just to me. Or Shay. Or Abby."

Spinning on his heel, Styx stomped across the room, his body trembling with the force of his emotions. "Damn you."

"Trust me, I don't like this any better than you," Viper continued to press. "Dante has been a brother to me for a very long time and Abby has become as dear to me as a sister. The thought of putting her in danger makes me want to ram my head through a wall. But can we destroy the world because we don't like the choices we're given?"

Styx wanted to block out the compelling words. An Anasso was supposed to protect his people, not put innocents in the direct line of fire.

A damned shame that Viper had a point.

Could he truly put the future of the world in jeopardy if there was the slightest chance to alter fate?

Feeling every one of his numerous years weighing down on him, Styx forced himself to turn back to his companion. "Even if I do agree to this madness and we manage to keep Dante from disappearing with his mate, we have no guarantee that the Dark Lord will give a shit about Abby," he pointed out. "The creature has to know the Phoenix is in the world, but she hasn't shown any interest in her before now."

Viper nodded. "True, but the Dark Lord has always been a victim of his"—he made a sound of annoyance—"I mean her bloated pride. If she caught a scent of the Phoenix near the rift, her desire for revenge might overcome her need for caution."

"That's a lot of *ifs*," Styx muttered.

"It's surely worth a try?"

Was it?

Styx scowled, not yet prepared to concede defeat. "Have you considered what happens if Abby or the goddess she carries inside her are destroyed?"

Viper studied him with an unwavering gaze. "What do you mean?"

"Right now we still have the hope that we can injure the Dark Lord's current form sufficiently to drive its essence out and she will be forced to retreat back to her prison," he pointed out, just as he had for Salvatore. "If we lose the Phoenix nothing will stop her."

Viper didn't hesitate. "And if we do nothing?"

Styx briefly contemplated the pleasure of rearranging Viper's perfect features. It wasn't the first time. Viper was one of the few vampires with the balls to stand up to him. Something that Styx didn't always accept with grace.

Instead he gave a shake of his head. "There has to be another way—" he began, only to break off as a shrill beep cut through the air. Digging the cell phone out of his pocket, he was astonished to discover his burst of power hadn't destroyed the thing. He almost wished it had when he caught a glimpse of the message waiting for him. "Shit."

"Now what?" Viper demanded.

"Regan heard from Jagr."

Viper curled his hands into fists, already sensing the news wasn't good. "Another rift?"

Styx tossed the phone on his desk. "Two more."

"We're out of time."

It was true.

As much as he hated to put Abby in danger, they had to find some means of destroying the Dark Lord before the hordes of hell overwhelmed them.

Now the question was how to get Abby to the nearest rift before it was too late.

"Get Levet," he abruptly commanded.

Viper blinked in confusion. "Why the gargoyle?"

"We have to get a message to Abby without interference from Dante. If he suspects we intend to use his mate as bait he'll do everything in his power to stop us," he said, grimacing at the knowledge Dante would never forgive him. "Levet is the only one who can reach directly into her mind."

The gardens at the back of Styx's mansion were just as rigidly formal as the rest of the estate. Perfectly manicured hedges that framed the individual rose beds, marble fountains circled by wrought-iron benches, and in the center of the flagstone pathways, a domed grotto that was bigger than most homes.

Lovely, of course, Levet acknowledged, but nothing compared to the gardens he'd known in France. No one could outdo the sun kings when it came to lavish excess.

Kicking a stray stone, Levet wandered aimlessly through the darkness, his wings twitching and his heart heavy. He hadn't wanted to contact Abby. Not when he realized that Styx was asking her to deliberately put herself in front of the rift to piss off an evil deity.

But what choice had he had?

The vampires had insisted that without the presence of the Goddess of Light the entire world was doomed to be overrun with evil. . . .

Rubbing his stunted horn, Levet wallowed in his misery, blithely unaware of the hint of brimstone that suddenly mixed with the scent of roses in the air.

So it was no wonder he nearly jumped out of his skin when a hand lightly touched his shoulder and a female voice whispered next to his ear, "Why so sad?"

"*Sacrebleu.*"

Leaping to the side, Levet glared at the small female demon with black, oblong eyes and a pale braid that hung nearly to the ground.

Yannah.

The female who'd bewitched him to the point of dropping everything to search for her like a Were in heat.

Imbecile.

"Hello, Levet."

"You." He scowled, in no mood to be teased. "Go away."

She blinked, her heart-shaped face a picture of innocence. As long as he ignored the sharp, pointed teeth that could rip through stone. Oh, and the power that thundered through the air.

"You don't mean that."

"I do." He tilted his chin, refusing to acknowledge the

sizzling awareness that burned through him. So what if he felt like he'd been struck by lightning every time he caught a glimpse of this female? Or that his heart soared with delight? He was finished making a fool of himself. "I have followed you from here to Paris and back again. And for what?" He lifted his hands, waving them in magnificent disgust. "Not so much as a kiss."

She tilted her head, looking like an inquisitive bird. "Would a kiss take away that frown?"

A kiss?

His heart gave one of those flutters, his blood heating at the mere thought of pulling her tiny body into his arms and tasting her brimstone passion. He had waited so long.

"It might—" He snapped his lips together. *Mon Dieu.* She had nearly done it to him again. "*Non.* This is no time for your games."

She pouted, but catching sight of his sour expression, she heaved a sigh. "Perhaps you're right."

He glanced around the shadowed garden, half expecting Yannah's mother to be hiding among the hedges. Which was ridiculous. Siljar was an Oracle, not a thief that skulked in the bushes. Not to mention the pertinent fact, she had the sort of power signature that could crush at a hundred paces.

If she was nearby, he would know.

He returned his attention to the tiny female who moved to stand in front of him, her white robe long enough to brush the paving stones. "Why are you here?"

"I sensed your unhappiness." She reached to gently stroke the tip of one stunted horn. "Tell me."

"I've done something I will never forgive myself for," he shocked himself by admitting.

It had nothing to do with her soft touch or the hint of

sympathy in her dark eyes, he assured himself. He wasn't that easily manipulated.

It was just . . . he needed someone to talk to.

Anyone would do. Even the marble statue of Neptune that spouted water out of his head.

Yeah, that was it.

"Ah." She wrinkled her nose. "You've called for the Goddess of Light."

Levet didn't bother to ask how the female knew he'd used his magic to speak directly into Abby's mind. Or that he'd urged her to travel to the rift. Yannah had more than one mysterious talent.

"*Oui.*"

"Why does that trouble you?" Yannah frowned, obviously puzzled by his distress. "It's the purpose of the Phoenix to stand against the tide of darkness."

"Because the Phoenix will not be charging into the battle alone," Levet said, his wings drooping at the mere thought of sweet, oh-so-fragile Abby standing face-to-face with the Dark Lord. "The spirit will take *ma chérie amie* along for the outing."

Yannah gave a faint shake of her head. "You mean along for the ride?"

"That is what I said, is it not?" he asked with an impatient frown.

"Yes, well, it's a time of change." Yannah tried to soothe. "We're all called to do our duty, whether we like it or not."

Levet pulled away from her distracting touch, pacing the distance between two ornate urns. "Well, I do not like it," he muttered, his tail whipping behind him. "I do not like it at all."

"Please stop, Levet," Yannah pleaded. "You're making my head spin."

"*Bien*." He came to a halt. Not because that's what she wanted. But how else could he send her a warning glare? "You have been making my head spin from the moment we met." He pointed a claw in her direction. "And, you punched me."

"It was a love-tap."

Levet made a sound of disbelief. "Love-tap? You broke my jaw."

"Do you want an apology?"

What he wanted was for her to kiss and make it better, a renegade voice whispered.

Kiss him over and over and over.

And not just on the jaw.

They could slip into the grotto where they would be all alone. He could at last indulge in the fantasies that had plagued him for weeks.

Non. Non. Non.

He folded his arms over his chest, just like he'd seen Styx do when he wanted to be an intimidating badass. "I want to be left in peace."

Yannah studied him, the dark gaze unnerving in its intensity. "This is more than guilt at calling your friend into danger, isn't it?"

He started to deny her ridiculous accusation only to find the words dying on his lips. Against his will his gaze shifted to the mansion where he could hear the rumble of vampires and Weres shouting orders.

"They are preparing for war while I am condemned to the gardens. You see, my skills are"—he searched for the appropriate word—"lacking."

Yannah regarded him with a shocked confusion that seemed genuine. "Why would you say that?"

"Because it's true."

"No." She gave a fierce shake of her head, the braid swinging from side to side. "It's not true."

Any other night Levet would have reveled in her fierce defense. Why not? He'd tried every trick possible to capture her attention only to be dismissed, abandoned, and forgotten.

Tonight, however, he'd been brutally reminded of his numerous inadequacies. With a grimace, he glanced down at his stunted body. "Look at me."

"I have looked," she assured him. "More than once."

He lifted his head with a scowl. "If I were one of my brothers they would beg for my assistance. I would be a powerful warrior with magic that would make even the Dark Lord tremble in fear."

She slowly stepped forward, her hands folded at her waist and the moonlight pooling around her. Despite her tiny size, she looked as regal as any queen.

"No, Levet," she said, her voice oddly somber. "If you were one of your brothers you would be hibernating in your lair waiting to offer your loyalty to whoever comes out the winner."

It wasn't at all what he'd expected and his pity party was suddenly deflated as effectively as if she'd stuck a pin in a balloon.

She was right. From all reports his brethren had retreated beneath the streets of Paris, ignoring Styx's call for demons to stand against the Dark Lord. Like rats fleeing a sinking ship. Gargoyles were infamous for bowing to whoever sat on the throne. Loyalty was not a word in their vocabulary.

"I suppose that's true," he slowly agreed.

She reached to place her hands on his shoulders, standing close enough he could feel the pulse of her power surrounding him.

"Besides, you have a weapon far more important than muscles or magic."

Levet found himself lost in the compelling darkness of her eyes. "What weapon?"

"A heart." Her hand moved to rest in the center of his chest. "The one power that can't be defeated by evil."

Chapter 24

The Dark Lord's prison

Gaius seriously underestimated the instinctive desire of any creature for survival.

He'd been convinced that he had nothing left to hope for. Nothing left but bitter regret and endless days of wishing for a swift death that would at last reunite him with Dara.

But the moment the Dark Lord had turned her attention to creating further rifts, he found his feet carrying himself forward, scouring the godforsaken surroundings for a way to escape.

A frustrating, not to mention, futile waste of time.

Although he still had his medallion, he discovered it no longer obeyed his commands. Not surprising. The Dark Lord wasn't stupid. She knew he would disappear at the first opportunity.

And while he could sense the doorways she'd ripped through the veils, and occasionally catch the scent of demons as they sought to use the openings to spill from their particular hell dimension, he couldn't push his way through them.

Perhaps this was his punishment.

To be trapped with the Dark Lord, all the while knowing that freedom lurked just out of reach.

It seemed fitting.

Standing near a stunted tree, Gaius flinched as a flare of heat seared over him, threatening to melt the flesh from his bones.

"Gaius."

He didn't want to turn. Not only because he was weary of her taunting, but because it made him nauseous to watch the strange spirit flickering around her.

But what he did or didn't want no longer mattered. Not since he'd bartered away his soul.

With a slow movement, he stepped around the dead tree and faced the female eyeing him with petulant displeasure. "Yes, Mistress?"

Her eyes smoldered with crimson fire while the misty outline of the Gemini haloed her slender body. "Were you hiding from me?" she demanded.

He wryly glanced around the empty landscape. "Where would I go?"

"I don't know, but you were plotting something," she accused. "I can sense it."

He stoically refused to react. Instead, he tried for a distraction. "Was there something you needed?"

There was a pause before she dismissed any thought of him with a wave of her hand. "The transformation should be complete," she complained. The lion's head flickered in and out of focus just behind her, as if being shorted out by some unseen electrical charge.

"Perhaps another sacrifice is needed."

"No," she glared at him with malevolent annoyance. As if the spirit's refusal to complete the binding was his fault. "There is something interfering. Or someone."

He took an instinctive step backward. "You can't think that I—"

"Of course not," she snapped. "Despite the treachery you harbor in your heart, you don't possess the power to halt my inevitable victory."

His lips twisted. All true.

Humiliatingly true.

"There's no one else here." He pointed out the obvious.

"Which means the interference must be coming from one of the rifts."

Gaius was motionless, his mind shifting through the unexpected revelation. Of all the possibilities he'd considered, he'd never once given thought to an outside force being able to penetrate this hellhole.

A gift. One he'd have to use with great care.

"Then close them," he offered the suggestion that she would be expecting. Anything else would immediately rouse her suspicions.

She reached to grasp his arm, branding him with her touch. "You'd like that, wouldn't you?"

He bowed his head, clenching his teeth against the blazing pain. "My only concern is for your welfare."

"Your only concern is saving your own skin. Pathetic worm."

"How can I prove my loyalty?"

"You can't."

Abruptly releasing his arm, the Dark Lord turned her attention to the vast expanse of nothingness bathed in a sickly yellow glow, holding out her hand as she walked forward.

Gaius fell into step behind her. Why would she have sought him out if she didn't want him to play devoted slave? But he was careful not to brush against the shadowy figure that surrounded her.

The thing was . . . unnerving.

They moved in heavy silence, their steps sending up tiny clouds of choking dust. Absently, Gaius wondered if this desolate land had been lurking beneath the white mists, or if the Dark Lord's almost-transformation had blasted it to this current wasteland.

Not that it mattered. One was as bad as the other.

Without warning, the Dark Lord came to an abrupt halt, her outstretched hand clenching into a fist. "It's here."

"Here" looked exactly the same as "there," but Gaius's disinterest was shaken as he caught an unmistakable scent drift through the thick air.

"Vampires," he muttered in shock, stepping closer to the elusive smell. "Could they be causing the disruption?"

"Don't be stupid," she hissed in fury. "Vampires are no match for me. As you've discovered."

He grimaced as her insult slid home. "Then what is?"

She dropped her hand, the halo around her seeming to fade to dull shadow.

"The Phoenix."

His eyes widened in surprise. "The Goddess of Light?"

"Ridiculous name."

Gaius barely heard her muttered complaint. Over the centuries, he'd listened to the Dark Lord's bitter complaints about the powerful spirit that kept him locked in his prison. But since the Dark Lord's resurrection into a new body, and with the threat of the looming transformation into the Gemini, Gaius had assumed that the Phoenix would go into hiding.

"Are you sure?"

"Of course I'm sure, you idiot." A sudden wind whipped around Gaius as the Dark Lord struggled to leash her temper. "Do you think I wouldn't recognize the bitch who stripped me of my powers and trapped me in this hell?"

He shook his head. "Why would she be so close to the opening?"

The crimson eyes flamed with an emotion that went beyond fury to mindless rage. "She's obviously arrogant enough to believe she can keep me trapped."

Gaius deliberately smoothed his expression to a bland mask. The Phoenix had the evil deity twitching.

So how did he take advantage of the unexpected gift?

Carefully, a voice warned in the back of his mind.

"Or . . ." He snapped his lips together, as if regretting what he was about to say.

As expected, the Dark Lord turned to stab him with a fiery glare. "What?"

He shrugged. "Nothing."

Gaius grunted in pain as the Dark Lord grasped his chin in a grip that crushed his bones. "Tell me, leech."

He paused. He couldn't overplay his hand. A hint. A vague suggestion. A pretense he was trying to lead her in one direction so she would bolt in toward the opposite. Just like a spoiled child.

"I can't believe they would bring the goddess so close unless they're convinced they could defeat you," he said as if the words were being pulled out of him. "Styx is an arrogant son of a bitch, but he isn't the sort of leader to make empty gestures."

"Defeat me?" The pretty features that should never have been on the face of such an evil bitch flushed with ugly outrage. "Impossible."

The agony of his shattered chin made it difficult to speak. "If you say so."

The crimson eyes narrowed. "I know what you're trying to do."

"Do?"

"You're trying to trick me into closing the rift."

"Certainly I am. My fate is now tied to yours." He said, his words holding enough truth to sound sincere. "If you're destroyed by the Goddess of Light, then my brothers will spend the rest of eternity making certain I regret my betrayals."

She released her crushing hold, the shadow surrounding her shifting in and out of focus. "My return can't be halted," she muttered, speaking more to herself than Gaius. "Not now. I'm too close."

Gaius narrowed his gaze at her stubborn insistence. His initial thought had been to keep her distracted long enough for the Goddess of Light to work her magic. Who knew? He might get lucky enough to slip away unnoticed.

Or at least be destroyed in the crossfire.

Now, he realized he had the perfect means to tilt the odds in . . .

Well, not his favor. But perhaps in the favor of the Phoenix.

He might have turned his back on the world, as well as his brothers, but he intended to do everything in his power to make sure the evil bitch standing in front of him was destroyed.

"What does it matter when it happens?" he asked with a small shrug. "Your worshippers will understand that you dare not risk a direct confrontation with the goddess."

The nearby stump burst into flames as the Dark Lord's fury swirled around her. The first thing her minions learned was never to speak of her ignoble defeat at the hands of the Phoenix.

And they most certainly didn't imply that the Dark Lord might be terrified of another encounter.

"Don't tell me what I can or can't do," she said, the pressure of her terrible voice sending Gaius to his knees.

He bowed his head, his chin still aching and his flesh beginning to singe. "Forgive me, but wouldn't it be better to send your minions to battle her?" he suggested softly. "Eventually, she'll be overwhelmed to the point you can defeat her."

The ground split open beside them, the stench of sulfur filling the air. "Are you implying I can't defeat her?"

He wisely kept his head lowered. "She did trap you here."

"Now I am the Gemini," she raged, seeming to forget the transformation hadn't been completed. "I am unstoppable."

"Let your servants sacrifice themselves," he continued to provoke, pressing at her weakest point. Her arrogance. "After the goddess is destroyed and you've taken over the world, you can write the histories to speak of your glorious defeat of the Phoenix." He glanced up to witness the veins of crimson that crawled beneath the pale skin of the Dark Lord. As if her blood flowed with fire. "Who will care if it's the truth or not?"

"I will know."

With a sharp motion, the Dark Lord lifted her hand and pointed it toward a spot just over Gaius's head. An earthquake shook the ground beneath him, widening the split until Gaius was forced to scramble backward.

"What are you doing?"

The Dark Lord continued to allow her power to build until Gaius was certain he would be crushed by the sheer force.

"When the goddess is destroyed it will be by my hand."

"You're going through?"

"No." Reaching down, the Dark Lord grabbed Gaius by the hair, holding on tight enough to warn she wasn't letting go. "*We're* going through, Gaius."

The heat of a thousand suns seemed to rush through him as he was jerked forward, shifting from one dimension to the next.

"*Merde.*"

At the rift

The cramped room in the basement of the abandoned warehouse had been made considerably larger by the simple process of knocking out walls and digging out the surrounding dirt so the warriors could position themselves for the upcoming battle.

And the battle was coming.

That was the one certain thing in a very uncertain world.

Despite the efforts of the Sylvermysts, as well as the exquisite Nefri, who had added her powers, the rift was widening with every passing minute, filling the air with the electric heaviness of a brewing thunderstorm.

Something was coming.

Something bad.

Standing on the fringes of the gathered crowd, Cassie ignored Caine's low grumbling to study the human female who was the chalice for the Goddess of Light.

She wasn't certain what she'd expected. Maybe a statuesque Amazon with a flaming sword riding on a chariot.

Instead, Abby Barlow was a slender female with rich, honey curls that framed her gamine face. Only the shocking blue eyes revealed she was anything other than mortal.

Dante, her vampire mate, on the other hand, was exactly what she'd expected.

Wearing black biker boots, faded denims, and a black leather jacket, he had a pale, aristocratic face and silver eyes that contrasted sharply with the shoulder-length black hair. With his loop earrings and massive sword, he looked like a pirate just waiting for an excuse to pillage.

The couple was standing closest to the Sylvermysts as they held the rift shut, with Styx and Salvatore standing beside them. Viper and the Ravens were stoically hovering at the sides.

The rest of the room was consumed by an odd combination of vampires, Weres, curs, fairies, imps, and a female Shallot that Viper watched with a blatant possession.

She had to be his mate.

Nothing else could explain that particular expression of exasperated concern.

The same expression was currently on Caine's face as he battled between the urge to toss Cassie over his shoulder and take her away from the danger and the certain knowledge she would simply return the second his back was turned.

"You're sure that's the Phoenix?" she asked, hoping for a distraction.

He narrowed his gaze, not fooled for a minute. "So they say."

"She doesn't look like a powerful goddess."

He lifted a brow, reaching to tuck a stray curl behind her ear. "I could point out that you don't look like a prophet who holds the future of the world in your beautiful head."

"This empty head, you mean," she muttered, that cold ball of dread still lodged in the pit of her stomach. When she'd discovered that Styx was planning to bring the Phoenix to the rift to provoke the Dark Lord into the world, she'd insisted on coming along. Somehow she'd hoped being near the action would jiggle loose whatever was blocking her visions. So far, however, her efforts had been a big bust. "Let's hope that Abby's power hasn't gone on vacation when she needs it most."

Caine reached to wrap his arms around her as the ground trembled and the air filled with a choking heat. "You shouldn't be here," he growled in her ear.

"Hiding won't protect me," she reminded him, allowing

him to keep her tucked tightly against him although her gaze remained on the rift. "Besides, if I have a vision we'll need to share it with the others. I can't do that locked in the cellars."

A growl rumbled in his chest. "It doesn't mean I have to like it."

"No," she softly agreed. "You don't have to like it."

The quakes intensified, buckling the ground beneath their feet and sending a shower of dust from the ceiling.

Whatever was coming was getting closer.

The demons around them tensed, and then as one they unsheathed, loaded, cocked, and aimed their various weapons as the air became too thick to breathe.

There was a moment, as if time was standing still.

Cassie pressed closer to Caine, taking comfort in his warm scent before she gently pulled out of his arms. The violence shimmering in the air would be calling to his wolf. She didn't want him hesitating to take his more powerful form because of her.

There were more tremors and then a collective cry as the Sylvermysts abruptly collapsed in unconscious heaps. There was the sound of cursing from a tall, dark-haired vampire who grabbed the wilting Nefri in his arms and carried her to the back of the room, as well as a cry from Jaelyn as she rushed forward to kneel next to her Sylvermyst prince.

In the midst of the chaos, Abby stood without flinching as a soft glow began to pulse around her.

The Goddess of Light.

The vampires took a step back to avoid the spill of power, but they stood firmly at her side while the Weres shifted in an explosion of fang and fur, forming a half circle around the widening rift.

Cassie sensed the minute Caine took his wolf form, the prickles of his power racing over her skin. He towered beside her, angling so he would stand between her and the shit that was about to hit the fan.

She glanced around him at the warriors standing like a living barricade against the oncoming evil, abruptly reminded of her vision that had infuriated the Dark Lord.

The tides of chaos break upon an impenetrable wall.

They stood shoulder to shoulder, ancient enemies all brought together against one common goal.

But would it be enough?

Her vision had hinted at this moment, but not the outcome of the battle.

Perhaps because the outcome had yet to be decided.

Not the most comforting of thoughts, she wryly acknowledged, gagging on the sudden stench of smoldering sulfur.

The Dark Lord.

The thought barely had time to flash through her mind when a figure appeared in the rift and then stumbled forward. Cassie frowned at the sight of the naked male who tripped over the unconscious Sylvermysts, his dark hair falling forward to obscure his face. Then, as he awkwardly scrambled to his feet, she grimaced.

Gaius.

And looking distinctly worse for the wear.

The vampire holding Nefri made a sound of infuriated disbelief, but before anyone could move to capture the vampire traitor, there was a blast of crippling heat.

Throwing her arms over her face, Cassie missed the grand entrance of the Dark Lord, although she felt the power of the evil deity sizzling through the room. When she at last lowered her arms it was to discover the familiar female form with long, dark hair and a disturbingly sweet face complete with dimples.

But there had been changes since she'd last seen the demented creature.

The cute sundress had been replaced by a flowing black robe and the eyes that had been a clear, innocent blue were now bottomless pits of crimson flames. As if they were the doorways to hell.

And they probably were.

Oh, and the peculiar outline of another shape flickered around her slender body.

Cassie tried to focus on the strange shadow, catching a hint of a lion head on top of a humanoid form before it flickered out of view.

Was that the Gemini?

Somehow she'd assumed that it would become an actual part of the Dark Lord.

The initial shock wave of her entrance forced the front lines to stumble backward. All but Abby, who stood firm, the glow of the goddess flaring toward the evil intruder.

The Dark Lord hissed as the glow surrounded her, but when the strange . . . spirit, or whatever it was that flickered around her, stopped the light from touching her body, she tilted back her head to laugh with a creepy delight.

"At last." The crimson eyes flared. "I've waited for this day for endless centuries. Now you'll pay for keeping me trapped in that hell." Her dimpled smile was just . . . wrong. "You'll pay for each and every hour I suffered."

Regaining their footing, the gathered demons loosened their ammunition, sending a barrage of bullets, silver-tipped arrows, and daggers flying in the direction of the Dark Lord. The creature gave another laugh, brushing aside the lethal torrent with a wave of her slender hand.

"I won't be stopped," she threatened, her gaze never leaving Abby. "Not this time."

She might have sounded like a cheesy blowhard if the rift hadn't chosen that moment to rip completely open, allowing the horde of nasty demons to spill out.

Cassie's heart squeezed in fear. Not at the sight of the hideous nightmares that crawled through the basement, but at the acceptance that the bloody battle was now inevitable.

They'd been hurtling toward this moment for . . . Cassie grimaced. For longer than she'd been alive.

Now there was no way to avoid the ugly fate.

As if able to read her mind, Styx held his massive sword in the air, his voice slicing through the thick air with a frigid blast. "Now."

With a combination of shouts and growls, the vampires and Weres attacked the approaching demons, using fangs and claws to tear through the horde.

Offering her a warning glance to stay put, Caine launched his massive body at the nearest enemy, his snarls sending shivers down Cassie's spine. Unable to watch the slaughter, she turned her gaze back to the Dark Lord, who faced off against Abby.

Their battle was less bloody, but no less brutal as their energies clashed with shocking force.

Cassie unknowingly backed up until she hit the crumbling wall behind her. Through the dust and smoke, she watched the savage melee unfolding, her stomach clenching in horror.

The cloying scent of death was almost overwhelming, but for all the killing on both sides neither appeared to be winning the war.

They were too evenly matched.

It could be a long, bloody stalemate that would be the end of everything.

Oblivion.

The trumpet of doom sounded in her mind at the precise same time the world around her went white. Gasping, she dropped to her knees and pressed her hands to her forehead.

The chaos around her faded away to leave a lone image burning in the center of her brain.

Scales.

The golden scales of justice.

And on one of the flat plates was a small stone.

Cassie momentarily floundered, unable to decipher the vision. Dammit, she'd been so desperate for a glimpse of the future.

Fate couldn't be so cruel to offer her that glimpse without the means to understand it.

Could it?

The vision remained, branding her synapses. But just as she was about to scream in frustration, the weight tilted. It was less than a millimeter. A breath of a dip by the plate with the stone. But it was suddenly as clear as if it was written in bold letters across the wall.

What they needed was something to tip the balance.

No, not something.

Someone.

Caine's warm, musky scent at last penetrated the white shrouding her mind, his lips brushing her ear as he tried to bring her back.

"Cassie." His fingers combed through her hair, his voice thick with concern. "Cassie, can you hear me?"

She leaned against his chest, smelling the wolf still clinging to his naked skin. He'd shifted back to human, but his beast was straining at the leash, maddened by his inability to reach her.

With an effort, she managed to force her eyes open, finding Caine kneeling beside her, his expression tight with concern.

"Levet," she managed to croak.

He scowled. "What?"

She shuddered as the sounds and smells of the raging

battle came crashing back. It was close. Close enough she could taste the blood in the air.

Clinging to Caine, she squashed the panic threatening to overwhelm her.

"We need Levet."

Caine gave a puzzled shake of his head. "The gargoyle?"

"Yes."

"Did you hit your head when you fell?"

She made a sound of impatience that was lost among the screams. "I had a vision."

Caine parted his lips, but before he could speak the body of a cur flew over their heads, slamming into the wall with a sickening thud.

"Shit," he muttered, tugging her as far away from the carnage as was possible in the cramped space.

She reached up to grab his face, knowing with absolute certainty that she held the fate of the world in her hands.

"Keep them away long enough for me to try and reach him."

"Reach Levet?" he muttered, still clearly baffled by her insistence that they needed the tiny demon.

"It's imperative, Caine."

"Fine." He glanced around the gory melee, turning back with a helpless frown. "How? With this much power a cell phone will never work."

She'd already figured that one out. Which meant she only had one option.

"An act of desperation," she admitted wryly.

He studied her for a long moment, and then with that absolute belief in her that never failed to melt her heart, he leaned forward to brush her lips in a tender kiss.

"That works for me."

Love spilled through her as she wondered what magical fate had ever brought this Were into her life.

"Be careful," she commanded, her voice gruff with worry.

"Always."

He stole another kiss before stepping back and shifting.

Cassie closed her eyes as he launched himself at an approaching demon, his fangs sinking into the creature's throat. Knowing that Caine was in danger was enough of a distraction without watching it in real time.

Instead, she allowed the image of Levet to form in her mind, sending him a silent plea to travel to the rift.

She didn't have a clue if her message was actually reaching the gargoyle. Or even if they had the necessary time for him to arrive.

But knowing she would be all but worthless in the battle, she continued to do the only thing that might help. A fine sheet of sweat coated her skin as she focused on her mental image, the heat and chaos in the room beating against her senses.

With such confusion, it was nothing less than a miracle that she felt the stir of air at her side. Even then she wasn't sure what to expect when she opened her eyes.

Panic. Mayhem. Nightmares from the pits of hell.

Death and destruction.

All very real possibilities.

What she found instead was a tiny gargoyle stepping out of thin air, his tail stuck straight out and his wings quivering.

"Levet," she breathed in shock, rising to her feet.

She wasn't sure if she was more surprised that she'd actually managed to reach him, or that he'd managed to arrive so swiftly.

The gargoyle, however, seemed unaware of her presence, let alone the battle raging only a few feet away, as he glared at the tiny demon who appeared directly behind him.

"You . . . I . . ." Wild-eyed, Levet pointed a claw toward

the small female wearing a long white robe. "*Mon Dieu . . .* Do not ever do that again."

The female remained unruffled, her almond-shaped black eyes holding a vast power. "You said it was an emergency."

Levet shivered, still trembling from his hasty journey. "*Oui.*"

"You've traveled by portal before, haven't you?" the demon asked, her curiosity holding more than a hint of amusement.

Cassie shook her head, wondering if the bickering duo were unaware of the war that raged around them.

Difficult to believe.

But before she opened her mouth to point out their danger, Levet was continuing his tirade.

"A portal is not the same as . . ." He waved his hands as words failed him.

"As?"

"As poofing."

"Poofing? Hmmm." The female tapped a finger to her narrow chin, her calm a direct contrast to Levet's agitation. "I suppose that's as good an explanation as any other."

"Arggg."

Cassie stepped forward. She didn't understand the argument. Demons were, after all, as baffling as humans.

But enough was enough.

"Levet," she said in firm tones.

On cue, the tiny gargoyle turned to offer her a bow. "Ah, *ma chérie.* I received your call." He straightened to regard her with a curious gaze. "You said you have need of me?"

Cassie waved a hand toward the dozens of demons who were currently shredding one another into gory little ribbons. "We all have need of you."

Levet followed the direction of her hand, giving a sound of distress as he fully took in the violent chaos.

Just in front of them, Caine was methodically chewing through the neck of an orc, his back marred with bloody gashes from the creature's claws.

Toward the front of the shattered room, Styx and Salvatore laid waste to any creature stupid enough to get near their savage attacks, the growing pile of corpses surrounding them like a wall of death.

Moving with a fluid speed, Viper danced among the carnage, his sword so quick most of the demons never saw their brutal end coming.

Further on, Ariyal, the Prince of Sylvermysts, was spraying a volley of arrows into the spreading rift, while his vampire Hunter mate, Jaelyn, stood back to back with him, her sawed-off shotgun blowing large holes in the strange, troll-like monsters coated in scales with raven beaks.

There was even an elemental fey who was mated to Cezar, who was using her powers to leech out of the air the lethal heat that pulsed from the Dark Lord.

This was the fate they'd all feared.

"*Sacrebleu*," Levet breathed. "As much as I wish to be of service, I fear I am no warrior. And my magic . . ." He grimaced with a bone-deep regret. "It is not predictable enough to use in battle."

Cassie bent down so they were eye to eye, reaching to grasp his hands in a pleading grip. "That's not why you're here."

He blinked in confusion. "It is not?"

"No."

"Then why?"

"I don't know," she grudgingly confessed. "But you were in my vision."

The gray eyes widened in fear. "What was I doing?"

She settled back on her heels, biting her lower lip as she realized how silly her explanation was going to sound.

"Tilting the scales."

"Scales?" Levet scratched his stunted horn, clearly baffled. "What scales?"

"Those."

Cassie pointed her hand to the center of the room where the combatants had cleared a space for the two females who stood face-to-face.

Although they were nearly obscured by the shimmer of combating energies, there was no mistaking the Dark Lord with her deceptively girlish beauty and her shadowed aura, or Abby, who was bathed in a soft glow, her eyes as brilliant as sapphires.

"Abby." The gargoyle gasped in distress as the Dark Lord lifted her hand and bolts of lightning shot toward the Phoenix, knocking her backward. Abby grimaced in pain, but with grim determination she forced herself to step forward, continuing to surround the Dark Lord in the power of the goddess. "*Non*."

With a flutter of his wings, the gargoyle abruptly charged forward, using his small stature to dart between the legs of the demons who were too busy to take notice of him.

"Levet . . . wait." Cassie straightened, her breath squeezing from her lungs at the fear she'd just sent the precious little demon to his death. "Crap, crap, crap."

"Don't fear." The female demon reached to pat Cassie on the back of her leg, the pulse of her power a tangible force. "I will protect him."

Cassie glanced down at the unpredictable creature, not entirely reassured by her promise. "Why?"

She flashed a smile filled with anticipation. And sharp teeth. Yow.

"Because I am not done playing with him yet."

* * *

"*Some are born great, some achieve greatness, and some have greatness thrust upon them. . . .*"

Shakespeare's words ran through Levet's mind as he narrowly avoided a spear that nicked the top of his wing.

He'd been convinced that nothing could be worse than to be condemned as a useless lump of stone and left to rot in Styx's garden. After all, he'd spent his considerably long life attempting to become a fierce warrior who would at last impress his brethren.

Now he realized that being a part of the battle was no better.

Not because he feared he would be killed.

Death was death. Inevitable, even to immortals.

No, what he feared was failure.

He'd always been the smallest, the weakest, and the least likely to become a hero. Even his magic was pathetic, if he was being perfectly honest.

How could he possibly be expected to "tip the scales"?

Taking a kick to the head and having his tail stepped on more times than he could count, Levet at last reached the center of the room. He skidded to a halt at the edge of the energy field that surrounded Abby and the Dark Lord like a bubble, the electric prickles crawling over his skin as the evil deity sent another bolt of lightning into her slender opponent.

"Abby," he cried out, close enough to see the blackened burns that seared her fragile skin.

She turned her head, looking every inch the Phoenix with her brilliant blue eyes and fierce expression.

"Levet." She frowned in bewilderment, then doubled over as another bolt struck her in her stomach. "Stay back," she gasped.

"*Non.*"

Darting forward, Levet abruptly found himself dangling

off the ground as someone grabbed him by the horn and lifted him upward.

"Dammit, gargoyle," a familiar voice snarled.

Levet was spun to meet a pair of furious silver eyes set in the face of a pirate.

Dante.

He wiggled, even knowing it was futile. Dante was like any other vampire.

Arrogant, annoyingly strong, and stubborn as a damned mule.

"Let me go," he commanded.

Naturally Dante ignored him, his expression so brittle that Levet knew it would take very little to shatter him.

"This isn't the time for your foolish bravado," he snapped. "Abby's fighting for her life." His gaze compulsively shifted to where his mate was bravely ignoring her grievous wounds to straighten and send a pulse of light toward the Dark Lord. "She's fighting for all of us."

Levet grasped the vampire's wrist, knowing he was teetering on the edge as he watched his mate being brutalized.

"Listen to me, Dante. I was a part of the vision."

He scowled, reluctantly returning his attention to the gargoyle dangling from his hand. "What vision?"

"Cassie's vision."

"The prophet?"

"*Oui.*"

"Shit."

"Let me go, Dante," Levet softly demanded. "Abby needs me."

The scowl remained. "If you—"

"I know," he interrupted, sensing the electricity building in the air. The Dark Lord was about to strike again, and there was no guarantee the Phoenix could survive another blow. "I'm here to help."

Without warning, he was lowered back to the ground, Dante's face white with fear. "Save her," he pleaded.

Levet nodded, forgetting his own doubts as he turned to step through the shroud of energy.

It no longer mattered what his purpose was, so long as he faced it with his head held high and his wings undrooping.

That was surely the definition of a hero?

He took another step forward, his skin crawling at the volatile power that slammed into him.

Mon Dieu.

He staggered to a halt. How could Abby bear the crushing pain?

Suddenly sensing his presence, Abby turned to regard him with unearthly blue eyes. "Levet?"

Before he could reassure her that he was there to help, he was distracted by the lightning bolt that sizzled past his horns.

"What's this?" the Dark Lord mocked, her eyes pits of crimson flame and her body surrounded by a black aura. "Have you come to be squashed, little bug?"

"I . . ."

His courage threatened to crumble. He was a little bug. A foolish little bug with delusions of grandeur.

Then, his glance skidded toward the battle that raged just beyond the bubble. He flinched at the sight of the warriors who fought. And those who'd already fallen. They didn't care if he was tiny, or if his wings were too frilly, or his magic as fickle as a fairy whore. They were sacrificing everything to halt the dark tide. How could he do any less?

He stiffened his backbone. *Hero, Levet. You're a hero, not a bug.*

"Well, gargoyle," the Dark Lord drawled. "Has the cat gotten your tongue?"

Levet tilted his chin. "I have come to kill you."

The crimson eyes narrowed. "Is this a joke?"

Levet felt Abby place a hand on his wing, the warmth of the goddess surrounding him.

"Levet . . . no. Please."

"Stay out of this." The Dark Lord launched another attack at Abby, driving her back several steps before turning back toward the quivering Levet. "If he wants to die, then who am I to deny his wish?"

The lightning flashed toward him, and with a curse he leaped to the side, his tail twitching. Some hero, he wryly acknowledged, sensing Abby escalating the power of the goddess as he darted from yet another bolt.

This wasn't helping.

So what would?

As the question was rattling through his brain, he made another dodge, his gaze catching sight of the strange form that haloed the Dark Lord's slender body.

Although most of his skills were questionable, the one constant was his ability to see through illusion.

Any illusion.

Squatting to avoid the latest strike of lightning, he ignored the fact the Dark Lord was forced to turn her fury back toward Abby, who was draining the last of her power into the wicked bitch.

Instead, he kept his attention locked on the aura that flickered in and out of focus around the Dark Lord.

There was something strange about it.

It was like the spirit was attached to the Dark Lord . . . but not fully integrated.

Or perhaps not fully committed.

Either way, he suddenly knew that this was his one shot.

Staying low as the two powerful deities continued their private battle, Levet inched his way forward.

The heat and pain pounded against him, but he forced

himself to put one foot in front of the other. The closer he was to the Dark Lord, the less chance his spell would backfire and hurt someone else.

Vampires were so testy about friendly fire.

A sickly smile curved his lips as he lifted his hands. This was it. Do or die.

Concentrating on the spirit hovering around the Dark Lord, he released the magic that was as ancient as the beginning of time.

At first there was nothing more than sparkles of color that danced over the silhouette of the Gemini. It was a pretty display, but it didn't even make the Dark Lord notice. Instead, she continued her ruthless attack on Abby, veins of crimson running beneath the pale ivory skin.

Stubbornly, Levet refused to concede defeat.

It was the Gemini protecting the Dark Lord.

Without that protection the bitch would be vulnerable to the Phoenix's attack.

He lifted his hands, but even as he was preparing to launch another spell, the sparkles began to sink into the dark aura. The darkness quivered, as if the pinpricks of light were causing it pain. Or injury.

Levet was hoping it was injury.

He released his second burst of magic. This time the sparkles struck directly into the aura, exploding like tiny firecrackers.

The scent of burned flesh mixed with the charred odor of sulfur and a foul stench of a rotting carcass. As if someone had just yanked open a grave.

The darkness shuddered, then like thick molasses it began to pull away from the female form.

Levet gagged, belatedly realizing the Dark Lord had sensed her danger and whirled in his direction.

"What have you done?" she screeched, her hands reaching for the ephemeral spirit as if she could physically hold on to it.

"Exactly what I promised," he croaked, drained to the point he could barely stand.

With an audible snap, the spirit pulled away from the Dark Lord, shooting away from the lights that danced in pursuit.

"No." The female stumbled backward, clearly aware of her vulnerability. "This is impossible."

"'The word impossible is not in my dictionary,'" Levet quoted Napoleon, a smile curving his lips as Abby stepped behind the female and wrapped her hands around the Dark Lord's neck.

"Die," Abby whispered softly.

"You . . ." Shuddering as the power of the goddess flowed through her body, the Dark Lord glared at Levet with a soul-deep hatred. "You will pay for this."

Levet was hoping it was an empty threat.

The evil *putain* was beginning to rot from the inside out as the goddess's power poured into her, her skin splitting open to allow the crimson flames to spill out.

But even as she was dying, she reached out her hand and pointed her finger at Levet.

He darted to the side, but he was a half beat too late and even as the Dark Lord was enveloped in a shimmering mist, she sent out a bolt of lightning that struck him square in the chest.

He cried out, an unbearable agony exploding through his tiny body. *Sacrebleu*. This wasn't the sort of pain a gargoyle could survive. Then, thankfully, he was tumbling into a waiting darkness.

His last thought wasn't of death or sacrifice or even the scent of Yannah that suddenly filled his senses.

It was that he'd finally done it.

He was a bona fide hero.

He hoped they'd write a song.

Chapter 25

Having inched her way toward the battling deities, Cassie was acutely aware of the moment the Dark Lord died.

It wasn't just that the entire room came to a silent halt. Or that the blinding lightning was no longer flashing.

Or even that the stench of sulfur was suddenly gone.

It was in the change in pressure that had been beating down on them. As if a terrible storm had passed over, leaving behind the fresh lightness of a spring day.

But she barely noticed as the evil creature was swallowed by a shimmering mist that obscured her from view. Her only thought was that Levet was lying motionless on the ground, his wings broken and his chest ripped open by the lightning strike.

"Levet." Reaching his side, Cassie dropped to her knees, grasping his hand as she glared at the tiny female demon who appeared at her side. "Dammit, you promised to protect him."

The demon regarded her with an unwavering black gaze, her expression giving nothing away. "I will take care of the gargoyle."

Cassie bit her lower lip. "Is he . . ."

"Don't worry." The female offered a mysterious smile

as she glanced over Cassie's shoulder. "You should brace yourself."

"What?"

There was the scent of anxious Were before she was pulled off her feet and hauled against a broad, naked chest.

"Cassie," Caine growled, his heart pounding beneath her ear. "I told you to stay put."

"Wait." She glanced over her shoulder, heaving an exasperated sigh as she realized the demon had already disappeared with Levet.

For the female's sake, Cassie hoped she took good care of Levet.

Otherwise, she intended to . . . well, she didn't know what she would do, but it would be bad.

Really, really bad.

"Cassie?"

"Never mind." She turned back to bury her face in the neck of her mate, breathing deeply of his welcomed musk.

He released a shaky breath. "You're going to be the death of me."

"Not anytime soon."

"Did you see that in a vision?" he teased, threading his fingers through her hair so he could tilt back her head and flash a smile that had melted a thousand hearts.

A thousand and one, she corrected as she lifted his hand to press it against the middle of her chest.

"No, here."

Lost in the wonder of one another, not to mention the realization they'd survived the end of the world, they ignored the demons fleeing from their lost cause, swiftly pursued by vampires and Weres.

And even the unexpected sound of crying babies.

It wasn't until Styx and Salvatore came to a halt next to them that they were pulled out of their brief illusion of privacy.

The two kings were looking a little ragged around the edges. Styx was coated in blood with his hair hanging in a tangled curtain down his back, while Salvatore had managed to pull on a pair of sweats to cover his nudity, his body still healing from a number of wounds.

"God . . . damn," the Anasso muttered, his gaze shifting behind Cassie.

"What now?" Caine rasped, setting Cassie aside as he straightened to face whatever new disaster was about to attack.

Cassie was slower to turn. She didn't want any more bad. Not for a very long time.

At first her gaze lingered on a weary Abby, who was being held in Dante's lap as he stroked tender kisses over her pale face. She looked drained, but amazingly unharmed considering she'd just battled the Dark Lord.

Eventually, she turned to see the vampire with the mohawk and fearsome beauty standing beside his half-Jinn mate, Laylah, as she held two babies in her arms.

Maluhia and his twin sister.

The babies created by the Dark Lord for his glorious resurrection who were now innocent children with the opportunity to follow their own destinies.

"Is it over?" she breathed.

"The Dark Lord is dead," Styx said, pointing toward the singed spot on the floor where she'd disintegrated beneath the power of the goddess.

"Really, truly dead?" Salvatore demanded.

"So it would seem."

They all turned to study the ancient vampire, but it was the King of Weres who spoke the words they were all thinking.

"You're not filling me with warm fuzzies here, leech," he said. "Are we safe or not?"

Styx gave a slow shake of his head. "I'm not sure. That kind of power . . ." He grimaced. "It just doesn't disappear."

Cassie understood what he meant.

At least vaguely.

Wasn't there a theory about black holes and the quandary of what happened to the energy that was sucked into them? If the universe refused to allow energy or information to be lost, then what about the power of a deity?

But at the moment, it was all too deep to process.

Thankfully, Caine felt the same way. With one fluid motion, he was scooping her off her feet and cradling her against his chest.

"That seems like something for kings to worry about, not us peasants," Caine assured them. He smiled down at her, a wicked promise in his blue eyes. "And I have a long overdue honeymoon."

"Take care of her," Salvatore warned, his voice gruff.

"I know, I know," Caine said. "She's the prophet . . ."

"No," the King of Weres interrupted. "She's a part of our family."

"Family," Cassie murmured, a warmth flooding through her heart.

She'd been alone for so long.

Now she had . . . everything.

Everything a woman could possibly desire.

"Whether you like it or not," Salvatore warned.

"We like it very much," Cassie said, giving her mate a warning pinch.

"Fine." Caine sent his king a warning frown. "But let's not plan any reunions for a century or two."

Clearly done with the conversation, Caine turned to make his way out of the bloody basement, holding her as if she were a precious treasure.

"Wait," she abruptly demanded, ignoring her mate's sigh of resignation.

"What now?"

She lifted her head to peer over his shoulder, meeting Styx's curious gaze.

"There's one prophecy I had years ago that I nearly forgot."

The Anasso was instantly wary. "What is it?"

"The vampire who can read prophecies."

"Roke?"

"Yes, he's going to be important for the future of the vampires. Keep him safe."

Styx's large body stiffened in instant alarm. "He's in danger?"

She shrugged. "I don't know. That's all I have."

"Wait . . ." The vampire moved forward as Caine resumed his path to the door. "I have questions."

"She's officially off duty," Caine growled, ignoring the chaos left behind them.

Cassie smiled, not at all bothered by his ruthless refusal to stop. She was more than ready to be just another female spending time alone with her mate.

"Where are we going?" she at last demanded as they left the warehouse and stepped into the moon-drenched night.

"Vegas, baby." His smile held a promise that sent her heart racing. "Vegas."

Epilogue

It was nearly dawn when the last of the vampires left the battleground, seeking the protection of their lairs.

Cautiously, Gaius crawled from beneath the stone wall that had collapsed on him after he'd been flung into it. A rather amazing stroke of luck, considering it'd protected him from the ongoing battle.

And more importantly from Styx and his goon squad, who would no doubt have killed him on sight.

Not that he was entirely certain he was glad to have survived.

His slavery to the Dark Lord might have ended, but he was a traitor to the vampires. He would have to spend the rest of eternity trying to hide from their wrath.

He was a pariah with no place to go and no one he could turn to for help.

Lost in his bout of self-pity, Gaius rose to his feet and glanced down at his bruised and bloody body. He would have to find someplace to hide, but first he needed to feed.

Taking a step forward, he was brought to an abrupt halt as a voice whispered through his mind.

"Gaius."

"No."

He gave a panicked shake of his head. It couldn't be the Dark Lord. The bitch was dead. He could feel it in his very soul. The one he'd once sold.

The voice came again. "Help me."

"No. Get out of my head."

"Gaius, it's Dara."

He stilled, his hands curling into tight fists. "That's impossible. You're a trick of the Dark Lord."

"No, Gaius," the voice reassured him. "Your mistress is dead, but her death brought me here."

He frowned. Was it possible?

The dimensions had been ripped open.

If the demons of hell could escape, why not the dead?

"You're here?" he asked cautiously, his desperate need to be reunited with his mate warring with the memory of the last time he'd been lured by the promise of Dara.

"Yes," she whispered.

"Where?"

"Follow my scent."

He hissed in shock as the evocative aroma of myrrh and cinnamon teased at his nose.

It was her.

No one else carried precisely that scent.

Only his mate.

Moving as if he were in a dream, Gaius stepped over the rotting corpses and forgotten weapons, headed toward a distant corner. As he neared, a black shadow seemed to shift, coalescing into a slender female form covered by a plain white gown stretched on the hard ground. His step quickened and the darkness again swirled to reveal an oval, honey-tinted face that was framed by a curtain of straight, blue-black hair.

"Dara." Falling to his knees at her side, Gaius reached to

stroke trembling fingers along the pure line of her jaw. "How is this possible?"

"We cannot speak now." Her smile pierced his heart. "We must get out of here."

Gaius frowned. "How? It's almost dawn."

She reached a slender hand to touch the medallion that still hung around his neck. "With this."

Gaius pulled back. Had her slender body briefly turned to mist?

No. He gave a shake of his head. It had been a figment of his imagination.

This was Dara.

His beloved mate.

His heart couldn't accept anything else.

"Where will we go?" he asked softly.

She offered another soul-stirring smile. "Anywhere we can be together."

"Yes."

Gathering her fragile body into his arms, Gaius laid his hand over the medallion and closed his eyes.